STILETTO

SUZANNE J. ROGERS

ISBN: 1536961566
ISBN 13: 9781536961560
Library of Congress Control Number: 2016913045
CreateSpace Independent Publishing Platform
North Charleston, South Carolina

Stiletto

This book is dedicated to my husband, John.
Always steadfast in his love and support,
heart of my "Hart."

~For encouraging me to challenge myself~

Thank you, Jordan Rogers.

CHAPTER 1

don't know anybody who prefers a whiplash day to a spa day. On spa days, peace and harmony carry you through your day, and your mind and body are in sync with the glorious universe. On the whiplash days, you're barely out of bed and problems come racing at you. You dodge one crisis, only to get blindsided by another; you curse the universe that's out to get you. There's only one way to deal with the universe, chocolate.

I was positive that today was a spa day. I got up early enough to still order breakfast at the fast-food drive-through window. Sometimes I think they change the time that breakfast is available the minute they see my car pull into the drive-through lane. "Sorry, we stop serving breakfast at six thirty a.m.," the guy at the window told me. "Would you like to try our rump roast with sauerkraut and sweet potato wrap?"

1

I gagged in response, and as I pulled away from the window, I looked into my rearview mirror and saw the drive-through-window guy handing the driver of the car behind me a bag that was so full of cinnamon rolls or egg muffins that they appeared to be almost spilling out onto the parking lot. They hate me.

Today the heavens had smiled upon me. Everything I'd ordered for breakfast was in the bag—even napkins! I happily munched my meal as I enjoyed a nice drive to the Haven, a local animal shelter renowned for providing sanctuary for animals of the predatory persuasion.

The sky was blue, the humidity low, and the subjects I'd come to photograph—the big cats—were providing me with just the photo ops I'd been looking for.

Every indication was that *this* was a spa day until it wasn't anymore.

There's a third kind of day that I haven't told you about yet: "spa/lash" days. This particular type of day starts out just peachy, and when you're all relaxed and feeling a false sense of security, it turns into the pits. There are moments when things briefly swing back to being peachy, but the stressful parts of the day are so bad that you're ready to call it a day and eat your weight in tootsie rolls.

I felt very relaxed as I strolled along, reveling in the warmth of a perfect spa day, when I saw a sign that said there would be a demonstration with animals at one 1:00 p.m. in the big tent. Who could resist learning "The Secrets of the Animal Trainer Extraordinaire?" In a few steps, I pushed my way through the heavy canvas flaps of the tent and felt the thick, heavy air that only an old-time, big top tent can wrap you in.

Finding a seat on the bleachers on the far side of the circus ring, I wedged myself in with the childless couples and retired seniors. As far as I'm concerned, these are the best seats in the house. The ones closest to the entrance were filled with squirmy kids munching on popcorn and cotton candy and frazzled parents trying to hang on to their children and their sanity until the day was over.

"Ladies and gentleman, kiddies of today and yesterday, welcome to the Haven!" The master of ceremonies' voice boomed through his microphone.

"Who wants to meet Marvin the Monkey and find out how he learned to do his tricks?"

Enthusiastic applause greeted Marvin the Monkey as he bounded into the ring.

"Marvin," said our host, "hop up onto this table, and treat our awesome guests to a little bit of your tap-dancing routine before we share the mysteries of the circus with them."

Marvin ripped his little tap shoes off and threw himself down on the sawdust that was scattered on the floor.

"Marvin!" Our host looked ticked off. *"Get up, and hop onto the table."*

Marvin was off the floor, and in a split second, he was out of his little monkey diaper and running around the edge of the tall fencing that separated the ticket-buying public from the "performers." As far as I could see, Marvin had only learned how to make rude gestures at people, but he demonstrated those with flair and great enthusiasm.

"Marvin, OUT!" Our host was sweating profusely and appeared red in the face with what I assumed was anger, but an unhealthy spike in his blood pressure was also a possibility.

Marvin knew "OUT." He stopped giving the audience the finger, collected his monkey diaper, did a slow trot over to the ringmaster, and slapped him in the knee with it. Smirking as only a monkey can smirk, he drew himself up to his full height of three feet and, in a dignified manner uncommon in most monkeys, proceeded to the animal exit gate without a backward glance. The crowd hadn't learned any circus secrets, but they had enjoyed Marvin immensely, and he was given a huge round of applause.

Little did we know that the next performer was going to be even more impressive. A hush fell over the audience as we watched the majestic king of the beasts make his slow, fear-inducing entrance into the performance ring. The ringmaster stood a respectful distance away from the star of the show and the trainer. We were about to be impressed.

It was quite impressive to learn that once in the ring, the giant cat could walk straight up to his trainer, smack him upside the head, knock him out, and look bored while he did it.

I was impressed with the fact that in one astounding leap, the kitty cat could clear the fencing of the cage and land in the top row of the bleachers.

I was also impressed with the fact that screaming and fainting were rather a specialty of the ringmaster, and several people learned how to emulate him right there on the spot.

I'm sure there are rules about how to behave around an escaped lion, but they weren't posted at the entrance when I paid for my ticket, so we all just kind of improvised. One roar was all it took for people to move like they never had before. Parents learned new ways to carry their children: by their legs, their hair…they were grabbing any body part they could on their offspring in order to get them out of the tent.

Some of us didn't have parents to carry us to safety, so it was up to our own legs and feet to learn to save us. Some of us were better at using those appendages than others, and when a few people fell on the way down the bleacher steps, a great number of us had too much momentum going to stop in time, and we fell on the people below us.

I wasn't too far down in the pile of people, when we came to rest at the bottom of the steps, but that was small consolation. When I got over the initial shock of the fall, I was acutely aware that my *very* personal space was being invaded.

"If I get a chance to look you in the face and find out you're not the person I'm in an intimate relationship with, *you're going to lose that hand*," I said, my voice expressing every drop of outrage I could muster.

A woman's voice blasted in my ear. "Shut up, you pervert! I can't help it! *You* landed on me! Now stop accusing me of sexually assaulting you, and tell me if that hideous thing is getting ready to *kill* us!"

I tried to focus my attention on checking out our situation, without inhaling. I had become acutely aware of the gross feel and smell of her sweat-soaked clothes pressed against my back, and it was hard to think about anything else.

Her cheese-grater voice brought me back to the situation at hand. "Are you awake up there? Is it going to attack us?"

"I don't know; I can't see anything, because there's a big heavy guy wiggling on top of me. Since he's pretty much covering my whole body, and the back of his head is on my chest, I'm having a little difficulty checking out our surroundings!"

"*Again* with the sex talk!"

"*I am not talking about sex!* I'm trying to tell you why I can't see where the lion is!"

"Well, he'd better quit wiggling and actually *do* something! Get him off of us so I can breathe! I'm running out of air!"

I was running out of the *desire* to breathe. The guy on top of me had a perspiration issue, just like the cranky gal under me. It was coming off him in sheets, and it was seeping its way through my blouse. I felt like the center of a sweat sandwich. He had landed sort of at an angle, and his head was just below my shoulder on my right side. My right arm was trapped, extended straight up over my head, and my left arm was pinned between my body and his. After quite a bit of effort, I was able to move a finger on my left hand a little bit, and I used it to prod the guy in the back. It took a second, but then he turned his face to his left and said hello…sort of.

"Have you ever heard the expression, don't poke the bear?" he demanded. "Well, right now I'm the bear, and the bear doesn't appreciate being called 'a big, heavy guy.' That's right, I heard you…everybody heard you. You pissed off the bear. Now…get your finger out of my back!"

Frankly I didn't care a whole lot about who was a bear and who wasn't; I was more concerned with the fact that I had a man speaking into my breast.

"I'd love to move my finger, but I can't. You're using your body to hold me hostage."

"Not anymore!" he growled.

I felt his arms move, and suddenly a woman was launched into the air. The poor thing looked like a brittle little bird, flapping her arms, making little screechy noises until she hit the ground. How could such a tiny thing have pinned him down?

Mr. Bear took off running right along with about ten other disheveled, wild-eyed people, who had been part of the pile of humanity. If anything big, toothy, and hungry needed something to chase, there were plenty of options.

Back to business…"You still down there, crabby pants?" I asked the woman who had spoken to me earlier.

"Where else would I be? Now…if no one is lying on your eyes, and you don't have any other excuse for not looking around, *is that wild animal getting any closer?*"

I'd had it with her. "With all due respect, you're an ass! So here's the 'you're an ass' report. I'm opening my eyes really, really wide, and it's amazing! I would never have known to do that if you hadn't told me. I can see the handlers, and they've got the lion on a long leash thingy. It's safe to get up."

The words were barely out of my mouth, before she pinched me hard where her hand was stuck.

"Save the sarcasm, sister. I want out of here!"

Her pinch made me spasm myself face-first onto the floor. I looked up in time to watch the back of my white-haired orthopedic tennis shoe wearing tormenter speed walking out the door of the big top. That's when the loud speaker came to life.

"We would like to invite our guests to leave the premises at this time and remind you all that you signed a waiver when you paid to come in. You can't sue us for the temporary escape of your favorite star, Handsome the Lion, and besides, he didn't hurt anyone this time."

I swore my way up off the gritty, debris-strewn concrete floor and used the bottom edge of my shirt to wipe off my tongue. I've never heard of anyone dying from accidentally eating dirt and gravel, but you can never be too careful.

CHAPTER 2

"Lady, could you move it? I got cleanup to do."

I turned around to find a surprisingly pimple-free teenager holding a large bucket and a lion-sized pooper-scooper. He was impressively calm, considering the drama that had just taken place. I gave him a closer look and decided that the reason he was so calm was because he was in *no* danger of becoming an appetizer for any wild animal. His clothes were hanging off of him, and he was just skin and bones and, I suspected, had a bad attitude.

"I'll be out of here just as soon as I find what I lost when I got caught in the stampede. Did you see a stuffed toy that looks like the animal that just tried to kill us?"

"Well, first of all, Handsome didn't try to kill nobody. Even if he wanted to, he'd have to gum them to death… he's only got two teeth. Second of all, once in a while he likes to jump the fence so that he can mess with the audience; that's what he was doin' today."

9

"What do you mean mess with the audience? Did he jump up to the top of the bleachers on *purpose* just to watch us freak out?"

"Yep, pretty much. You folks was lucky...last week he got right up close to the fence and sprayed everybody in the first three rows with his eau de pee pee."

My nose crinkled up. I could almost smell Handsome's "pee pee." Magically I felt a whole lot better about the choices that Handsome had made today.

"I'd better get out of here so that you can get to work... Did you see a stuffed lion anywhere? It's kind of a lucky charm."

"That's kinda ironic, isn't it? Callin' that thing your lucky charm? Don't look like it brought you any luck today. You got cotton candy in your hair, you smell, and your knees are bleeding through your jeans...in case you hadn't noticed."

I took a deep breath. "I'd love to stand here all afternoon listening to your flattering compliments, but...*did you see the stuffed lion anywhere?*"

He shrugged his skinny shoulder toward the exit. "It's right over there by the popcorn machine."

I started to walk away. "Love the scooper, by the way... nice that they put your picture on it right where you pick up the doody."

"That sounds kind of like an insult the way you said that. Almost makes me want to forget to show you *this*."

He was pushing my camera bag toward me with the toe of his scuffed, dusty boot. I snatched it off the ground and had a heart palpitation.

"Oh no! I'm so sorry."

"No problem. My feelings weren't all *that* hurt. Don't forget your lion on your way out."

I muttered a thank you in his direction and got my feet moving. No way was I telling him that I had apologized to the camera bag and not him. Who knows what he'd say to that.

I was feeling embarrassingly close to crying...the camera...well; it's just a part of me. "Come on, London," I whispered to myself. "A man-eating beast could have made a meal of you and a lot of other people, yet nothing...no screaming, no fainting. But forget your camera, and it's the end of the world." I squared my shoulders. Talking to myself again, I made myself move. "On to the popcorn machine, camera girl. There's a stuffed lion to save."

I walked a whole five feet and picked up my lost lucky charm. Now that I'd found my own toy Handsome, I was ready to get out of there. I turned around, and damn if I didn't find handsome again. This one was living, breathing, to die for...*handsome*.

The second "handsome" that I had found was long, lean, and looked as if he'd walked right out of a magazine ad. You know the ads I'm talking about...the devastatingly handsome man, who sits almost arrogantly on the back of a magnificent-looking horse, wearing blindingly white polo pants and a tight black polo shirt. A few stray strands of hair hang down over his forehead, and he has the jaw-line and cheekbones of a Greek god.

Impossibly thick eyelashes that surround a smoldering gaze could make us buy anything the company was selling.

There was no smoldering taking place in the eyes that stared at me. These eyes, shaded with gold and brown and bronze were on fire. The heat from that fire licked across the empty space between us, and I began to feel the need to rip my clothes off.

You can never be too careful when there's a risk of spontaneous combustion, and the chance of it happening to me at that moment was off the charts. A basic instinct for self-preservation kicked in, and I made myself tear my eyes away from his. He wore black jeans, which fit too well, and a long-sleeved light-blue shirt that was having a prob-lem containing his muscular arms. All the volunteers wore the same shirts, except nobody else was having a biceps issue.

He had kind of a safari hat thing on, and if he had hair at all, it wasn't showing itself. Did I forget to mention that he was also wearing about a gazillion tons of sex appeal? Oooh baby.

When I registered that, my neck felt as if it had been scalded with hot water. I pulled my eyes away from the amazing male specimen and made for the exit. I wasn't sure if he was still watching me, but I worked my "sexy walk" all the way back to my car, just in case.

I quickly unlocked the jeep, swept the fast-food debris off the passenger seat, and settled my gear and my lucky charm in for the ride home. I held my breath and braced my butt for contact with the fiery-hot driver's seat...summer in Florida is not for the faint of heart.

After the initial searing of my posterior, I turned on the air conditioner full blast.

CHAPTER 3

I hope I didn't run anybody over on the way home. You know that thing where you drive home and when you get there, you don't remember anything about the drive? Yep, I did just that. My mind was on other things, like, did my sexy walk leave a lasting impression?

My name is London Hart. I'm a photographer, and I hadn't been at the big-cat sanctuary just for the cotton candy. I'd gone hoping to get at least one great shot to finish off my portfolio for an important job interview. An image of a lion or a tiger was a natural first choice for me. My family history is, shall we say, interesting, and a large part of my childhood was spent around the big cats.

My father had been a famous animal trainer in England until the biggest circus in the United States made him an offer he couldn't refuse. My mother is French and was traveling with a ballet troupe that performed in London as part of their tour schedule before my dad had made the move to the States. It always sounds like a movie to me. Beautiful French woman dancing on stage, handsome Englishman goes to the performance because his male coworkers want to go see the pretty French girls dance in their tutus. He sits in a crushed velvet seat in the audience and falls in love with the beautiful ballerina. He fast-talks his way backstage after the show, and one year later, little me, London, is born.

I wish I could say that I have my father's snazzy-sounding accent or my mother's elegant French accent. I have a slightly southern accent with the tiniest little twist of… something. What do you call a mixture of a French and English accent? Doesn't matter; I don't have enough of it that it needs a name.

It had taken me about twenty-five minutes to get home to my little hole in the wall apartment. Snugged in just a block away from the main drawbridge that connects the island portion of Venice, Florida to the mainland, it was small, but I could clean the whole place in about ten minutes, which was a definite plus. The big negative about the place was its proximity to two drawbridges…something I failed to consider when I rented the place.

I jammed my key in the door, and as soon as I got inside, I sank onto my lumpy, comfy, old sofa and pulled my cell phone out of the side pocket of the camera bag. I needed to make a call, but the sofa felt so comfortable, so snoozeable. I closed my eyes and kicked off my shoes.

Forty minutes later I woke up from my little nap. It took me a minute to fully wake up, and I lay there trying to get my brain to remember what it was I'd been doing before I fell asleep.

I sat up, and the cell phone slid off my stomach onto the floor. *That's* what I was supposed to be doing...checking in. I had barely touched the number on speed dial and the call was picked up. She didn't waste any time getting to the point.

"*London!* Did you get the shot? Tell me you got the shot!"

"Slow down, CC. First, do you have more than a minute to talk?"

"I'm just about to stick the last pin in the client from hell. Can I call you back in just a little bit?"

"Go finish torturing the poor woman and give me a call when you're done."

"No hanging up until you tell me if you got the shot that's going to make you rich and famous!"

"My lips are sealed...now go get busy!"

"You know what? I'm driving down as soon as I finish. I'm picking up a vibe...the 'I need chocolate' vibe. Am I right?"

"There might be a little vibe. If you do stop for chocolate, stop and get at least six brownie bites from the bakery in the grocery store. Make that eight. Make that ten; I'll save some for tomorrow."

"Right...just like you *always* save some for tomorrow."

"Don't get all snarky on me, princess! Go stick a pin in the wench, and get down here."

There was only radio silence on the other end of the line. The best gown designer in the country and my best friend in the world would be burning up I-75 in no time.

I needed to clean up, but first I took Handsome and put him on the night table beside my bed.

"I think you show great potential as a lucky charm, little mister. You led me right to that mouth-watering man. It would have been nice if you would have arranged for the luck to take me to the point of talking to the man...but you're new at this. Get all rested up; I'm going to need you to work some magic for me when I have my job interview with the magazine editor." I looked into the little black eyes. "We're going to make a good team."

Chapter 4

It was time to get rid of the "stranger sweat" that had dried onto my skin. I shuffled into the bathroom and scared myself. I'd made the mistake of looking into the mirror after I'd been asleep. I have hair issues...bed head, hair issues.

I also have "I hate the color of my hair" issues. I have "my hair's too long, it's too short, it's too messy" issues. I now had the "I just took a nap with cotton candy stuck in my hair" issues. Hopefully a shower would help.

I turned the setting for the water temperature all the way over to it's coldest. No matter how much I complain to the landlord, he never manages to adjust it so that the water doesn't immediately come out hot enough to boil my skin off.

Twenty minutes later I was sparkly clean, my skin was in love with my new Goldleaf body wash, and my hair was sugar free. I pulled on shorts and the first T-shirt I could lay my hands on. Unlike CC, I'm not really fashion forward. I'm kind of "fashion stuck in a rut." Back in the living room, I pulled my camera out of its bag and ejected the memory card and fed it to the computer. Images started streaming onto the screen, and I watched picture after picture parade in front of me. I realized I was holding my breath...I had gotten the shot I needed!

Before I went any further, I pulled two thumb drives out of my camera bag and saved the images on them. No way was I going to take a chance on having to go through the heartache of accidentally erasing the images from the camera and not having them backed up...trust me, it's happened.

Furious pounding on my front door finally pulled me back to the here and now. I yanked the door open, and five foot eleven inches of elegant sophistication shoved past me. C. C. Covington moved like a flower floating down a stream. She should have been a ballet dancer, but she had a thing against tutus.

"I thought you were dead!"

"Why in the world did you think I was dead?"

"London, I've been knocking on your door for twenty minuths."

Translation, thirty seconds...CC tends to exaggerate just a little. On another note, the way she said "minutes" made my antenna go up.

"Well, surprise, here's me...not dead. Do you have the brownies?"

"Yeth…"

Stupid question; she had one in each hand and the last bit of one in her mouth.

"Tell me you didn't eat all of them."

"Do you think I'd show up here with chocolate on my lipths and none in the bag? Do I look like thomeone with a death wish?"

"Gimme."

She flipped the bag holding the remaining precious cargo toward me, and it fell on the floor. "Take them! Why should you have any concern for the fact that I didn't have time for lunch and only ate a few of the divine little confections? And I didn't mean to throw that; I'm having a little sugar surge."

Picking up the bag, I issued a warning. "These better not be all smooshed." With one eye closed and the other eye open, I peeked into the bag…"Cee, how many did you have when you left the store?"

"I had eight."

I couldn't help myself; I snapped at her. "*You ate five!!??*"

"I did pretty good, didn't I? Look at me. I'm wearing white capris and a silk blouse, and I dare you to find one little spot of chocolate on me anywhere."

"That's not the point, CC. The point is that you ate *five*!"

Ignoring me, she headed for my bedroom/office. "So? Did you get the shot that you needed for your portfolio?"

I'd taken a second to pull a brownie from the bag and stuff it into my mouth. Another second was required to fully savor the richness of the fudge topping, and one more second was needed to rinse my fingers off at the kitchen sink.

"Hello?? Are you going to show me or not?"

"I'm *coming*! God forbid you should have to wait one millisecond…I still have a brownie lodged in my throat… is that fast enough for you?"

I hit the refresh button on the computer, and the images popped up on the screen.

"You got it…you got *them*," she whispered. She pulled the little footstool, which I keep by the bed, closer to the computer and sat down. I eased myself into my chair and scrolled through the pictures.

"This is Handsome. I just can't get over how beautiful he is. King of the Jungle doesn't do him justice."

CC was studying the image as intently as I was. I scrolled more images across the screen, and we were about ten images in, when I heard CC draw in a breath. She looked at me with her big eyes slightly glazed over and then she looked back at the computer screen.

"Who is *that*?" she asked.

"Who is who?"

She tapped the man in the background of the image with the tip of her elegantly manicured fingernail.

"*That* who! *Who* is that man?"

We both stared at the image. It was the man with "the eyes." I hadn't realized that I had captured him in the

background of one of the shots. Without enlarging the image, CC couldn't see the eyes the way I had seen them...I couldn't help it...I shivered. Just that slight shiver broke the spell, and CC turned and stared at me.

"Who is he?"

I wasn't comfortable with the way she said those words...I could hear CC; she had "the hunter of men" in the tone of her voice. For some reason, I didn't want her hunting this particular man.

"I don't know," I said truthfully.

"You saw this man, this gorgeous man, and you didn't find out who he was?"

"Now just who was I going to ask?" I said. "The guy selling marshmallows on a stick that you can feed to the bears for a dollar?

It's not as though the place was crawling with staff just hanging around holding signs that read 'ASK ME WHO THE GORGEOUS GUY IS!' Besides, I'm not sure I want to know who he is. We made eye contact, and...he made me feel uncomfortable."

"He made you uncomfortable. Uncomfortable how?"

I hesitated for a minute and then threw all caution to the wind. I jumped up and paced back and forth.

"CC, you should have seen his eyes...I've never seen eyes like that before. They just kind of grab you...and they're, like, three different colors. I had some kind of primal reaction when he looked at me...I got all...I can't explain it...just uncomfortable."

"Ooooh, I like this! Somebody finally got through the walls you put up...so are you going back, you know, to see if he's there again? If he *was* there, you could kind of just trip and fall into him, or ask him for change to feed the goats; there were goats there, right?"

My defense system kicked in too late, and I realized that I had activated CC's "let's find London a man" switch. I was now mentally kicking my own ass, but I did get a little comfort out of the fact that her "hunter of men" vibe was gone.

"CC! What difference does it make if there were goats? Enough already. It was just a chance meeting. There were no fireworks. (I'm such a liar.)

"I didn't hear music playing. Cupid didn't whack me over the head with a red bow and arrow...now let's just drop it. Do you want to see the other shots or not?"

I must have put a little extra growl in my voice, because she snapped her mouth shut and swallowed her next comment. She flipped her eyes back to the images on the screen.

"You're going to get the job, you know...unless the editor is a total fool."

"I hope you're right. I'd love to work at the magazine and make enough money to move."

"I never could understand why you picked this location. Those bells clanging every time the drawbridges go up and down would drive me crazy," CC said.

"The price was right, and it's not so bad in the summer; just in the winter when the snowbirds are taking their boats up and down the intracoastal."

We'd devoured the rest of the brownies…but I was still hungry. I looked around for my car keys. "Want to drive down to the beach and share something at Sharky's?"

Stupid question, for sure…CC can keep on eating and never gain a pound…I don't know how we stay friends.

Chapter 5

Ten minutes later we were seated on the deck outside of Sharky's, watching the sun go down and enjoying a huge platter of seafood nachos.

"Remember the restaurant in Islamorada where we met, CC? They had the best nachos I've ever had, except for here."

"You know I don't remember anything about that place. I remember riding home in your car; that's it. You're an obnoxious friend, London Hart…when are you going to get tired of torturing me with this story?"

I ignored her…I was having fun. "You don't remember those waiters? They were wearing those crisp white aprons and black shirts and black pants. You told me they had 'seductive faces and they moved as if to music that no one else could hear.' You were quite poetic."

"I was?" She flicked the end of a strand of her long brown hair between her fingers. Then she chewed on it.

"You never told me the part about being poetic before… usually you just remind me of the stupid stuff that I did that night."

"Like drinking that third white chocolate martini and pinching the waiter's derriere."

CC pointed her fork at me. "Let it go, London…it's been five years."

"Just let me finish. I love this part…remember I had some kind of business meeting there?"

She put her head in her hands. "*No,* I *don't* remember."

"Well, I was there for a meeting, and eventually I noticed that the whole restaurant was watching you…nobody even tried to be subtle about it. So I started watching you, and I saw you pinch the waiter's butt—twice! After that the waiter wouldn't come back, so the owner of the restaurant came over to deliver your dinner, and you reached out for a whole handful of 'cheek.' You missed, slid off your barstool, still holding your martini glass, and that was the end of the show. Do you remember everyone applauding?"

She ignored my recitation of her antics. She had a more important question for me.

"I never asked you this, but was the waiter's ass worth so much of my attention?"

"I have no way of answering that…I don't spend a lot of time rating the behinds of random men."

"Where were you when they were handing out the estrogen?"

I almost dropped a nacho that was dripping with cheese, as it was halfway to my mouth. "Excuse me?"

"You just don't salivate over men the way some of my other friends do."

"A lot of your 'friends' verge on being hazardous to a man's health…they're animals. I don't think there's anything wrong with acting like a lady, even though that seems to be going out of style."

CC stuck her tongue out at me and ate the last nacho. "So blah, blah, blah, you being the kind-hearted, concerned citizen that you are, you helped me off the floor, refused to let me drive my car, and you 'hauled my designer-clad butt home.' You've got to stop telling this story." She put her hand on her stomach and groaned. "I ate too much. I'm going to have horrible heartburn! I can feel it. Are we ready to go?"

I flagged down our waitress and asked for the check. CC passed the time going from table to table, asking people if they had an antacid.

Just as the waitress brought me my change, Cee flopped back down in her chair.

"Thank God that guy with the biker dudes had something for my stomach."

"CC! Did you eat something that he gave you? Do you even know what it was?"

"Relax, London, it tasted chalky like all those tablets do. It's fine. You worry too much."

"If you get high and start getting crazy on me, I'm going to lock you in a closet until you're normal again. Dear God, why did you take something from a stranger?"

CC just rubbed her stomach and burped. "See...it's working already!"

An hour or so later, CC was on her way home, and there was no indication that she had been drugged by our fellow diner. I had developed a slight case of indigestion of my own, and I was in bed tossing and turning...only ten hours until I opened my portfolio, and the editor of the magazine had the chance to change my life. I think I counted every hour until it was time to get up.

CHAPTER 6

"I'm here to see Mr. Brant," I told the receptionist at the huge curving desk. "I'm London Hart."

"Please have a seat, Ms. Hart."

I'm quick in social situations, and I stopped myself from giggling at the woman; it's just that her voice was so unexpected. She had a very high-pitched, little-girl voice. A mouse would've had a hard time matching her decibel range. I pressed my lips together and sat down.

She jabbed a button on some kind of futuristic-looking desk thingy and looked me over.

"Would you like a mint while you wait? I found a store that carries these awesome mints; they have a candy-coated outside and chocolate in the middle." She shoved a huge bowl toward me that was piled high with multicolored candies.

I took one, solely to make her happy and to make a good impression. It had nothing to do with my need to self-medicate with chocolate, because I was so damn nervous.

She popped one into her mouth, and crunching furiously, she introduced herself.

"My name is Sophie. Is there anything that I can get you while you wait? Water? Latte? Chai tea? Energy drink? Energy Bar? Coffee?" As she listed the available goodies at warp speed, I began to suspect that she had already consumed a *lot* of things that contained caffeine.

"I'm fine; thank you, Sophie. I had coffee on the way in."

"Well, I'm going to help myself to just a little more of the hazelnut blend."

She sprang out of her seat and stood up...I think. She was *tiny*. Her nose was tiny and dainty, and she had little ears that came to a rounded point at the top. They were very similar to the ears on those holiday-movie elves. If I had to guess, I would've said she wasn't even five feet tall. Everything about the woman was little, except her hair. She had it teased and tossed and whipped up into a towering brown frenzy...I half expected to see little faces looking out of it. I'm not kidding, I'm not exaggerating...it looked like a family of chipmunks could live in it and still have room for their cousins to move in. My brain snapped back to attention when I realized she was asking me a question.

"Now are you sure that I can't get you anything?"

I don't know why I did it, but out it came. "You don't, by any chance, have a pack of cigarettes and a Scotch around, do you?"

She blinked at me...once, twice, thrice. Finally she answered—very slowly, "No, I'm sorry I don't...but if we go to the mail room, we can buy some pot from Blandon, our tech guy."

There was a pause of about ten seconds, while I just stared at her; then she started laughing in that girlish voice. She went on laughing until I was afraid she was going to throw up that cute little celebrity mouse that lives in Orlando.

Finally, wiping her eyes, she looked down at a red light that had begun to blink on her high-tech communication… thingy.

"Oh! Mr. Brant is ready to see you…just go along the hallway right outside these doors, and take a right."

I picked up my portfolio, carefully shook her little hand, and headed out the doors. Turning, I found before me a hallway that led past offices with glass walls. Not just one wall…every single wall was glass, floor to ceiling…I got the strange sensation that the people working away in these little see-through boxes were kind of like animals being displayed at a pet store.

Ten offices down, I was greeted by a man waiting expectantly outside black glass doors. Mike Brant was definitely Mr. Boss Man…he had privacy. Unlike the see-through walls of his minions, the walls of his office were black glass, very cool, very power hour…very impressive. He wore a gray suit, black shirt, and gray tie.

There was no room for a family of chipmunks on his head. His black hair was buzzed short and suited his slick look. Looking at the whole package, he kind of reminded me of a shark.

"Ms. Hart, it's nice to meet you!" The grip he had on my hand as he shook it was almost painful, and I was glad when he let my poor little paw go.

"I've heard a lot about your work...Come in, have a seat." He pointed at a large black chair that looked extremely uncomfortable. It was all sharp angles, and there wasn't an ounce of padding on the thing. It was obviously an expensive piece of furniture, but it was totally ridiculous. Brant circled back behind a desk piled high with magazines, mints, random papers, pens, two computers, empty coffee cups, and what I was hoping was white powder from a doughnut. I gave a quick glance at his nose...he looked cocaine free, but you never know.

"So tell me about yourself. I've heard you do a lot of freelance work. Tell me about that." He dropped down into what I assumed was a desk chair. All the stuff piled on the desk made a nice little privacy fence. He peered at me with an unblinking intensity. I was already nervous, but his eyes, the color of coal, really made a person feel like a butterfly pinned to a board.

I swallowed hard and crossed my fingers. I didn't think dropping to my knees and saying a quick prayer that I'd get the job would be appropriate at the moment. Finger crossing had to do.

"I've been freelancing for the last five years. I started out shooting senior photos for high-school kids, and not too long after that, I started doing anniversary, engagement, and wedding photos for newspaper announcements. Two years later I started getting job offers from various corporations in Sarasota to cover their society events. That's where I'm at right now. I love the work, but I need something full time." I paused to take a breath, and he took the chance to shoot me a question.

"Do you think you'd be comfortable doing architectural-type stuff? There wouldn't be a lot of portraits involved, maybe just a little shot of somebody now and then to stick somewhere in an article." He opened a desk drawer while he was talking and pulled out a pair of black trendy glasses.

"I wouldn't have a problem with architecture. The buildings we have in this area, old and new, are so interesting. I always wonder about the old ones, what their secrets are."

He jammed his glasses on. "We're not really interested in finding out what secrets the buildings have; we're not a ghost-hunting business."

"That's not what I meant. I…"

He cut me off with a flap of his hand, waving aside any other comments I might make.

Great…He thought I had visions of being a ghost hunter.

"We're still putting together a plan of exactly what we want to showcase for our readers," he said. "It might be commercial buildings, residential properties, or civic centers; we're not sure yet. What have you brought for me to look at?"

I dug around in my pristine black "business" bag and brought out the thumb drive with my portfolio of images on it and handed it to him.

"I've got a little of everything on here—portraits, landscapes, street photography, and wildlife."

He pushed his glasses farther up on his nose, shoved the thumb drive into his laptop, and focused on business. I sat in my great big "alien spaceship" chair and quietly studied him. Well built, tall, suave, and intimidating. I wouldn't have put him at forty yet, more like midthirties. He didn't exude friendliness, but then I wasn't there to find a new buddy to go shopping with.

He scrolled through my portfolio a second time and then stopped abruptly. Brant must have had some kind of pager system on his desk. I hoped so because he was looking down at his desk and talking in a raised voice.

"Sophie, get in here!"

That woman could apparently move like greased lightning. She popped through his office doors almost immediately.

"Yes, Mr. Brant?" she asked.

"I want you to take Ms. Hart back out to your desk." He stood and extended his hand to me. Obviously our meeting was over.

"I, uh, I appreciate your giving me the opportunity to show you my work. It was a pleasure meeting you," I stammered.

He handed back my portfolio, dropped back down behind his wall of magazines and papers, shoved some clutter out of the way, put his feet up on his desk, and closed his eyes. I backed out of the room, confused by the abrupt dismissal and his need for a nap. As soon as we'd gotten a few feet away, I looked to Sophie for some answers.

"Sophie, what just happened in there? Did I do something wrong? Did he hate my work or like it?"

"Oh honey, he liked it! He never says anything when he likes somebody's work." She patted the sides of her rat's-nest hairdo. "If he likes what he sees, he just has me get the contact info of that person, and we go from there. Mr. Brant and I have sort of a shorthand way of operating. He's very good at recognizing talent, and he's almost never wrong about a person's potential. He's giving you the chance to show him what you can do! I'm going to set up an appointment for you to do a photo shoot. Then I'll send you an email with all the details. We've had our eyes on a beautiful estate that would be the perfect place for you to start. It's not too huge, and you can get a feel for how you'd work on a site if you get the job. I want to set you up for a shoot in Matlacha first thing Monday morning if I can. Don't you just love all the little art galleries there? Now you just let me take care of everything, and I'll be in touch. I just knew things were going to go well for you!"

"How did you know that, Sophie?" I asked.

"You picked a lucky mint from the candy bowl when you first got here, and they always work." She had a self-congratulatory smile on her face.

OK then, magic mints, how fabulous. We stopped at her desk, and I gave her my email address. I couldn't help it. I snuck a peek at the bowl of mints. I really wanted another one, but I had a feeling that Sophie would disapprove if I picked another lucky one by accident. She probably had a rule about only one per customer. I pulled my keys out of my bag and headed for the door.

"It was nice meeting you, Sophie. I'll look forward to hearing from you."

"Welcome to our little family, Ms. Hart!"

I did a happy dance all the way to the jeep. I was one step closer to landing the job.

CHAPTER 7

The first thing I did to celebrate was stop at the chocolate shop downtown. I left with chocolate-covered marshmallows and a pound and a half of milk-chocolate caramels. I think it was also possible that I left with a contact high from the delicious smell of the very air that you breathe when you're in there. The shop has everything a chocoholic could want...from ice cream to fudge to boxed and individual pieces of chocolate. There's a separate case that holds the fudge that they make right there in the shop. If you time it right, you can get there and watch them making it, but I stopped doing that...I never left without two pounds of fudge and a little drool running out of the corner of my mouth.

Clutching my bag of celebration treats, I hadn't gotten too far down the row of shops on Venice Avenue, when I ran into Brenda...a dynamo of a woman. She was a savvy business owner, and she owned one of my favorite shops on the island. Sparkling blue eyes and a radiant smile charmed even the toughest of customers.

"London! Sweetie! I haven't seen you in two weeks. Where have you been?"

"I've been shooting here, there, and everywhere. You look amazing! That blue blouse is spectacular with your eyes." I gave her a quick hug and held the bag of caramels out toward her. "Caramel?"

"Yum! Thank you! I love everything they sell in that delicious shop."

She reached into the bag, and when she pulled her hand out, half of the caramels went with it…Wow…really?

She leaned in close, shoved a caramel in her mouth, and chewed furiously. She stared into my eyes. "Now tell me, how's your love life?"

"Wow, Brenda, talk about getting straight to the point. My love life is fine. It's non-existent but fine. How's *your* love life?"

"You sassy girl, asking me such a personal question. Are you sure you want to know? Because if I tell you how I spent Saturday night, your chocolate's going to melt." She did a little wriggly move with her petite self and fluffed her short spunky hair with her fingertips.

"Don't tell me anything! I'll get embarrassed, and then my hands will sweat, which will jeopardize the chocolate."

"But you're one of my girls! A person is supposed to be able to tell their homegirls anything."

Brenda had homegirls, and I was one of them? I needed to find out what I was obligated to do as a home girl, but that would have to wait…Brenda had launched into her story, and I began to suspect that she didn't really care about my chocolates at all.

"You know Alex? He's the charmer who has the ice-cream shop two doors down from me…Remember? The guy who wears the Rolex and drives the Bentley? Well, we had a date last Saturday, and we went to the movies. Alex wanted to sit all the way in the last row, so we did, and when the lights went down…"

"Time out! I have a feeling you're going to say something that I won't be able to unhear, and our friendship would never be the same!"

She rolled her eyes at me, licked her coral-painted lips, and started talking again. "Well, the previews came on, and he reached over and…"

"La-la-la-la-la-la-la!" I stuffed my fingers in my ears and started singing loudly. (Don't worry…I had the bag of chocolates in a death grip.) She tried to pull my fingers out of my ears, but I was too quick for her. I scooted just far enough away to stay out of her reach.

"I really do have to get going, Brenda…but we'll get together soon. Maybe we can do a girl's night at the movies sometime soon…as long as you promise not to tell me any intimate 'Alex' stories."

She flashed me a mischievous smile. "Now why would I make a promise I know I can't keep?"

I rolled my eyes and pointed my finger at her. "Behave."

I dodged between moving obstacles as I made my way down the sidewalk: a woman in tight red spandex shorts rollerbladed past me with inches to spare…a couple pushing their pride and joy through the crowd in a top of the line stroller moved at a snail's pace due to all the people who wanted to get a look at their little darling. I did a double take when I realized their stroller baby was a small dog wearing a large diamond bracelet as a collar. I imagine trying to walk down the street on four little legs with that weight around your neck might be a challenge. A stroller was a brilliant solution to the problem.

Chapter 8

Needless to say the chocolates didn't make it home. I'm a stress eater, big time. They barely made it back to the jeep. With all the tourist traffic, it took me fifteen minutes to drive the four blocks back to my place. Every time I had to stop for a pedestrian, I dug around in the empty bag, hoping that I'd missed a chocolate.

When I finally got to my place, I was feeling the after-effects of a sugar high, and the minute I got in the door, I walked to the sofa, sank down onto it, and waited for my energy to return. I did have the energy to use my phone, and I dialed CC's number.

She didn't bother saying hello. "I've been texting you for the last hour. You've got to start looking at your phone once in a while, London."

"I get distracted and forget to check it. Did you just want to tell me that you sent me a bunch of texts, or do you want to know how the interview went?"

"Give me the details."

"You are now talking to the almost-new photographer for the magazine."

"What do you mean 'almost' new photographer?"

"I'm being sent on a trial assignment…if I do well, I've got the job."

"What's the job, London? Where are you shooting, what are you shooting?"

"They're sending me down to Matlacha to shoot a private home. I've got the weekend to get ready, and then first thing Monday morning, it's Showtime."

As the words came out of my mouth, I slapped my hand to my forehead. Crap, I'd just made the photo shoot ten times harder…I knew what was coming next…and there it was.

"Ooooh! Can I come along? I love to see what design elements people incorporate into their houses. It's fun to see if they've got style or just a lot of money and the decorating sense of a jelly doughnut."

"You can see pictures of the house when they're in the magazine—*if* Brant decides to publish them."

"Do I have to beg? I won't be any trouble. I don't have any appointments on Monday, and I could help you! I could be your assistant or something."

I listened to myself start to cave in to her argument for going along. "You've got to have what looks like a legitimate reason to be there. You can't just stand around gawking. You're actually going to have to help me if I let you come along."

"Define the word 'help.'"

"You can carry the tripod and any other equipment that I need help schlepping around. You'll also have to peel me a grape if I decide I want a snack and braid my hair if I ask you to."

"Are you being for real with the grape and hair stuff?"

"No, you dope. You really don't get my sense of humor, do you?"

"Does anyone?"

I sniffed to indicate my hurt feelings. She didn't care.

"So when do you pick me up? When do I need to be ready?"

"You need to be ready when you drive to *my* place, and then I'll drive us the rest of the way. We're going south, you're north...why would I pick you up?"

"Okay, smarty-pants...what time do you want me on your doorstep?"

"Get to my place no later than eight, and make sure you eat breakfast before we leave. We're not stopping for anything on the way there—not a stick of gum, not a muffin, not a breakfast burrito...nothing."

"I'll have something from the boulangerie across the street sent over first thing before I leave for your place."

"How did we suddenly start talking about Halloween? Why do you need 'boo' lingerie? I was talking about breakfast."

"A boulangerie is a *bakery*. Didn't your mother teach you *any* French? They make the most delicious baguettes...

and their croissants are to die for! Oh dear God, I'm going to have to run over there right now, before they close. I'll talk to you later."

I think it took about fifteen minutes after we'd hung up for the calls and texts to start.

Every call and text went something like this: "Should I wear flats? You know that I always wear heels, but I could make an exception. I think I'll wear flats; I've got a really darling pair, but I'm not sure that they look 'assistant-ish.' You shouldn't have given me such short notice about our job, London. I'm just not prepared…I need to go shoe shopping and maybe just pop in to get my hair trimmed. By the way, you have *got* to try one of these croissants some-day. They're so light, and they serve them warm…I think they must release endorphins or something when you eat them. I feel so *good*! Now I have to cut you off, London; I can't listen to you chat all day."

That call got to me…I hadn't said one syllable! I'm positive that I hadn't uttered one syllable.

CHAPTER 9

Sunday morning I accidentally woke myself up. I hate when that happens. I could have slept all day, but I must have been tossing and turning all night, and my sheet had twisted around my ankle. My foot had gone to sleep, which caused me to be "not asleep." I let my foot dangle off the side of the bed to get the blood moving again, and after the zing from the "pins and needles" had worn off, my thoughts turned to the blueberry frozen waffles in my freezer. I decided that I was so hungry my shower was going to have to wait; I padded to the fridge in my black fuzzy slippers and nightgown. I'm not one for long nightgowns, as they tend to get twisted around my waist when I'm sleeping, and that kind of defeats the purpose of them being long. I wear knee-length ones; they're long enough that I can hop out of bed and not show the world my nether regions…not that the world, or anyone else, was looking.

I carried my waffles back to the bedroom when they were done toasting and climbed back onto bed to eat them. Before you go telling me that the syrup was going to be a problem, let me explain. I just put a little margarine on the edges and eat them like toast, so aside from some crumbs, it's no problem. I snuggled back under my covers when I was done eating and thought about Brenda and CC.

Things seemed to be flourishing for both of them in the romance department—with CC, that was always the case. I hadn't shaved my legs in a month...what does that tell you? It's not for lack of trying to put myself out there in the dating world. I'm just getting pickier where men are concerned. I've had one too many dates with men who have Peter Pan syndrome. There seems to be an overabundance of guys out there with arrested-development issues...mentally, not physically...they wanted to be frat boys forever. I was looking for a man...a grown-up, self-assured, intelligent, honest man.

I'd set my phone to vibrate, and I'd been so deep in thought that I hadn't noticed that it was "dancing" itself off the table until it fell to the floor. I didn't even have to look at the phone to know who was sending me a text...CC had lost her mind. Who knew that going with me to the shoot was going to send CC into a full-blown frenzy over what clothes to wear? I knew that she was, at this point, fully prepared clothing wise, shoe wise, and hair wise. She was going to chew me out for not responding to her, but if I had, I wouldn't have been able to get *myself* ready for the shoot. I really didn't have that much to do, except to make sure that my camera batteries were fully charged, that I had plenty of SD cards, etc. I just needed time to let my brain clear and focus on my plans for the shoot.

I got out of bed and pulled open my camera bag. Just for luck, I took Handsome off the bedside table and got him ready to be tucked into the jeep when I left.

"Your job, little mister, will be to guard my camera and sprinkle some good luck on it. I'll do the rest."

The rest of the day passed in a lazy Sunday kind of way. I showered, read the paper, watched a movie, and decided to have a frozen pizza for lunch. Two hours of television later, I was ready to pack up for the photo shoot. It didn't take long...I've learned what cameras and lenses, and so forth, work best for me. I am pretty sure I could pack in my sleep.

I made one last trip into the kitchen, grabbed an ice-cream sandwich, set my alarm for seven o'clock, and climbed into bed. I was as ready as I'd ever be. Pulling my sheet and blankets up over my head, I slowly exhaled and eased off into dreamland.

I woke up to the sound of my cell phone ringing. I forced words out of my sleep-numbed mouth. "Explain yourself."

"Are you positive that I don't need to take a pair of night-vision goggles?"

"It's four in the morning, CC. Do your brain a favor, do *my* brain a favor, *and go to bed!*"

I never did get back to sleep.

CHAPTER 10

C and I shared a silent drive all the way down to Matlacha. I didn't trust myself to talk to her, talking might lead to forgiving her for waking me up in the middle of the night, and I wasn't ready for that. She'd pulled up to my place, locked up her car, and climbed into the jeep without a word. I focused on the road, and she pretended to admire the scenery. The landscape isn't all that exciting travelling south on I-75, and it's somewhat the same once you've left the interstate and you start to head down Burnt Store Road. That area is changing, though.

It used to be that you'd drive past miles and miles of flat, scrubby land. A few years back, a gas station appeared… an oasis beside the long stretch of hot road. Now with the improvement in the economy, new homes are popping up, the road is being widened, and decorative palms sway in the breeze. The closer you get to Pine Island Road, man-made channels with homes crowding up to the edge of the water provide boaters access to the Gulf of Mexico. The houses always make me think of thirsty camels that have finally found water after crossing the desert.

Once you reach Matlacha, things change. It's not a big area at all, but it's still very much natural Florida. There's a residential area packed with "jungle" foliage. The main road through Matlacha is narrow, with just two lanes, and a causeway takes you west over to St. James City. Lined with really small, quirky, whimsically painted art galleries; authentic bait shops; and a restaurant or two, deep blue water surrounds this strip of civilization, and it's a nature lover's paradise.

Our "trial run" photo shoot home was tucked away in the residential area, and at long last we pulled in and parked in the designated guest lot.

CC broke the ban on talking. "So who's the owner?"

"Says on my info sheet, Richard and Toni Palumbo."

The front yard was environmentally friendly, meaning a mowed lawn of beautiful grass was nowhere in sight. Native plants and trees lined the path that led to the front door. Both the path and the parking area were made up of crushed shells that had been bleached white from the sun. They were so brittle that they made a nice little crunchy sound as you stepped down on them.

"Who does their walkway like this?" CC said. "These people must live in flip-flops and don't have to worry about what happens to their shoes." She was calculating every step she took, trying to avoid as many of the little things as possible.

"These crummy shells are slicing little scratches into my Michael Kors!"

"We went over what shoes to wear a hundred times. I said *practical*…now suck it up. You've got, like, five hundred pairs of shoes…you'll live."

I'd been stopping every three feet to let her catch up with me, taking a few snaps of the house as I waited.

"We're going to have to stop on the way home so that I can get some new shoes…What would Prissy Hardcastle say if she saw me wearing shoes with shell dust all over them?" She lifted a foot and held it out for me to examine her shoe.

I stared at her. "Are you kidding me? Since when did you start caring what Prissy Hardcastle thinks? Last month you told me that if she yapped on one more time about her pet pig and the pedicures she gets for it, you were going to vomit in her purse."

CC just squinted at me. "I have an ulterior motive when it comes to Prissy. Have you seen her brother? He's visiting from Brazil, and for the last week he's been coming along while we have our design meetings, Ele e divino…I could be in love with him in about five minutes. I don't want Prissy telling her brother that I prance around in dirty shoes…some people care about those things."

I rolled my eyes so hard it made my head hurt…"You don't have to be so subtle, I get it…I'm a mess most of the time. So now you're after Prissy's brother. Have you ever gone five minutes *without* falling in love?"

Hands on hips and jaw thrust out, CC went on the defensive. "You know perfectly well that my mother had me tested when I was seventeen, and the doctor said that I was normal, that my tendency to become infatuated would just taper off as I matured.

She spent all that money for three weeks of testing, and to this day, she still refuses to accept the diagnosis! She drives me nuts...did I ever tell you that she kept a chart in her bedroom closet of the number of boyfriends I had and how long the relationships lasted? I found out she and Dad used to place bets on when the breakup days would be. What kinds of parents do that?"

"Did you ever tell her about that time, four years later, when you ran into the doctor at that bar and you spent the next two days, you know, 'in love'?"

CC's lips curled into a slightly wicked smile. "Good Lord, no! Sometimes 'seeing the doctor' isn't something a mother needs to know about."

She got a dreamy look in her eyes. "When we were together, he told me he was really glad that he had misdiagnosed the length of time it would take for me to grow out of my 'enthusiastic' phase. But he told me again that I was in the normal range for libido...I'm in the ninety-nine percentile group, the high end, but *still* normal."

I just shook my head. "Your poor mother."

CHAPTER 11

We reached the front door, and I grabbed a few shots of it. I had never seen anything like the Palumbo's front door. No way was I leaving this job without pictures of something so unusual. It was *huge*...made of mahogany; it was stunning. It had strands of seaweed carved into it, and smack in the middle of all the seaweed was a mermaid. Her head was tilted back to look over her shoulder at arriving guests, and her hair was carved to look as if it was floating all around her. Her tail was flipped up, and she held a conch shell in one graceful hand.

"Damn, I want to be that mermaid," CC said.

I looked around for a doorbell and finally found it. It was right in front of my face...on the bellybutton of the mermaid.

I appreciated the placement. (Did I mention that this princess of the sea wasn't wearing her seashell bra?) They could have put the buzzer somewhere more personal and that would have messed with my head a little. I gingerly pushed on the button, and the tinkly music announcing our arrival had barely sounded two notes, when the door was yanked open, and a tall exotic-looking woman with super-short white hair stood peering down at me.

I was looking at one of those women who make you feel inferior immediately by looking you up and down whenever you're together. They start with your shoes and work their way up. They judge your shoes, clothes, make-up and hair. The most important area of judging is saved for your jewelry or, in my case, the lack thereof. And the whole time they do this, they seem oblivious to the fact that you're totally aware of what's going on. Idiots.

Finished with me, she gave CC the once-over. I put the time to good use by deciding to run the rude chick through my own checklist.

Expensive hairstylist on call…check.

Expensive leopard-print running suit to give the illusion that she exercises…check.

Diamond-covered cigarette case…check.

Diamond chips manicured onto each fingernail… check. (wowza!)

I was snapped out of my assessment of her when she cleared her throat loudly and moved on to her next bit of rudeness.

"Get your Asses in here! You're late!" she snapped.

(Raspy cigarette voice…check.)

I wasn't going to argue with her and tick her off before we even got started. She waved the drink in her hand at me. "Are you the photographer?"

"I'm London Hart, and this is my assistant, C. C. Covington."

"I'm Toni. Welcome to my home."

She ushered us in as she used up five seconds being gracious and then reverted to her authentic personality.

"Now we need to do this quickly…my husband, Richard, is ticked that I agreed to do this, so he's sulking out on the dock, *pretending* to fish."

I had wasted a lot of time the night before, worrying about how to make conversation with the homeowner. That was definitely not going to be a problem. I wasn't prepared for the verbal avalanche that started flowing out of her.

"The man doesn't know the first thing about fishing! *I* know about fishing." Her voice was getting louder and harsher. "You want to know *how* I know about fishing? I grew up working on my dad's tuna boat and learning everything there is to know about the fishing industry. I run the company now, and it's *my* family's money that bought this house and everything in it! *I'm* the one in this family who gets respect. You know what they call me? 'Toni the Tuna'! Wanna know what I call my *husband*? Richard the *Dick*."

She paused to slurp down the rest of her drink. "I was *so* excited about this photo shoot, and he had to go and take the fun out of it for me. I have half a mind to stick a fish-hook in his ass and run him up a flagpole."

Well, there was a mental image I could have done without.

Toni licked the inside of her empty glass, and just to be sure she hadn't missed anything, she swiped her finger around in it. "Let's get started, girls; I've decided that we're going to take our sweet time and to hell with Ricky. Let's start with the copper room."

CHAPTER 12

was mulling over what a room made of copper might be like as we made a left. Crowding up behind Toni, we passed through a door that, I swear, had bars built into it. I could see them protruding a little at the top. The door was dark and reminded me of the dungeon scenes that I'd seen in too many Saturday-afternoon movies.

"So what's with the door, Toni?" I said. "Up there, those things, they look like they're made of metal."

"That's for security. You never know what could happen...remember what happened at Jurassic Village!"

CC looked at Toni. "So you must have a yellow brick road around here somewhere, in case you want to go to Oz and shop the outlet malls."

Toni's back stiffened. "I was making a *joke*. I'm aware that there isn't a real island somewhere with manic dinosaurs." She turned to me. "Your friend thinks I have a screw loose. Tell her not to speak to me again."

I glared at CC, and she sniffed and became busy in-specting her fingernails.

Toni had come to an abrupt halt, and CC and I were penned in-between her and the closed security door. I stood on my toes and peeked over Toni's shoulder. Car-sized potted plants and live palm trees crowded the space in front of us. It looked like a jungle...a jungle with about twenty pairs of eyes the color of brand-new pennies peering out of it at us. So much for a room made of copper...it was all about the copper eyes...totally creepy.

Toni moved forward into the room, with CC and me nervously crowding her. She paused and lowered her voice to a whisper. "Now nobody make any fast moves...you'll scare them."

The words were barely out of her mouth, when a herd of small black muscular animals burst out of the dense greenery and charged toward us.

"Oh dear God, leopards!" CC shrieked. Two of the leopards attached themselves to her slacks like Velcro, and she lost it.

Even in times of crisis, she still had her priorities. "Get off me, damn you! You're ruining my Cavallis!

She ran off into the palm trees gyrating like a crazed belly dancer, trying to shake the leopards loose. I lost sight of her, but it sounded as though she was crashing into most of the palms, and there was an awful lot of thrashing and swearing going on.

Toni's whisper had disappeared, and she was shouting toward the palms that were dropping coconuts like mini bombs. "Stop running! Stop running! Those coconuts can kill you if they hit you on the head!" Those helpful words only increased the volume and creativity of the swearing coming out of Toni's private jungle.

Toni hadn't moved a foot, probably because she was covered in leopards. They were sitting on her shoulders and dangling off her arms. One had wrapped its front legs around her neck and was hanging on her like a necklace.

I stood rooted to the floor, and so far the leopards hadn't noticed me. I became vaguely aware of a weird, primal screaming that seemed to be coming from a distance. The horrifying noise got closer and closer, and suddenly a monkey flew toward Toni and me as if it had been shot out of a cannon. It had come prepared for battle, because it was flinging some kind of "monkey ammunition" at Toni and, because I was right behind her, at me.

Whatever the leopards had planned to do to us was no longer an issue. They leapt off Toni, propelling her to the ground behind me, and they hauled ass for the safety of their jungle home. I pivoted like a pro ice skater and went...nowhere.

"I told you two not to make any fast moves!" I looked down to find that Toni had latched onto my pants legs as she lay on the floor.

I tried to swat her hands away. "You can't blame this on us! CC only moved after she got mugged by the leopards!"

She pulled me to the ground and held tight. There was only one way to escape her grip and the monkey poo...I unzipped my pants and started to shimmy out of them.

She immediately objected to my plan of action. "Don't you dare! Don't you dare get naked in front of my babies!"

Get naked in front of her babies? Obviously her sanity had left the building, but I didn't have time to worry about that. I shimmied some more.

"If you don't want me getting naked, then let go of me!"

CC burst out of the dense foliage, and Toni lost her grip on me. CC grabbed my hand as she ran past me and tried to pull/drag me along behind her. I was all caught up in my pants, stumbling and tripping, and decided to make the ultimate sacrifice.

I dropped her hand. "It's okay, Cee, go on without me...save yourself. Run, *run*!"

We were in various forms of full retreat from the jungle of death. Toni had somehow gotten off the floor and darted past me, leaving me to bring up the rear as we escaped through the Jurassic door. As soon as I was clear of it, Toni jumped behind me and slammed the door shut.

CC had made her escape barefoot and stood clutching her shoes to her chest. Looking down at her ripped and torn slacks and her coconut-milk-covered blouse, she shot Toni an angry complaint. "Robbie made these custom for me."

Toni flicked a little monkey poo off her shoulder. *"And I should care right now that 'Robbie' made them for you?"*

CC's voice was shaking with anger. *"Cavalli!! Roberto Cavalli! Yes, you should care!!"*

"Well, excuse the hell out of *me*," Toni said. "That'll teach you to wear expensive clothes to a photo shoot. Why don't you dress like your boss...what'd you say your name was...Paris?"

"My name is London. CC can wear whatever she wants, *and I want to know what just happened in there!"*

Toni made a big show of ignoring me and made her own request. "Shall we start again?"

Chapter 13

"**S**tart again? I'm not going back in with those vicious leopards! No, ma'am," I said.

"Don't be ridiculous! Those weren't leopards. Those were my pet Bombay cats, and they're not vicious; they're my babies. They're very affectionate and loving...you saw how close to us they wanted to be." She ran her hands through her hair, and one last monkey "pellet" fell to the floor. "Now where do you want to start taking pictures?"

"Not so fast, lady," CC said. "*Explain the monkey!*"

"The monkey is Rufus. He fancies himself as the protector of my herd. He doesn't like me."

CC shot her a look. "No shit, Sherlock."

I didn't care about the monkey. I realized my pants had fallen down around my ankles again. Mentally promising to buy myself half a dozen brownie bites on the way home as a reward—should we survive the rest of this photo shoot from hell—I pulled up my pants and got down to business.

"All right," I said. "We'll try this again. But first, I want to wash my hands and face off."

Toni was surprisingly helpful. "Stay right here. I'll get some baby wipes; I buy them in bulk."

She left us for about two seconds and was back with a packet for each of us. We put the wipes to good use and then checked each other for any monkey ammo that we might have missed. Toni gave the copper-room door handle a jiggle to make sure it was securely shut.

"You girls want some orange juice? I need a sugar boost."

"Not right now, Toni; thanks. What I would like is to get outside and shoot the pool and lanai. Once that's done we can start again on the interior of the house. But just to be clear, I'm not taking any pictures of the Bombay cat room."

I didn't care if she got offended or not. The woman needed to know that I had boundaries. While I was making my little speech, a maid appeared before us with a tall glass of juice for Toni.

"Understood. Follow me this way. *Richard! We're starting the shoot!*" she bellowed. "Come on, girls."

We followed her even more cautiously than we had the first time, passing through a large living area.

The woman had taste, no doubt about that. The carpet was cream colored, and the border of it had large exotic flower patterns woven into it. The reds and oranges and greens of the flowers were a perfect complement to the soft green fabric on the sofas and chairs. Paintings with a laid-back island theme adorned the walls, and palm-frond-shaped paddles on the ceiling fans moved the gentle breeze from outside into the house. I could see a bit of the kitchen, and I got the impression that by the time she'd gotten that far in her decorating, she'd lost her sense of taste. I was looking forward to seeing more of that room.

Toni had stepped up her pace, and I hurried to follow her as we passed through retractable glass doors and reached the pool. Talk about gorgeous! It was crystal clear, and the water appeared to be moving ever so gently away from us. It was like one of those resort pools...you know the kind. You can float around on a raft or a pool noodle thingy, as if you're floating slowly down a stream. They must have achieved some kind of engineering miracle. I'm not much of a water person, but with a body of water like that to float around in, I could become one. There were groupings of comfy-looking lounges scattered here and there beside the pool, with small tables just the right size for holding your tropical drink and fabulous snack. Everything was white. White cushions and white pillows had been tossed strategically on them; a white towel was draped over a lounge.

Enclosing this tropical paradise was a huge pool cage that went all the way to the top of the second floor of the house. You could leave your doors totally open to the gulf breezes and not worry about wildlife or insects getting inside. An enormous dock the width of the property ran along what appeared to be a canal, and a tall man was working at a fish-cleaning station…Despite Toni bellowing toward him, he remained standing just as he was with his back to us. I could see a bit of his profile; he had that rugged "Marlboro Man" thing going for him. His shirtsleeves were rolled up, and he was deeply tanned.

"Richard! *Richard!* Don't you dare pretend you can't hear me! We're going to start the photo shoot, and you have to get that mess out of sight. Don't make me tell you again."

That got a response. Richard turned and walked through a screen door into the pool area, carrying a fish in one hand and a bucket of fish guts in the other. He stopped five feet in front of Toni. In a low voice that would have gotten the attention of any animal in the jungle, he growled at her…"I'll be done when I'm done, and not before then, you bitch."

Chapter 14

Was this guy a born diplomat or what? He sure knew how to handle Toni the Tuna…not.

My instincts kicked in, and I raised my camera just in time to capture Richard's expression as his face caught the drink his wife had thrown at him.

We had passed an enormous ceramic elephant when we'd first walked out onto the lanai. Seeing Richard's face transform into something out of a horror movie, CC and I instinctively backed up…smack into the elephant. A split second after Toni bounced the drink off his face, Richard went into action.

He raised the fish in his hand and pointed it at her. "YOU WANT YOUR PRECIOUS POOL IN A MAGAZINE? HOW ABOUT WE ADD A LITTLE COLOR SO IT'LL REALLY *POP!*"

With that, he threw the fish into the pool, followed by the fish guts in the bucket. The beautiful aqua of the pool instantly became transformed with ribbons of red.

I'd been busy firing the camera, and CC had decided to crawl under the elephant. She was keeping herself busy emptying the flask she had pulled from her purse, by pouring the contents down her throat. I had taken a second to glance over at CC and was relieved to get a thumbs-up from her. I was ready to join CC under the belly of the elephant, when Toni brought my attention back to the action with a skin-peeling scream. She was running for the stairs at the side of the pool. She raced up them and through another retractable door into a room that turned out to be their bedroom. In seconds, she came out of the room with her arms full of golf shirts and shoes. Leaning over the balcony, she hurled them down and into the pool.

"*You bastard!*" she shouted. "You'll pay for ruining this for me! You know how much I wanted this house in the magazine! *Paris!* Get ready to take some action shots of his precious golf clubs!"

"*London!*" CC called out from under the elephant. "*Her name is London!*"

I gave CC a death stare and held my fingers up to my lips. We didn't need Toni's wrath aimed at us.

Toni had raced back into the house; returning with an armful of clubs, she began hurling them one by one over the railing. Some of them landed in the pool, but others were deadly missiles raining down all around us. I turned to crowd under the elephant, with CC for protection. Clothes are one thing, but heavy metal rods…that's a whole different ball game.

My plan to take shelter fell apart, when for some reason, CC started to crawl out from under the safety of the elephant. Not the best decision she ever made…she got knocked out cold by the golf bag that had followed the clubs over the balcony railing.

I lunged for CC, but my right foot made contact with a slippery, bloody fish part that hadn't made it into the pool, and my feet went out from under me.

Toni the Tuna must have moved onto emptying her husband's jewelry drawer, because the last thing I remember seeing as I fell backward was a Rolex watch and a gold-and-diamond-encrusted cigarette lighter doing a swan dive toward the pool.

Chapter 15

I **was having** a nice little dream about buying a hat. The hat was smooth and slick and red and moist. Moist? That couldn't be right. The dream started taking on a sinister quality when my fingers told my brain that it could add gel-like and slippery to the materials that the hat was made of. My eyelids fluttered, and I left the dream behind. My hands were on the top of my head, so I felt around for the dream hat. No hat, just a glob of filleted fish tangled up in my hair and a splitting headache. I tried hard not to gag.

Trying not to think about what was on my head, I forced my mind back into focus, and it replayed the "Toni and Richard show" for me, ending with an image of CC out cold under the elephant. I jerked my eyes over to where I had last seen her. Just inches away from me, halfway out from under the elephant, CC was on her stomach, looking at the pool with her face the color of chalk.

She whispered at me out of the side of her mouth, bare- ly turning her head. "London…do you have your phone?"

"It's in my pocket."

"Well, now would be a really good time to call the po- lice," she said.

"Are you hurt?" I tried to get off the ground. "Where are you hurt?"

"I'm not hurt…just call nine one one. Do it *now!*"

Her tone gave rise to goose bumps on my arms. "If you're not hurt, why do we need the police?"

"Because somebody has to do something with those two, and it isn't going to be me. I don't deal with dead bod- ies. I like bodies when they're warm."

I shot a look at the pool, and it felt like my heart stopped. I made my fingers work, and I fumbled for my phone. "What was that number again, CC?"

"Nine…one…one."

I punched in the numbers and nearly dropped the phone when a voice spoke into my ear. "Nine one one… what is your emergency?"

The dispatcher spoke with that donkey voice from "Winnie the Pooh." She sounded bored, depressed, and maybe constipated.

I cleared my throat and tried to keep my voice from shaking.

"We've got bodies, two bodies."

"Okay…you've got bodies…is there an emergency with your bodies?"

"No...*yes!* Well, some of us here have an emergency with our bodies'...hell! Let me try this again...There are two bodies in a pool, and they might be dead!"

"Two bodies in a pool. Are they on little floaty rafts just relaxing, or are they being serious?"

"I'm thinking they're being serious."

"So do you think they drowned?" Madame dispatcher asked.

"*I don't know!* You're the police! You're supposed to tell me!"

"I've got officers on the way, but it would be helpful for us to have as much information as possible before their arrival."

CC was getting fed up with all the small talk on my end of the conversation. "Go over there and look at them, London. At the rate she's going, the woman won't be satisfied until you've done a complete autopsy on them. *Just go look!*"

"I heard that!" snapped the dispatcher. "You've got your phone on speaker."

"*Hang onto your thong, sister!*" CC took offense so easily. "My friend is doing her best! We're up to our necks in dead bodies here, and we're practically unconscious."

I could hear the sound of laughter coming through the phone from more than one person on the dispatcher's end.

I worked at crawling to the edge of the pool, but it was slow going. I was keeping one hand over my eyes most of the way. I really didn't want to see anything nasty. I kept my eyes on the ground for a second or two, screwing up my courage, and then peeked through my fingers at the pool. Yep, there was definitely something scary in the pool. Two bodies were bumping up against each other in the middle of the bloody water.

"CC, tell the dispatcher there are two bodies in the pool. They're not moving. Well, they're floating, but they're not, like, *intentionally* moving. Do I have to do anything to the bodies before the police get here?"

CC relayed the information. "She says to try to find out if they have a pulse."

"Are you *kidding me*? I don't want to touch dead bodies!"

CC had turned the volume up on the phone, and the dispatcher's voice reached me easily. She was losing patience with me. "If they're not dead, and you don't check for a pulse so we can help them, it's all on you. It will be your fault if they kick the bucket."

"Dammit! Hang on a minute. I've got to find something I can use to pull them over to the side of the pool."

The dispatcher decided to be my helper. "They got a fishing pole?"

"The dead guy had one earlier. I'll try to find it."

The dispatcher was now my "snarky" helper. "Take your time. I'm going to run across the office and get a latte while you get the pole…maybe even do my nails."

"There's no need to get sarcastic. I'm sorry if I'm not moving fast enough for you! I don't find dead people every day."

"Ma'am, you still don't know if they're dead...go get the fishing pole!"

Gritting my teeth, I pulled myself to my feet by grabbing onto a nearby patio table that still had the remnants of breakfast on it. A piece of greasy bacon was abandoned on the tabletop, and buttered grits had apparently missed somebody's mouth.

A casting rod with a large lure was resting against the pool cage right next to the table, and I didn't waste any time getting the lure into the air. It took me two tries to snag Toni's soggy blouse, and reeling in the two intertwined bodies had the muscles in my arms screaming. When I finally got them to the side of the pool, I went to CC and handed her the fishing pole.

"Whatever you do, don't let go of the pole."

She let go of the pole, and Toni and Richard the Dick started floating gently down the pool. I didn't care.

I was back on the phone with the dispatcher. "I'm pretty sure they didn't drown."

"And you know this because..."

"Well, it's only a guess, but unless an enormous amount of water seeped in through the bullet holes in their heads, they probably didn't drown. And I'm not checking them for a pulse...no way do they have a pulse."

"Fine, forget it. Just stay on the line until our officers get there. We don't have to talk, but it will save time if you're still on the phone with me if you decide there's something else you need to tell me."

I was thinking that was a *really* good idea, because a nasty thought had occurred to me.

Keeping the phone clenched in my hand and my eyes glued to the dense jungle growth that surrounded the pool cage, I wondered if we were being watched.

That's when CC decided to come out of her horror-induced trance and state the obvious at the top of her lungs. "THEY'RE DEAD! THEY'RE DEAD! THEY'RE DEAD!"

I hissed at her. "Why are you screaming now? You already knew they were probably dead! Do us both a favor and *shut up*. We don't know if the killer is still out there, and we don't want him or her to come back, do we?"

CC snapped her mouth shut and crawled back under the elephant. It seemed like a good idea to me, so I wedged myself in beside her.

Chapter 16

It didn't take long for the police to get there, and then the place was swarming with them.

CC and I were quickly separated and taken inside the house. I didn't know whether to be comforted by the fact that I was accompanied by several lawmen and women or intimidated. My "friends" escorted me into the kitchen, and I had a bird's-eye view of the pool area. I felt as though I was watching an old episode of the Twilight Zone as I watched CC being escorted into the house by her own herd of police officers. Once she disappeared from view, I turned my attention to my surroundings.

The kitchen/interrogation room was certainly odd. It was done in a "tiki-hut trash" motif, or maybe the look Toni had been going for was, "Tarzan and Jane got drunk and decided the jungle didn't have enough Corona beer neon signs, tiki torches, African fertility masks, and souvenir shot glasses" motif.

Toni had definitely enjoyed mixing elegance and kitsch. I don't think she could have squeezed one more Sloppy Joes Key West coaster onto the kitchen counter if she'd tried. An EMT, who had come along with an officer, and I shoved a pile of coasters aside on the counter and cleared a spot for his equipment. Serious and very professional, he ordered me to take a seat on a thatched barstool. My vital signs were quickly checked and declared normal.

The EMT didn't think I had a concussion, but I did have a very tender, swollen, egg-shaped lump on the back of my head and a small cut on the "egg," which was what had caused all the bleeding. I had to give my caregiver a "cross my heart and hope to die" promise that I would get the cut looked at if it became red and hot to the touch. Satisfied, he slapped a butterfly Band-Aid on the wound and handed me off to my interrogator, Officer Doccifer. I'm not kidding, that was his name! Try saying that three times, real fast.

Taking my statement wasn't a time-consuming event. I hadn't seen anyone else around the pool, I hadn't heard anything unusual, and I didn't see a gun of any kind. A heavy feeling of uneasiness settled over me as we talked. I was realizing that we might look less than innocent. After all, the orange juice maid, CC, and I were the only other people who had been there as far as I knew. Not exactly a plethora of suspects.

Officer Doccifer hinted that the TV drama "don't leave town" warning applied to me and let me go. If I'd been on my own, I would have been in my car and gone in under five minutes, but I wasn't alone. I needed to find my traumatized "assistant."

I found CC curled up on an overstuffed lounge chair down by the dock, and the look on her face told me she was more than okay. She was getting her pulse checked by an EMT with a perfect tan, pearly white teeth, and aviator shades hiding his eyes. She was smiling and twisting the end of her long brown hair around one of her fingers as she gazed adoringly up at him.

"Is she okay?" I asked another EMT who was standing nearby.

"She's fine," she said. "I'm more concerned about the condition of the officer who's taking her vital signs. As soon as he's done with her, I'm checking *his* vital signs…I have a feeling his pulse is going to be *very* rapid."

Judging by the bright red color of his face, I'd say his pulse rate was off the charts. He handed CC his cell phone, and she tapped in what had to be her phone number. Oh Lord, help me! She'd found another man.

I was risking my own safety, but I went ahead and broke up their cozy little moment. "Cee, we need to go."

I recognized the spark that flashed in her eyes; she wasn't happy with me. "Just another minute, London. You go ahead on to the car, and I'll catch up with you."

Once we were finally in the jeep and on the way home, I got "the look" from her.

She added words to her glare. "I don't know why we had to leave."

"We had to leave because I'm not comfortable being around people who think I've *killed* someone!"

"Well, I think you could have given me a few more minutes with that gorgeous hunk of man. Mark is the first nice guy I've met in a long time."

"I seem to remember you meeting 'the one' at a coffee shop just last week. What was his name? Bradford Moneybags? You told me he was the love of your life and that you were going to give up the boutique and grow *raisons* on a farm together, and by the way, contrary to what you told me, raisons don't come from raison seeds. Then there's Prissy's brother...what's his name—'Doofus the Third'? You told me, like, an hour ago that you had plans for him."

CC just gave a shrug of her shoulders and dug in her purse for her lipstick.

"I'm pretty sure that Mark might have been Mr. Right...I hope he calls me, because if he doesn't, I might have to experience an emergency. I could call and ask them to send him to help me."

"CC, you can't use 911 as a way to shop for a date! You're not supposed to use it like you were ordering carryout."

I could tell she hadn't listened to a word I'd said. Happy with the game plan she had for her love life, she went on to her second favorite topic. "I don't know about you, but I think I'm suffering from shock...I could use a drink."

"Where do you want to go…? And it has to be some-place with food. Finding dead bodies apparently makes me hungry."

She didn't hesitate for a minute. "Let's go to the Nest. They've got the best martinis."

I steered the jeep north, and we headed for sustenance. Once again we had a quiet drive—well, except for when I was quietly swearing at the cars that kept cutting me off at the last second. CC's angry driving advice of "Don't let them squeeze in! Don't let them squeeze in!" took my swearing to a whole new level.

Chapter 17

When we finally got to the Nest, the parking lot was packed. I had to park down at the jetty and take my chances that the pelicans roosting in the trees above the jeep wouldn't use the poor thing for target practice. We grabbed a ride on the restaurant shuttle, and in seconds we were inside the soothing darkness of the bar. It looked as though every table was taken, and there were a lot of names on the chalkboard wait list next to the door. It was going to be a while before we got a seat.

We were debating whether or not to add our name to the list, when the hostess came to our rescue.

"If you girls don't mind sitting at the bar instead of a table, there are two seats at the far end on the right."

"You're a lifesaver, honey," CC said. "Come on, London, I'm in need of a very large olive at the bottom of a very large martini."

"Forget the olive, CC; I need one of those little muffins that they serve with butter. I wish they'd give a person more than one with each meal."

"You should order the grouper nuggets, and I'll get the one-way salad. Each of those comes with a muffin, and I'll give you mine. If you get a martini, will you give me your olive?"

"The only drink I'm having is pink, which goes by the name of lemonade. See if you can get the bartender's attention. I want to order our food at the same time that he takes our drink order."

CC fluttered her eyelashes, and the bartender instantly materialized before us.

"What can Bob get you two lovely ladies?" he questioned.

"CC's going to have a dirty martini and a one-way salad," she purred at him.

"Lemonade with two cherries, please, and the grouper nugget appetizer." I had no purr in me and no desire to be flirtatious after the morning we'd had.

"Gotcha." He turned his back and got to work on our liquids. As soon as he was out of earshot, I asked CC the one-million-dollar question.

"Did what happened this morning, really happen?"

"Oh, it happened all right." She fiddled with her napkin and then started twisting it in her hands. "I keep seeing Toni and Richard the Dick in the pool, and it doesn't seem real. I mean, one minute they're fighting like cats and dogs, and the next…they're dead. Really *dead*…I've never seen anybody so dead."

"I keep wondering if maybe there was someone else there, someone who was hiding in the plants and stuff outside the pool cage. Somebody was somewhere, armed with a deadly weapon. Why didn't they kill us too?"

She shushed me. "The bartender is coming."

Bob dropped off our drinks and promised that the food would be out soon.

CC fished the olive out of her drink and chewed it thoughtfully. "I think whoever it was didn't shoot us because we were unconscious. We weren't going to be able to tell the police anything, so we're weren't a threat." She drained her glass and looked for Bob, hoping for a refill.

"Do you think the maid could have done it?"

"I suppose she could have, London, but that darling officer told me that they found her knocked out and tied up in the laundry room. If she was helping the murderer, why would they whack her on the head and tie her up?"

This time I shushed CC. "Heads up…here comes our food…the police didn't say if we're allowed to tell anyone about what happened, so we'd better not discuss it in front of anybody."

"Here you go, ladies," Bob said. "Let me know if you need anything else."

"I need something else," CC said. "I need another martini and an order of fries. I don't think this salad is going to do it for me."

"Coming right up." Bob bowed and headed for the kitchen. He must have swiped somebody else's order because he plunked a basket of golden, crispy, French fry perfection in front of her in less than a minute. Her martini followed a half second later. Bob was a wizard.

I was deep into buttering my muffin. I bit into it and savored the deliciousness. I tried a bite of a nugget, but it was way too hot. Leaving the fish to cool, I poked at the ice cubes in my lemonade and considered the maid's guilt or innocence while I watched CC finish her second drink. She ate one fry and shoved the basket an inch or two away from her. She was flagging Bob down again.

"Do you know what happened to us today, Bobby?"

So much for not discussing the murderous events of the morning.

"Enlighten me." He leaned on the bar and gave her his full attention.

That's all the encouragement she needed. "Have you ever seen a murder, Bob? I mean a *real* murder—blood, guts, and *everything*?"

She didn't wait for him to answer but just jumped into a recitation of our morning. She really put some "oomph" into the telling. Starting with the traumatic attack of the leopard cats, she wound up her tale of terror with the horrific conclusion of our visit…the murders. I don't think Bob was too impressed and probably didn't believe her because he'd started polishing glasses about halfway through the story.

"So you're telling me that all this happened to you this morning?" he said.

"Exactly!" CC said. "Not even two hours ago!"

He leaned back against the shelving that contained row upon row of liquor bottles. I could see our faces in the mirror behind him, and we looked pretty sloppy. More proof that the morning had been real. CC would never go anywhere looking less than her best unless something earth shattering had happened.

"So if I turned on the news, you two ladies would be on there, standing by some yellow crime scene tape or whatever?" he asked.

"You don't believe me!" CC gasped. "I can prove it right now!"

"London probably has a concussion, and she should have had *stitches*! Show him the back of your head, London! Show him where your head cracked open like a *coconut*!"

"My head did not crack open like a coconut," I said. "I have a cut, no cracking of the head; just a cut."

Bob had suddenly become very interested in the subject of stitches, and he looked kind of worked up. He put both hands on the bar and jutted his face up close to CC's.

"*Stitches!* You want to talk about *stitches*?? I'll bet you can't guess how many stitches I've had! I had *fifty* stitches when I lost *this*!" With that dramatic pronouncement, he held up his left hand and fanned out his fingers…half of the middle one was missing.

CC's eyes rolled back in her head. Her face went green, and she went facedown into her basket of fries.

Chapter 18

Bob saved the day and brought CC back to consciousness by waving a bottle of peach schnapps under her nose. Once her head came up off the bar, I blotted French fry grease off her face with a napkin and gave her a minute to get her bearings.

"Feel up to heading back to the jeep and then to my place?" I asked. "Your car's there, but I can take you home, and you can get the car later if you want."

"Let's just go back to your place, if you don't mind, London. I hate to admit it, but I'm not real excited about being alone right now. Do you think the killer followed us or anything?"

"Why would he? Like you said, we're no threat; we can't identify anybody, and he's long gone by now."

"Why do you think it's a he?"

"He, she, it, they, whoever…I'm sure they don't care about us."

CC got off her barstool and put a tip down on the bar. "Love the finger, Bob," she called over to him. "Sorry I was so rude about it. Save me a martini; I'll be back."

We squeezed past the tables full of locals and pushed open the heavy doors. I liked the doors, even though it was a challenge using them. They were heavy due to the weight of the stained glass windows at the top and the huge brass door handles. The brass head of a sea captain on the top of the handles caught my attention every time I ate at the Nest. No nearly naked mermaids on these doors like at Toni and Richard's. I wondered if the next owner of the Palumbo house would appreciate the doors or take them down.

CC had been asleep on my couch, curled up under my favorite fleece blanket, having a nap for the last half hour. I was in my bedroom at the computer, looking over the images I'd managed to get before the murders. It made me cringe when I thought about my scheduled meeting with Mike in just two days. I didn't have a lot of shots, and most of them were not the kind of thing you'd put in a magazine, what with the blood and all. I looked over at Handsome perched on the nightstand and sighed. My little friend hadn't been much of a good-luck charm for me as far as I could tell. Not that I blamed him in particular...it's hard for a good-luck charm to go up against domestic insanity and a mystery murderer.

"London, are you here?"

"I'm in here, CC. Are you feeling better?"

"I feel like I need food. I guess I drank my lunch."

I stopped myself from saying something that I shouldn't and went out to the kitchen. "How about a sandwich?" I asked her. "I've got a deli ham and cheese, or I've got some cold chicken."

CC came out to the kitchen, pulled a chair out, and took a seat at my little two-person table.

"Chicken, please, and a bottle of water, if you have it."

I pulled a plate out of the cabinet, grabbed a bottle of water, forked some of the chicken in the fridge onto the plate, and handed it to her. I pulled a half-eaten bag of chips off the counter, stared down at the dishes in the sink that had accumulated over the past day or so, and started shoving chips in my mouth. Stress eating...if murder isn't a good reason to do it, I don't know what is.

"I don't know about you, CC, but I'm not going to be able to sleep tonight. I'm afraid I'll have nightmares."

I pulled out a chair and joined her at the table. "Do you think it's possible that we saw something or heard something suspicious and just didn't realize it?"

CC shook her head. "I know I didn't. I couldn't take my eyes off Richard and Toni. I just kept looking back and forth from him to her, her to him. I couldn't believe what they were doing. The only thing I looked at other than the two of them was you...until I got knocked out. After that all I saw was a lot of 'dead.'"

I asked her the question that had been bothering me. "That's the part that really gets to me. Why aren't we dead, why are we still walking and talking?"

She picked up her plate, walked to the sink, and rinsed it off. "I know…it's bothering me too. I know we said it's because we were unconscious and didn't see anything, so there was no need to kill us. But there are other possibilities. Maybe the killer only brought two bullets because they thought just the Palumbos would be there."

"Why would someone only put two bullets in their gun? What if you missed the first time?"

CC rolled her eyes. "I don't know anything about how a killer packs when they're going off to murder somebody; I'm just guessing here. Two bullets, four bullets, I don't even know how many bullet compartments a gun has." She stood up and carried her empty plate to the sink. "I'm going home. This murder stuff is exhausting. I need a nice hot bath, and then I'm going to watch something stupid on TV until I forget about this—at least for tonight." She gathered up her purse and car keys and jammed on her sunglasses.

I unlocked the front door and watched her walk to her car, both of us pretending that we weren't looking into the shadows for a nut with two bullets in their gun.

Before the sun set, I made myself take a little walk down the boulevard, passing under the Spanish moss that swept down from the trees. Usually the inquisitive squirrels that scampered through the branches watching me put me in a good mood. But today, even they couldn't take my mind off the frustrating situation I found myself in. Any way I looked at it, there just weren't enough good images to show Mike at our next meeting. There went my dreams of a career *and* finding a different place to live. I didn't even eat dinner, so you *know* I was depressed. It was lights out at eight…then lights on at ten…then lights out at one.

I must have gotten hungry at some point during the night and walked to the kitchen in my sleep, because I woke up in the morning and found gummy candies under the sheets with me.

CHAPTER 19

had to find a way to fill my day, or I was going to go crazy. I was stressed about my upcoming meeting and the photo shoot failure, and I was still a little freaked out about the murders. I decided to treat myself, so I walked over to the Crust Café and Bakery. This is a dangerous place for me. Large trays of scones in the front window invite you into the bakery, and if you let yourself go through the door, you find yourself in front of their display case. Cream cheese brownies, regular brownies, chocolate chip cookies, lemon squares, all oversized and all delicious, perch on their white doilies and attempt to seduce you into buying them. Past the display case are cute little tables with white tablecloths and feminine touches that make you think "tea time."

I won't describe their breakfast and lunch menus, as I start to drool when I do describe them, and it's embarrassing for me. I restricted myself to a raspberry scone that I knew would never make it home and a chocolate chip cookie for later. Clutching my brown bag I decided to stroll past the Island Nook and see what Brenda was up to.

I saw Brenda at the same time she saw me. She was at the back of the shop, and the moment we made eye contact, she rushed toward me. Skidding to a stop, she grabbed me by both arms.

"*London, are you OK? Where were you shot?*" She spun me around in front of her. "*I don't see a bullet hole! Where's the bullet hole?*"

"I don't have a bullet hole, Brenda...I didn't get shot. I just have a little bump and a cut; I'm fine."

"You're not fine! You got shot, and then the murderer tried to bash in your head with his golf clubs!"

"No golf clubs were used on my head! Everything you just told me is wrong...who told you all this?"

"It may come as a surprise to you, but I *do* keep abreast of current events! Everybody's talking about the murders, and Toni Palumbo was actually a customer of mine. She'd drive in, and we'd talk about our golf games, and then she'd buy some of her ocean breeze candles...said they put Richard in a romantic mood."

"Richard and Toni still got romantic with each other? They acted like they hated each other's guts!"

"They had a real volatile relationship. One minute they were all lovey-dovey, and the next it was Richard Burton and Elizabeth Taylor at their worst. They didn't care *who* was around when they started to fight."

"They fought in public?"

"Where didn't they fight? I was at a charity thing on a yacht one weekend up at Marina Jack's, and they really went at it. They nearly pushed each over the railing and into the bay, before some of the men pulled them off each other."

Brenda's description of the battling Palumbos was something to think about. I wondered if they fought with other people, making enemies who would be happy to resort to murder.

"I think I might have to buy a big dog."

I hadn't expected our conversation to take such a random turn, but that's Brenda.

"Brenda, how are you going to get a big dog into your little fiat? That car's almost too little for *you*!"

"I'm not going to take the dog anywhere…it's for protection at my condo. If the beast needs to see a veterinarian, I'll just pay one to come to my place. They make house calls, don't they?"

"Protection? Did something happen?"

"Something fishy is going on next door." She lowered her voice. "You know how the place next to me is owned by somebody from up in Tampa? Well, up until recently, there's almost never been anyone there. Once in a while on a weekend, I'll hear the door slam and see a car parked in their carport space, but that's only for a few hours at the most. Now there's somebody staying there, maybe living there, because there's a car in the parking spot every night, and a few times now I've seen this young guy wearing a fancy suit going in the door. He carries this big square briefcase...it looks like the Space Age kind they use in the movies."

"You're losing me here, Brenda. What kind of briefcase do they use in the movies?"

"You know the kind. They used to be leather...that's in the older movies. It seems like they make the bad guys carry stainless steel briefcases now...or maybe they're made out of aluminum...it doesn't really matter. The point is, the thing's all shiny, and when the bad guys open the briefcase up, it's, like, full of bundles of cash. Then, again, sometimes its diamonds...sometimes the briefcases are just packed full of diamonds. I'm telling you, London, I think this guy going in and out of the condo next door is Mafia."

"How did you come up with him being in the mob?"

"I just have this feeling—this 'mob' feeling."

I could see that she was truly worried, and the Brenda that I know doesn't sweat the small stuff. Maybe something odd *was* going on with her next-door neighbor.

"Call me sometime when he's there. I'll come over and spy on him with you." I was half kidding, but she took me at my word.

"The next time he's there, I'll call. Maybe I could distract him, and you could go snoop around in his car!"

"I said I'd come over, not commit a crime! I'll *look* in the windows of his car and see what I can see; that's it." My protest fell on deaf ears, because the shop door had burst open, and a group of eager shoppers were fanning out in every direction. Brenda was already moving away from me.

"Touch base with me later, London, but first go home and take a nap. It's important to take one after you've almost been killed."

I smiled at her retreating back as she went to greet her customers. She and the gals who worked for her could be outnumbered six to one and still make sure that every customer's needs were met. I knew the bubbly shoppers would all leave the shop feeling as if they had just made new friends.

Brenda's suggestion for a nap sounded better and better, but it wasn't even noon yet. I decided to walk the rest of the way to the beach and enjoy my scone sitting on a bench and watching other people work up a sweat playing volleyball.

CHAPTER 20

Wednesday I dragged myself out of bed, climbed into the shower, prayed that the water wouldn't scald me and took the fastest shower on record. It was time to get dressed for battle, but I already felt defeated. I pulled on the black slacks that I had picked out the night before to wear for my meeting with Mr. Brant and stood at my closet, trying to decide on a blouse. Finally I just pulled a long-sleeved black top off a hanger and slipped it on. The photo shoot had been such a disaster that I was in mourning; wearing black seemed like the natural choice. I still had hair and makeup to go, but first I saved the images from the photo shoot to a third thumb drive that I'd give to Brant. Looking at the images one more time, I decided that I did have a handful of images to show for the day that weren't of total insanity.

I had the shots I'd taken as we made our way up the driveway to Toni the Tuna's house, *before* the fish fight between the couple had started. I had the images of the belly-button doorbell. In the interest of full disclosure, I included all the pictures taken at Toni's house—the good ones, the bloody ones, and the ones of "just plain crazy." At least I could prove that we'd been there…(as if the police report wasn't proof enough).

I had tried all morning to keep my anxiety level down, but finally I needed to leave for my appointment, or I was going to be late. I was driving down Venice Avenue with tension building in my knuckles as I gripped the steering wheel, and my stomach was doing cartwheels…I was just so damn nervous about meeting with Mike. Why don't the drawbridges ever go up when you need them to? I mean, if I was late because of situations beyond my control, who could find fault with me? Too soon, I found myself standing in front of Sophie, about to face Mike.

Sophie greeted me by making tiny little sympathetic noises with her tiny little mouth. She had seen the news and me standing beside a police officer, pointing toward the pool. She was full of helpful remarks.

"I couldn't believe it when I saw the news and there you were…you really should have run a comb through your hair before you let them film you. Anyway, what did you do when you found the bodies? I hate when they don't show the dead bodies…I mean, if they're not going to show you the bodies, how do you know the people are really dead? I believe in conspiracies, don't you? Do you think the Palumbos are really dead?"

"Trust me, those two have taken their last breaths."

"If you say so, London; I just met you, but I trust you. The important thing is that you're okay; and the television didn't make you look fat at all. You know they say it adds ten pounds, but you looked good—well…maybe a little bigger in the butt…Turn around, let me look."

When I didn't swing my behind around for her consideration, she hopped up from her desk and circled me.

"It's true!" she squeaked. "Your butt's not nearly as big as it looked on TV."

Well, great. Now on top of everything else, anyone who watched the news was going to think that my butt was *huge*. Before I could dwell on this happy turn of events, she grabbed me by the elbow.

"Come on, honey, Mike will be ready for you in just a minute, but I can take you to his office now. Don't you worry; nobody is going to look at your butt."

I wanted to slap her. I followed along as she babbled her way down the hallway. We reached Mike's office, and I sank into a chair, heaving a sigh of relief after she patted me on the arm and left, closing the door behind her.

There I sat, waiting for Mike. I was pretty sure I was going to hear the dreaded words, "Don't call me, I'll call you," by the time the meeting was over.

I waited for a long time…just before I was ready to start wandering the halls looking for a vending machine with *any* kind of chocolate in it, Mike shoved open the doors, strode over to his desk, and threw himself into his chair.

"So show me…what did you get?"

He stuck his hand out and snapped his fingers…I pulled the thumb drive out of my purse and slowly held it out toward him. He practically had to pry it from my grip.

"Things didn't go quite like I had planned…you know how some days your lucky charm works and some days it doesn't?" Yep, it was official; I was now babbling.

"What the hell are you talking about? Hang on; let me get this opened up."

Mike shoved the stick into the side of his laptop, and up popped the images. You could have heard a pin drop. He sat and stared, and stared some more. At least twenty images of "Toni gone wild" stared back at him from the computer screen. It took a few minutes for him to find his voice. He turned very slowly away from the screen and looked me dead in the eyes.

"Would you mind explaining to me just what it is that I'm looking at?"

"Well, if you want me to be accurate, two crazy people, some bloody fish, and a lot of overpriced clothes."

"I saw this on the news, but I just couldn't believe that they were talking about the house that I sent you to…Are you okay? You didn't get hurt, did you?"

It was nice of him to ask, but I wasn't sure that *he* was okay…. he had lurched from his chair and was pacing back and forth, back and forth.

"I'm fine; I just hope that I still have a job."

I sat waiting for him to say something, anything to let me know I was still on the payroll, but I heard nothing. Finally he looked up and let out a big sigh.

"Well, we're in the toilet for sure. Tonight's the deadline for images to be inserted into the article, so if you'll excuse me, I've got to go talk to the team and see how we can salvage this mess."

Without another word, he got up and left the office. I took this as my cue to leave. I retraced my steps back to the office door and gave Sophie a half-hearted wave good-bye. She just gave me one of her signature "I'm happy, happy, happy" smiles. She had a bunch of her mints lined up on her desk and was popping them into her mouth, definitely working on her sugar high. I was going to go find the biggest box of chocolate I could fit into the jeep and eat myself into a stupor.

Chapter 21

Half an hour later I pulled up in front of my apartment. Piles of empty wrappers slid out with me and landed on the ground at my feet as I got out of the jeep. I was beginning to think that eating all that chocolate, on top of the stress of watching my new job go up in smoke, hadn't been a good idea. I was having heart palpitations...and a caffeine-induced urge to clean out my purses. I do my best cleaning after a chocolate binge.

I decided to start my frenzy with the purse I had in my hand. I'd loaded it down with everything I might possibly need at the meeting with Mike and a lot of stuff I would *never* need. Ten minutes later, everything in the purse was scattered all over my kitchen table. I'd dug out ten dollars worth of change, a nice big pile of receipts that I methodically ripped into shreds and had licked the remaining sugar off about twenty empty mint wrappers, when the phone rang. I didn't recognize the number displayed on my cell phone, but I answered anyway.

"London?" barked a voice into the phone. "This is Mike. We need to talk."

I dropped down into the nearest chair and held my breath. Mike didn't waste any time getting to the point.

"I've got a proposition for you. I showed the images to the team, and they saw an opportunity to enhance the magazine as a result of what took place at the photo shoot. They think we could use you in two different ways. One way is to keep sending you out on architectural shoots. You know, still feature the beautiful homes, the pretty pools, the pretty kitchens…blah, blah, blah. The second way we want to use you is *really* cool. We want to have you keep your eyes open for the drama that goes on in the background, pick up on the vibe between the people who live there. Do a little chatting with the staff if you can get some time alone with them.

"You could pick up on a little gossip here, a little craziness there, and then a few weeks later, we could use that info on a tabloid page. We wouldn't use any photos that you took at the shoot in the "tab" articles, so the homeowners probably won't realize that you're the one who fed us the dirt on them. We're thinking that if we add the tabloid stuff, we'll pick up new readers…it's a no-brainer!"

Mike was talking so fast that I was truly impressed… he actually ran out of breath at the end of this marathon sales pitch.

He continued. "Now I know I'm suggesting a change of focus for the job and that there's a little 'risk factor' involved, so I'm willing to talk more money."

My brain registered the phrase "risk factor." I was pretty sure he was referring to the fact that an unhappy homeowner might figure out that I was the one who blabbed their secrets and do to me God knows what.

"How about we bump up the salary I originally offered...say an extra five thousand a year? We're going to go ahead and print the usable photos from the Matlacha shoot tonight. You know...just the standard architectural-type stuff...none of the actual fish-fight shots. We don't need a lawsuit on our hands. So the ball's in your court, London. If you want in on the tabloid stuff, I'm going to need to know as soon as possible."

"How long do I have to think about this?"

"Let's say two days? I'll give you my cell phone number. You've got the office number already, so just let me know in the next forty-eight hours...if you decide you don't want to do this, I've got to find someone who does, ASAP."

Without so much as a "see ya, love ya, or catch ya later," he was gone. I sat frozen in my chair, weighing my options.

Pro...More money, more money.

Con...Potential death, potential death.

Pro...I turn down the job and continue to feel like a legit photographer.

Con...I take the job and feel like a Paparazzi poop head.

Pro, Pro, Pro...Money, money, money.

Twenty minutes later I'd reached a decision. I'd rationalized that there was surely only a minute chance that someone would figure out that I had been the source in a tabloid article, right? I decided that the "minute" part of this deal justified my upping the ante with Mike.

He picked up after the first ring.

"So what's your answer, London? Are you on board?"

"I'm on board if you bump the salary up another seven thousand, not five thousand."

An unhappy grunt sounded in my ear and then a sigh of resignation.

"You've got it…make damn sure you earn it."

Did I hear the sound of angels singing? I was rich! (Well, hardly, but I felt like it at that moment.)

We'd meet a week from that coming Monday, by which time there would be a contract ready for me to sign. On that Wednesday, there would be a meeting with the team so that they could fill me in on just exactly what this new job was going to be all about. Mike had given me a check for the Matlacha job, and the first thing I did was pay some bills that were just a little late. I still had enough left over for a deposit and two months' rent…apartment hunting, here I come.

I felt so confident about my future that I ran out, got boxes, and started packing a few things, just to see what it felt like. It felt great, so great that I got carried away, and before I knew it, the day had flown by, and I had worked off a lot of excitement. When I finally went to bed, I laid my head down on my pillow, surrounded by cardboard boxes all packed up with nowhere to go.

Chapter 22

woke up feeling more tired than I had when I went to bed the night before. I'd had the craziest dreams all night, all of them having to do with finding a house to rent.

In every dream I would find a place that I thought would be perfect for me.

When I called for information, they'd say it had already been rented. In one particular dream, I was so frustrated with being told this that I went to a house I'd wanted to rent, armed with a spoon and a large magnifying glass that had a long, straight silver handle. I pounded on the front door, and when it opened, a family of five stood staring at me...each one of them had binoculars held up to their eyes, and they studied me silently. This struck me as extremely rude, and I swung the magnifying glass menacingly above my head as if it was some kind of ninja weapon. The residents charged out of the house and ran away down the street. I moved into the house with my magnifying glass and spoon, which was all I had…nothing else.

Did the binoculars symbolize my decision to become pseudo paparazzi, i.e., a disgusting snoop? Did the magnifying glass represent how hard I was going to have to look to find a house or apartment that was just right for me? Then there was the spoon; did it represent digging into someone's private life or simply a craving for a pint of double-barreled chocolate bon-bon ice cream?

I'd eaten my way halfway through a box of cereal, pondering the mysteries of my gray matter, when my cell phone started ringing. Brenda's face was looking up at me from the screen as I swiped open the call.

"London, is that you?"

"Who did you think you were calling?" I asked.

"You! I was calling you! Can you come over, like, right now? The guy next door is back, and he's not alone; there's a giant with him!"

"What's going on, Brenda? Have you had something to drink?"

"*I haven't been drinking!* The glass is totally empty!"

"So there *is* a glass involved. What's the glass doing?"

She sighed into the phone, and her exasperation came through loud and clear. "I'm holding the glass up to the wall so I can hear what's going on in the neighbor's condo. You said you'd come over and check out his car the next time he was here…well, he's here, and he has some *gigantic* guy with him…Is there any way you can come over now?"

"Give me ten minutes, and I'll be there. Tell me which car is his; I'll check it out before I come to your place."

"He's parked in space one hundred and two; the other guy parked in the guest parking down at the far end. Just look for a big black van. That's what he was driving."

"Got it…you just sit tight, and I'll be right over."

"I'm going to give you a seven-minute start, and then I'm going to create a distraction. That way you can check out the cars, and nobody will notice."

"I don't think that's necessary, Brenda. No one is—"

She cut me off. "You just worry about the cars. I'll take care of the rest."

The phone went silent as I grabbed my keys and my purse and slammed out of the apartment. What was Brenda's idea of a distraction? That had me worried… Brenda never did anything halfway, and occasionally that had backfired on her. I should have worried less about Brenda and paid more attention to what I was doing.

Without hesitation I jumped into the jeep and grabbed the blistering-hot steering wheel…I had no idea that I even *knew* some of the words that came out of my mouth. I wasted two minutes sitting in the jeep with my hands pressed against the air-conditioning vent, cooling off my crispy fingers.

Once I finally got on the road, I had to contend with fire engines. I pulled over four times to let emergency ve-hicles pass me, and I was way late getting to Brenda's. Way *too* late.

Brenda hadn't been kidding about a distraction. The emergency trucks that had passed me were all lined up in front of her condo when I pulled into a guest parking space. If I was going to take advantage of her dramatic efforts, which hopefully did not include setting the building on fire, I needed to hurry. I started my investigation of the cars that belonged to "the bad guys," with the van parked two spaces down from me. After I'd checked the van, I found the car parked in space one hundred and two...just like the van, the windows were tinted so dark I couldn't see a thing inside it. I just saw me looking back at me.

I knew Brenda was going to be disappointed, but looking through the windows was all I'd promised to do. I walked back toward her place and realized that Brenda's door had been bashed open, and there were people gathered in small groups, watching the firemen. There didn't seem to be any frantic activity, and no smoke or fire was coming out of her place. I gave a little sigh of relief. It looked like her plan hadn't caused any damage that could earn her prison time.

I pushed my way through the crowd that had gathered and tapped the shoulder of a guy wearing a fireman's coat that had "Captain McDewy" printed across the back of it.

He swung around, and his frown was enough to make me start backing away. I'd only gone about two steps, when his frown disappeared, and he reached out and grabbed my arm.

"Tell me that you're London."

"I'm London. How did you know?"

"The lady who's stuck in the ceiling did a good job of describing you."

"Excuse me?"

"Here's the situation…your friend crawled up into the attic of this building. You see how there's one common roof for all these units? Well, there's an attic that runs all the way across, and for some reason your friend went up in there…she won't say why. There's nothing stored up there, but up in there she goes, and she manages to slip off the rafters and put her legs through her neighbor's ceiling. Are you okay with going up into the attic and talking to her?"

I started to sweat just thinking about how hot it would be up in the attic. I don't really handle heat all that well, and Brenda had been trapped in it long enough for it to become a serious threat to her health.

"Show me how to get to her," I said. "She must be a wreck by now."

"Far from it." The captain laughed. "I could use a woman like that on my crew…from what I've seen, I'd say she's a bit of a warrior. We wanted to start extricating her right away, but she refused to let us touch her until you got here. She even threatened to bite me when she got loose. Apparently I was 'giving her a look.'"

Hearing Brenda described as a warrior made me laugh in spite of the circumstances…the biting part didn't surprise me all that much.

"I hadn't thought of her like that before, but I think you're onto something."

Captain McDewy led me to the emergency stairs that were on the backside of the units, and we climbed up to a small access door that stood open. A few pieces of plywood had been put down just inside the open door to provide a small solid spot to stand on; everywhere else it was just rafters and insulation. Light from a single bulb illuminated a five-foot circumference, and after that it was pitch black, almost.

Quite a bit farther down from where we were standing, I could see lights bobbing around, and firemen standing on the attic rafters, holding onto the roof joists to keep their balance. As we gingerly inched our way farther into the attic, I began to see the outline of something rising out of the insulation on the floor. Talk about creepy...the thing on the floor wasn't moving, and the attic was as silent as a tomb; no one spoke a word.

"She's conscious, isn't she?" I whispered to the captain. "Why isn't anyone talking?"

"She got upset when they asked her questions," the captain whispered. "My men decided the best thing to do would be to just keep everything as quiet as possible so that she'd stay calm. If she moves too much, she'll go the rest of the way through, and I've seen people end up in the hospital with some pretty nasty wounds from being cut up on their way down."

We reached the silent group, and there was Brenda… eyes closed…the picture of calm, collected, and sweaty.

"Brenda," I whispered, "I'm here. Can you hear me?"

Her eyes flew open. "Well, of course, I can hear you!" she shouted. "I'm not *deaf*!"

Two firemen jumped at the sound of her voice and disappeared out of sight. They did a lot of yelling on their way down.

Chapter 23

An hour later, Brenda had been hoisted to freedom. The firemen were all gone, two in ambulances, while the others rode back on the horses that had brought them…the fire trucks. Aside from the door-replacement company employee who was putting the finishing touches on her new front door, we were alone.

Taking no chances on being overheard, we went into her kitchen to talk things over. Brenda went straight to the refrigerator and got us each a bottle of cold water.

I got right to the point. "So…I think that in the future, should the need arise, maybe you could create a smaller distraction."

"That wasn't supposed to be the distraction. I just decided to take a different approach to hearing what my neighbor was saying, and it turned *into* the distraction. I have to say, I am kind of proud of myself—I definitely had everybody's attention. You got a chance to check out the cars, right?"

"Brenda, I couldn't see inside them…the windows were all blacked out."

"You couldn't see anything, nothing? There's got to be a way to get some kind of clue as to what's going on with these guys." She massaged her temples, hard, as if she could make a clue pop right out of her brain.

"I'm going to go online and order a professional listening device, like a 'bug' or something, one that actually *can* hear through walls, and then I'll give it another try. I might have to call you again, London."

"I'm not making any promises. I don't want to have to go off, who knows where, the next time you get stuck somewhere. There could have been big old spiders up in that attic. Now I'd like to take a minute and ask the obvious question. How did you go from trying to listen to your neighbor with a glass held up against the wall to being stuck in his ceiling?"

"It's complicated," Brenda said. "You already know that I couldn't hear any sounds coming from next door using the drinking glass. I'm starting to think that's one of those 'urban myths' that people keep falling for. Anyway, I went outside to watch for you, and I heard voices coming from the guy's open upstairs window, but I couldn't make out what he was saying. I knew listening with a glass was a waste of time, so I thought I'd just attack the problem from a different angle."

"Personally I think I would have picked a different angle."

"*Anyway*, I read somewhere on the Internet that the sound of voices travels up, so I went up into the attic and walked across those board things to get right over his second-floor area. I wanted to get as close to his ceiling as I could, to listen, so I started to crouch down, and then my feet went out from under me, and there I was…stuck."

"What happened when you poked holes through the ceiling with your legs? What did your neighbor say?"

"Nothing! There was just total silence until the firemen got there."

"How did the firemen find out you were in trouble?"

"Well, I had my phone in my blouse pocket, and once I pulled myself together, I called the police. They said they'd *already* gotten a call and that help was on the way. The only way somebody would know that I needed help was if they were *in* that condo! The next time I'm going to do something that forces whoever is in there to come out."

"Does there need to be a next time? Maybe this whole episode was a sign…you know…a 'leave your neighbor alone' sign."

"Don't be ridiculous, London. I proved that there's something weird going on next door. I'm not going to stop *now!*"

"What proof do you have?"

"Well, nothing concrete, but wouldn't a normal reaction to seeing fire trucks roll up in front of your house be to come outside and see what's happening? If the door next to you were being broken down with a battering ram, wouldn't you want to know why? If somebody's legs were hanging out of your ceiling, wouldn't you yell up and ask if the owner of the legs was in trouble? Wouldn't you try to do something or at least let the legs know that you called for help? No one did any of those things! Someone was in there, because *someone* let the ambulance people into that condo to rescue the guys who fell through the ceiling. Someone didn't want to be seen."

I had to admit she had a point—several, in fact.

"I need a shower," she sighed. "Now seriously, London, can I call you if I come up with a new plan?"

I sighed. "I guess, but remember my rule—I'm not doing anything criminal."

"You leave that up to me." She laughed.

She held open her brand-new door and nudged me outside. I gave her a snappy salute and made a beeline for the jeep. Having done my good deed for the day, I was going to head home and start the search for a new place. A place that didn't have a shared roof or an attic sounded like a really good idea.

Chapter 24

think I spent most of the next day and a half checking out rentals and eating shortbread cookies. It was about noon on the second day when I began to realize that I had spent so much time on the computer that I was having trouble straightening my fingers. I stood up and tried to stretch my body like a cat would, every little inch of it.

Even though it was ninety-three degrees outside, the humidity had dropped, and it was actually bearable outside. I needed to breathe some air that hadn't been cooled by an air conditioner, so I scooped up my keys and shoved my debit card into the pocket of my shorts. I had just walked out the front door, when I ran into a neighbor...Karen always had her finger on the pulse of our little town.

"I heard a rumor today that you're looking to move, London. Are you?"

"If I can find a place…everything is getting snapped up so fast, it's starting to look like I might be staying right here."

"I might have an idea for you." She shot me a happy smile as she tried to capture the strands of her long hair the breeze insisted on playing with. "I've got this friend, and *she* has a friend who owns a horse ranch south of town. There's a little house clear at the back of the property, and it just became available."

"Seriously, Karen? That sounds exciting!"

"I thought you might like the idea. It's a really cool little place, and it's always really hard to get a shot at it. The minute it's listed, it gets snapped up."

"I didn't see it online," I told her. "Why isn't it on there?"

"Because when I say it just became available, I mean it *just* became available. The renters who were living there cleared out in the middle of the night…I'm talking *last* night. My friend called me this morning to see if I knew anyone who would be interested in moving in—mid-month—and do a prorated rental for the last two weeks and stay on after that. It's not listed with a realtor yet, so you could swoop right in and snatch it up."

"Do you know why the renters left?"

"It turns out they had an allergy…an allergy to paying the rent. They were two months late. They snuck out before the sheriff came and booted them out."

"Who can I contact about it? I guess I could take the time to check it out." I was trying to act all cool and calm, but I was mentally chewing my fingernails.

"Let me run back to my place and get the contact info." She zipped off, and I paced the sidewalk.

She was back in five minutes and handed me a business card. "Now call right away. I've heard the place is just the cutest!"

I resisted the urge to blow kisses at her as she went on her way and nearly broke an ankle in my rush to get back inside my apartment to call the number on the card. Hoping for a lucky break, I held my breath while the call connected.

Had Handsome worked his lucky-charm magic…? I thought so, because Wednesday morning found me moving into a tiny little house that had a tiny little porch, with a tiny little white porch swing. The house was painted a green that I decreed was "soft tropical green"…CC called it, "sea-foam green." Whatever it was, I loved the color, and the house felt welcoming and calming and sat in the middle of a group of palm trees that were busy dancing in the breeze.

Cream-colored walls made a nice background for a pretty yellow sofa and love seat in the living room. A coffee table with black metal legs sat before them, and it had a really cool top. It actually had a drawer that pulled out from under the glass tabletop. You could put all kinds of things in there for people to look at.

At the back of the living room, there were French doors that opened into a very small den…perfect for a studio. Arched windows looked out over the little garden in the backyard, and sunlight spilled into the room.

Down a tiny hall off the living room, a single bedroom was proclaimed "butter yellow" by CC.

"That's not butter yellow, CC," I argued. "It's more of a daffodil yellow."

"There's no such thing as daffodil yellow. I have never, in all my years as a designer, heard of a color called daffodil yellow." She narrowed her eyes and glared at me.

"Calm yourself nutso. It's only a color; call it whatever you want." She'd been helping me all morning, and I wasn't going to blow it by arguing with her just because, in my opinion, she was colorblind.

I opened a box and pulled out a cami—just what I had been looking for. I clutched the top in my hand and took a minute to admire the white dresser tucked into the far corner. I was in love. It could have been neon green, and I would have still been happy; it had big drawers, little drawers, drawers with drawers in *them*! My old place had plastic cabinets, and they had worked fine, but a dresser…this was living.

My queen bed looked right at home up against the east wall, and when we moved my spindly legged bedside tables in and added my lamps, the room felt really cozy. The one and only bathroom in the house was just feet away from my bed, and that was going to be awkward when a guest needed to use the facilities, but it would just have to do.

I headed back to the kitchen to help CC. The kitchen was small, but I felt like Goldilocks…it was just the right size for me. It had the littlest stove I'd ever seen in my entire life, and it was obviously quite old. Amazingly, it was still bright white with shiny black knobs, the burners were original, and the cute little clock on it ticked along happily. The walls were painted the same cream color as the living room, and CC peppered me with all kinds of suggestions for accent colors.

There was a two-person breakfast table and chairs, a little on the small side, but as long as I had a place to sit down and eat, I was happy. I loved every inch of the place, including the Gardenia-scented air that floated through the windows.

CC and I had made a certain amount of progress in the unpacking of my stuff…we might have made more if I hadn't had to go back and redo everything she'd done. I'd found my bras in the refrigerator and my panties in the freezer…I was afraid to go back and look in my dresser drawers.

We placed the last box of my things in the house after what seemed like hours of unloading, and finally I collapsed onto the front-porch swing. *I* may have been exhausted, but CC still had the energy to chatter away.

"I never even knew this ranch was here! I mean, who would have guessed that a ranch this size, with one of its borders being the Gulf of Mexico, was this close to town?"

She looked across the fields sectioned off with white fences that enclosed acres and acres of land. Men and women on horseback were obviously seeing to the business of caretaking the property, and you could tell that the ranch was serious business.

Not too far from the front porch was a huge fenced area that just happened to have some beautiful horses grazing fairly close to the front and side of the house. I couldn't believe that I was sitting on my front porch watching horses. If I had to pick only one subject to shoot for the rest of my life, it would be horses.

"Look at those beautiful animals...you got *so* lucky when you found this place. I like city life, but this is pretty divine!"

"There's one more thing that's pretty divine about this place. If you follow that path over there, it takes you right to the gulf and a white sandy beach."

"How perfect! You could take a drink and a handsome man to the beach, and it would be a fantasy. A man, the sand, ooooh...just think of the potential for romance."

I knew what was coming...more advice on my love life. Rescue from this tiresome topic came in a very unexpected form. CC had wandered off the porch and was moving in the direction of the path and the beach beyond.

"Well, what the *hell*?" she yelped. "I just stepped on a freaking road apple...You've got horse shit in your driveway!"

She'd done a pretty thorough job of it...both shoes were firmly planted in a gift left behind by an anonymous horse. She dropped down onto her knees and awkwardly slid her feet out of the shoes. Barefoot and ticked off, she got off the ground and tried to tug her shoes loose from the manure. As they finally came free, they made a yucky suction noise.

"Oh sweet mother of Versace!" she shrieked as she held the stinky shoes as far from her as possible. "This is so gross!"

She pinched her nose shut and, holding the shoes with one hand, changed direction and headed for her car.

"I'm out of here," she snarled. "This smell is getting into my pores! How am I going to walk into the lobby of my building? The doorman will vomit when he smells me!"

I was all set to tell her it wasn't that bad as she inched along, but then it happened. She was just a foot away from the safety of her car, but so was another collection of horse doody. CC's bare feet were drawn to it as if it was a magnet…oh, the horror.

Swearing up a storm, she threw her shoes in a wide arc. They came down to earth over in the field next to some very surprised horses. She pulled tissues out of her pocket, wrapped them around her toes and yanked the door of her car open. Angling herself into the driver's seat of the gleaming Mercedes, she gave me a look of agony. I was pretty sure it was because she had to press down on the pedals with her icky foot.

"I love your new place, London, and I'm really happy for you, but I'm going home to clean the lovely country 'atmosphere,' which is oozing between my toes, off of me."

"You can wash your feet off here. You don't have to drive all the way home like that."

"No way! Who knows how many more little plops I'll step in if I try to get back over to the house? Crap, now I'm going to have to sell my car!"

She put the car into gear, pinched her nose shut tight with two fingers, and the car jerked and lurched up the winding driveway as she got used to driving barefoot and filthy.

After CC's car had disappeared from sight, I spent another hour digging through packed boxes, looking for my pajamas, toothbrush, etc. so that I could change and climb into bed when I was ready.

Organized for the night, I decided to follow the path to the beach and enjoy watching the sun go down over the gulf…I kept a close eye on the ground until I was sure I was out of the horse droppings danger zone. Reaching the beach I realized that I couldn't remember being this happy in a long time. I sat in the sand, enjoying the gentle gulf breeze, and after the sun was gone and the orange and pink streaks left behind were fading away, I retraced my steps back to the house.

Quiet…peace and quiet…no drawbridge bells clanging…no ambulance sirens…just quiet. The distant sound of the waves washing onto the beach whispered to me through the windows. I was going to enjoy getting used to that. I locked up for the night and crawled under the covers. My grown-up life was finally beginning.

CHAPTER 25

I **woke up**, and it took me a minute to figure out where I was. Waking up in a strange place is always disconcerting for me. The door is in the wrong place…the walls aren't where they're supposed to be…it's such a weird feeling. I grabbed a quick shower and washed the weirdness out of my head. I had four days to get settled, and I was going to enjoy every minute.

I grabbed my favorite pair of worn-out jeans and Cape Haze T-shirt and got dressed. I knew I'd be changing later when the day would get hotter, and I'd have to do some digging then to find the box that I'd packed all my shorts in. Right now, I didn't want to take the time. I *did* take the time to dig out an old pair of worn-out cowboy boots that I'd had for years. After CC's unfortunate experience with the horse litter, I was taking no chances.

I was now clean, dressed…I was Super-Motivated Girl! I took my unstoppable self to the kitchen, where, with any luck, I'd find something for breakfast in the kitchen. My super senses told me that the chocolate-milk container was trying to push the refrigerator door open, so I helped it out, poured a glass of the delicious nectar of the gods, and carried it in to my little studio. I switched on my laptop and watched the circle thing go round and round on the black screen for a minute. No matter how fast it pulls itself together and is up and running, I'm too impatient to stand around waiting for it. Satisfied that it was waking up, I took a moment to go out and enjoy the view from the front porch.

I let my eyes wander over the fields where I'd seen the horses the day before and was surprised to see one standing right near the fence…I had the distinct feeling that I was being judged…by a horse…a horse who didn't seem very impressed with the human it was looking at.

I was, however, *very* impressed by the horse I was looking at. It was a big, beautiful bay, and it had a commanding presence. I walked over to the fence…the horse took a few steps backward as I approached, so I had to stand on tiptoe to stretch my hand out far enough so that it could take a sniff. I guess you could say I was letting it check my ID.

I must have checked out fine, because it moved closer to the fence, and I was able to reach out and lay my hand on its neck.

"Good boy…aren't you something?"

I was so focused that I didn't hear the sound of someone approaching until a voice behind me made me freeze just where I was.

"Looks like you've made a friend, but if I were you, I'd move my hand away real slow and take a step back."

The voice behind the words was deep, with just a hint of some kind of accent. I didn't question what was obviously an order. I was pretty sure that I'd made some kind of major mistake…sneaking one quick pat on the horse's neck, I turned around to face the music for whatever I had done wrong. Looking down at me from the back of a coal black horse was the owner of the voice. It was a good thing I was holding onto the fence. I was looking at someone right out of a romance novel.

White cowboy hat…blue jeans…chaps to protect long, long legs during a day of riding…white cotton T-shirt…and well-worn boots. The aviator sunglasses he wore to protect his eyes against the brilliant Florida sun, in addition to everything else, made him…well…(whisper this next word with me)…*sexy*. I was having a hard time swallowing.

Did I swoon, falling to the ground like a graceful swan, causing him to leap from the stallion and sweep me up into his arms?

No, no, I did not. This is real life…but my legs got a little weak…just for a minute.

What I *did* do was blurt out the first thing that came to mind.

"He started it!" What the *hell* was I talking about?

"Excuse me?" The low voice sounded amused, which immediately irritated me.

"I just meant that the horse was already standing there, and, well…who doesn't go over and pet a horse when it's standing there looking at you?"

Well, that just made *so* much more sense than "he started it"…I felt like a fool.

He studied me for what felt like a year and then shifted in his saddle…He tipped his hat back, and locks of black hair fell out and over his forehead, halfway covering his sunglasses. When he spoke, he spoke slowly, as if gently correcting a child.

"Well, I'm really glad that you wanted to be friendly, but it's always a good idea to be careful around an animal that you don't know. Your new friend is named Reckless. He's a retired military horse, and it's a pretty good idea to leave him be. He's not always in the mood to be social."

I tilted my chin up, I knew there was no reason for it, but I was feeling defiant. "Well, he didn't seem to mind my petting him." I was still feeling defensive, and besides, it was the truth.

"I still can't quite figure that one out. Either you're very lucky, or I've just met the only other person on this ranch that Reckless has ever liked…I think maybe I should introduce myself." In one smooth motion, he was off the horse and walking toward me. He was tall—really tall. And here's the thing; I knew this guy…well, I knew this guy's body. Not *that* way…really, you people with your dirty minds…I recognized his body. Oh hell, I give up.

He reached out and took my hand. "I'm Ryder. You must be the new tenant."

With him suddenly so close to me, I was having a hard time remembering *who* I was. He smelled of leather and the warmth of the sun…I know there is no warmth of the sun's smell, but how else am I going to describe this? He just smelled…*delicious.*

We had finished with the handshake, but he stood looking down at me, not letting go.

The warmth from the palm of his hand where it pressed into mine was spreading through my entire body…slowly I tugged my hand free and held it behind my back. It was still pulsing with…something.

It took me a minute to stop concentrating on the sensation in the palm of my hand and to remember how to speak English.

"Yes, I'm the new tenant. I'm London, London Hart. Are there any other hidden dangers here on the ranch that I should know about?"

Everything in me was telling me that *he* was one of those hidden dangers.

"Reckless is the only horse and the only thing here that you need to be cautious with. Everything else is harmless enough."

As he spoke he walked to the fence. That was all it took for Reckless to move right up to him and stretch out his neck. He bobbed his head up and down and placed his muzzle on Ryder's outstretched hand. I gave a little shudder…I knew what it felt like to feel the heat from that hand.

"He sure seems comfortable with you. Do you two have a history?" I asked.

"I've been here for five years, so we've had plenty of time to get to know each other."

He took a minute and ran his hand over the horse's neck and mane. "So what's your story? Reckless is a smart horse, and if he trusts you this fast, there's a reason."

"I don't have much of a story. Let's just say that over the years I've learned to read an animal's body language. I know when an animal is better left alone, and I know when they're approachable. Reckless isn't a threat to me."

He stood and studied my face, and then he lowered his sunglasses and looked down into my eyes. "There's something about you, London Hart…I'm going to enjoy finding out just how well you do read body language."

He turned, and in a few fluid strides, he was beside his horse and swinging up into the saddle. He looked at me and tipped his hat, just like something out of a movie. He whirled the horse around and left me watching him ride down the winding drive.

Standing there staring after him, I realized I was absolutely reading his body…language. Oooooh baby…my hands were sweating, and I thought maybe I had a fever. I didn't even want to *think* about what my body language was telling me.

Chapter 26

I'm going to come right out and admit that I spent the next few days daydreaming about Ryder. I had no control over it. I didn't make a conscious decision to savor every moment of our meeting; it just kept happening. It was embarrassing. By Sunday night I was finally able to force myself to focus on my upcoming meeting with Mike and the aspects of the job that hadn't been addressed yet.

Monday rolled in, and I spent two hours with Mike, discussing my salary, benefits, and all that wonderful heavenly stuff. In a few days we'd meet again, and I'd get introduced to the rest of Mike's team and learn more about the actual plans for my photo shoots. I think I may have danced my way back to the jeep.

Years ago, I developed a bad habit of rewarding myself with food. Today I felt that I totally deserved a reward for landing such a great job…for handling myself like an adult at the meeting with Mike…for not eating a candy bar from the vending machine on the way out of the building…therefore, I deserved cheesy popcorn. I zipped into the grocery-store parking lot, ran inside, and grabbed my favorite brand of delicious popcorn. I found a checkout lane that was miraculously empty and kept my eyes fixed on the conveyor belt that gave my snack its ride toward the scanner.

I refused to look to my right, as that's where the candy bars were…there's got to be a special place in hell reserved for the evil genius that thought up that product placement. It was bad enough that I knew the candy was right beside me, calling my name, but then Janice, the checkout gal, went to work on me. "You wanna buy a candy bar today, honey?"

I'm tough, so I knew I could handle her. "No, thanks, just the popcorn."

"It's buy two, get the third one free."

"No, thanks, I'm a recovering sugarholic."

"Tell ya what." She snapped her gum and adjusted her bra strap. "You buy two, and if you don't want the third one, you can give it to me, and I'll eat it for you. The management don't care what happens to the candy as long as I make my sales quota for the day on these things."

"I'm really sorry, but if I buy those, I'm just going to eat them, and I'll blow my one day of sobriety, although technically I guess it's a half day."

"You want me to lose my job?" She put her hand on her hip and gave me a disgusted look. "I got three cats to support. What'ya got against cats?"

"I don't have anything against cats *or* you. I don't want to get fat just because you have to meet a quota."

She threw my purchase at me. "Next time you come in here, don't get in my lane."

I stalked out of the store and climbed into the jeep, ripped the popcorn bag open, and stuffed a handful of it into my mouth. Two more handfuls of popcorn later, I gave myself a mental slap. Stress eating had gotten me again. I jammed the key into the ignition and roared out of the parking lot. The rest of the way home, I moved my hand to the bag, grabbed a little popcorn, and ever so casually dangled my hand out of the window. What? If the popcorn just happened to accidentally slip from my fingers, leaving a trail behind me, was that a bad thing? It was biodegradable and I wouldn't gain five pounds in one afternoon.

Ten minutes and ten cheese-stained fingers later, I was home with half a bag of popcorn less than I started with. Yes…if you must know, I did lick the salty, cheesy leftover stuff off my fingers…it's allowed…you don't want to get that all over your steering wheel…you know you'd do it, too, so stop giving me a hard time.

Anyway, something was different when I pulled up in front of my cute little house…it could have been the large horse standing by the front porch, but that was just a wild guess. Taking my time, I got out of the jeep and slowly walked toward Reckless. Sudden moves didn't seem like a good idea. You never know when a horse is having a bad day. I finally reached the porch and decided that a casual conversation couldn't do any harm.

"So…how about them Colts? I mean the football team, not, you know, the colts over in the field."

I hate it when a horse thinks I'm dumb. Reckless was obviously not impressed with my small talk, because he just kept right on eating grass and ignored me. I climbed the stairs onto the porch.

"Don't go anywhere; I'll be right back."

I let myself into the house and made a beeline for the kitchen. I grabbed an apple and a carrot and decided against taking him organic grapes. I went back out to Reckless with my bribes and solemnly passed a carrot over to him.

"What do you say we go for a walk and figure out how you got here?"

He didn't seem to have a problem with that, and munching away on the carrot, he followed me over to the side of the house. I'd seen a small gate in the fence just off the side yard when I first moved in but hadn't paid much attention to it. The minute we rounded the corner of the house, I saw the gate standing open. The latch had been moved to the side, and I didn't see any one around who might have opened it.

I stood and stared at it, and while I watched, Reckless walked past me, back through the gate, and into the pasture. Turning around, he put his neck down over the top of the gate and pulled it closed. I dropped the apple. Did I actually see what I just saw? It took me a minute, and then I picked up the apple, walked over, and slid the latch. Without saying a word, I handed the apple to Reckless.

I spent two days trying not to obsess over cheesy popcorn, avoiding sugar and keeping an eye on Reckless, I wanted to figure out how he got the gate open. I would sit on the porch and pretend to read a book, peeking over the top of it once in a while to see what he was doing. He never did anything exciting; he was just very busy being a horse. Once, he got close to the gate, and I was sure that I was finally going to solve the mystery. No such luck; he wasn't giving up his secret…he just walked to the gate and, hanging his head over it, gave me a bored look. Finally I had to abandon my surveillance. The next day was Wednesday, and I had to go to my meeting with the team.

Of course, the big day arrived, and I woke up late. I dressed in record time, skipped breakfast, and grabbed a carrot out of the fridge. I gathered all my things together, jerked the front door open, zipped through it, locked it, and trotted down the steps.

I found Reckless in his usual spot by the fence and offered him the carrot. Instead of my usual report to Reckless on how I was going to spend my day, I made our chat super short.

"Hey, bud, wish me luck; I'm off to get my first assignment. Hold down the fort until I get back, and *no* opening the gate unless I'm here to see it."

Reckless chewed on his carrot and gave me a stern look.

Chapter 27

The traffic gods had smiled on me, and I'd made it through every light on the way into town. Right on time, I was sitting in front of Sophie's desk, waiting for her to show up so that she could tell someone that I was there and ready for the meeting. Behind Sophie's desk was the main computer/file room for the office...Like almost every other area of the place, the walls were all glass, and everything about that room was very high tech, ultramodern, and intimidating.

I was scrolling through my phone to kill time and didn't hear Sophie come out of the file room until the doors made a soft little "whoosh" as they closed behind her. She took a few quick steps and invaded my personal space...apparently she needed to study me at close range.

"Hi! How are you? I love that purse! I meant to tell you the other day that I like your hair...is that red your natural color, or are you getting it done? My sister has red hair; well, it was red, but now it's kind of brown...Anyway, she colors it all the time, because she's got a ton of white hair...she's only thirty! It doesn't seem fair that she's got white hair when she's so young. How old are you? Have you got any white hair? Here, let me look!" She reached out and started spreading my hair apart at the roots with her fingers.

I slapped her hand away before I could even think... never let it be said that I have slow reflexes. Drat...! The poor woman was turning as red as my hair. One second I was ready to take her towering hairdo and load it and her into a shredder, and the next second I'm apologizing to *her* for fondling *my* hair! What was wrong with this picture?

"Sorry, Sophie, I have this thing about people picking through my hair, and I didn't expect to have someone getting intimate with me so early in the morning and...sorry, I didn't mean that the way it sounded."

The more I babbled, the more irritated I got, but the babbling seemed to be helping Sophie. Her color had started to fade back to a nice normal pink, and she looked as if she was making a nice recovery. Somewhere a buzzer buzzed, and she grabbed my hand and jerked me out of my seat.

"Let's go, London...I don't know about you, but I'm *so* excited to get started!"

She opened a door and shoved me through, and I was looking at "the team." Sophie rattled off everyone's name so quickly that I knew I wouldn't remember a single one. They were friendly enough and seemed excited about taking on a new project. By the end of the meeting, I had my secret spy-mission details. Sophie would take care of scouting a location, contacting the homeowner, and arranging a date for the photo shoot. She would e-mail me all the info and answer any questions I had.

When I was done with the onsite part of the job and had the images ready for Mike, he and I would connect, and I'd give him the files and any tabloid-type stuff I'd picked up. That's when the team would take over and decide what they were going to do with everything. As we left the meeting, Sophie was practically skipping, and she looked like a ten-year-old on a sugar high.

"Ooooohhh…I just love this!" she squealed in her tiny little voice. "I'm officially an assistant to a spy. I mean, I know I'm not *really* your assistant, but I do get to send you spy emails! This is just so awesome!"

"You do know I'm not what you would call a real spy, right, Sophie?"

"Well, not technically, but you're sort of going to be one…I've watched a *lot* of television shows and movies that had spies in them…and you're going to do sneaky stuff like they do."

As we reached her desk, and I headed for the front door, she did a quick spin, gave me a huge hug, and skipped toward the ladies' room. "Little Miss Zippy on speed"… that's what I was going to call her from now on. Yes, sir, she was one strange potato.

It had only taken about two and a half hours to complete the meeting with the team, and since I had two days to prep for the job, I decided to drive up north to meet CC for lunch. I didn't even call her to see if she was free…if she was busy, I knew a place where I could get an awesome chocolate-chip cookie, and I'd skip lunch.

The normally hushed tones of the boutique didn't exist when I walked through the leaded crystal doors of the shop. I could hear raised voices on the second floor, but all was quiet on the first floor. This floor was the stuff of dreams.

Customers could wander among the samples of CC's work that adorned mannequins throughout the main-floor gallery. The walls of the gallery were all white, and the floors were of gleaming white marble. The mannequins struck haughty poses and seemed to have a lifelike awareness of the beauty they presented as they showcased the gowns. The gowns shimmered and glittered, and an almost overwhelming desire to touch the silk and gossamer fabrics settled in your fingertips.

For those waiting for their appointment with CC, there was a separate lounge where champagne and a manicure were available for those who wanted to relax a bit. You could even get a little Botox discreetly done. When the magic moment arrived, and it was your turn to spend precious time with CC, you ascended a gorgeous white marble stairway that curved from the first floor up to the second. At the top of the stairs you would be met by one of her staff and whisked through the leaded crystal doors of the inner sanctum. For some, walking through those doors was the supreme validation. If you had C. C. Covington designing your gown, you were part of the crème de la crème.

The voices coming from the second floor were becoming even louder. The doors to the design area were cracked open just a little, and it wasn't hard to hear the words that floated down the steps, not with that marble all over the place.

"Eduardo! You're cutting into my time with CC. I need her to focus on *me*. I didn't make this appointment just so that she could spend all her time prying your paws off her!"

"But my darling, darling sister, she adores me, I adore her…what can I do? It is beyond our control; this passion that burns with the heat of a thousand embers…this love that will never die…this—"

CC cut him off. "Prissy, he's not taking my focus off you…I've got all the measurements that I need, and I know just what I'm going to design for you. Eduardo darling, I'm afraid the heat of a thousand embers has caused our love to burn out…now get your hands off me, or I'll have Bruce from security dropkick you to the curb. Prissy, you'll get a call when it's time for a fitting…Eduardo, I'm keeping the earrings and the necklace."

Did CC know how to handle drama queens, or what? The doors were swept open, and the squabbling pair didn't seem to notice me as they passed me on the staircase and took their argument outside. It suddenly dawned on me that Eduardo was Prissy's brother from Brazil. This was the guy CC thought she could fall in love with in five minutes…the guy who was "Ele e divino." From what I'd overheard, so much for divine.

"Am I wrong, or did you have your hands full with that pair?" I threw myself down on a chair upholstered in some kind of expensive-looking silk and ran my hand over the fabric. "This is nice. Would you like to give it to me?"

"More like Eduardo was trying to get *his* hands full… he's a total ass. And no, I wouldn't like to give it to you."

"Sorry, things didn't work out with Eduardo. Why don't you come grab some lunch with me…drown your sorrows a little."

"I am *so* up for getting out of here. Let's drive over to Saint Armands Circle…I haven't been to the Columbia in a while, and I'm dying for some of their guacamole. As far as Eduardo goes, there's nothing to drown, except maybe him."

I was heading for the door. "Get your purse, girly; we're out of here. The traffic for the bridge didn't look too bad when I passed it on the way here, so if we hurry, we should be ahead of everybody else heading over to the circle for lunch. I just hope there aren't too many people using the bridge for exercise today. The women pushing strollers and jogging at thirty miles an hour *really* make me feel like a wimp."

"Everything makes you feel like a wimp, London. You get intimidated watching the mall walkers." She picked up her cell and stuffed it in a bag just big enough for the phone and a credit card.

"Have you seen the calf muscles on those women? They look like they have grapefruits stuck under their skin! I don't think I even *have* calf muscles."

"I don't have the strength for your pity party today, London…Eduardo used up my last ounce of patience, so move it! I need guacamole, and I need it bad!"

Chapter 28

We were over the bridge and looking for a place to park in ten minutes, and despite an art festival that was taking place, we were able to score a parking spot only a block from the restaurant.

"This *never* happens!" CC happily chirped. "Now all we have to do is snag a table for lunch and we're golden."

"If we have to wait, I don't mind…there's something that I want to talk to you about, CC."

Her antenna went up immediately.

"What? What is it…is it a man? Tell me it's a man! Is it that man you met at the lion place? Did you find out who he is? Tell me, tell me, *tell* me!"

While CC hammered me with questions that I didn't answer, we walked the short distance to the restaurant. Somehow we managed to get there without getting crushed by the crowd of tourists licking ice-cream cones and looking at everything except where they were walking.

The hostess stood at the door brandishing menus, and we were immediately whisked off to a table. Within a minute of being seated, a waiter appeared at CC's side, and before he could speak, she rattled off our order.

"I'll have a glass of Merlot…and don't bring me any baby half glass; I want a full glass. She'll have water with two cherries. We want two large orders of guacamole, two baskets of chips, and an enchilada with two forks." Flapping her hands at him, she waved him off and gave me her full attention.

"London, spill…what's going on?"

"Well, here's the deal…I *did* meet a man, and *this* time I know who he is."

I practically whispered the words…I didn't want other people to overhear me…I don't know why.

CC whispered back. "You did? Who is he?"

"His name is Ryder, and I met him on the ranch."

"Well, at least you found out this one's name…tell me more."

CC was giving me her full attention, which was amazing considering that our food had just arrived, and she *never* ignores guacamole.

"There isn't much to tell. He rode up on his horse, I made a fool of myself, and he got more gorgeous by the minute."

"He's gorgeous? Gorgeous is my favorite personality trait in a man. Go ahead, describe him for me…was he dressed like one of those cowboys in the movies, who look yummy when they're all sweaty and dirty?"

I couldn't deny it. "Pretty much."

CC had started moving a huge chip loaded with guacamole to her mouth but dropped it back onto her plate. She sat back in her chair and crossed her arms across her chest.

"Is he married?"

"There was no ring. Whether that means anything or not, I don't know."

She flapped her hand dismissively. "If he is, we'll find out. We'll run a background check on him. I should have done that with Eduardo, but I fell for his stupid accent and threw caution to the wind."

"I'm not running a background check on the guy, CC. I may never see him again, and all we did was talk a little."

She ignored me. "This is the second time you've stumbled on a prime specimen without even trying. I think that from now on where you go, I go...you seem to be a man magnet right now, and I need to find a new one. Now spit it out...what else happened with this guy?"

"I was just petting a horse, and he rode up and warned me to be careful around that particular horse. It was all very...nothing. I'm not suddenly irresistible to men... they're not being magnetically drawn to me, and we also don't know if he's 'prime'; he could be an ass." I stopped to take a breath...this next part had me rattled. "I also need to tell you that it's only been *one* man. This guy was the same guy from the animal haven place—the guy with those amazing eyes."

"Are you kidding me?"

"It's the same guy, CC…it's the same guy, and he's even more beautiful up close. And he still makes me uncomfortable."

CC was up and out of her chair. "Let's go, let's go right now! You run and get the car, and I'll take care of the bill. I want to see this guy…if you don't want him, I call 'dibs.'"

"Sit down. I'm not going to go get the car. We don't even know if he's there right now. I wouldn't want you to meet him right now, anyway. You're so charged up you'd probably kill him with the wall of estrogen that's practically oozing out of your pores."

CC sighed and threw herself back down into her chair.

"Fine, but I'm not done with this subject…I'm going to need to know more about this guy…*and*…now I'm even more determined than ever…where you go, I go. If you so much as go to the bathroom…I'm going with you."

"How am I going to meet a man in the bathroom, CC?" I laughed. "Can we move on to what I wanted to talk to you about in the first place? I need a little input."

CC sat back and picked her chip up again.

"This is about your new job, right? What's the problem?"

"I'm not so sure that I'm OK with it. Part of the deal is that I'm supposed to sort of spy on people while I'm in their houses. I'm going to feel like a skunk spying on the homeowners and letting the world know things that these people would rather keep private. I wanted to be a serious photographer, to do something that I could be proud of. With this change in the job, I just feel...skunkish."

Telling her just that little bit of information was stressing me out. I loaded a huge forkful of guacamole onto a chip, wolfed it down, and repeated the process. My stress eating was officially under way.

"I don't see how you have any other options right now," CC said. "You need a job, and this way you can pay your bills, have a decent place to live, and do some legitimate photographic work. You can decide how much dirt to share with your boss...you don't have to tell him everything. That way you can still feel like a decent person."

She stared at me for a second and added, "But you do have to tell *me* everything, and you do have to put the fork down. You're eating the paper liner in the bottom of the guacamole basket."

I looked down at the soggy paper stuck to my fork, and I wondered if eating paper was going to be hazardous to my health. I tossed the fork onto the table.

"So I've got a question for you, Cee. You know that thing you insisted on a little while ago—'where you go, I go'? Why don't you come with me on the shoot Thursday? Who knows, you may meet someone."

"Are you suggesting this because you love my company, or because you're just the tiniest bit nervous after what happened to the floating Palumbos?"

I slouched down in my chair. "I feel stupid saying this, but, yes, I'm a little nervous, and it would be nice to have company."

CC got a worried look on her face, and concern filled her eyes. "I wish I could go with you, but I've got an appointment at nine with Mercedes Fontaine. Will you feel safe going by yourself?"

"I'll be fine. I'm just being silly. So…why don't you tell me about your appointment? I feel like I've heard you mention Mercedes before."

She ran her hands through her hair and frowned. "I probably have. I'm doing her gown for that charity thing that's coming up next month, and she's driving me crazy. She has her 'empath' come with her to our design sessions so that she can pick up on my emotional energy. If she thinks I'm giving off negative energy when they get to the appointment, they walk out…they've done it twice so far, even though Mercedes gets charged five thousand dollars each time she bails on me!

"Did you know that she carries her pet goldfish around in her *purse*? She calls it 'Tulip.' I swear…if she flakes out on me again, that goldfish is going to end up on a cracker with cream cheese."

"You just heard yourself threatening a goldfish, right? Maybe it's time we get you back to work."

I tapped the sleeve of a passing waiter and asked for the check. As soon as we got outside, CC took my arm and gave me a coaxing smile.

"Want to run over and grab some ice cream before we head back? I just love the ice cream in that shop over on the back street…Big Oley's, or whatever it's called."

"Are you kidding me? I just ate a whole bowl of mashed-up avocados! Where do you *put* all the food you eat? You eat more than anybody I know, but you're still thin…where is the justice in that?"

She gave me a hurt look. "It's not my fault! I don't know why I can eat so much; I'm afraid that someday my metabolism is going to let me down, and my eating habits are going to bite me in the butt."

She looked over her shoulder and twisted around, trying to see her backside.

"Do you see any changes back there?"

"I'm not checking out your behind with a million people walking by!"

CC sighed and decided to skip the ice cream. We headed back to the jeep, and when she wasn't looking, I checked myself out in the storefront windows. I *wasn't* happy with *my* butt. When your underwear starts riding up in places you never knew it could, it's time to take a break from sugar.

Traffic was a mess when we pulled out of our parking space. It seemed like everyone was leaving St. Armands at the same time. I zipped off the main road and took the back streets, trying to avoid just sitting in traffic, crawling around the circle inch by inch.

I loved the little exclusive area tucked just off the roundabout. If you never got off the main drag, you'd never know that just seconds away from the craziness of the circle sat quiet residential streets with the most amazing mansions...sitting like jewels among their gorgeously landscaped lawns. It would be so cool to be able to walk out the door of your house, browse the shops, eat in fabulous restaurants, walk the bridge, watch the boats in the bay, and be just a few minutes away from a beach.

I wasn't feeling jealous, mind you...I'd found a little slice of heaven just under an hour's drive from all this. It might not be a mansion, but it was serene and surrounded by its own kind of beauty, with the Gulf of Mexico just steps away...that was more than good enough for me.

Chapter 29

Thursday morning I was up before the alarm went off. It was prep day...I had camera batteries to charge, cameras and lenses to clean, just general crosschecking to see that everything I would need was ready to go.

It didn't take me long, and the only thing left to do was to wait for the e-mail from Sophie with the location for the shoot.

I still had some chocolate milk left, so I grabbed that and finished it off. I *know*...I was supposed to be watching the sugar, but chocolate or not, milk is milk, right? I still had to make sure that I got all my nutrients.

I must have checked my email three times by noon... nothing. I was going to go stir-crazy waiting for "Little Miss Zippy on speed" to put her fingers on her computer keyboard.

I finally gave the Internet a break and made popcorn with cheese sprinkled on top of it...don't start with me...

when you make the popcorn yourself, it counts as a healthy food choice. Popcorn is a grain, cheese is a protein…there you have it, a fabulously healthy meal.

I took my lunch out to the porch swing and got comfy. What a day, it had a perfectly cloudless blue sky; the temperature was neither too hot nor too cold. I'd finished my popcorn and realized that I was starting to doze off, so I dragged myself into the house and brushed my teeth. Popcorn stuck between your teeth is not a good look… even if it's only you who's doing the looking.

Once I was all beautified, I went outside to visit my boyfriend, Reckless…As soon as I approached the fence, I saw him start to make his way across the field to me. We were definitely friends now, and he had me on a schedule…ear scratches first, and then I could tell him about my plans for the day. I'd finished the mandatory scratching on his right ear and was starting on the left one, when I saw Ryder coming down the drive. Not on horseback this time…this time he was driving a pickup truck that had seen better days. He pulled up just as I gave Reckless one last good scratch.

Ryder leaned out of the window, pushed his hat back on his head just a bit, and gave me a smile that sent a little jolt into the middle of my chest. The deep voice that made my heart…or something…go pitty-pat…had a question for me.

"If I wouldn't be interrupting the two of you, I wondered if I could borrow you for a few minutes…a new foal was born last night…Want to ride over and meet the newest member of the ranch?"

"Are you kidding? Just let me grab my camera."

I zipped into the house and grabbed a large denim bag that I like to use when I'm traveling "light." I grabbed my camera and cell phone and shoved them into the bag.

I locked up the house and jumped into the truck. Now this was a real farm truck. A woven blanket was thrown over a tear in the seat, and bits of straw were all over the inside of the cab…on the seat, the dashboard, the floor, pretty much everywhere.

Ryder threw the truck into gear, and we headed toward a section of driveway that I'd never been down. It was too quiet in the truck. I get antsy when it's too quiet…time to make small talk.

"This is such a beautiful place…would you mind if I ask you some questions about it?"

"Ask away, London."

"I was talking to the real-estate broker who had the place listed for rent, you know, asking the kind of questions you do before you sign on the dotted line. She really didn't seem to know much about the place. She didn't even know who actually owns the ranch. She just deals with the ranch accountant. She said she gets an email whenever the place is going to be available…she takes care of the listing, does her real-estate thing, and that's about it. Do you know anything about the history of the ranch?"

"There's not much that I can tell you…I know that the land for the ranch was purchased six years ago and that the ranch itself was built a year after that. I worked for the general manager of the ranch when I came here, learning all about the farm, and about a month after I came on board, we went over a 'ten-year' plan that the owner had come up with. The game plan was, and is, for me to develop the ranch…improve the breeding program, oversee the operation of the stables, etcetera."

We had pulled up in front of a barn as he talked, and he brought the truck to a stop. Reaching across me, he pulled up on the door handle.

"This one kind of sticks," he said as he leaned across me. I found it impossible not to notice the well-muscled arm that brushed ever so lightly across my T-shirt.

I slid out of the truck and looked up to see a man striding toward us from the barn.

"Glad I caught you, Ryder," he said. "I'm making a run-up to Ocala to check out those trailers. You're only interested in the slant load models in the six-horse setup, right?"

"We're good on everything else," Ryder said. "The other trailers have only got five years on them at the most. Trey, I want you to meet London Hart. She's living on the ranch now…London, this is Trey Danner."

Trey gave me a smile that was half polite and half-dirty. I didn't know it was possible to do both at the same time, but he managed it. Yuck.

"It's a pleasure to meet you, Miss Hart. I can see I'm going to need to be stopping by your place to give you a 'feel good' welcome real soon."

He made my skin crawl and my palm itch. It was itching to slap him. Ryder took me by the elbow and steered me past the idiot.

"You're running late, Trey," Ryder said, without looking back at him. "I wouldn't make any extra stops if I were you."

Without another word we crossed the rest of the way to the barn and stepped into a quiet equine world. Ryder stepped in front of me and led me to the far end of the barn, where we peered over the top of a stall door. Standing close to its mother on wobbly little legs was the new foal. Its body was deep black, as was its mane, but the tail was equal parts black and white.

"I've never seen a horse with markings like that. Have you had any like this before?"

"Never," he said. "It ought to be a very handsome horse when it's fully grown."

"Is it okay if I take a few pictures?" I asked him quietly.

"If you can do it with no flash, go ahead."

He moved over just a little to give me more room, and I captured a few shots of just the foal and then a few of the foal with its attentive mother. I didn't get to enjoy the experience for long…I could feel my cell phone vibrating in my bag and had to step outside to take the call. It was Sophie.

Chapter 30

S ophie's voice squeaked into my ear. "I just sent an email with all the info you'll need, but I wanted to call to make sure that you check your email. You should be good to go...let me know if you need anything else. Are you excited? Do you feel like a spy yet? I do, and I'm not even going to be there with you...I think I'm going to stop on the way home and get, like, a black trench coat and a pair of really big black sunglasses and maybe a black scarf. I'm just really feeling this spy stuff, you know? Do you want me to get two of each thing so that we can dress alike if Mike calls us in for a meeting?"

I thought I'd stop this flow of verbal diarrhea before Sophie told me about her plan to take up smoking cigarettes and pretending that her tube of lipstick was actually a teeny tiny spy camera.

"Thanks, Sophie...I'll pass on the trench coat, and I'm sure I won't need anything else, but if I do, I'll let you know."

Just as I ended the call, Ryder followed me outside.

"Problems?"

"No, just an overeager coworker...I should probably get back to my place. I guess I've got work to do."

"No problem, just let me do one more quick check on the newborn, and we'll head back." He turned, and I admired the view as he walked back to the barn. I'd just gotten situated in my seat, when Ryder walked out of the barn and climbed into the truck. He had a question for me.

"You heard a bit about what I do today. Why don't you tell me what it is that you do?"

I hoped he was the kind of guy who wasn't bothered by the "sin of omission," because I really didn't want to tell him everything that my job involved.

"I'm a photographer. I'm doing some work for a magazine—architectural-type stuff...nothing all that interesting."

And that's all he needed to know...I hoped there wouldn't be any more questions that I would have to dance around.

I didn't have to worry about what his next question would be. As he pulled away from the barn and circled back in the direction of my place, the sun was blinding, and I pulled down the visor to block it. The windows were down, and as I lowered the visor, a ton of straw that had been caught behind it showered out. The breeze from the window picked up the straw, and in a second I was covered with the stuff...in my hair, all over my blouse, and down my arms. I sat spitting out the pieces that had found their way into my mouth. The truck jerked to a stop, and Ryder cleared his throat...then he looked away from me and stared out the window. Well, of course, laughing came next. Just between you and me...he had a *great* laugh.

"I'm glad that you find me *so* amusing."

The laughter stopped immediately.

"I find you much more than amusing, London."

He turned toward me and took off his sunglasses.

The moment that I looked into those amazing eyes, my hand froze in the act of pulling a piece of straw from my hair. That doesn't mean there was no movement at all. I realized that I reached to touch his face with my other hand. Halfway there, he reached out, took my hand the rest of the way, and held it against his cheek.

I was totally rattled. I've read historical romances, well, all right, I'd read one...and it had seemed *so* over the top, so exaggerated, so ridiculous.

Now here I was, and I was afraid I wouldn't be able to stop myself from saying, "Sir Cranberry, you must stop gazing at me with such an ardent glow in your eyes. You must desist or I fear my heart will go on a wild rampage."

What I was experiencing in real life...what I was seeing in his eyes...was something warm and uncertain, and I *felt* it. Whatever "it" was, in that moment it reached out, and ever so carefully, it touched my heart.

I don't know what would have happened next. The curse of technology intervened, and his cell phone rang and then rang again. He let go of my hand, and I dropped it to my side. He blinked, and the spell was broken.

He picked the phone up off the seat where it rested between us.

"This is Ryder."

He listened intently as he slipped his sunglasses back on. Still listening, he put the truck back into gear and headed toward my place. His end of the conversation consisted of yes and no while we made the short drive, and I became very focused on picking all the straw out of my hair. When we pulled up next to the house, he ended the call and turned to face me.

"You said you had work to do, and it looks like I'm going to be taking a drive up north. I was about to ask you if you'd let me grill you a steak for dinner, but it looks like that's out of the question...are you free tomorrow night?"

"I've got a photo shoot tomorrow, but I should be done and back here by five o'clock."

I was hoping that the little cartwheel my heart had just done wasn't showing on my face when I answered him. When he flashed me a smile, my heart got to do another cartwheel, a *big* one.

He surprised me by getting out of the truck and walking around to my door. Opening it and helping me out landed me toe to toe with his cowboy boots. He did that awesome tip of the hat thing as he looked down at me. I made my way around the truck toward my front porch, and he followed, and then he stopped and leaned against the truck with his arms folded, waiting as I got the door unlocked.

I gave him the tiniest wave good-bye and stepped inside. I spent a few seconds standing with my back resting against the door, and then I peeked out the window to watch him drive away. He was still leaning against the truck, a smile on his lips.

Chapter 31

I was really tempted to write it all down so that I wouldn't forget anything, especially the part about him putting my hand up against his cheek. Such a small thing, but maybe the most romantic gesture I'd ever experienced. I'd been in his presence all of two or three times, and there was no way to deny that we had connected on some deep emotional level.

After he actually had driven away, I came back to the present. I tossed my bag on my bed and pulled everything out of it, setting aside things that I would need. I was going to use my big leather bag the next day at the photo shoot, and it would be transformed from everyday citizen bag to "secret spy" camera bag…Damn, Sophie was rubbing off on me. Before I got distracted and did anything else, I headed for the freezer; it had been awhile since my popcorn lunch, and I was starving. I heated up a low-cal meal and carried it over to the computer. As promised, Sophie's e-mail had arrived and was waiting in the Inbox.

I clicked it open, and there were my instructions...I'd be shooting on Manasota Key, a twenty-minute drive to the south. I really love this area. Too small to be overbuilt, you travel along a narrow road and pass under several tree canopy sections to reach the other end of the key.

The description of the home to be photographed was short and sweet. It was perched twenty feet above the gulf, was "eclectic," and there were giant stone lions at either side of the driveway gate.

The owner wanted to be sure that the beachside cabana was included in the photo shoot...apparently it was her favorite part of the property. Monique Summers was listed as the owner, and I recognized her as a woman known to be extremely active in charitable organizations and also quite the party girl. Married and divorced five times, she had accumulated a lot of wealth.

I emailed Sophie and thanked her for the info...within minutes she shot an email back, asking if I was sure I didn't need any help. She just *knew* that Mike would let her off work to help me if I needed her. I assured her again that I could handle it and that I'd worked solo for a long time, so no worries. I hated to burst her little spy bubble, but I didn't think I could listen to that childlike voice for several hours and keep my sanity.

I'd just sent the message, when my cell phone rang. Brenda...my thoughts about Sophie evaporated, and my curiosity kicked in.

"Brenda! Anything new going on with your neighbor?"

"You get right to the point, don't you, London? As a matter of fact, that's why I'm calling. Up until now it's been pretty quiet next door. No one's been staying at the condo…but the accountant showed up about an hour ago. He had that briefcase with him again."

"How do you know he's an accountant?" I asked.

"Well, I don't; he just looks like one, you know? Anyway, I called so that you could talk me out of peeking in his windows when it gets dark. I have a new neighbor two doors down, and he's a cop; he walks his dog every night, and there's a chance he could see me peeking and arrest me. It wouldn't be good for business if I got arrested."

"You don't need me to talk you out of snooping; you just told yourself the very things I would have told you."

"But I don't listen to me. It's kind of like those commercials where someone has an angel sitting on one shoulder and the devil sitting on the other shoulder. The little guy in red always has a more convincing argument for why I *should* do something. The angel needs some backup, someone who can help make me listen. You're that someone."

I sighed. "So I'm supposed to be your conscience?"

"You are officially on the side of the angels, London. Now tell me I can't go drag a trash can under the accountant's window, climb up on it, and spy on him."

"You can't go drag a trash can under the window, climb up on it, and spy on your neighbor."

"Thank you, London. I appreciate your helping me…I sincerely mean that."

I sighed again. "You're going to climb up on the trash can, aren't you, Brenda?"

"Damn straight I am. Wish me luck!"

I listened to the dial tone for a minute after she hung up, wondering if I had enough money to bail her out of jail after she got arrested.

Resigned to the fact that my friend was turning to the dark side and on her way to becoming a career criminal, I did the little bit of cleaning up I needed to do. I patted myself on the back for not eating any chocolate after my stressful talk with Brenda and decided to walk down to the beach and watch the sun go down.

As I walked down the steps of the porch, I glanced over and saw Reckless grazing along the fence. I called over to him as I started down the path. "Aren't you supposed to be heading back to the barn by now? You're supposed to be in bed by eight."

Amazing! I must be turning into a horse whisperer... Reckless looked at me for one long minute, turned around, and headed for the barn.

Sitting by the gulf, watching Mother Nature at work, I relaxed so much that I was suddenly exhausted. I got to my feet, when I realized that the sky was growing darker, and I regretted not bringing a flashlight with me for the walk back to the house. Aside from getting smacked in the face by the occasional palm frond when I veered off the path every now and again, I was doing a pretty good job of finding my way.

I was occupied with thoughts about the way the darkness creeps out of the low-growing bushes and grasses as soon as the sun disappears, like a pack of night spirits, when I heard a sound that made me jerk to a stop. I was sure that the sound had come from just behind me, somewhere among the trees. I tried to convince myself that I was just hearing chameleons skittering through the dead, dried-up palm fronds that littered the ground. I couldn't make myself turn around to see if anything else might have made the noise. I shook off my unease and continued down the path. That's when I felt a hand touch my back...softly...I took one breath, and then the hand twisted into the fabric of my blouse, and I was yanked to the ground.

I screamed so loud and so hard that I could taste blood. That scream took up all the air in my lungs, and I couldn't do anything but lay where I had landed. I braced myself for the worst, knowing that I couldn't fight off my attacker if I could barely breathe, but nothing happened. I listened for any movement, but there was nothing—not the sound of a human, ghost, or raccoon. I wasn't going to wait until there was a something to hear. I'd gotten some air back into my lungs, so I scrambled to my feet and ran the rest of the way to the house.

I don't remember unlocking the front door or how I ended up with my phone in my hand. I do remember that my hands were shaking so badly that I couldn't punch any buttons to make a call. I spent, I don't know how long, huddled on my couch, watching the locked front door and listening for any unusual sound. Finally I decided that if anything was going to happen, it would have already, and I dragged myself to the bathroom to check for real or imagined injuries. Except for scratches on the backs of my legs and elbows, it looked like being pulled to the ground hadn't caused any other issues. A little soap and hot water, some antibacterial gel, and I was as good as new—my legs and arms were, anyway. I couldn't put a Band-Aid on my brain, and it really needed one…it was freaked out.

I stripped off my clothes, grabbed my phone, and wrapped myself in a brown robe that was my version of a security blanket. I'd had the robe forever, and when times were tough, the softness and warmth it provided was the ultimate Band-Aid. Sleep was going to be impossible for a while, so I tried to distract myself from my fear. I climbed into bed and plugged my phone into its charger. I wasn't going to take the chance of having a dead battery if I had to call 911. Rolling onto my side, I came face-to-face with Handsome, the stuffed lion. I could talk to him…that would help…maybe.

"OK, Handsome, we're going to stay calm; we're going to take deep breaths and not jump every time we hear a noise, right? Not that there's any reason to be nervous. Everything's good, everything's cool…we're cool, right? I'm going to talk out loud for a while, if you don't mind; I had a little scare outside, and talking to you will make me feel better," I told the soft little face. "Okay, here I go, talking about nice, non-scary stuff. I had a moment with the human 'handsome' earlier…it was so weird. One minute we were talking, and then he took his sunglasses off, and

I started operating on pure impulse…it was almost ridiculous, how out of control I felt. I wonder if that's how CC feels all the time?"

I picked up my furry lucky charm, fluffed up his fur, and sat him back down in his appointed place. My mini chat with Handsome had calmed me right down, until the phone rang, and my fight-or-flee instinct kicked in, and I fell off the bed. I'm not sure if that was a fight-or-flee response, but it didn't really matter. I lay on the floor, phone clutched in my hand.

"Hey, Cee, what's up?"

"Do you still want some company tomorrow? Mercedes waltzed in with the Empath, without an appointment, to do a *pre*appointment check of my aura! She plopped her stuff down in *my* desk chair and proceeded to prowl around with that fake vibe reader! I was on a call with a fabric house in the back room, and when I walked out, they were telling one of my assistants that she needed to start using beetle-prong body wash to improve her love life. *What the hell is beetle-prong body wash?*"

"Did you kick them out?"

"I didn't have to. The Empath informed us that she felt 'an illness of sizeable impact' bearing down on her and that she couldn't possibly work tomorrow. She and Mercedes charged out of here as if the bubonic plaque was hot on their heels. What's really sad is that Merce left her purse in my chair, and there's a snooty-looking goldfish lounging in its fishbowl at the bottom of the bag."

"CC, you are not going to hurt that goldfish."

"I would *never* hurt an animal, London!"

"That's a trick statement, Cee; I know you don't consider fish animals."

I heard her sniff on the other end of the call. "You'll never convince me otherwise."

"Just call Mercedes to come get her fish, or have a courier deliver it, or something."

"I will, after I find a drink and some crackers and cream cheese. If the goldfish happens to pay them a visit, there's nothing I can do about it."

"Cee! Don't you touch that fish! Get that assistant of yours to call Mercedes while you go eat some chocolate or something, do Pilates, yoga, just chill!"

"Fine," she huffed. "Am I coming with you tomorrow or not? I'll go plan my outfit and leave the fish alone if you let me come along. Oh…and tell me who the homeowner is. Anybody I know?"

"The owner is Monique Summers. Now go plan your outfit. You're coming."

I know, I told Sophie that I could handle the job solo. I hadn't been attacked when I told her that and now, since CC had offered, I was really, really glad to have company. I didn't want to be alone on the drive to the shoot. It would give me too much time to obsess over the phantom of the night that had attacked me. It would also be easier to break the ice with Monique if she was with me…I was pretty sure that she was a client of CC's.

"I'll pick you up at your place this time. Be ready at twelve thirty, and you're carrying the tripod again," I told her. I cut CC off as she was beginning to whine about her nails getting ruined. I was afraid if we talked longer, I'd tell her what had happened to me on the path. If we started talking about that, I'd never get any sleep.

CHAPTER 32

Right on time, my "assistant" climbed into the seat beside me and pulled on a long white pair of opera gloves.

"Would it be inappropriate of me to ask why you're wearing the gloves?"

"Sun protection, London," she explained. "I'm planning on having the best-looking arms and hands you ever saw on an eighty-year-old."

"You do know about that thing they call sunscreen, right?"

"Yes, smart ass, I've heard of sunscreen...it doesn't work for me. My pores just seem to get sealed shut when I use it, and I end up sweating like a pig at a hog roast."

Well, there's an image I could have lived without. We had just crossed the drawbridge onto the Key and were approaching Blind Pass Beach. It was all I could do to keep driving and not pull over and park—the lure of my favorite hobby was calling, but CC read my mind.

"Keep going, London," my passenger ordered. "We're not stopping for you to go shark-tooth hunting. Once you start, you'll just keep going all day long, so just keep driving."

"I'm driving; do you not see me driving? I am coming back here, though…when I've got more time and less passenger."

"Don't be rude, London, and anyway, don't you think twenty-five thousand teeth is enough?"

I couldn't help myself…I had to correct her. "It's over twenty-five thousand now, and I enjoy it, except for the occasional naked beach walkers. That I don't enjoy."

She turned to me with big eyes. "I thought they'd put a stop to that!!"

"Apparently not. The last guy was like ninety-five…naked as the day he was born, except for a pair of neon orange walking shoes. He wasn't the only inappropriate walker that day. There was another guy—maybe a little younger than ninety-five—walking along in these oversized, saggy, tighty whities."

I couldn't bring myself to tell her that his "tighties" weren't the only things that had been sagging.

CC was not a fan of this kind of beach activity. "That's disgusting…they should arrest those people, not only for nudity…it's sexual harassment, and who knows, you might be suffering from posttraumatic stress disorder. They should have to be registered as sex offenders."

"I can see them being registered as visual offenders… but not sex offenders, although maybe that falls under the category of a sex offender."

"Just drop it, London; you know this will make my blood pressure go up. Are we there yet?"

We were now well past Blind Pass Beach, and I needed to start watching for the house.

"It should be along in here somewhere, CC."

Her rant about naked beach people was instantly forgotten, and she was on high alert. We'd only driven another quarter mile, when I saw the house on the right.

CC summed things up pretty well, I thought. "Whoaaaa…! Monique has done all right for herself."

I pulled into the drive at exactly one o'clock, hit the brakes, and sat staring out of the windshield. In front of us was a mansion with a huge welcoming veranda. What I could only describe as turrets like you would see on a castle, covered in ivy, anchored each corner of the house…I expected to see a damsel in distress with long flowing hair leaning out of one of the windows, sipping on a mint julep.

Sitting in the jeep with my mouth hanging open was not getting us any closer to the house, so I put my foot down on the accelerator and followed the discreet little signs that directed cars to a parking courtyard. We grabbed my gear and made our up the stairs of the veranda to the front door. We were definitely expected, because the door was opened before I could ring the doorbell.

Monique Summers was some kind of something. Her hair was blond and twisted into the tightest bun I'd ever seen…it had to hurt. It was pulled back so severely that I expected it to just snap off at her hairline and leave her standing there, bald as a baby's butt. The rest of her was well toned and expertly pulled together. She was wearing a beautiful yellow suit that probably cost more money than I was going to make in the next six months.

She smiled and grabbed my hand. "You must be London, and is that you, CC? How long has it been? I don't think I've seen you since you did my "divorce" dress! Love the gloves…they're so *you*. I loved them last season, when they were in style."

I think I saw actual flames light up CC's eyes. Taking a shot at CC's designer expertise was a dangerous thing to do.

"Darling Monique! You look fabulous! What have you been doing—core stability, total strength, the bar method?" CC asked through clenched teeth.

"Oh honey, don't be silly; I haven't changed a bit." She smoothed her hands down over her hips and smiled smugly. "Before I forget, I need to come see you. Can you set me up with an appointment? I need a dress…I'm getting married, and I need something spectacular. I was thinking something…you know, virginal."

I nearly gagged; the woman had been married five times, and she wanted something "virginal"…I wasn't going to be the one who mentioned it, but that ship had sailed. I opted for a change of subject.

"Monique, is there somewhere that I can put this equipment where it won't be in the way?" I asked.

"Of course, London! Where are my manners? Just put it over there in the corner by the ugly chair that looks like a throne. *Oh!* I shouldn't say that, should I? Here you are, ready to photograph the house for a magazine, and I start off the day by calling the furniture ugly. But it is ugly, isn't it? It's all kinds of ugly, and it took a lot of work to get the look just right."

She turned in a slow circle, and she had a very satisfied look on her face as she surveyed the hideous furniture that surrounded us.

"I suppose I'd better explain. This house belonged to my last husband. It was in his family for seventy years, and he was an insufferable snob about the history of the furniture, the artwork…blah, blah, blah…I got the house in the divorce, and, of course, he was furious. I, on the other hand, couldn't have been happier. Even though I hate the house, I really, really wanted it. The only reason I got it was because the detective I hired found out that my ex had been having an affair with my best friend through most of our marriage, not to mention the other flings he'd had.

Apparently, being a politician can be such a burden… seems the poor man didn't want me to let his constituents know about his 'zipper' problem, and he had to let me have the house and everything in it, in exchange for my silence."

I was following along with her story, through its little twists and turns, but I was also doing a happy dance in my mind. So much for having to dig for dirt for the tabloid page at the magazine. She was giving me plenty.

Monique was totally unaware of how easy she was making my job...her mind was on her manicure. She had paused briefly to examine the tips of her nails, and for someone revealing so much personal drama; she seemed perfectly comfortable and relaxed. Looking up from her nails, she flashed me a malicious smile and picked up where she'd left off.

"During the divorce I learned that he intends to marry my backstabbing 'best' friend," she said sarcastically. "So this is my revenge...my revenge masterpiece. I got the house that my ex, the jackass, loved so much, sold all the furniture and art that belonged to his family, and filled the house with this medieval crap, or whatever it is. Now you're here to document my labor of 'love,' and as soon as the article is published, I'm going to send him a complimentary copy. My only regret is that I won't be there to see his face when he sees the photos."

I didn't know what to say to her. Congratulations on destroying family heirlooms? Congratulations on finding such a creative way to express your rage? I really didn't know what to say...somebody else did.

"I'll say one thing," CC said. "You're definitely going to be the newest member of the 'revenge served cold' Hall of Fame. Let's get started shooting this divorce triumph of yours. I think everyone will be dying to see your handiwork."

Monique slicked her hands over her hair and patted imaginary stray hairs back into place.

"Prepare to be amazed," she chirped. "You'll be the first to see my ex's worst nightmare."

Patting her hair into place once more, she crooked her finger at us to follow her, and we were off…about to see the fury of a woman scorned, expressed in interior design.

Chapter 33

The architecture of the house itself was wonderful, nothing horrible about it. On the main floor, tall arched stone windows faced the gulf and treated the viewer to a magnificent view of the rolling surf and the towering clouds that floated above the water. Seagulls and pelicans created a constantly moving piece of art as they soared and then dove into the water, over and over.

Unfortunately there was no ignoring the revenge of Monique inside the house. The living room was a mishmash of color. Red-and-purple-striped fabric hung from long curtain rods fixed at the very top of the walls and cascaded down to the floor. It made me feel slightly nauseous if I looked at it too long. When Monique wasn't looking, I tugged a piece of fabric aside, and behind it was gorgeous mahogany paneling. Obviously that had to be hidden, it was way too tasteful and elegant. The carpet was gold with an emerald-green diamond-shape pattern running through it.

There were two "salons," one on either side of the living room, which must have been used for after-dinner pursuits…smoking in one salon for the gentlemen…and what? Inhaling second-hand smoke for the ladies in the other? Velvet wall coverings were once again used, this time in shades of pink and yellow. The carpet was the same ghastly design and color that was used in the living room. The whole effect reminded me of a treat that we tried to break our teeth on at Christmas and sometimes Easter… ribbon candy.

As we moved from room to room, Monique spent her time trying to pry socialite-related gossip out of CC. I could have told her not to waste her breath. CC was a master of deflection and Monique learned nothing.

We spent about two seconds in the kitchen, but I found it kind of fascinating.

The room was huge, and everything in it appeared to be original. The walls were covered in tiny faded white tiles and so was the floor; the range had a little clock on it that was very similar to the one on my little stove. Just like mine, it was doing a good job of keeping time. There was one concession to modernity, and that was the refrigerator. I was glad that Monique had left this room alone and had preserved most of the original features and fixtures, and so forth. Strange to feel glad about it, but I was starting to feel sorry for the poor house for being treated so badly by Monique. Just off the kitchen was a laundry room with state-of-the-art washers and dryers.

Yes, I said washers and dryers plural—there were two of each appliance. A large linen closet was built in next to them, and to the right of the closet were a counter with cabinets below and a sink on top.

Next up was the second floor. We zoomed through the rooms—and we're talking *lots* of rooms. There was a music room, crammed with drum sets and life-sized cardboard cut-outs of the three stooges…don't ask me why. We peeked into a private study…everything in it, including the walls, was black. Monique explained that the use of black was representative of her ex-husband's heart. We passed three bathrooms with toilets filled with men's footwear—no explanation for that design choice was forthcoming from Monique. We were only shown one bedroom, and it lacked a bed. It had a barnyard motif, and it was filled with every size and shape of ceramic pig you can imagine. Another nod to the ex, I assumed.

Monique concluded our tour and led us back to the living room.

"I'm going to head down to the beach to make sure that everything is ready for you to shoot the cabana. When you've finished in here, come down the steps to the beach…just go around to the south end of the house, and you'll see them."

As soon as she was out of earshot, I looked at CC. "Have you *ever*…in your *entire life*…seen such ugly furniture, such ugly *everything*?"

"Oh man, she hates the ex-husband big time," CC murmured back to me.

She was looking apprehensively at the large sofa that she was leaning against…it had legs with evil gargoyle faces carved into them and wings…huge wooden wings with feathers glued all over the armrests.

"This sofa thingy would give me nightmares." She stepped away from it and walked to a door discreetly tucked into the wall. The door had the word "cheater" painted all over it in neon orange. Pulling the door open, she peeked inside.

"London," she whispered at me, "I don't want to be too critical, but who makes a toilet out of a carousel horse? It might be okay for us girls, but how is a man supposed to use something like this? You have to put your foot in a stirrup to swing yourself up on top to sit on the seat…nobody can just stand on the floor and use it. A guy would have to aim up and hope to hit the target!"

She stood and stared at it, finger to her lips. "And how does it flush? Where does everything *go*…down the leg?"

She closed the door and plopped herself into a chair that had five nice, neat rows of spikes about four inches long sticking out of its back.

"How are you ever going to make this house look good? It's a freak show."

I used my "I'm totally confident" voice (which was a lie) when I answered her.

"I'm going to focus on doing the best I can with what I've got. The windows are architecturally fantastic, and the exterior is definitely going to grab the reader's attention. I can focus on the pretty stuff, and that will balance out the ugly, depending on what images the magazine chooses to use."

"London, did you *see* any 'pretty stuff'? I know I'm just the pack mule, but I can't for the life of me see how they can make an article using just pictures of windows and the outside of the house."

"I'm keeping my fingers crossed that there's a lot that I can do with the cabana shoot. I hope that she used better taste in it, since she specifically asked that it be photographed."

With that said, I got down to work and covered the main floor as quickly as I could. I was glad when we had finished the downstairs and I completed the second floor in record time.

The exterior was going to be more fun to shoot. I was eager to get some shots of the turrets and the massive front door, as well as the landscaping around the veranda. CC plodded around the perimeter of the property as I worked, finally coming to a stop a whole two feet from me where she hovered. She'd been carrying my camera bag for me, and it contained just a few items. You would have thought there were a small pony and a bear with three cubs in the bag, the way she was complaining.

"This is *so heavy*! Why is it *so heavy*? I'm getting a hump on my back from carrying this. I can feel it! Put your hand on my back and feel it, London…do you feel the hump? *Oh dear God, I'm gonna have a hump on my back!!*"

"OK, Madame drama," I said, laughing, "I'm almost done. All I have to do is shoot the cabana and I'll drive your poor little exhausted self home."

As I stood looking at her, I realized she was short one piece of gear. "CC, where's the monopod?"

She made a little pouty face. "I left it in the back of the jeep, because I couldn't carry *everything*. I figured I could run and get it if you needed it, but, honestly, London, can we just do the cabana and finish already?"

I rolled my eyes at her, and she marched off, huffing and puffing her way to the south end of the house. When she reached the stairs, she dropped back and let me take the lead down to the cabana.

Designing the stairway that descended the steep hillside must have been quite a challenge. Chunks of earth would have had to be cut away and removed to accommodate the massive pieces of slate that served as steps. On each side of the slate, layered stone created a natural-looking retaining wall. The whole effect was quite beautiful, but beauty and safety are two different things; my vote would have been for safety. I don't know if it was simply for the purpose of aesthetics, but there was no handrail to hold on to.

About five feet from the bottom, the steps curved sharply to the right. I kept watching my feet as I made the turn, I didn't want to fall and damage my camera, or anything else for that matter. As CC made the turn behind me, she let out a scream that was probably going to give me permanent hearing loss. She threw herself onto my back and grabbed me with both arms. That's all it took to send me tumbling down the stairs. When we reached the bottom, she had me pinned...but not to the ground. She had me pinned to a body. Pinned to a body that was giving a good impression of not being alive.

They say adrenaline can give you incredible strength. It must...because *something* gave me the strength to raise CC *and* myself up and off the body. I rolled both of us into the sand and broke the death grip CC had on me. We both lay on our backs, completely silent...for about one second. At exactly the same time, we both opened our mouths and screamed. I looked at her, she looked at me, and we screamed again.

I didn't want to move. I barely wanted to breathe. I hoped that if I stayed exactly as I was, I wouldn't have to look at the body. I kind of wanted to scream again, but CC beat me to it.

"SHE'S DEAD! SHE'S DEAD! SHE'S DEAD!" she shrieked.

"CC, shush! We don't know if she's dead. Stop saying that; she might hear you!"

"She can't hear me; she's dead! Look at her; she has dead written all over her!"

She had rolled toward me and had me locked in a death grip again.

"CC, you're drawing blood! Let go of me, and I'll check her."

She pulled her fingers off my arms and stared down at the blood on her fingertips. "Gross."

Twisting away from CC and leaning all the way forward, I put my hands in the sand and pushed myself up off the ground. It took all the willpower I had, but slowly I turned and looked at the body that was face down in the pristine white sand…pristine if you didn't factor in the blood coagulating around Monique's head.

CC had apparently run of out screams and had her eyes shut tight. Just as I leaned over to check the body to see if there was a pulse, CC rolled over to push herself up off the ground and rolled herself into the back of my knees. *Oh, dear God, I was lying on Monique's body again!*

CC's eyes flew open, and she let rip a scream that should have brought a possibly dead Monique back to the land of the living. Not pausing in her screaming, Cee, who at a later date swore she actually levitated off the ground, pulled me off the body, hurling me backward onto the sand once again.

I sat in a daze and, looking down, saw that I was now covered in blood and sand from my shoulders to my knees. CC stood frozen with her hands over her mouth, and I slowly got up off the ground. This time I kept my distance from the body that was starting to cool and stared at the scene in front of me.

Monique lay sprawled on the beach; beside her lay a long tubular black rod with an attachment on the end…the attachment was covered in blood and other stuff that was too gross to think about. It wasn't the blood or the "other stuff" that made my head spin as if I'd just gotten off a merry-go-round. It was the fact that the long black rod was my monopod.

"Cee, this isn't good…this really isn't good," I whispered.

CHAPTER 34

Well...it wasn't good, but it was different. Granted, being questioned by the police regarding murder was the same as last time. But the difference this time is that the murder weapon was on the scene, and it belonged to me. I don't even remember calling the police. One minute I was standing looking down at Monique's body, and the next I was being helped into the back of a squad car. This couldn't be real. Was I really sitting in a little room with just a table and chair and a soft drink at the police station? Granted, the soft drink belonged to the cop, not that I would have wanted one, even if he *had* offered me one, which he hadn't. I'd been questioned for forty-five minutes, and then the officer had excused himself and left the room. (He probably had to use the little boy's room after drinking all that soda that he wouldn't share with anyone else.)

I'd gotten the same questions as the previous time... did I see anything suspicious? Did I hear anything odd? Did I know the victim?

I got fingerprinted again...I don't know why; they already had my prints from the first homicide scene. It had been what? A week? My first set of prints should have still been fresh! Twenty minutes later the officer came back into the room with another can of soda in his hand and told me that I could go. Just like with the first murders, I got the "don't-leave-town" speech.

I walked out of the police station to see CC waiting by the side of the jeep. I crossed the street and unlocked the doors.

"Are you okay?" I asked her as I put the key in the ignition.

"You know the last time we were at a murder?" she asked. "Do you remember what we did afterward?"

"We went and ate, CC. where are you going with this?"

"I want to skip the eating part and go straight for some drinks. I need a martini, possibly two. If they don't know how to make a white chocolate martini, somebody's going to get hurt."

We were at the Nest in twenty minutes.

After her second drink, CC was ready to talk. "I think I'm done going to photo shoots with you," she said, giving me a fairly direct look. I say 'fairly' because her eyes were beginning to cross a little. "I'm not liking this murder stuff. So far we've been lucky...we haven't been shot, and we haven't been clubbed over the head. I don't want to take the chance that this is a three strikes and you're out, kind of deal."

I rubbed the spot where my dull throbbing headache was beginning. "Don't worry about it, CC. I'm going to ask Mike if they've got any other job openings at the magazine. I've got the images from this shoot, and Monique gave us enough dirt for the tabloid…but I don't know if they can even use it at this point. As far as I'm concerned, it would be tacky to rat out a dead person. I think that my job with the magazine as a photographer is probably over, which is fine by me."

I massaged my baby migraine. I felt sick and shocked and exhausted.

CC looked into the bottom of her empty glass and then held it up to her eye, looking for more Martini, I guess. "Poor Monique…just over four hours ago, she was a woman looking forward to her revenge…and now…"

I jumped out of my chair. "Over four hours ago? It's after five? CC, I have to go; I have to go *now*! Can you take a taxi home?"

"You've got to *go*? You've got to go *where*??"

She sat up straight in her chair and slammed her glass down on the table. "After the day we've had, you're abandoning me? What's the deal??"

I grabbed my purse from where it was hanging off the back of my chair. "I've got a date, and I'm late! I forgot all about it, and I've got to get going. Can you get a ride home?"

CC slammed her glass down on the table yet again.

"She's got a date! She's got a date!"

Yelling over to the bartender, she bellowed the news one more time. "Hey, Bob! *She's got a date!*"

I looked over at Bob and gave him the signal to cut CC off.

"No more drinks for my little friend tonight. Can you get her a cab and make sure that she doesn't leave here with anyone but the taxi driver?"

He raised his hand to his forehead and gave me a very serious salute. "You got it!"

Problem solved, I charged out the door and ran for the jeep.

I made the trip home in ten minutes. Ryder was leaning up against the fence, feeding Reckless a carrot, when I pulled up, and the smell of steaks grilling filled the air. If the full impact of the murder hadn't started to hit me, I might have tried using my sexy walk...this was a man who deserved a sexy walk. He was wearing black jeans, a black polo shirt (the bulging muscles in his biceps were still there), and black boots. The black hair, which I had only glimpsed before, fell just past his shoulders; his long bangs swept back from his forehead in thick waves.

I became acutely aware that I was still wearing the outfit that I had left in that morning. Falling onto a dead body—*twice*—and pulling myself out of the sand wearing someone else's blood was not exactly going to enhance whatever sex appeal I possessed.

Ryder took a good long look at me as he began to move toward me.

"London?"

He covered the last ten feet in a few long strides and took my face in his hands. His eyes swept over my face, and out of nowhere, tears began to fall down my cheeks.

"She was dead, Ryder, she was dead."

"Who was dead, London?"

"Monique…Monique was dead. CC was right."

My legs started to go out from under me, and with one quick movement he swept me up and carried me into the house. He took me straight to the bathroom and ran the shower until it was hot, keeping me propped against him. He adjusted the heat a bit and then looked me in the eyes.

"Are you okay to get yourself cleaned up?"

I sniffled and nodded yes.

He cupped my chin in his hand. "I'll be in the living room."

As the warmth of the water washed away the mess the day had made of me, I was starting to get a grip on my emotions. A little makeup and slipping into a pair of capris followed by a soft green T-shirt with a little lace trim at the bottom had me feeling like I'd stripped off the last remnants of murder. All I had to do was walk to the living room and sit down beside Ryder, and I was crying again.

He held me against him as I cried, and with my head against his chest, I felt protected, safe.

I finally had cried myself out, and I looked up to find myself looking into the warmth of gold and bronze, edged with the blackest of black eyelashes. He bent his head, and raising my chin with the tips of his fingers, he lowered his lips to mine. He gave me a small tender, comforting kiss. For some reason, I hiccoughed. He laughed, and we went for kiss number two.

There were kisses, and then there were kisses. This kiss was going to go down in history. My mind, heart, and body were all wrapped up in that kiss. I was where I wanted to be for the rest of the night (maybe even longer), when Ryder sat up with an oath, released me, and ran from the room. It took me a minute to catch the scent of something starting to burn on the grill. The steaks were on fire (they weren't the only ones).

While Ryder put the fire out and salvaged the steaks, I headed out to the kitchen. Opening a bottle of wine, I sliced a loaf of French bread into small pieces, brushed a little olive oil on them, and waited for the broiler in the oven to get hot. I'd made a quick pit stop on the way home and picked up a salad from an awesome Italian restaurant in town. I'd just pulled the French bread from the oven, when Ryder walked in the door, balancing the two charred steaks on a plate.

We both stood and stared down at the poor burned steaks as they cooled, and then I did what came naturally.

Even burned, they still smelled delicious, so I picked one up with a fork and licked it.

The golden eyes watched me as I licked the steak again, and then he picked up the other one. After removing some of the worst of the charcoaled outer edge, he licked *his* steak. I had found my soul mate.

I tend to get a little carried away sometimes when I think something's funny, so I pulled the steak apart with my fingers and nibbled around the edges where there was some slightly tender meat. As I chewed, a little juice escaped my mouth and ran down my chin.

He was fast...before I could blink; he had licked it off my face. He didn't have any juice on his face, so I decided to fix that. I reached over, put my finger in a little olive oil that had spilled on the counter, and wiped it onto his cheek. There it was, on his cheek; what's a girl to do? His cheek tasted salty, just like you'd expect it to, and it was smooth...really, really smooth.

His next move kind of took me by surprise. He stuck his hand in the salad and fished out a cherry tomato. Without any hesitation, he dropped it down the front of my blouse.

I'm not telling you anything else. Oh well, just a little more, but that's it...I mean it.

Things happened, okay? You know what kind of things. I found out what kind of cologne he wears and that it tastes good. I found out if it's boxers or briefs. I found out he has just the right amount of hair on his chest and none on his back. I found out that I want to burn steaks more often and that I'll never look at a cherry tomato the same way again.

Chapter 35

When I woke up the next morning, the birds were singing, there wasn't a cloud in the sky, and I skipped through the forest, while the bluebirds perched on my shoulder.

Not really. It did look like it was going to be a really nice start to the weekend, though, and I could see Reckless outside standing by the fence, close to the house. I jumped in the shower and was a little surprised to find a small piece of tomato in my hair. Well, that did it…I was looking for bluebirds and butterflies to come flittering my way…I was *happy*.

I grabbed a quick breakfast, and for a healthy start to my day, I enjoyed whole-grain toast with a dab of butter. OK, the truth…I was out of chocolate, so I was forced to be healthy. Tossing my crumb-covered napkin in the trash, I sashayed my happy little self out to visit Reckless.

I have a confession to make. About a week or so ago, I'd kind of given myself permission to climb the fence so that I could walk in the field with Reckless. Why didn't I just open the gate and walk through, you ask? Where's the fun in that? Sometimes I took my camera along and shot images of him as he grazed, but lately I'd just been talking with him and getting his opinion on my major life decisions. Today I definitely needed my "Reckless time."

As soon as I climbed the fence, Reckless started heading across the field toward a hill that was a favorite of his, and I followed. I enjoyed sitting on the top of the hill, watching him, so I found a comfy-looking spot and sat down in the sun. That's when the glow of the Ryder-induced happiness started to recede a little, and the reality of Monique's demise crept back into my brain. Reckless hadn't wandered too far from me, so after a little back-and-forth debate with myself, I decided to tell him about the murders and that horrible night in the woods. I didn't think talking about murder and mayhem would upset him too much.

"Things have been kind of scary lately, Reckless. You know how I've had these photo shoots to do for work… well, each time there's been a murder. I know, it sounds like I'm making this up, but I'm not! The first time, two people were killed, and this last time, one person was killed. So we're looking at three deaths. I'm telling you, Mr. Horse, I'm getting really creeped out."

Reckless edged closer as I went on with the details.

"I mean…it's not like they just passed away while they were sitting in a chair sipping a glass of wine…that might not have been so upsetting. The scary thing is, these were violent deaths…blood, guts, and everything! I was in the same space, at the same time, with a murderer."

Reckless tilted his head and gave me a questioning look.

"Don't give me that look! I know what you're thinking…you're thinking do I really want this job so badly that I'd risk my life? Well, the answer to *that* is a big fat NO. I'm going to tell Mike on Monday that I can't do this anymore. I don't want someone to find me dead at the bottom of a cliff, or in the bathtub turning purple with a poison dart sticking out of my neck. And there's something else I want to talk to you about." I took a deep breath. "That night I asked you if it wasn't time for you to be getting off to bed. Well, someone was in the woods when I took my walk to the beach. I was coming back just as it got dark, and I heard little noises. I told myself it was just a little animal or something, but then out of nowhere somebody pulled me to the ground. The next thing I knew, they were gone."

Reckless stood close to my foot, chewing very slowly and keeping one eye on me.

"Could it really be a string of coincidences—the attack, the murders? I've thought about this a lot, and you know, except for what happened to me in the woods, CC and I were together when these people got killed. Could somebody be after *her*? Could somebody be trying to frame her for the murders? I need to ask Cee if she's got a customer who's mad at her.

"Maybe someone is unhappy that they look fat in a gown that she designed. People always want to blame her for that, even though the truth is they used food to design the fat themselves. The romance department is more likely to be the area of her life that would drive somebody crazy. It's more than possible that she flirted with someone's boyfriend or husband and they're out to get her. Then, again, it could be a brokenhearted ex-lover...there must be fifty of those."

Reckless snuffled the grass and ignored me while I strained my brain, thinking over the possibilities.

"I started thinking about it today, and I keep going back to the affair CC had with Tralenka Portia's father. I've got to quit calling him that, now that we know he *wasn't* her father. Anyway, CC only dated him for a month, and then she found out that he was a total jerk."

Reckless seemed to be sucking on his teeth, but he was now giving me his full attention.

"That dirty rat was 'dating' Tralenka at the same time he was romancing Cee. She only found out he was two-timing her because a concerned client couldn't resist letting CC know that there was another 'woman.' The really disgusting part of all this is that the other 'woman' was barely *eighteen years old!* You don't know her, Reckless, but CC's heart was broken. Well, it was broken for, maybe, forty-five minutes. She doesn't waste a lot of time crying over lovers who turn out to be losers. She dumped him in a heartbeat.

"So anyway, when 'the rat' dumped Tralenka and tried to win CC back, Tralenka turned into a teenage mutant psycho. One afternoon when CC left work, Tralenka jumped out from behind a really fancy-schmancy shrub that was beside the door and spray-painted CC's hair, face, and knees, red. Don't ask me why the knees…why does a psycho do anything they do? Thank God CC was wearing her Christian Dior sunglasses. Tralenka was kicking and screaming like a banshee, when the cops dragged her nutso ass off to jail. Maybe she's the one trying to frame CC for murder."

I turned that idea over in my mind for a minute.

"Darn it, Reckless, the problem with that theory is, if somebody *was* after CC, why would they try to hurt *me*? Why try to grab me on the path, come to my house on *purpose*? Obviously they only wanted me…this is so damn confusing…maybe they didn't want CC, after all."

Reckless must have started getting bored with my story, because he started chewing on my hair. That was enough to end my trip into "detective land."

I gently pried my hair out of his mouth and got up off the ground.

"All right, big boy, I get the message…enough of all this drama. I know you don't really want to hear any more of this craziness…but if you could spare me just one more minute…and this is totally off the subject…I wanted to ask you what you thought about Ryder. What do you think? Do you approve?"

Reckless just nudged my leg. I wondered what a nudge on the leg meant...yes, you two make a seriously perfect couple...or no...this has "train wreck" written all over it.

He hadn't had much to say, but I was still grateful. "Thanks for the talk, mister; I feel like I can tell you anything."

Giving me one more serious look and passing a little gas, he turned and trotted off across the field to join the rest of the herd. It was official...we were now close friends...I had been blessed with "eau de horse stinky." I shot a quick look around the field and the yard around the house. I felt pretty safe in the daylight, but it was going to be a long time before I took any more walks to the beach.

CHAPTER 36

I'd come back down to earth from my "bluebirds on my shoul-der" mood, and I definitely wasn't skipping back to the house. Troubled and stressed, I let out a long sigh, and then suddenly a thought occurred to me...maybe some choco-late had mysteriously hatched in my kitchen. I walked a little faster. I searched the whole house. An invisible choc-olate chicken had not stopped by to lay any eggs, so I de-cided to review the images that I had taken at Monique's.

Looking at the images of the house, you would never guess that it was soon to be a house of murder. It wasn't dark and foreboding looking...no bats hung upside down from the turrets, and no creepy butlers had lurked in the hallways.

I examined every image a lot more closely than I nor-mally do...was there a dark shadowy figure somewhere in the background? Had I overlooked a scraggly, tooth-less, deranged-looking handyman shooting deadly looks at

Monique? I checked every photo again; zip, zilch, nada. No clues, nothing. The images were going to look great in the magazine, if, and that was a big IF, Mike used them at all.

I burned the images to a disc, including the images of Monique lying dead in the sand. Yes, that's right; I took pictures of the dead body. I took them to protect myself. I wanted to have proof of exactly what the murder scene had looked like...don't ask me why.

I sent Sophie an email and asked her to set up the meeting with Mike. I had the shots and wanted to meet somewhere outside of the office as we'd discussed.

I didn't dread this meeting as much as I had the one after the first murder. This wasn't my first rodeo; after all...I was murder experienced. That thought made me pause. What was happening to me? Was I actually getting comfortable having meetings to look at pictures of places where there'd been a homicide? I worried about that for about a second and then reminded myself how gut wrenching the whole experience had been...I was a long way from being numb to the sight of murdered bodies.

I stopped obsessing on the murders for a minute when I realized that I was going to need a new monopod, and that meant a quick shopping trip to pick one up. The police still had the one I took to the photo shoot, and I *never* wanted it back. *Boom....!* I was right back into dwelling on the murders.

Thinking about the monopod, I realized something that made the little hairs on my arms stand up. CC had been wearing her opera gloves…she'd handled the monopod, but she wouldn't have left any fingerprints. Would my prints be the only ones found on the murder weapon?

I didn't want to think about what that might mean for me…I gave an involuntary shudder. I needed to get my mind off murder, and I didn't have chocolate…so my main coping mechanism wasn't an option. I could always daydream about Ryder, but that would cause a *whole* lot of frustration and lead me right back to wanting chocolate.

Before Ryder had left Friday night, he had told me that he needed to take care of some business up in Sarasota and that he wasn't going to get back until Monday. I wondered if he was going to be at the Haven again. Had he told me that he volunteered there? I couldn't remember for obvious reasons…I'd gotten so swept up in our "dinner" that I forgot to ask him about that day. I kind of hoped he'd remember my sexy walk and comment on it.

I thought about driving up to take more pictures of the big cats but thought better of it. I didn't want to run into him and have him think that I was some kind of stalker chick. Instead, I planted my rear in front of the computer again and checked my e-mail. Sophie had sent me a response, so at least I could make plans for my meeting with Mike.

I hadn't even thought about the fact that the murder would have been front-page news. I also never dreamed that the pictures I saw a neighbor of Monique's taking with their cell phone would be on the Internet and in the paper.

Sophie's e-mail was in all caps. "OH NO! NOT AGAIN! I SAW YOU IN A PICTURE WITH THE POLICE ALL AROUND YOU! I WANTED TO CALL YOU, BUT I THOUGHT YOU MIGHT STILL BE UPSET…THOSE PICTURES OF YOU WITH THAT BIG RIP IN YOUR PANTS AND YOUR UNDERWEAR SHOWING JUST WEREN'T ATTRACTIVE.

P.S.: YOU MIGHT WANT TO CONSIDER ELECTROLYSIS. IT LOOKED LIKE YOU HAD A MUSTACHE IN ONE OF THE SHOTS."

Crap, I had a *hole* in my pants, and I went to get drinks with CC like *that*? I looked like I had a *mustache*, and it was all over the *Internet*?

Sophie's e-mail went on to say that Mike hoped that I was OK, and since I wasn't lying on the ground covered with a sheet, he had assumed all was well. (Well, golly, didn't I have the most caring boss ever?) I was supposed to meet him for lunch the next day at a small restaurant that was not in the touristy area and somewhere that local business people weren't likely to lunch.

With my meeting with Mike arranged, I decided to zoom into town and find an inexpensive monopod. I closed up the house and tossed my purse into the back of the jeep. I'd only gotten a little way down the driveway, when I stopped to let a rider on horseback cross in front of me. I watched the dapple-gray mare move slowly closer to my jeep and then stop right in front of it, preventing me from moving forward. I looked at the rider and locked eyes with Trey. A dirty old man in the body of a good-looking "thirty something."

I rolled my window down. "Trey, would you mind letting me pass?"

"Well, that depends, Miss London…would you let me *make* a pass?"

I rolled up my window and glared at him. He threw his head back and laughed…removing his cowboy hat, he swept it down and to the side. He actually did a little half bow toward me and then smacked his hat against the mare's flank. They shot past me, and I hoped the horse would throw off the jackass she had perched on her back. I stomped on the accelerator…would I let him "make a pass?" What a cliché. Trey was blond and green eyed, well built, and with his personality, he couldn't have been more unattractive to me.

I made the trip to town as quickly as I could, bought a monopod that cost more than I wanted to spend, and then made a beeline for home and the kitchen. I was going to plant myself in front of the TV and just let my brain chill. That's when Brenda called.

"London, are you OK? I just heard about the murder!"

"I'm OK."

"You must be traumatized! I mean, how many murders have happened, and you were *right there* when the murderer was!"

"Too many…I'm beginning to feel like I'm the angel of doom."

"Don't be silly, London! There's no such thing. It's kind of ironic that you mentioned being an angel of doom, though…I asked you to be on the side of the angels the other day, and you were…and I didn't listen. I should have."

"You went ahead and peeked in that guy's window?"

"Yeah…and I got caught."

I sucked in a breath. "What happened?"

"Well, I waited until it got really dark outside, and then I snuck over and moved the trash can."

"Did you see anything?"

"Oohhhh yeah…all the living-room walls are covered with blue fabric, and he only has folding chairs to sit on. There was a big closet on one side of the room, but the door to it was closed, so I couldn't see what was in it."

"Was he in there?"

"I didn't see him, but my new neighbor, the cop, saw me! He came out of nowhere and yanked me off the trash can."

"What did he do, what did he say?"

"He gave me a verbal warming, and then he let me go home."

"I think you mean a 'verbal *warning*,' Brenda."

"Well, whatever, he scolded me…and the result was a *warming* as far as I'm concerned. He was cute."

"So are you going to stop stalking your neighbor now?"

"Well, it's going to be a lot harder to watch him now. The cop said he better not catch me doing it again, because if he did, he'd arrest me. He said I'd be a repeat offender!"

"Time to retire, Brenda…maybe find a new hobby."

"Oh, I don't think so! I'm having too much fun! Now, I've got to go, but you need to be careful…keep your eyes open for murderers whenever you go out; they could be anywhere."

"I'll remember that, thanks." Great…my paranoia had an immediate growth spurt.

Brenda had hung up.

There was only one thing to do. I went to the kitchen, ripped open a bag of prepopped popcorn, found a big bowl, and filled it to the brim. Once I'd sprinkled grated cheese on it and turned on a movie, I threw myself down on the couch and rationalized that it was either eat the popcorn or pluck my eyebrows and check for a mustache. *Aaaaggghhh*…I was *not* going to let something that Sophie said get inside my brain. I was not going to let Trey's creepiness make me stress eat…five minutes later the popcorn was all gone. Damn you, Trey.

As soon as the movie was over, I wandered into the bathroom…I'd resisted looking as long as I could. I was almost positive I was going to see a mustache when I looked in the mirror. Damn you, Sophie.

Chapter 37

Why does Monday have to be so hard? I had slept like the dead, and even though I was on my way to lunch with Mike, I was still trying to get my brain to fire up. I wasn't looking forward much to this meeting, but I *was* looking forward to eating. The little restaurant by the bay in Osprey had awesome food and was never too crowded. Thinking about my meeting with Mike this morning had felt like déjà vu all over again. I was nervous and worried just like before. What wasn't the same was that I wasn't worried about losing the chance to work for the magazine. I knew I was going to quit, and I was more worried about finding a new job.

I pulled up in the parking lot and saw Mike pacing rapidly back and forth near the entrance. The minute he saw me, he turned and gave the hostess a look. She must have made him wait for a table until I got there, and I got the distinct impression that he hadn't been happy about it.

The minute she got "the look" from him, she handed two menus to a terrified waitress who had obviously been watching Mike pace like a caged tiger. Mike is a big guy, probably around six foot three and built like a football player...that makes for an intimidating presence even when he's *not* irritated.

Menus in hand, she was off like a scared rabbit, and we had to hustle to keep up with her. She made up for Mike's having to wait, by taking us to a table that provided all the privacy we could have wanted. She brought the iced teas that we ordered in no time flat and left us to study the menu.

As soon as she was gone, Mike put down his menu and leaned way forward, his eyes shifting from side to side to make sure that no one was listening.

"What do you think is going on?" he asked, so quietly that I had to lean in to hear him.

"I think I'm having lunch with you," I whispered back.

"Don't be a smart-ass, London. So what's your theory? Why do you think these people are getting murdered every time you show up?"

Talk about getting right to the point. I definitely didn't have a snappy comeback for that remark. I couldn't think of *anything* to say to that remark. So I just sat there, looking at him. I guess he wasn't expecting me to say anything, because he went on to his next question.

"Did you bring the CD?"

I took it out of my bag and handed it over.

"Were you able to get any shots before 'it' happened?"

"I got pretty much everything except the cabana. I even got shots of the body."

He almost choked on his tea. *"You got pictures of the body??"*

"Yes, and I'm not saying that I'm proud of that. Sometimes instinct just kicks in, and you keep shooting." I'd explained this to him before, but I felt he needed to be reminded. I didn't want him to think I was some kind of ghoul. "It's almost as if I'm disconnected from what's really happening."

I braced myself, waiting for a disapproving stare, or the complete opposite, an inability to look me straight in the eyes.

I was a total jerk for having photographed the body, and I knew it…I didn't get either of the reactions I was expecting. He stood up, leaned across the table, and kissed me smack on the lips. Well, ewwwwwwwwww!

"You are brilliant!" Mike hissed at me.

I wasn't feeling brilliant at the moment; I was feeling slightly violated.

He went on, while I wiped my lips with the back of my hand.

"I can't believe I forgot to bring my laptop with me so that I could look at the images…but that can wait…tell me everything."

I don't know if he was aware of it, but he was rubbing his hands together…in excitement? Anticipation? Who knows, but it made me a little nervous. There was only one place to start, and that was somewhere near the beginning. I plunged into the details. It didn't take too long to cover the actual shoot itself, but then I gave him what he was waiting for.

"It was just pretty routine, except that she really, really hated her ex-husband and wanted to get revenge, because he cheated on her with her best friend and now he's going to marry that same 'friend.'

"CC and I finished up with the house, and then we took the steps down to the cabana. That's when we found Monique lying in the sand...dead."

Mike had fixed a laser-like stare on me. "Who's CC?" he asked.

"C. C. Covington, the designer to the stars of Sarasota. She's my oldest friend, and she's gone along on the shoots as my assistant."

"Covington...I've heard of her...I'd like to meet her sometime...maybe do a story on her. I've heard she's a real babe."

I threw him a disgusted look.

"There's a lot more to C. C. Covington than her looks."

"Yeah, I've also heard she's never met a man she didn't love. Anyway...we can probably still do the photo spread if we only use the exterior shots...so long as the police department clears us to use the images. We can give the history of the property and include some images of the former owners...then we get to the juicy part. People love a mysterious murder, and the fact that our photographer was there at the actual moment the crime was committed would really grab their attention, so we'll throw that info in too. So…that's enough about the article. I wanted to talk to you about your future with the magazine. I want to go in a different direction with you."

I held up a finger to indicate that we needed to pause for a moment.

"Before we discuss this and that, could you just pinky swear that you'll make it clear in the article that I didn't murder Monique?"

"Don't be ridiculous, London; we wouldn't print anything that would implicate you! Now let's talk about your job."

I had been planning on quitting, but I was curious about what he had to say. It would be nice to still have a job, as long as it didn't involve risking my life. Our "little rabbit," the waitress, probably wondered why I was shredding my napkin when she chose that moment to return for our order. I have a bad habit of destroying paper placemats, including the little paper wraps on straws when service is slow or I'm stressed, or if I'm bored or if I'm breathing… I'm fidgety sometimes; what can I say?

After our waitress skittered away from the table, I had no idea what I had just ordered. She hadn't gotten ten feet away from us, when Mike leaned in close and began to talk in a near whisper. I really wanted to ask him what kind of cologne he used and recommend that he never buy it again.

Mike was an attractive man. He kind of had a Cary Grant look going on. From everything I'd heard about Mike, he was a really good guy with a heart of gold. All that good stuff goes out the window, though, when a man smells like an old shoe. I didn't have to think twice about what to get him for Christmas…December first I'd be standing at the men's cologne counter, picking out the latest Gucci for men. I tried to concentrate on what he was saying and *not* how he smelled.

"These murders got me thinking, and as a result I've been talking with some editors who work in the tabloid business. I don't really have a background in this stuff, and I'm trying to learn because I think the magazine needs some kind of spark. I've changed my mind about the type of tabloid reporting we'll do. I don't want to do shots of local celebrities driving out of Debby's Donuts with powdered sugar all over their face. I want to dig up some *big* stories, and that's where you come in."

I was really curious to find out how I was going to fit in with his plan, and I had questions, one of which had already been answered…if I wanted to keep my job, I could.

Little Rabbit trotted up with our food and trotted off again. Another question had now been answered…I'd ordered alligator bites for lunch. Ewwwwwwww!

Chapter 38

Mike took a huge handful of fries and stuffed them into his mouth. "I want to blow all the other magazines out of the water by solving a mystery. I've had this idea for a while, but I didn't know how to pursue it, and then...you came along."

It was amazing...I'd understood every word he said, despite the chewing of the fries.

"Look, Mike, if this involves blood or shooting or stabbings, you can count me out."

"No, no, no! It's nothing like that. You handled yourself really well when these murders took place. You proved once again that you can keep your cool, and that's what I need...someone who can stay calm and gather information...even when things get a little crazy."

Obviously the sound of CC and I screaming our guts out hadn't travelled *all* the way back to town from Monique's place. Oh yeah...we stayed *real* calm and cool.

"You got shots of a crime scene, even after you rolled all over a dead body! If that had happened to me, my pants would have had to go straight to the dry cleaner."

Another image I could have lived without.

"Here's the deal, London. There's a mystery billionaire living in Saint Armands. Nobody knows what he looks like, but *everybody* wants to know about him, especially the women…they're beside themselves hoping to meet him. He's single, supposedly very handsome and has *bigggg* money. But he's like a ghost…practically invisible from what I hear. Every media source that you can think of has tried to get pictures of the guy, but so far zip, zilch, nada…no picture of him…nothing."

Mike was getting more excited as he talked. "So I'm on a mission. I want to get pictures of this guy, 'the Prince of Saint Armands.' If we can get at least one image of him and do a story about him, everybody will be talking about us, and we can take this magazine national. So that's where *you* come in…you're going to get the pictures."

I leaned back and folded my arms across my chest.

"I'm supposed to somehow get the pictures that have been impossible for anyone else to get?"

"Exactly."

"And just how am I supposed to find this invisible Prince?"

He leaned so far over the table that I was afraid he was going to launch himself face-first onto my plate. There had been an awful lot of leaning over plates during this lunch. As a result, Mike's tie had food spotted all over it.

He shouldn't have ordered the baked mac and cheese. It didn't look so hot on his black tie.

"Like I said, we're not going to do stuff like park on the street outside of his house, waiting to get a shot of him. We're going to be clever and approach this from a different angle…a personal angle. We know one thing about this guy for certain; he believes in giving back. He gives a ton to charity, so I'm sending you into his mansion on the pretext of doing a photo shoot for a charitable event." He sat back, pleased with his plan.

"So what you're really saying is, you have something against this guy, and you're trying to get him killed. With my record on photo shoots, if you send me in there, he's as good as dead."

"Don't be ridiculous," Mike snapped. "Don't even *joke* about that."

"I wasn't serious," I said. "Well, at least not one hundred percent serious."

Being the intuitive person that I am, I decided Mike wasn't in the mood for "funny" and got back to business.

"Are you telling me that you already have arrangements made for me to get into his home?" I really wanted to say "mansion," but that just seemed like a totally unreal word to use.

Mike sat a little straighter in his chair and got a gleam in his eye.

"This guy—let's just call him 'the Prince' from now on—is really, really involved with charities, like I said.

He's been actively giving since he moved here. I should mention that he's not really royalty…at least as far as we know. So anyway, Sophie volunteers for a lot of charities around town, and she knows the score on what's going on and what's happening where and when. There's a big event coming up in a month called 'the Strength of the Stiletto.' It's all about 'girly power' or something like that."

I should have smacked him right then, but I don't like doing that to people in a public place. I settled for wondering if he really was a chauvinist or just harmlessly clueless.

"The money raised will help women in need on a variety of levels. The charity provides job training, and they buy them nice clothes, nice shoes, whatever they need to accomplish a nice professional look. They even pay for childcare while the women go out to apply for jobs. The Prince is a big supporter of charities that benefit women in particular, and Sophie said it was *huge* news when it was announced that the event would be held at his place. I guess they needed a place with lots of security, you know, to protect the shoes."

My attention had wandered just the littlest bit while Mike was talking…I was really impressed by something he'd said. Little Sophie was involved with charity work. Who knew? I hadn't given her enough credit…I had gotten the impression that she spent her off hours watching James Bond movies, dreaming of the day that she'd be a for real spy. Wait a minute…had Mike just said they needed security for *shoes*?

"What do you mean they need to protect 'the shoes'?"

"Well, of course, there are the shoes that are being auctioned off...all kinds of designer shoes contributed by celebrities that will be sold in a silent auction...and then there will be *the* shoes." Those are the shoes that need protection."

I was going to be patient; I was not going to reach over and pinch him or grab him by the neck.

I needed clarification. "Let me get this straight...there are 'shoes' and *the* shoes? What are *the* shoes?"

"The jewel-encrusted stilettos that are supposed to be worth ten million dollars."

"Are you kidding me, Mike? Actual shoes? *Worth ten million dollars?*"

"Can you believe it? I didn't know shoes like that even existed!"

"Ten *million* dollars...what a person could do with ten million dollars. So tell me how Sophie got me access to the house."

"Sophie just got on the committee recently, and she volunteered our photographer—you—to take photos at the event and to visit the house beforehand to get a few shots for publicity purposes."

"Did you just say that I'm the photographer for the *event?*"

"Yes, and beforehand...like, a couple of weeks before the event. They need time to get the pictures out to the media and the other advertisers so that they can get tickets selling in advance. You'll go to the mansion again the night of the big Shoe Fest…events like these always have photographers lurking around, grabbing shots of the socialites who are there…you know, candid shots of couples dancing, pictures of groups seated at their tables enjoying dinner. They use those shots for their brochures and info packets for the rest of the year. Having you in place at the event is our plan B. It will give you another opportunity to get a picture of the Prince if you don't succeed at the mansion."

Mike was finally out of dramatic information to surprise me with and was sitting waiting for some kind of reaction from me. I didn't know which one to give him. I had a whole list of reactions to his news…I felt a little nervous, I felt a little intimidated, I felt a little manipulated, I felt a whole lot *excited*!

I'm not a high-society type of girl, even though I was raised around wealthy people. I know which fork to use while eating my salad and to break small pieces off a dinner roll and eat just the small bit instead of taking a huge bite out of the roll. Knowing those things comes in handy from time to time, but I'm the kind of girl who would rather be out with my camera than sitting by the pool at 'the club' spearing cherries out of a fruity drink with a teeny, tiny plastic pirate sword.

For some reason the scenario Mike was spinning sounded like fun. The mansion photos…okay…kind of interesting…but the part about trying to track down and photograph an elusive billionaire? *Very* interesting…that part of the job kind of appealed to the wildlife photographer in me. Watching and waiting for my subject to make its appearance and then capturing an image of the beautiful male of the species...woo-ha! Now that's my idea of fun! I decided to put Mike out of his misery.

"I have one request." I could see him clench his jaw just the littlest bit. "I want CC to go to the 'stiletto night' with me."

Mike's eyes lit up, and a huge smile spread across his face.

"Done! No problem! Call Sophie tomorrow, and she can give you all the details for phase one...the mansion photo shoot. London, we're going to make a great team... this is just the beginning!"

As we stood up, Mike did one more big lean across the table...but this time I was ready for him. I took two steps back, and his tie dragged through what was left of my side order of applesauce. He looked down with big sad eyes at the tie. It was now pretty much the equivalent of a messy baby bib.

Well, it made no sense at all, but that made him even more attractive. I was definitely going to have to introduce him to CC—even though he had called her a "babe." With the whole Cary Grant vibe going on *and* the fact that he wasn't at all pretentious, the man had potential...yep, if I had anything to do with it, Mike's world and CC's were about to collide.

Chapter 39

By the time I climbed into the jeep, there was still plenty of time left to get things done. The first thing I needed to do was swing by the grocery and pick up supplies. I made a mental shopping list...I knew for sure that I needed brownie bites. I'd learned my lesson; I'd been caught without emergency chocolate in the house one time too many lately. It was time to stock up. What else was on my list? Popcorn and shredded cheese, carrots for Reckless, and some little tomatoes...just in case Ryder stopped by. At the thought of tomatoes, I blushed the color of another vegetable...the beet...I could feel myself turning beet red. I'd never acted so impulsively with a man before. Our relationship had gone from nothing to *something* in a heartbeat. I had no idea how to act the next time that I saw him.

By the time I reached the bakery, a horrible thought had occurred to me. I was going to have to watch my sweets intake...in just over a month, I was going to have to slide myself into a gown for "stiletto night," and eating brownie bites was probably going to have to be crossed off my list of fun things to do.

I didn't have the heart to tell the sweet lady behind the counter that I had changed my mind, so I forced myself to accept the bag of 'bliss' she handed me. These would be my last bites for a month. Don't sit there laughing at me… it's not polite. I have amazing willpower…people mention it all the time.

I had stored my groceries and was sitting in the jeep, peeling the chocolate shell off the chocolate fudge on a "bite," when a pickup truck pulled into the space beside me. Holding the fragile shell between two fingers, I glanced over and promptly dropped the melting chocolate onto the front of my blouse.

Ryder strikes again…every time I see the man, it's as if I get a little electric shock. He had his window down, and he motioned for me to put mine down. I lowered the window, and with a little smile playing at the corner of his mouth, he raised the temperature in my jeep about thirty degrees.

"I could help get that chocolate off there if you'd like." He grinned.

I nervously brushed my fingers across my lips and brushed my hair back from my forehead. I didn't know what to do with my hands…they seemed to have a mind of their own, and their mind was telling them to run their fingers through his hair, which would be totally inappropriate in a parking lot in broad daylight. I ignored his generous offer and tried to steer the conversation in a direction that would make my brain focus on something other than the fascinating physical reaction I was having to him.

"Did you get everything done?" See, I was able to form words and everything when I looked at him.

"Pretty much. I was at the Haven most of the time, and they always have a lot for me to do. I'm going to have to go back up to Sarasota again this weekend…this time for ranch stuff. I was going to ask you if you wanted to meet me up there Saturday. We could have dinner, maybe even combine that with a sunset cruise."

I'm not sure, but I think I answered him before he got the word "cruise" out of his mouth.

"I'd love it."

"Good."

Those damn sunglasses. I wanted to see those eyes…it was becoming a "thing" with me. I couldn't just say, "Take off your sunglasses…I want to melt into your gorgeous, beautiful, dreamy, delicious eyes." So I just sat and stared at him like a dope and lost track of the conversation…although at that point I don't think we were having a conversation any longer…my mind had gone off into "Yes, I'll have your baby" land.

"London?"

I loved it when he said my name.

"You might want to take a look in your mirror."

I glanced up into my rearview mirror, and my mouth dropped open. I had chocolate smeared across my lips, on the sides of my face, and on my forehead. All that nervous fussing with my face and hair had been done with chocolate covered fingers. Crap.

I heard the truck back up, but no way was I going to wave bye-bye. I picked up the bag of brownies and squeezed and squished the evil contents into nothingness…there… no more brownie bites. It took me about a minute, and then I opened the bag, swiped up some of the brownie mash with a finger, and popped it into my mouth. I was hopeless…and I was starting to wonder if I'd actually said, "Yes, I'll have your baby" out loud. Crap.

When I was sure Ryder was long gone, I pulled a facial cloth out of my bag and wiped all the chocolate off my face.

As always, I had my camera in my bag, so I pulled it out and checked it to see if any chocolate had fallen in and melted on it. Trust me, it could happen. I still hadn't gotten over the time that I went to use the camera and discovered that half a piece of crab Rangoon had somehow fallen into my bag and smeared crab paste all over the lens. That was *not* something that I wanted to repeat.

For the first time in a long time, I took a good look at the bag. The inside was trashed. Luckily today I hadn't dropped any chocolate into it, but there was dried chocolate on the inside from a previous snack. Somehow I had managed to tear a hole in the lining. Putting my finger through the hole, I found an open tube of lipstick that had melted. It was definitely time for a new bag.

Road trip! What better excuse to drag CC out shopping with me than buying a new bag. I wanted something that sent out a vibe…you know, something that looked professional, successful. One that quietly conveyed to all who looked my way, "That's right, I photograph megabuck mansions of the rich and famous."

Come to think of it, I'd need a bag for the night of the gala. For the gala I needed a bag that *screamed*, "Yes, I *am* the important snobby photographer whom you want to impress, and don't I look fabulous in my gown?" A bag for every photo occasion…ooooohh…why didn't I think of this before??

I'm not a big fan of shopping for clothes, but purse shopping I *love*. This could be fun. It would give me a chance to tell CC all about the stiletto gala and introduce the topic of Mike. Doing a little matchmaking and shopping for a couple of new bags…hopefully that would get my mind off the mortifying chocolate incident with Ryder.

Chapter 40

My purse shopping got delayed almost immediately. I'd been trying to do better at checking my messages as a result of CC's complaints, and it was finally becoming a habit. I had joined the rest of the human race with my compulsive phone monitoring. Three messages from Brenda, each one more insistent than the previous one, waited for my review. The gist of the messages was, "get here now." I flashed back to her getting stuck in the attic and felt my stomach twist a little. The use of the word "urgent" in her messages had me worried. I wasn't giving up on the purse-shopping expedition, but delaying it a bit seemed like a good idea.

I navigated my way through the parking lot, giving the distracted pedestrians plenty of space. You bump one guy hooked up to one of those oxygen tank thingies, and you never hear the end of it.

I found Brenda standing on the sidewalk in front of her place, smoking a cigarette.

"You don't smoke, Brenda; put that out."

"It's part of my disguise." She took a puff. "Look over to your right."

I swiveled my head to look at the people having lunch at the tables in front of Carney's.

"So…I'm looking…still looking…what am I supposed to be looking at?" I asked.

"Third table down on the right…young guy, black T-shirt. Eating the quesadilla." She got the words out just before she had a small coughing fit.

"Put out the cigarette…the guy with the two behemoths?"

"*Exactly!* That's my neighbor and his mob buddies."

I tried for a relaxed, normal, casual posture as I maneuvered myself up against the wall next to her.

"They don't look like mob guys," I whispered. "It is odd though that they're both wearing black suits in heat like this."

"Now you see what I *mean*! Who else would do that? In every documentary I've ever seen, the mob guys always have suits on…no matter what they're doing."

"You do realize that at the time most of those crime guys were wreaking havoc, it was the *style* for men to wear suits. For instance, normal guy 'Joe' who sold handkerchiefs in the department store wore a suit to work."

She ignored the voice of reason. "The baldheads I can't figure out; maybe it's something the younger generation of mafia guys do. Now that I think about it, wasn't Marlon Brando bald in that famous movie?"

"He wasn't bald in *Streetcar Named Desire.*"

"No, no, no…the mafia movie, what was it called…*The Great-Uncle?*"

"You mean *The Godfather*…I don't know if he was bald in that movie. I heard something bad happens to a horse, so I never watched it."

"Well, something bad is happening here; I can feel it," she murmured.

"How long have you been standing out here?"

"Not long enough. They've been here awhile, long enough to finish their meal. I glanced out the shop window ten minutes ago, and that's when I noticed them. I've been listening to their conversation…well, the parts that I can hear, anyway. I'm listening for clues about what they're up to."

"What have you heard?"

"I heard them say 'guillotine,' 'cement job,' and 'riding the leg.'"

"Dear God! The last one is too weird…I can't believe they're sitting right out in the open talking about this stuff."

Brenda sucked on the cigarette and started to choke. "They're getting up! Don't look at them! Don't look at them!"

We whipped around and pretended to window shop; that's when I noticed the pack of cigarettes Brenda had stashed on the window ledge. I waited three beats and casually looked over my shoulder, and our suspicious crime suspects were gone.

"They're half a block away, Brenda; we can turn around."

She whirled back around and marched over to their table. Without a shred of embarrassment, she picked up the restaurant copy of their receipt and put it in her pocket.

"What are you doing?" I hissed. "You can't do that!"

She gave me a sly smile. "I just did."

"Put that back, and get rid of that cigarette."

She kept the receipt and flipped the cigarette out of her fingers. I felt sorry for the woman who had to pick it out of her salad.

"What kind of clue are you going to get from that receipt?"

"Well, ta-da! His name is signed at the bottom. Now I know his name, and I can find out more about him!"

"That's actually not a bad idea, but you've got to give back the receipt; the restaurant needs those."

"Fine, I'll run inside my place, jot the name down, and give the receipt back."

"Good. Now why did you need me here?"

"When I call the FBI on these guys, there needs to be two of us reporting them. They'll take it more seriously if multiple people are suspicious of them."

I shook my head. "I don't think two people are going to get them interested in this. Look at how many reports of UFOs they get sometimes, and they don't flip out and send in the National Guard. I don't think any law-enforcement type is even going to look up from the doughnut they're eating over this.

Why don't you just let your neighbor and his friends do whatever it is they're doing and be done with it?"

"Because I can't. I think these guys are a threat to our community, and I'm going to find out what they're up to!"

I lifted the pack of cigarettes up off the window ledge. "Be careful, and let me know who 'receipt guy' is after you research him. And *no smoking*!"

She shrugged at me and disappeared through her shop door and into the comfort of air conditioning.

I shoved the pack of cigarettes into my purse and tried to get the image of Marlon Brando in his super-tight T-shirt yelling 'Hey…STELLLLA!' out of my head. I glanced into a clothing store as I headed back to the jeep, and a cute purse caught my eye. As soon as I got the cheese from the grocery store home and into the refrigerator, it was road-trip time!

Chapter 41

As the front door of CC's boutique silently dropped shut behind me, I heard loud voices emanating from the design area upstairs. One of the voices belonged to Bobbi, a seamstress trained in France. She had only been with Cee for a little over six months, and she was still going through an adjustment period. I stopped in my tracks…I didn't know whether to make a little noise to let everyone know that someone was now in the boutique…or whether to say and do nothing and accidentally eavesdrop on what was obviously a heated argument. I'm no saint; I figured if they were being that loud, then they didn't care who heard them…so I sat down in a nearby chair and decided to enjoy the show.

"*But, Madame!*" Bobbi shrieked. "*I had no idea! I did not see any special notations made on your dress order! I am not zee mind reader! I do not work for zee circus and look into zee crystal ball!* I HAVE NEVER HEARD OF SUCH A THING! Who in zere right mind would design an evening gown with *pocketz*??? It would be a *travesty*! *A travesty!* I, Madame, studied at Zee 'Ecole de la Chambre Syndicale de la Couture Parisienne,' and I tell you zis eez just not done! Madame CC's establishment does only haute couture...she would have my head if I were to do as you inseest!! I must also advise you, Madame, that if I were to sew zee gown as you demand, the whole design would be changed, and your butt, it would look like zee giant *bubble*!"

I didn't know about the client, but if someone told me *my* butt was going to look like "zee giant bubble," I might back off on my demand for pockets. All I could hear was a deep, threatening tone...pretty deep voice for a woman. After the voice stopped, all was quiet...for one, two, three beats, and then Bobbi called for backup.

"Madame CC! Madame CC! I need you at *once*!"

If things didn't work out at the boutique, Bobbi could use that piercing voice in a career cutting glass or diamonds...she wouldn't have to lift a finger...just raise that voice and "zee" job would be done.

I could hear the click of CC's heels as she made her way down the marble hallway to the design area. All had fallen silent between the two combatants. Bobbi certainly had seemed to have the power of hysteria going for her. Her opponent hadn't seemed to be intimidated and obviously had great control over their emotions. That ability, combined with a steely determination, could be enough to win the battle. Would there be "pocketz," or would there be no "pocketz"? I was beside myself with anticipation about the outcome…not.

CC's voice floated down the stairs, soothing and pleasant.

"Now, now, my darlings, what has caused all this up-set? I can see that you both could use some refreshment. Flor! Flor!" (Flor was her assistant and go-to guy when there was a crisis at hand.)

He ran past me and flew up the stairs two at a time in his skintight black slacks and zebra-striped shirt…the man was a marvel; not one strand of his platinum-blond hair popped out of place. He threw open the doors at the top of the stairs and disappeared…perfect…I could hear everything a little better now.

"Yes, miss…"

"Flor, be a dear, and bring two glasses of champagne and a bit of that lovely Brie de Meaux."

"Certainly."

Back he came, flying down the marble staircase.

I wasn't sure what Brie de Meaux was, but I thought I might grab a chunk or a lick or a slurp as soon as Flor raced back up the stairs with it…lunch with Mike seemed as if it had been hours and hours ago. I had pretty much lost interest in the outcome of the battle royale, so I decided to follow Flor to the kitchen. CC could catch me up on all the details later. Right now I wanted some Meaux. I was pretty sure Meaux was cheese, but I was so hungry it didn't really matter what it was.

"Sweetie pie, I don't know how you do it," I said to CC as we climbed into the jeep.

CC blew out some air. She had calmed the storm and settled everybody down while I was in the kitchen eating cheese. When I suggested a road trip, she had simply picked up her purse and headed out the door.

"It's actually pretty easy to handle difficult clients. You can soothe a lot of ruffled feathers with the right drink and the right nibble."

"That may work for the client, but how about the employee? How do you make them happy?"

"I slip an extra fifty bucks in their pay for the week… that usually puts a smile back on their face."

"Bobbi certainly deserves it…If it had been me, I would have been tempted to slap the client across the face and yell, '*I do not have to put up with zee likes of you! I depart herewith!*'"

"I definitely need to keep Bobbi happy. She's an amazing talent, and I'm lucky to have her."

"So…can you tell me the identity of 'pocketz,' or would you have to kill me if you told me?"

CC gave me her "I've-told-you-this-a-million-times-before face."

"You only know about Prissy because you showed up when she was having her fitting. My clients are supposed to be confidential."

I gave her *my*, "I've-told-you-this-a-million-times-before face."

"And *you* know that you end up telling me who they are eventually. So who is 'pocketz'?" I said.

"I'm *not* telling you this one...when somebody is making a fool of themselves, I'm not going to tell you who they are. It was a bad situation, and I don't want to make it worse by telling anyone. You're not the only person I talk to, you know, and if I tell too many people, it's going to get back to the client. The fastest way to put yourself out of business is to embarrass a client...no one will trust you after that."

I could see that I wasn't going to win this argument, so I decided to drop it for now. CC was done with the whole conversation, anyway, and was busy putting on her lipstick.

"Where are we going?" she asked mid-application.

"We're going to find a purse for me and a man for you."

"*What?*" She whipped her head toward me and painted a nice long scarlet line from the corner of her mouth to her ear.

"We're going to get a purse—actually two purses for me—and a man for you."

CC had a slow smile spreading across her face and a little bit of a crazy look in her eye.

"What in the name of Gucci are you talking about, London?"

I had started to doubt my plan of fixing her up with Mike, but there was no turning back now. I decided to plunge right in and start with the matchmaking.

"There's someone I'd like you to meet, CC. It's Mike, my editor. We had lunch today. I think you'd like him."

I'd barely finished my sentence, when she shot out her first question.

"Sex appeal...yes or no."

"Well, yes...I know you, Cee; I wouldn't be stupid enough to suggest someone who didn't have that going on."

"Tall or short?"

"Tall."

"Hair?"

"Plenty of hair."

"To die for?"

"Come on, Cee...how am I going to be certain that he's 'to die for'? 'To die for' is in the eye of the beholder."

"Kissable lips?"

"Ewwww...! I don't know...he's my boss!"

"When do I meet him?"

Well, that went better than I thought it would.

Chapter 42

Ten minutes later we were at the mall, and now *I* had the crazy look in my eyes. I was nearing my idea of heaven... my favorite department store with the best purses ever!

In the short discussion with CC about Mike, we hadn't even gotten to the part about the gala and the billionaire. CC slid to a stop and bumped into me when I paused to decide which purse to look for first. Gorgeous, sophisticated "work" bag...or gorgeous, sophisticated, "Night of the Gala" bag.

CC was trying to get my attention.

"Hey, crazy purse lady...what kind of purse emergency are we shopping for?"

"OK, I've already told you that I had a lunch meeting with Mike today. You know how you and I talked about how I'm not going to do anymore photo shoots, because everybody keeps getting killed, right?"

"Right."

"Well, Mike has this really kind of cool idea. He wants to take the magazine national...but he's got to make a big splash somehow so people will take notice. Long story short, he's got it set up for me to photograph some mystery billionaire's mansion and then be the official photographer for a gala that's going to happen at the mansion.

"I'm supposed to somehow get a couple of shots of this guy so that Mike can plaster it all over the magazine...he beats out the other media by showing the world what the Prince looks like and bingo-bango-bongo...the magazine gets lots of buzz, a whole bunch of new subscribers, and Mike is a happy camper."

"London, why do you keep calling this guy 'the Prince'? Is he royalty?"

"As far as I know, Mike just wanted to call him that. Apparently everybody on Saint Armands and in Sarasota is in a total swoon over him. Rich, good looking, likes to spend his money...what's not to swoon over?"

"Wait a minute. Are you talking about the invisible guy? The one who has the mansion on Saint Armands?"

"Yeah, CC. That's the guy. Have you heard about him, too?"

"Who hasn't heard about him? The rumors are flying all over town. I've heard everything...He's incredibly handsome, he's really ugly, he's tall, he's short. He's a hermit, he's tied to the mob, he's Superman. Nobody really knows anything about him...I don't know how he's managed to fly under the radar for this long, but you're right, he's a mystery man."

I had missed the last part of what she was saying. I'd seen a purse that was calling my name. She was only able to prevent me from going into a full-blown purse trance because she was asking about the need for a bag.

"London, you still haven't explained the importance of the purses."

I was running the palm of my hand over the butter-soft leather of a purse big enough to squeeze my camera into, along with a few batteries. I know, I know…you're not supposed to walk around with your camera so unprotected, but I'm a shoot-from-the-hip kind of photographer. I work fast most of the time, and I get bugged by carrying too much equipment. I do some of my best work with just a good-sized purse with the camera stashed in it, including the batteries and media cards.

I finally answered CC. "The first bag that I need is one to take to work. It needs to be a little nicer than the ones I usually carry, and it needs to look professional. I want a purse that looks as if it's at home in a mansion. Don't look at me like I'm nuts; I know myself, and on a job like this I need to 'feel' the part. A fabulous bag will add credibility when I walk through the door.

"You know how people like that can be…if I'm going to be accepted by the snobs, I need to look like a snob, act like a snob, command respect."

CC gave me a disgusted eye roll. "Don't be ridiculous. First of all, that's the most ludicrous justification for buying a purse that I've heard in a long time. Secondly, a fair amount of these people are *not* snobs, and if you go in there with some kind of fake act, you're going to turn people off. I mean it, London...If I catch you going all snobby on me, I'm going to slap you naked and hide your clothes."

I had no idea what she was talking about, but I didn't like the sound of it.

CC picked up a really awesome black bag with a nice long strap. It had one long, long strand of rhinestones that was attached by a silver ring on each side of the bag.

"Hand over the bag, CC."

Without a word she handed it to me. She knows how I am. I'd give you the shirt off my back in most cases...but when it comes to purses...I'm a little scary.

"Take it, it's yours." CC held it out to me with just two fingers. "Okay, we've got one bag taken care of. Is this going to be the 'gala' bag or the 'mansion' bag?"

"I don't know, Cee...the mansion bag? I have to get a gown for the big event, and whatever bag I get has to fit a gown sort of occasion. This black one feels businesslike."

CC had a look on her face that was suddenly very intense.

"I'm doing it."

I looked her up and down.

"You're doing what? Should I be scared? You aren't one of those people who never knew they were pregnant and now you're giving birth, are you? They have rules here in the purse department…you can't give birth in the purse department!"

CC reached out and pinched my lips together. "Shut up."

I nodded my head, shutting up.

"I'm making your gown for the gala…*that's* what I'm doing."

I saw little stars and glittery lights dancing above her head. My Fairy Godmother had finally arrived. And then reality snuffed out the stars and dimmed the glittery lights. The smile that had plastered itself across my face shrank down to nothing.

"Cee, you don't know how much that means to me, and I'm really, really grateful…but I can't afford you."

"You can't afford me? What has that got to do with anything? This is 'Cinderella goes to the ball'! This is my gift to you. I'm going to make you a gown like no one's ever seen…ooooooooohhh…I'm *so* excited! I can't wait to get started!"

I grabbed her by both arms.

"Do you really want to do this, CC?"

She grabbed *me* by the arms. "Yes, yes, yes!! I want to do it!"

We began to jump up and down as if we'd won the lottery and lost twenty pounds on the very same day. I stopped jumping halfway through a spectacular twisty maneuver, which kind of hurt, because it made CC pull on my arms a little hard as she came to an abrupt halt in her jumping.

"What? What? Why'd we stop jumping?"

"CC, I forgot to tell you…you're coming to the gala, too! I got Mike to agree that you could come with me. You need to make a dress for *you*!"

"Oooooooohh, London! You know that I go to these things all the time, but going with you is going to be *so* much fun!"

We began our happy dance again and ignored the saleswomen who were glaring at us. I was just about to add singing to our spectacle, but then I saw it…the perfect bag for the gala.

I let go of CC's arms and made a mad dash for the gorgeous bag that I had spotted. CC followed, still doing little hops up and down as she wiggled over to me. She came to a complete stop when she saw the bag that I had snatched from the glass display.

She said it before I could. "That is the most beautiful, perfect bag ever."

"Isn't it?"

It *was* perfect. Every inch of the bag was covered with tiny teardrop-shaped clear crystals. I turned the bag this way and that. The light caught the crystals, and they sparkled like diamonds. I decided that it was meant to be…I was meant to have this bag, because on top of being "sparkly," it was large. I'd never seen a bag like this in any size other than "evening" bag size—you know, something small enough to put your lipstick, mirror, keys, and emergency money in. This bag could hold all those things, plus my camera and all the little odds and ends that I'd need to shoot with. A dream bag, if ever there was one.

"I know I said I wanted to settle on a gown first, but what do you think, CC?"

"I think, buy the bag."

Chapter 43

We were back in the jeep and heading to the boutique. CC had an appointment in an hour and a half and she said there was something that she wanted to do before the client showed up. Once we got inside the shop, I found out that getting me stripped down to my underwear was what she wanted to do. She wanted to get my measurements so that she could start planning my gown. We were headed upstairs to the design area when Flor popped out of nowhere waving his cell phone at CC.

"Madame! Pardon! May I interrupt you for zee tiniest minute, Madame?"

CC turned on the stairs and looked down at him.

"Flor, why are you speaking with a bad French accent? You know as well as I do that you were born in the Bronx."

Covering the cell phone with the palm of his hand so that he wouldn't be overheard, he continued mangling the language.

"Madame, zee customers expect an air of elegance, of sophistication, of zee exotic. And besides, it got 'Meez' Bobbi a bonus, so if a French accent is what it takes, then a French accent is what I'm damn well gonna have!"

CC wasn't one to suffer fools gladly.

"Flor, drop the accent right now, or the only bonus you're going to get is that I won't march down these stairs and smack you upside the head. Now what did you want?"

"Miss Chesty Hills is on the phone. She wondered if there was any way that you could fit her in this afternoon for a quick confab. She's going to some shoe gala and wants a gown and a hat!"

"That crazy loon…She wants a *hat*?" CC closed her eyes and counted to three quietly…her exasperation under control, she gave Flor his answer.

"Tell her that I can squeeze her in if she can be here in an hour," CC said. Then she muttered under her breath, "Squeeze being the operative word."

I couldn't resist; I had to know…"What do you mean 'squeeze being the operative word?'"

CC closed her eyes and pinched the bridge of her nose. "Chesty Hills has a figure to match her name. She's had several bust 'enhancements' done over the years, and as a result, she's really difficult to design for. I don't think she ever eats, so she's a toothpick from the chest down, but she's too much girl on top. She carries a lot of 'boobage'; there's a lot to 'squeeze' in."

I wasn't sure if I wanted to still be at the boutique when this miracle of science showed up. Who was I kidding? I was dying to see the amazing "boobage."

Flor disappeared as magically as he had appeared, and CC and I got down to the serious business of assessing my assets. I'm definitely not a "Chesty Hills." I'm more what you would call, "Adequate Hills." CC stood with her finger pressed against her lips, considering me from every angle.

"I'm planning on losing some weight before the gala, so, you know, you can design the gown in a size smaller than I am now."

"Uh-huh." She gave me a look. "That's what they *all* say. I happen to know that you have a serious brownie addiction, and I don't see you losing a dress size in the next six weeks."

"You don't give me enough credit. I once gave up pixie-sticks cold turkey for a whole week! Of course, I ate half a bag of sugar that week, but still, I did have discipline when it came to the pixie-sticks!"

CC just shook her head. I could tell she was going into "designer mode," and I decided to let her have all the quiet she needed.

Forty-five minutes went by, and we hadn't spoken a word. CC had taken all my measurements and told me to get dressed. She had then taken me into a back room full of fabric that I had never known existed. She led me from fabric to fabric and had me stand next to each of them. She would stand and stare at me with a slight tilt of her head, and I knew she was seeing something that no one else could. The fabrics were so beautiful…they almost had an unearthly quality to them. The spell was broken when Flor tapped discreetly on the door and announced the arrival of Miss Chesty Hills. CC gave her head a little shake and gave me a thumbs-up.

"We're good. I know what I want to make for you, and you're going to look totally stunning."

"I don't know what to say, CC. 'Thank you' seems pretty lame."

"Don't worry about it; you're taking me with you… we're going to do our spy thing, and it's going to be the best evening ever!"

I gave her a hug, and we went back into the design area. I stopped dead in my tracks. Standing in front of me was the living, breathing embodiment of "boobage." No superstar celebrity that I had ever seen had a figure like this. I didn't know where to look…Straight ahead was not an option. If I looked straight ahead again, I wouldn't be able to stop staring, and I'd embarrass Chesty *and* myself.

CC grabbed me by the wrist and dragged me over to be introduced.

"Chesty darling! How are you? It's been simply ages, and I've missed you!"

She gave Chesty a great big hug…well, sort of a big hug. She couldn't quite get her arms around the girl because there was so much mammary projection that she could only lean in and do that fake cheek kissing, hello stuff. Chesty was a little taller than me, and CC was right…her legs were like little toothpicks wrapped up in pink Capri pants. I finally looked at her from the waist up, and she was wearing a pink silky top covered in pink sequins. She was a sight to behold.

"Chesty, sweetie, this is my dear friend, London."

Suddenly I was smothering. Chesty had swept me up in a huge hug, and I was now "lifting and separating" her "booblets." Just when I was sure I had used up the last bit of oxygen I had, she thrust me away from her and held me at arm's length. While I gasped for air like a fish out of water, she looked me up and down.

"Girl, you are just adorable! However did you get such a gorgeous complexion? Your cheeks are so pink, and your little nose is even pinker!"

Something told me it wouldn't be polite to point out the fact that my "pinkness" was probably a mixture of the early signs of bruising from her crushing hug and the little scratches the sequins had etched onto my face. A face can't suffer that kind of frontal-area impact without suffering some kind of injury.

"Where did you get that gorgeous red hair? I'd give my right arm to have that beautiful color."

I decided to overlook the liberties she'd just taken with my face and be polite.

"My hair color was a gift from my mother…I come from a long line of redheads. I guess I can thank my DNA."

"*DNA?* Is that the new product that they're using down at Philippe's salon? I've heard it's just wonderful!"

"I'm not sure what they're using at Philippe's, but I'm pretty sure it's not DNA. I was talking about genetics."

"*Geneticks?* You got that hair color from some kind of a tick bite?"

I gave up...time for a new topic. CC stepped right in and distracted her.

"Chesty, tell me what you need."

Chesty lit up like a Christmas tree. "I'm so excited! As you know, CC, I'm on the board of the charity that is dedicated to helping women do...'whatever.' The gala's only six weeks away, and it's gonna have all those beautiful shoes for us to bid on. Then there's going to be yummy, yummy food and great music. The best part is that it's going to be at my boyfriend's house, and it's just *the* most amazing, gorgeous place!"

Chapter 44

I was afraid to breathe. I was standing in front of the girl-friend of the mystery Prince of St. Armands. I had so many questions for her that I didn't know how or where to start. CC wasn't helping me much.

"Why, Chesty honey, it sounds like you're going to have lots of fun. Now I want to hear more, but tell me what kind of dress you had in mind."

My mouth was shut, but my brain was screaming, "Ask her about *him*! Ask her about *him*!"

"We want the men to wear their tuxedos, of course, but the ladies can wear whatever color their little hearts desire. We want the gala to just *glow* with beauty...the shoes that will be there for bidding on will be every color you can imagine. I've seen pictures of some of them, and they're beyond beautiful! All the important people are going to be there, including the mayor. He's going to make a little speech, and then I'm going to introduce everybody to Iggy.

People are so curious about him…it's like I'm not only dating a gabillionaire, but a celebrity too! After I introduce him and thank him for having the gala at his place, that's when we're going to auction off the free gown made by you. Bebe Baranski will be on stage with us, modeling one of your gowns during that part."

"Well, that all sounds just lovely, Chesty, but it doesn't answer my question about your gown."

"I want something in pink, CC…gorgeous, earth-shatteringly beautiful pink. And to set it off, I want touches of orange. Find the most fabulous, glittery orange possible. And I want a hat. I want a really, really big hat with a feather on it!"

I could see that CC was struggling with herself. She had a look in her eyes that could mean trouble, so I took over and steered the conversation in another direction.

"Chesty, the event sounds just amazing," I gushed. "I'm going to be the photographer for the event, and CC's going with me!"

Clapping her hands together, Chesty reached out to grab me for another hug, but I jumped behind CC for protection.

"Oooohh! I'm so glad you girls are coming! It's gonna be wonderful. My adorable Iggy is pulling out all the stops for this." She then leaned in and whispered, "He's loaded, you know…I mean with money, not from drinking."

She got the giggles over that one and did a little hop.

"Oooh, CC, where's your little girls' room? I think I just tinkled a little."

CC silently pointed to her right, and Chesty did a little Marilyn Monroe walk down the hallway…knees tight together.

How lucky was I? The one customer who needed to see CC "today," and it was the one person who could give me info on the Prince. We were finally going to find out who the mystery billionaire was…I couldn't wait for Chesty to get back from freshening up to find out more. CC, however, obviously still had the orange-and-pink hat simmering in her brain. She was muttering and chewing on a fingernail.

"CC, stay calm…it's just a hat…she isn't the first customer you've had who hasn't got any taste or style. Just focus on what's important…getting Chesty to tell us stuff about the Prince. Don't you want to find out more about this guy?"

"Not really. This whole area is full of rich guys, and this is just one more. I'm already rich, and he doesn't sound like my type."

"How do you know that he's not your type? We don't even know anything about him yet."

"We know that he dates Chesty. That tells me a lot."

"She seems nice enough…if you overlook her atrocious taste in clothes and artificial projectiles."

CC fluffed up her hair and gave her shoulders a shake. "I don't want to bad-mouth a client, but let's just say that Chesty has an 'edge' to her."

I wasn't going to find out what the "edge" was, at that moment, because Chesty came strutting back down the hallway. Apparently she was no longer having a problem… strutting your stuff could be a dangerous thing when you're having bladder issues.

She shook her finger at us. "Nobody make me laugh; I'm all out of my little tinkle catchers."

I immediately put on my most serious face. "Chesty, you lucky girl…you've got the catch of the year! You have to know that everybody wants to know all about your man."

"Well, they're not going to hear about him from me! I've already said too much. You two are the only people who know I'm seeing him. Promise me you won't say a word to anybody."

Drat…so she wasn't going to tell us any details. Forget "drat"…damn.

"Can you at least tell us his whole name?"

Chesty was admiring herself in one of the full-length mirrors that were scattered around the room. She pulled out a lipstick and applied pink lipstick to her overly plump lips…I'm not making any accusations, but they looked like duck lips, and you know what that means.

"I guess it couldn't hurt to just tell you his name. But I'm not kidding…tell a soul before the party and I'll hunt you down and kill you."

CC leaned over as Chesty checked herself in the mirror one more time. "There's the edge I was talking about," she whispered. "She's not kidding about the having you killed part; I heard she actually did it once."

Satisfied with her lips, Chesty turned back to us and gave us the Prince's real name.

"Jett Brannigan, but I call him Iggy…just to drive him crazy."

I couldn't help myself…"Couldn't you call him Biggy? I guess that *could* be kind of risky, though…that might lead to embarrassing comments…he'd have to be really secure about his anatomy."

Chesty let out one little giggle and immediately grabbed her crotch. With a little shriek she was off and "Marilyn Monroe'ing" it back to the bathroom. CC was calling for Flor, and in seconds, he popped his platinum tresses around the corner of the door.

"Yeez, Madame?"

"Oh my Lord, will you stop using that accent!!! Go get an ice pack…my head is killing me!"

"Yeez, Mada—" He saved himself just in time. "Yes, Miss CC. I'm on my way."

I decided that this would be a good time to make my exit. Chesty was losing her bladder, and CC was quickly losing her temper, so it didn't seem like a good idea to hang around. I gave CC an encouraging hug and headed for the staircase, right behind Flor. We were both lucky we didn't plummet to our deaths…CC made us both jump when she bellowed another order.

"Flor! Bring a mop! She had a full glass of iced tea before she got here!"

With that happy announcement ringing in my ears, I escaped through the front doors.

I swung up into the jeep and pointed it toward home… so it was "Prince Jett"…who'da thunkit? As I made my way back to Highway 41, I glanced over to the west to get a quick view of the Ringling Bridge that takes you over to Lido Key and St. Armands Circle. Before long I'd be over there…skulking through a mansion, looking for Prince Jett.

Chapter 45

The day had been stressful. The meeting with Mike, the meet-up with Ryder, and Chesty and her bladder issues. I knew I couldn't just drive on home. I was going to have to make a stop…an illegal stop…well; illegal as far as my diet went. I didn't have any brownie bites…I'd eaten them all in the parking lot earlier. Could it really have been only three hours ago? It seemed like two days ago. I pulled into a grocery store chain that I love in Sarasota to pick up the essence of life…the brownies. I think this is the coolest store…you can park underground, and when you're done shopping, you can put your cart, loaded with your grocery bags, on its very own little escalator as you ride down right next to it on the "people" escalator. They've got an elevator too that you can use, but why in the world would you want to do that?

I got all the way to the bakery department and had talked myself out of my chocolate treat by the time I got there. I had to lose weight for the gala...bleh. So what could I eat? Oooh! I had forgotten all about the yummy narrow ice-cream bars on a stick...you know the kind of stick...it looks like the tongue depressor that the doctors use when you have to say "ahhh," except smaller.

The ice-cream bars were made and sold by a famous weight-loss program, and I *loved* them! You could eat two and only consume one hundred calories. I swooped down on the ice cream aisle and snagged a box. Just a few aisles over I grabbed up an inexpensive cooler, and up near the checkout they had ice. My purchases completed, I snuggled the ice-cream bars down into the ice that filled the cooler.

By the time I got back in the jeep and was doing the five o'clock traffic, stop-and-start dance on Tamiami Trail, I was tired. It had been such a busy day, busier than I was used to. Finally I was home and hauling the cooler out of the jeep. The ice cream bars had made the trip in pretty good shape and were only slightly thawed...I crammed them into the freezer and dragged myself down the hall-way to the bathroom. I smoothed down Handsome's fur as I went by the bed.

"You didn't miss much today, mister. Purse shopping, brownie eating, and gator bites for lunch...just an average day. Oh! And Miss Chesty...let's not forget Miss Chesty, my new best friend."

Twenty minutes later I was warm and clean and hungry. I pulled the last clean T-shirt out of my closet and slipped it over my head...I had to put back on the jeans I'd worn the day before…tomorrow was definitely going to be laundry day. I was too tired to do laundry tonight…this had to have been the longest Monday in history.

Like a homing pigeon I made my way to the refrigerator to see what was for dinner. I already knew the answer. Those heavenly ice-cream bars. I pulled two out of the freezer and got comfortable in my favorite chair. I switched on the laptop and peeled the wrapper off both the bars. I'd barely started checking my e-mail, when I realized that I'd finished the ice cream…back to the fridge for three more.

I was only eating the chocolate coating off of them, so I know I wasn't getting too many calories. Back to the chair and the laptop. I keep a nice little table beside the chair, so when I finished eating the outside off one healthy snack, I just dropped the remaining ice cream onto a paper towel that I had put on the table to use as a plate. Halfway through the last bar, the doorbell rang.

I carefully sat the laptop on the floor and walked over to the window next to the door. The memory of being attacked in the woods came rushing back, and I moved back the closed curtain with just the tip of my fingernail and peeked out. Either the ice-cream treats were giving me palpitations, or it was the fear of who might be outside my door. What was standing on my porch wasn't an unknown danger…I knew this type of danger. It was Ryder.

I jumped back from the window and smiled…I guess my chocolate-covered face from earlier in the parking lot hadn't scared him off, after all. I had the door unlocked in a heartbeat and stood looking at him with a big grin on my face…I couldn't help it…he just makes me smile.

He reached up and tugged on his cowboy hat. "Howdy, ma'am."

When was I going to stop getting that little zap in the heart every time he looked at me with those eyes? While I was getting zapped in the heart, Ryder hadn't said another word. He stared at me with a strange look in his eyes, and I started getting nervous. Slowly he raised his hand and, with one finger, pointed at my chest. Well, that seemed kind of rude.

I looked down at where his finger was pointing, and there it was, one of the little tongue depressor sticks from an ice-cream bar. Somehow I had managed to drop the damn thing, and it had attached itself to my shirt just below, and I'm talking, *just*, below the most delicate area on one of "the girls." There was a slight breeze in the room, and the little stick was actually rotating…like a plane propeller…or a tassel. I wanted…to…die.

"Saving that for later?" he asked.

OK, I'd heard that line plenty of times before, but for some reason I got the giggles…the giggles only got worse when a breeze came through the window and made the "propeller" spin, before it blew off my chest. That did it…Ryder's eyes started to water, and then he let out the laughter that he'd been holding back. We laughed until the room ran out of air. Once I was able to get a couple of deep breaths in me, I made myself leave the room without looking at him. I knew I'd lose it again if I looked at him, so keeping my eyes straight ahead; I took off for my closet to find something, anything, different to wear. By the time I'd dug up something semi clean to put on, Ryder had gone outside to wait for me.

"Okay, let's try this again. What's up, Ryder?"

He was walking down the steps of the porch and heading for the side yard. Once more with the finger pointing... except this time he was pointing toward something other than me. I leaned over the railing to see what he was pointing at. Big surprise...Reckless was hanging out in the yard again.

"Did you open the gate for him?"

"No, my friend, I did not...what we have here is an escape artist."

"What?"

"An escape artist...he's done this before."

"He's done this before? When?"

"Just a while back. I came home, and he was standing in front of the house."

Ryder walked over to Reckless and gave him a stern look. "You've got some explaining to do, mister."

Reckless gave a snort and then walked to me and sniffed at my pocket.

"London..."

I didn't like where I thought this conversation was headed.

"Have you been giving him treats?"

"I might have. It depends on what you call a treat. I didn't give him any chocolate, or pie, or popcorn. He tried to talk me into giving him French fries last week, but I said no. He might have had a nice healthy snack or two…but *no* treats; absolutely none."

Reckless gave me a bump from behind. I bumped him back.

"Don't say a word, Reckless; I've got him almost convinced."

Ryder slowly walked toward me, reached around me, and took hold of Reckless.

"I can see that I've got a lot to learn about you two and your relationship. Come on, Reckless, let's get you back where you belong."

The two of them walked to the gate, and Ryder turned to me.

"How's he getting out?"

"I'm not sure how he's getting out, but turn him loose, and you'll see just how talented he is."

Ryder stepped aside, and just like before, Reckless walked through the gate and turned around. He gave Ryder a lovely demonstration when he put his head over the gate and pulled it shut.

"Did you lock the gate the last time he did this?"

"Of course, I did. Somehow he's getting it open."

"Well, I hate to be the one to spoil his fun, but the party's over. Tomorrow we'll get a new latch on it…something he can't open. Reckless, you're spending the night in the main barn. I need to look at the latch on your stall to make sure you haven't been getting that one open, too." He got Reckless back out of the field and closed the gate behind him.

"I'm going to walk him on over to the barn. Do you want to run into town and have dinner after I get him settled?"

Guess who wasn't tired anymore.

"Just let me run in and put on my twirly-whirly T-shirt, and I'll be good to go."

The look on his face made a shiver run up my spine.

CHAPTER 46

We were sitting in a little restaurant downtown that has it all. You can eat outside on the sidewalk, you can sit inside at a window booth and watch the world go by, or just sit at the bar. This was our lucky night; we got to sit inside in a booth by the window and watch the setting sun light up the tops of the palms along Venice Avenue. A chicken quesadilla...that's all I could think about... well, almost all I could think about. Ryder was sitting *this close* to me, and I was having a few thoughts that I really don't think it would be appropriate to share with you. We'd placed our order and were just people watching. The huge glass windows were folded back to let in the air, and tourists meandered by, enjoying the cool of early evening. I was enjoying having my day finally slow down and having Ryder next to me. A fingertip placed on the end of my nose got my attention.

"So…what were you up to earlier this morning? Besides enjoying your brownies?"

Drat…between the brownie-bite debacle and the twirly-whirly stick attached to the front of my blouse, I'd pretty much blown any chance of impressing him with my sophistication. Not to mention the first time that he saw me when I had cotton candy gumming up my hair.

"I had a meeting with Mike, the editor I've been working with."

"A good meeting, I hope."

"Actually, it was kind of a *great* meeting. I'm pretty excited about an idea that he's come up with. It's really…"

I lost my train of thought because the waitress had just delivered my quesadilla and Ryder's burger. Ooooooohhh, lots and lots of melted cheese and black olives, chicken, tiny diced tomatoes, and scallions. They serve the quesadilla flat…more like a pizza than anything else, and it is amazing. It's beautiful just sitting on the plate. Every time I order this when I'm sitting outside at one of their little tables, I hear people walking past me, talking about my food: "What's that? What do you think that is that she's eating?"

Before I even had a bite of the first piece, I was thinking about ordering one to go so that I could have it for lunch the next day. Ryder reached over and put his fingertip on my nose again.

"So go on, tell me. What's the assignment?"

I appreciated his interest, but he needed to pay more attention to his food…I was pretty sure that I was going to snag one of the outrageously good fries on his plate. I moved my hand ever so slowly toward a really yummy, crispy-looking fry, and he pressed the tip of his fork gently against the top of my hand.

"I wouldn't do that if I were you."

I pulled my hand back ever so slowly and picked up a slice of my meal. Taking a bite, I turned to him and gave him my sexiest/innocent wide-eyed look. He reached over to me and placed his finger against my lip.

Ooooooh, what was he going to…crap! He was pulling a long, long strand of cheese off my lip and the side of my neck. What is *wrong* with me? Why can't I eat half way neatly, like a normal human?

"Getting back to my *job*…Mike has this plan to take the magazine national. He needs a big story, so I'm going on the hunt."

"You're going on a hunt. What kind of a hunt?"

"I'm hunting a human."

Ryder sat down his burger and handed me a fry. "Am I allowed to ask you why you're hunting a human?"

"He wants me to get some shots of the elusive new billionaire on Saint Armands. No one knows much about him, which is really odd with all the information that you can get on the Internet. I tried entering his name and doing a search, but there's just no personal info on the guy at all. I'm going to go to his home and take pictures next week, and then a few weeks later I'll be the photographer at the gala that will be held there. If I can get pictures of Jett Brannigan, Mike will have the story he wants." I looked at him with my big wide-eyed sexy look again, and he handed me another fry. Then it hit me...I'd just blabbed the Prince's real name. I knew when Chesty warned us against revealing it, that I'd eventually slip up, I just didn't think it would be so soon. Now I had one more thing to worry about. Ryder brought my thoughts back to the here and now.

"When you look at me with your eyes crossed like that, you look just like a pug puppy that my mother had...every time I saw those goofy eyes, I fed her a snack...man, she got huge."

I handed him back the fry. Looking like his mother's dog wasn't exactly the look I'd been going for.

"Are you sure this guy is going to be happy with you if you take pictures of him when he's in the privacy of his own home? From what you're telling me, he's agreed to photos of the house but not of himself. Suppose the guy is a little 'off'? Hiding away and keeping your identity a secret isn't exactly normal. I'm concerned for your safety, to be quite honest, London."

Ryder was worried about me?

"He's not nuts, just probably shy or something, and I'm not going to take pictures of him looking undignified. If he's running around in the maid's underwear, I won't take the shot. I'm going to tour the house and take pictures, and what happens, happens. If I don't get a picture of him when I'm there, then I'll get it the night of the gala. I always get my man."

Ryder slid a little closer to me.

"Isn't that interesting? *I* always get my woman."

I choked on an olive and took a breath. Here came that fingertip again…he placed it on my lip.

"You've got a little sour cream…right there."

The next thing I knew he leaned over and licked it off. Was it getting hot in here? I needed cool air…like *immediately*!

"Are you ready to go?" I asked. "Because I'm going outside to pour these ice cubes down my shirt."

I got up and headed outside, carrying a "to-go" cup of ice cubes. He had paid the bill and was right beside me, before I'd gone ten feet down the sidewalk.

He reached over and took the ice cubes away from me. "I don't want you putting these down your blouse and getting arrested for public indecency. You've had too many visits with the police as it is."

We were walking back to the truck. Easy, right? Wrong. I had to get to the corner without being sucked off the sidewalk and into the ice cream and fudge store by the heavenly smells that wafted out of the open door. Ryder must have a sixth sense. He reached out and held my hand just as we neared the chocolate danger zone, and I immediately forgot all about ordering bubblegum ice cream and a slice of rocky road fudge.

As we drove back toward the ranch, Ryder reached over and held my hand in his. He ran his thumb over and over the ends of my fingernails. I liked it. We drove along quietly for about five minutes, and then he gave my hand a squeeze.

"London…I wasn't kidding when I said I wasn't comfortable with your 'spy' mission. What if I came along with you, or better yet, what if you just didn't go at all. Stay home and rest that busy little brain of yours."

"Rest my busy *little* brain?"

I let go of his hand, and he tried to grab it back.

"That came out wrong…I'm sure you have a fine brain, normal sized, larger than normal probably."

"Save it, Ryder, I'm a big girl; I'll be fine. I don't need you to come along, and I don't need you to tell me if I can go or not."

We drove the rest of the way back to the ranch in silence, and I hopped out of the truck before it had even come to a complete stop. He could just kiss that sunset cruise good-bye.

Chapter 47

The next morning I had a hard time getting down the steps to my jeep, because I was kicking myself for messing things up with Ryder. I woke up three times during the night… feeling stupid for overreacting to Ryder's concern. Each time I woke up, I gave myself a mental slap. I was exhausted, and it was 9:00 a.m.

I had decided that I needed to get out and take a drive to clear my head, when I heard a soft whinny behind me. There was Reckless, standing inside the fence where he was supposed to be for a change.

"Well, look at you, friend. Looks like they've got a brand-new latch on the gate, and from the looks of it, I'd say you're not going to be wandering over to my front door, looking to borrow a cup of sugar any time soon."

He didn't look like a very happy horse, so I walked over and scratched his ears and gave his neck a little hug before I left.

I drove aimlessly, my mind going in a million different directions. I cruised past the small airport and then drove out to the jetty and watched the surfers for a while. I finally decided to drive into the magazine's office and talk to Sophie in person instead of getting my spy orders over the phone or in an e-mail.

I pushed open the doors to the office and found Sophie hard at work on her computer. As soon as she saw me, she literally bounced around on her chair and squealed. *Squealed.* I don't usually have that effect on people, so it kind of took me by surprise. Was I supposed to squeal back? I settled for saying hello.

"Hi, Sophie, I hope it's okay if I just stopped in without calling."

She clapped her hands together. "It's more than okay! It's super-duper! Are you excited about the gala? *I'm so excited about the gala!!!* Some nights I can't even sleep because I'm so excited! What are you going to wear? Are you going to get your hair done or just wear it all wild and crazy like you usually do? Are you going to color it? Are you getting your nails done? I'm getting my nails done. Are you going to go get electrolysis? We talked about that before, right? I know you're comfortable with that big old black hair growing out of your neck, but on an occasion like this you might want to have someone trim it back. Oh, what am I saying...why would you want to pay someone to do that when I can do it?"

She went to the door to the hallway, and throwing it open, she yodeled to some invisible person. "Angie! Bring me my tweezers from the bottom drawer of the doughnut cabinet in the kitchen…It's right there under the box of powdered doughnuts. London is finally going to let me get rid of that hair we named Sally!"

She hippety-hopped back over to me and started staring at the thing my head sits on.

I slammed my hands up on either side of my neck and then felt the front and the back…there was no hair growing out of any part of anything. I had a hard time resisting the urge to take my hands off my neck and put them around Sophie's neck…and I wasn't going to be checking for a hair named Sally.

Fortunately for me, the tweezers couldn't be found. In an effort to distract her from her desire to pull hair out of my body, I asked her for my instructions about the mansion job. Her fingers were now flying across the keyboard of the computer, and the printer was starting to spit out a sheet of paper.

"I'm just giving you this information so that you have a copy for yourself, but the plan is really simple. We're going to drive up to Saint Armands, and while I keep the butler busy, you're going to go around the mansion and take pictures."

"Wait a minute…you're going to go *with* me?"

"Well, sure. If I don't go with you, the butler or whoever is going to stick to your side the whole time you're trying to find the Prince. I'll create a diversion. You know, like, I'll trip and 'hurt' my ankle or something. I could feel faint and need water and stuff…and if that doesn't work,

I'll use my sex appeal to lure him into a study or something with me."

"What if it's a butleress?"

"I've never heard of a 'butleress'...I wonder if you have to go to a special school to be one...like when you want to be a fancy chef...what do you suppose they do when they're not waiting around to open doors for people?"

I was confused. "Who? The chef or the butleress?"

"Well, the butleress, of course. Why would a chef be standing around waiting to open a door? I've always wondered if they're allowed to sit down...you always see them standing by a door...or holding a silver tray with a letter on it."

She was off on another one of her crazy trains of thought, and I was getting a headache.

I interrupted her. "OK, you're distracting the butler and I'm sneaking down the hallways trying to get a picture of our mysterious man. Am I supposed to just pop open doors and yell *aha*!?"

"No yelling *aha*. We don't want a picture of him looking goofy. We want a picture of him looking handsome and mysterious and rich."

"I wasn't being serious, Sophie...so let's cut to the chase. Whatever picture of him I can get, Mike will take?"

Sophie actually spent a moment on the same planet that I was on and gave me a straight answer. "Short of catching him coming out of the bathroom with his pants down, we'll take anything."

Chapter 48

woke up the next morning with a whopper of a headache... that could only mean one thing...a storm was coming. I don't know what it is, but my head forecasts the weather better than any meteorologist. When lightning is on the way, my head starts to pound. I dragged myself out of bed and looked out of the window. The sky was blue, and the clouds were puffing along like little happy marshmallows, but they weren't fooling me...it was going to get ugly.

I'm not a big coffee drinker, so I don't have any of those really cool magic machines that make delicious coffee. If I need it, I have to go get it. One shower later I was in the jeep and about five minutes away from a drive-through that could sell me the headache cure that I needed...not the coffee but the doughnut that I always ordered with it.

I was licking the sugar off my fingers, when my cell phone rang. It was the police. I was asked very politely to come downtown to the police station. I circled around the fast-food building and went through the drive-through again...I was going to need another doughnut.

Four hours later the doughnut was nothing more than a fond memory, but I was a free woman. Not that I'd been arrested, but I kept expecting to be. I realized as the hours crawled by that the police weren't totally satisfied with my explanations of what happened at the two separate murders. The part that really made me nervous was, just as I had feared, they had only found *my* fingerprints on the monopod that was used to kill Monique.

CC's opera gloves were a problem. We were only apart a few minutes at Monique's, when CC went to put the equipment that she didn't want to carry back in the jeep. She had the monopod as we began the shoot, and I had to tell the police that when they questioned me. Wearing the gloves made her look suspicious. What better way to prevent accidentally leaving fingerprints on a murder weapon? Did it look bad for both of us?

We didn't have to worry quite so much about the first murder, because they hadn't found the gun responsible for killing that happy couple. My headache hadn't gotten any better, and now the sky was getting black, and the clouds were riding low. It had been hours since my drive-through breakfast, and it was now officially afternoon. I pulled into a parking space at the "Nest" and darted inside just as the first fat raindrops started falling. I had my choice of tables, but I decided to have lunch at the bar. As I walked toward it, I recognized a head full of long brown hair and the woman pulling at it. I plopped myself down on the barstool next to CC and ordered an amaretto sour.

"What's the matter with you?" CC snapped. "You almost never drink, and it's like what? A quarter past noon?"

"Don't start, CC. I just spent the last four hours with my best friends, the police. To put the frosting on the cake, I've got a killer headache. I think there's something about the orange slice that they put in the drink that gets rid of the pain."

She was definitely in an ornery mood. "Orange slice, my eye…it's the alcohol that gets rid of the pain."

I decided to go on the offensive. "If it's not too personal, what are you doing here, and just exactly how *long* have you been here?"

She was slurring her words just the tiniest bit, and she waved around her martini glass, sloshing the drink onto the bar.

"My whole life. Why are you asking me how long I've been here? You know I was born in Florida, little Miss Punkin Head."

Well, that was a new one. I hadn't been called a "punkin head" before. I sighed and sipped at my drink.

CC stopped in the act of flipping a cracker with cheese on it at the bartender and, instead, flipped it squarely onto the side of my head. This day needed to be over. First I had to spend hours getting grilled by the police and now CC was flinging cheese at me. Could this day get any worse?

"Mind if I join you?"

Well, what do you know…just like that my day got worse. I had wanted Mike and CC to meet, but this wasn't exactly what I had had in mind. For one thing, I had imagined them meeting when CC was *sober*. There was nothing to do but introduce them.

"Mike, I'd like you to meet a friend of mine…C. C. Covington. CC, meet Mike, my boss."

Mike reached across me and shook CC's hand.

"I've heard great things about you, CC. I was hoping that we'd get a chance to meet."

CC was working hard to focus her eyes. She had to be making a great impression, considering she was eating cheese out of the pot that it had been served in…with her thumb.

"Shame."

Mike looked confused. "Excuse me?"

"Shame," CC said again.

"I'm afraid I'm not following." Mike looked totally baffled.

"SHAME!" CC bellowed. "SHAME HERE! GLAD TO MEET 'CHU! DON'T 'CHU UNDERSSSHTAND ENGLISSH?"

Oh Lord, help me now…she was in worse shape than I thought. Mike's face was turning red, and I had a feeling that wasn't a good sign. I was right.

CC had rubbed Mike the wrong way. "*Look*, Miss Covington, there's no need to cause an uproar!"

"WHO ARE YOU CALLING A WHORE?" CC shrieked.

You could have heard a pin drop…silence, absolute silence…everyone sat waiting, waiting to see what would happen next. They waited until she jumped up off her bar-stool and fell on the floor. She had dropped tons of cheese on the floor under her chair; apparently she'd been trying to consume as much of that as she had the booze. All it had taken was for her to put one wobbly foot on the floor, and she was gone. Mike tried to help her up, but she was having none of it.

She was back to barking at him. "Don't touch me, you jerk! I'm jusss fine!"

"*Good!*" he snapped back. "London, I'll see you later... CC, *I hope I* DON'T *see you later.*"

With that he started for the door. CC had pulled her-self halfway up off the floor and managed to grab his belt as he stomped past her. Off he went, pulling her behind him as if he was a boat pulling a skier. I threw some money at the bartender and ran after them.

They were in the parking lot, nose to nose, scream-ing at each other. I couldn't hear a word...that might have had something to do with the lightning and thunder that was crashing down all around us. My head had been right again...a nasty storm had blown in...make that two nasty storms—CC and Mike were definitely having their own.

I took one look at the crazy fools and ran for my jeep.

Chapter 49

I ran little errands for hours after that. I needed time by myself...nobody talking, nobody freaking out. I finally pulled up in front of the house around five, glad to be at the end of a really weird day. I hadn't been home for twenty minutes, when there was a knock on the door. I didn't even get a chance to answer it, before I heard a voice that I knew all too well calling my name. Or should I say *squeaking* my name.

"London! London! Are you in there?"

Was she actually twisting and turning the doorknob? I yanked the door open.

"Sophie! What's wrong?"

Little Miss Sophie rushed into the living room...out of breath, eyes bugging out of her head. She threw herself down on my couch. Out came her story in her tiny little voice.

"Mike came back to the office and was furious! He said that he'd run into you and a friend of yours and that

SUZANNE J. ROGERS

he wanted to kill somebody! He was dripping wet, and his pants had cheese on them from the knees down. What happened?"

"Unfortunately he met my friend CC when she was three sheets to the wind."

"Your friend CC was doing laundry in the wind when he met her? Why would that make him mad?"

"Sophie...she was 'three sheets to the wind,' 'pickled,' 'trashed,' 'bombed,' 'ripped'...you know, 'kerschnickered.' She might have insulted Mike accidentally."

"Oh! Kerschnickered! Why didn't you say that in the first place!"?

"Did you come all the way here just to ask me what was up with Mike?"

"Oh, I hope you don't mind! He was just so mad that I didn't dare ask him what was wrong after he shouted out that stuff about you and your friend. I was afraid to call because I thought he might catch me on the phone, and I didn't e-mail because you never know who might snoop through your mail! So anyway, that's why I drove out...I got your address from your payroll records...you don't get paid very much, do you?"

Again with the cheap shot...what is it about the woman? Every time she saw me, she had to insult me!

Sophie jumped up from the couch and walked into the kitchen.

"Thanks for telling me about your drunk friend, London...I hope Mike doesn't run into her again...he was so mad; he was *scary*! You don't think he'd actually hurt someone, do you? He's so big, and he's really strong."

"I don't think he'd hurt anyone, Sophie, but I don't know him all that well."

"Do you have any crackers? Ooooh...how about marshmallows? I *love* marshmallows...they fill me up, and they don't have a lot of fat. You know what I do with them? I put three on a small plate and stick them in the micro-wave...they get really big, and if you eat them real quick, it's a lot of fun."

That girl could change topics faster than anyone I'd ever known. I opened all my cupboards...no crackers... no marshmallows. I decided it was time for Sophie to go home, so I walked outside onto the front porch and just as I'd hoped, she followed me like a puppy. I started down the steps, intending to walk toward her car, when she let out a squeaky little scream. She had turned toward the field and seen Reckless, and now she stood frozen with her hands over her eyes.

"What is that? What is that horrible beast?"

"It's called a horse, Sophie. You've never seen a horse before?"

Reckless stood looking over the fence. I could swear he was sizing her up, and then suddenly he stuck his tongue out at her.

"I don't like it! It's going to spit on me! I've seen that on TV. They come up to you, and then they spit on you!"

"Oh, for crying out loud, Sophie! Get a grip!"

I should have saved my breath…she had raced across the driveway to her car in a panic and was roaring up the driveway. I gave Reckless a long look. There was only one thing to say about his scaring her off, more than likely, never to return.

"Thanks, buddy, I owe you one."

After that, I didn't hear a peep out of anybody for a week. Mike…I didn't want to hear from…I hoped he would cool off and forget about his run-in with CC before I met up with him. Sophie was probably sitting at her desk covered from head to toe with a rain poncho…on the lookout for random attacks by spitting horses. CC probably didn't remember the whole episode with Mike and, I assumed, was hard at work designing dresses for her clients.

I spent a few days photographing the horses on the ranch, and one afternoon as I left the pastures and cut through the main barn compound, I saw Ryder leaving one of the barns. He looked tired, and his usually spotless black jeans were dusty and dirty. He looked up, and when he saw me, he immediately began to walk toward me. Just about that time, my luck ran out.

I felt two arms wrap themselves around me from behind, and I was lifted off the ground in a big bear hug. Oh, dear Lord…it was Trey. I hadn't seen him, since he used the horse to block my jeep in the driveway.

Ryder stopped where he was…even from a distance I could see his eyes go dark. Just as he started to move toward us, the new wrangler, who just happened to be not unfortunate looking, walked up behind him and slipped her arm through his. The moment he turned to look at her, she held up her phone and pointed up to the office. He turned, and she continued to hold onto his arm as they walked away. It was totally irrational, I know…but all I could think was, "she'd better not touch his hair."

The arms around my waist held me tighter.

"Baby girl, where you been?" Trey breathed into my ear.

"Around."

"You do play hard to get, don't you? What've I got to do to get you to talk sweet to me?"

"Not gonna happen, Trey. I never talk sweet to anybody who calls me 'baby girl.'"

I dug my fingernails into his arms and wrestled myself free of him. I walked home in a fury and wrestled with my jealousy the whole way…She'd better not be touching his hair.

Chapter 50

After what seemed an eternity, the big day had finally arrived. Sophie and I were only a few blocks away from the mansion, and the palms of my hands were sweating.

"Now you remember what we're going to say, right, London? My cover story is that I came along because I represent the committee and to assist you in any way that you might require. The butler won't have any reason to doubt that, and then I'll just use my sex appeal to distract him, and you can start spying."

I'm not sure how he was going to notice her sex appeal when she was covered neck to ankles in a black trench coat. It was ninety-five degrees outside, but Sophie was embracing the "spy" scenario 150 percent. She had scarlet lipstick on and her fake eyelashes were so huge that I'm not sure how she kept them from getting stuck together. The woman was 300 percent crazy.

We were on the south side of St. Armands on a quiet street that seemed a million miles removed from the bustle of the Circle. In reality, it was just a few blocks away. We waited while heavy black iron gates swung slowly open for us after we'd been buzzed in, and that's when I think I stopped breathing. Huge shade trees and beautiful green grass rolled out before us. Way in the distance I could see the sparkling blue of the bay, where palm trees dipped low as if sipping from the water. Taller palms stood beside them, standing guard.

The mansion was the crown jewel. The house was constructed of some kind of gorgeous gray-blue stone that graced every inch of the façade, and the lines and flow of the house were breathtaking. I counted eight sets of French doors…each set twelve feet high, on the first floor…four on each side of the front door. They sat back, recessed a bit into the exterior of the mansion, and they were trimmed in stone. The second floor boasted French doors with balconies that were in perfect alignment with the French doors on the first floor. In each upstairs window, there were dark heavy floor-length drapes tied back at the sides.

Just as we were about to reach the mansion, the driveway split. If you went to the left, the drive led up to three cascading steps. The steps became a large terrace that showcased the massive wooden front doors. The drive continued past the steps and then swung left again, morphing into a large circle that had the biggest fountain at its center that I had ever seen.

The front doors were beautiful and arched and made of a dark heavy wood with glass in the center of them so that you could see into the grand foyer.

On the second floor directly above the front doors was a very large balcony with a slightly smaller set of arched French doors. There was even a chandelier hanging from the ceiling of this porch area. I half expected to see the queen of England standing with one hand gripping the stone railing, waving in a queenly fashion at us.

On either side of the front doors and the balcony doors, there were beautiful ornamental potted trees. And then there were the stone columns. Three columns on either side of the front door supported the balcony above, and three columns on each side of the balcony itself supported the wide roof above it.

Standing a bit in front of the house were Italian cypress trees…from the driveway they looked taller than the mansion. Like sentries, there was one on each side of the front door, and then there was another one farther down near the end of each wing. Yep, there were even more windows…I felt as if I was looking at a castle…sort of.

I crawled up the drive to take in as much of the house as I could, before we broke off and followed the right branch of the drive…it stayed a little farther from the house and eventually led us to the back.

There were French doors on the back of the mansion, just not as many as on the front. There was some kind of wide rectangular door at the far end, which led to what? The garage? I parked, and we slowly got out of the jeep.

It took the two of us a second to stop staring and start fumbling around for the things we'd brought with us.

Sophie gave me a bug-eyed look and whispered at me, "London, I'm scared."

"This is no time to go getting cold feet on me, Sophie. Put on your big-girl panties, and let's do this."

She made a little mewing sound, you know, like a tiny kitten meow. I pressed the button on the security box next to the entrance.

"Yes?" a deep butler-ish voice came through an intercom.

"London Hart and Sophie..." Cripe! I didn't know Sophie's last name!

"Dudby...my last name is Dudby!" Sophie shouted into the speaker.

"Sophie, you don't have to shout...I'm sure he can hear you just fine!"

She scrunched up her nose at me, just in time to impress the man who stood with one hand on his hip, staring at us.

"Enter, please." There it was again...the deepest of deep voices; it had a classic butler sound to it.

"Thank you."

In we stepped.

CHAPTER 51

"**I**'**m London, this** is Sophie…it's a pleasure to meet you."

"I'm Adam, but you can call me Mr. Adam. I must tell you right away that I'm new to buttling, so if I neglect to offer you anything that you need, just tell me."

He was fairly tall, slim but muscular. His clothes were subdued; he had on gray slacks and a gray sweater with shiny black shoes. I didn't know *what* to think about his hair. It came down to his shoulders and was done up in all those little braids that you see people wearing. I snapped my focus back to the matter at hand when Sophie took control of the conversation.

"Mr. Adam, it's so kind of your boss to let us take photographs of his home. We're just so thrilled and excited to be here!"

She licked her lips and stuck out her tiny bust…which was buried somewhere inside her trench coat.

She purred at him. "Is there someplace that I could hang my coat? I'm just so *hot*...I don't know if I've ever been this hot. Are *you* hot?"

I couldn't believe what I'd just heard. I stood staring at her with my mouth open. It got worse...the butler's eyes had gotten a glow in them, and he was *unbuttoning her coat for her*!

"Allow me to take your coat, madam."

He made the unbuttoning process last *forever*, and then he whisked the coat off her like a magician. Now two of us stood staring at her. She was dressed in a scarlet dress that matched the color of her lipstick. The dress was cut down to *there* and cut *way up to there*, and somehow it covered just enough of her to avoid being totally indecent. Little Miss Sophie was one hot mama!

I trailed in their wake as Mr. Adam led Sophie to an office. I'm surprised he didn't trip over his tongue on the way there...he was practically drooling. Once we got to the office, I started in on my lame story about the order in which I wanted to photograph the house, but I didn't get very far.

Sophie went into her routine...she tripped and "hurt" her ankle, pulling down a pile of documents that had been on the edge of the desk. She made little "I need help" sounds from underneath the mound of paper. Mr. Adam jumped into action. He waved his hand at me to go.

"You just take all the time that you need, Miss Hart. I've got someone, *something*, that I need to do...so you just feel free to roam the house."

I didn't wait for him to change his mind…I grabbed my gear and headed toward the door. As I made my exit, I heard Mr. Adam murmuring consoling words to Sophie. I wish I could unhear them.

"Now, now, Sophie, let's just get you out of that dress… I mean *mess…let's get you out of that mess.*"

I didn't actually pay attention to where I was going when I charged out of the office; I just wanted out of there. Sophie definitely had the situation in hand.

I went down the hallway that we had followed to the office and passed a number of rooms without even pausing. I was still mentally replaying the mating dance that I had just witnessed…I wasn't doing it on purpose…I just couldn't make it stop. Finally I made myself slow down and told my mind to focus on what was right in front of me and actually look at my surroundings.

I had assumed that the mansion would be beautiful… but you know what they say about the word "assume"… when you assume, you make an "ass of u and me." I felt a little like an ass…I had just assumed that the mansion would be somewhat like the homes we had gone to for the other shoots. I was *so* wrong…I had wandered into a room that was way beyond what I had expected.

I came to a stop and stared. French doors stretched out along the far wall in both directions.

I walked across the room and gazed through the glass of one of the doors…I hadn't noticed when we drove up that between the French doors and the driveway was a beautiful garden. Tropical flowers bloomed in an explosion of vibrant colors, some low and close to the ground, some waist high. Stone pathways wound through the flowers and small ornamental trees. I could see large fountains tucked into quiet, shady corners with the incredibly huge fountain in the driveway completing the picture.

I wasn't sure if the committee would want pictures of the garden, but I was taking them anyway…it gave me an excuse to soak in the wild chaotic beauty. I had taken a few shots and was trying to get a good shot of one of the fountains, when I got a surprise. A two-foot-long black snake poked its head up from the bottom of the fountain and then started to make its way toward me. I've never been all that afraid of snakes, but this one made me a little nervous. It seemed to be curious about me and was getting a little too close for comfort. I took a few more shots and reentered the mansion.

I went back to studying the rest of what I'd decided to call "the great hall." I wasn't sure what a room like this would be used for. It was such a huge, huge, huge room. The walls were a rich golden color, and all the thick moldings that were at the bottom and top of the walls were probably two feet high and had intricate carvings on them. They were a glossy, brilliant black, which complimented the glossy marble of the floor…it was like walking on a black mirror.

As far as furniture went…well, there wasn't much. At the south end of the room, there were a few very large leather couches and four comfy-looking leather chairs. The chairs and sofas were a deep gold, and a substantial leaded crystal coffee table was settled in the middle of them. Somehow I got the feeling that putting your feet up on the table to rest one's weary feet would be frowned upon.

Centered behind the furniture was a massive oil painting. It contained every color of the vibrant flowers in the garden and pretty much looked like flowers gone wild. I loved it.

Behind me, little alcoves of varying sizes were set into the long wall. They provided cozy nooks for intimate conversations. There were gold love seats in each alcove, along with a few armchairs. Wall sconces would create just enough light to soften the features of the individuals lucky enough to lounge in their glow.

I shook myself free of the spell the rooms had me under and got down to work. I was positioning my camera in the main room by the sofas and had started to back up to move the tripod, when I tripped over an ottoman that I hadn't noticed. Somehow I managed to land on my back on a sofa instead of the floor. I didn't get up. I looked from one end of the great ceiling to the other and back again...about three times. I was counting and then recounting...yep...eight chandeliers...eight...*massive*...chandeliers. There was one in front of each French door.

CHAPTER 52

Shooting the great hall took a long time, there was so much to shoot, but eventually I'd taken all of the shots that I needed. I started quietly down a hallway that led toward the back of the house and happened upon the kitchen, it was beautiful. The tiles on the floor were a glossy white with black ceramic tiles forming a square in the center of the room. All of the appliances were stainless steel and sparkled as the result of meticulous care. Just like the great hall, it was gorgeous. I took a few shots but found no elusive billionaire.

I was having a hard time opening doors and going into rooms without someone giving me permission, and I had decided to give myself a talking to. "Someone else besides Sophie needs to put on her big-girl panties and start getting down to business."

I threw my shoulders back and yanked open the door nearest to me...Oooooh...the billionaire's guest bathroom…surprise…no billionaire. I spent an extra minute checking out what I suppose would technically be called the powder room. The room was so beautiful that if it were in my house, I'd want to use it as the living room… I'd want to show it off and impress people. I know…I'm weird.

I decided that I needed to hitch those big-girl panties up a little higher and try another floor of the house. Where would a reclusive Mr. Moneybags hide out? Someplace away from everyone else…somewhere down in the depths of the private world he had created.

I worked my way back to the great hall and headed for the staircase at one end of the room. The stairs were big and wide and wound up and wound down. They were also glossy black marble…steps that could kill you, in my opinion. I decided to act like the spy I was supposed to be and crept down the steps ever so slowly, making as little noise as possible. Step by step, step by step…until I was at the bottom and looking at more hallways with more closed doors. To hell with being quiet…there was nobody here but us chickens.

I walked about forty feet down the hallway to the left. All of a sudden I was seized with the feeling that I was close, very close to the secret hiding place.

I was drawn to the door just ahead of me on the right, and I slowly advanced toward it. Sucking in my breath, I grabbed the doorknob with a determined grip and gave it a forceful turn. It was locked…I gave it a little kick...damn door. I moved on to the next room and decided to use my mounting frustration to power the door open at any cost if it should also be locked...I grabbed the doorknob, twisted it, and it politely let me in.

I found myself in a wine cellar. Dimly lit wall sconces gave it sort of a mysterious atmosphere. I always thought wine cellars were these dark dusty rooms...kind of like a cave with cobwebs everywhere. This room was no cave.

In the center of the room was a long, wide table... my best guess was that it was made of rosewood. There were enough chairs covered in rich dark cherry-colored leather to seat twelve guests at one time. The table was the centerpiece of the room, and fanning out from it in five different directions were wine racks. The racks were rosewood to match the table and chairs, and they were lit with tiny recessed lights that were tucked into the ceiling. The layout of the wine racks looked a bit like a maze, but not one you'd get lost in...I could see over the tops of them. They were only about four and a half feet tall and probably eight feet long.

The room was *so* quiet that it felt kind of spooky. I set up my tripod and camera and took enough photos of the room to make the gala committee happy. I *should* have left and gone on to the next room, but I couldn't help it...I wanted to explore the maze. I kept my camera with me but left my tripod by the door, and then I started exploring the rows of racks. It was so quiet...the floor was covered with thick carpeting, and every step I took made no sound at all.

I have to admit it was kind of fun snaking my way around the room, looking at all the amazing wine. I don't know a lot about wine, but I know enough to recognize expensive labels when I see them…there must have been thousands and thousands of dollars wrapped up in those bottles of mutant grapes. I'd seen enough to have plenty to tell CC, so I decided to walk along behind the ends of the racks and curve around the side of the room to get back to my stuff. That's when an interesting thought occurred to me. Why were the lights already on in this room? I hadn't turned them on, and I hadn't seen any-one else in the room. I had to abandon this unsettling thought to focus on another.

It's a funny thing about dead bodies. You find them in the most unexpected places. I was almost back to where I'd left my things, when I tripped over a large man slumped down against the wall.

You would think that I would have screamed or fainted, but you would be wrong. Don't forget that I was becoming an old pro at finding dead bodies…no scream-ing for this crime-scene expert. Nope, no screaming for me…I just threw up all over my shoes (and his) instead.

I didn't want to do it; really I didn't, but I slumped down next to the dead guy. I laid my cold sweaty fore-head down on my knees to pull myself together. I was just starting to think that I might keep down the rest of my breakfast, when a hand reached over and grabbed one of my knees. That was it…I lost it. Well, *you* would have, too! The dead guy had his hand on my leg!

Much hysteria later, we were both up in the gleaming kitchen with cold cloths pressed against our foreheads. It turned out that Reynaldo wasn't dead, after all. "Rey"— as Mr. Adam called him—was the mansion property manager and had been knocked out cold by person or persons unknown.

Aside from a bruise on the side of his forehead and a pair of now ruined, smelly shoes, he seemed to be okay. He'd been doing the monthly inventory for the cellar and had almost finished, when he turned a corner, and someone bashed him on the head. After that it was lights out for him until I did my little vomiting number.

Between the two of us, Rey and I had helped each other upstairs and into the kitchen. I'd been in no condition to lug both a tripod and a camera up the stairs, so I'd just left all my things lying on the floor of the wine cellar.

I'd been yelling for help all the way up the stairs, and we'd barely walked through the door of the kitchen, when the cavalry arrived. Rey and I were rushed into comfortable chairs…Mr. Adam was dithering around and finally decided to call the mansion security team. They wanted to talk to Reynaldo, but that was going to have to wait. He was as white as a ghost and still weak.

Sophie had been fussing over us like a lunatic mother hen…offering us cold water, wine, coffee…neck massages and a sponge bath.

I don't know how Rey felt about the sponge-bath offer, but I definitely wasn't interested, and I needed to go back to get my camera equipment.

I wasn't thrilled about going back downstairs with Rey's attacker still on the loose, but it had to be done. I slipped out of the kitchen and returned to the stairs. Taking a deep breath, I raced down the stairs, into the wine cellar, grabbed my things, and was out of the room in a red-hot minute.

I went back to the kitchen to check on Rey. I was a little afraid I'd interrupt Sophie giving him a sponge bath, so I knocked on the doorframe before I put even one toe inside the room.

"Who's knocking?" Sophie called out. "Is that you, London? If you're not London, then whoever's out there, identify yourself, or I'm going to unload this shotgun all over your nasty ass. Are you listening, burglar man or woman?"

"Don't shoot, Sophie. It's me!"

"Oh thank God! I don't really have a shotgun...I just have a carrot and a stick of butter!"

"Is it safe for me to come in?" I wasn't taking any chances...I wasn't sure I trusted her...even with butter. A deep voice called out to me.

"It's okay, Miss London. It's me, Rey, and nobody has a weapon."

Rey looked much better than he had when I'd gone back downstairs. His color was back to normal, and he was just hanging up the phone.

"I just talked with security, and they found the garage door open. It's possible someone accessed the house from there."

"What's security going to do now?"

"There's really nothing they can do...they'll do a sweep of the house, and if nothing is missing, they'll just report it to the police so that it's on record."

I let out a little sigh...at least this time there would be no chatting with any cops.

"Miss Sophie, thank you for your help," Rey said. "Is there anything else that I can assist you with here on the property, Miss London?"

"I was just going to ask Sophie if she was ready to leave. I think I have everything I need."

I gave Sophie a look that I hoped said, "Let's get the hell out of here." We had all left the kitchen and were walking back toward the great hall for one last look around. I glanced down toward the seating area and the couches and decided that Sophie needed to leave the room immediately.

"Sophie, didn't you have a coat? I think you left it in the office."

I was hoping that I sounded casual, natural. With a little squeal Sophie latched onto Mr. Adam's arm and pressed against him, getting as close as she could.

"Adam honey, I'm just so turned around...this house is so big that I don't think I can find my way back to the office. Will you take me?"

She was fluttering her fake eyelashes so much that one of them finally flipped off. Well, that just completed her look…I had noticed her smeared lipstick earlier, the floozy look was a done deal.

I was pretty sure that Sophie wouldn't have responded well to my next question, so I was relieved when she and Mr. Adam left arm in arm for the office.

"Rey, why is that black snake lying on the couch? I saw a snake just like that outside a while ago…and now there's one in here…on the couch…looking at me."

"We only have one snake in residence, Ralph. His home is out in the garden but every once in a while he likes to come in and visit. We find him all over the house, but this room is his favorite. He's harmless, and he seems to like people…he's not your typical snake."

Ralph had lifted his head up and placed it on the armrest of the couch. He was looking in our direction, sticking his little tongue out, tasting the air…picking up our scent.

"Do you mind if I take his picture? He's the coolest snake I've ever seen."

Rey nodded his head in Ralph's direction.

"Go ahead, but you'd better get your picture now; I think he's getting ready to leave."

Ralph had draped his head and part of his body over the armrest, so I fired off two quick shots. The minute I lowered the camera, he slithered the rest of the way off the couch and headed right toward us. We stood and watched him come to within two feet of us…he stopped there, his little tongue flicking the air again. A black snake, lying on a black floor, it was kind of creepy, but it was also kind of cool.

"Ralph, how are you?" I asked.

I know it was probably a stupid thing to say to a snake, and I didn't really expect an answer…but I felt like I had to say something; he was obviously expecting some sort of acknowledgment of his presence. I guess he was satisfied with my hello, because he came right up to me, circled my feet, and then slithered back toward the French doors. I watched Ralph go to the second door and pass out into the garden.

"Rey, was that door locked before? I don't remember it being open."

"I'm sure it was locked. I check the doors myself in the morning and at night. They're connected to the security system that indicates a breach if they're tampered with. Unless an event is taking place and access to the garden for the guests is desired, they're always locked. I need to talk to security to see if the system is functioning properly."

We both stood and stared at the door that Ralph had passed through. Had the attacker left through the French doors or through the garage exit? As Rey walked me out, I would have liked to have asked him which way he thought they had gone, but he was looking pretty beat up and tired, and in my professional opinion, he really should have seen a doctor.

Rey and I now shared a bond...we'd gone through a trauma together, and I was worried about him. I hoped Ralph the snake would keep an eye on him.

On the ride home Sophie told me more than I wanted to know about her time spent with Mr. Adam. She was all but purring with satisfaction. She had kept "the hot butler" occupied, and she was now considering a career change.

"London, I'm going to go home and research jobs for spies, on the computer. Wasn't I awesome? I think I'm just totally cut out for this line of work...think of it, I could buy a whole wardrobe of spy dresses and coats. I might even dye my hair blond...or maybe black...black is more of a spy color."

I took a glance at the mousy brown mess on her head and thought a change of color might do her good. Some time with a comb and a brush wouldn't be out of line either...she and Mr. Adam had squashed down the towering structure that she usually managed to create with her hair, to just a fraction of its normal height. Sophie had sort of been reading my mind, backward.

"You know, if I were you, London, I'd spend some time at the beauty shop getting your color fixed. You must have too much iron in your water, because your hair is just so red! And you need to style it...you need to tease it up, give it some body…you know, care about how you look a little bit."

It's a good thing that I have a lot of self-control. We'd just pulled up in front of the office, and Sophie was about to get out of the car. Thirty more seconds of listening to her trash talk my appearance and I would have planted my foot in her posterior as she exited the jeep.

"Remember what I said about your hair!" she yelled after me as I drove away. "And you might look into breast augmentation while you're on the computer tonight. I hear plastic surgeons can work miracles on somebody with problems like yours!"

My self-control was hanging by a thread. It was all I could do to restrain myself from putting the car into reverse and backing over her.

When I got back to the ranch, I looked over the images, and they hadn't turned out badly at all. There were lots of shots that the committee could use for advertising the gala. Unfortunately, I didn't have an image of the Prince to give to Mike. Luckily I still had plan B…the night of the gala. At that point it was late; I was tired and hungry. I was dying for a brownie bite, but I made myself heat up a low-cal meal and ate it unhappily. Twenty minutes later I was in bed and thinking about the gown I had to wear…I had two days left before I had a fitting with CC.

Handsome gave me a look that said, "Come on…one little piece of chocolate won't hurt us." As punishment for his treachery, I turned him around on the nightstand and made him look at the wall. Never trust a stuffed animal...even if it *is* a lucky charm.

Chapter 53

woke up wishing that I could have slept for twelve hours; eight just wasn't going to be enough. I really needed the rest, but I started dreaming about Abraham Lincoln pouring a glass of wine for Sophie, and both of them were wearing trench coats. My new friend, Ralph the snake, was wearing President Lincoln's hat and sticking his tongue out at me. That woke me up. I planted myself in front of my laptop and looked at the pictures of the mansion again, in particular, the wine-cellar shots.

There they were, rows and rows of wine racks cradling the heavy bottles. There was nothing in the shots to indicate that a man lay unconscious just out of view. I scanned the images once more, just to make absolutely certain that no part of Rey's anatomy was embarrassingly exposed. I mean a hand, a foot…get your mind out of the gutter… I mean something that would be embarrassing to *me*. A decent photographer does his or her best to hand over a flawless product.

I scrolled to the last two pictures and realized there was "dust" on the shots. Dust can be actual dust that got into the camera, but I use the term loosely. Any little marks caused by a smear on the lens, and so forth, is "dust" to me. I started to zoom in on the images to clean them up, and my cell phone rang.

I picked up and heard the deep voice of Reynaldo.

"How are you today, Miss London?"

"I'm fine, Reynaldo; it's good to hear your voice. You sound a lot better than you did yesterday."

"That's actually why I'm calling. I don't know that I thanked you properly for helping me."

"You shouldn't thank me, Reynaldo; after all, I ruined your shoes."

"Be that as it may, I wanted to say thank you and extend an invitation."

"An invitation?"

"Yes. Anytime you would like to come back to the mansion and spend time in the garden or visit Ralph, you have only to ask."

I could feel a smile spread over my face, and I hoped that he could hear it in my voice.

"Thank you, Reynaldo; I might just take you up on that."

"I hope that you do. Thank you again."

I stood looking at my phone for a second, wondering why getting the chance to visit Ralph again made me so happy. I'd been off the computer long enough for the crazy-patterned screen saver to pop on...with a sigh I got back to work.

I copied the images to a CD for Mike; made a backup CD of all the images for myself, filed it in storage, and grabbed my bag. I was sure that Sophie had told Mike all about our big adventure and expected an impatient text from him any minute. Yes, I could have just e-mailed the images to him, but I wanted to postpone disappointing him with nonexistent pictures of the billionaire for as long as I could.

I grabbed a carrot for Reckless and hurried out onto the porch. Leaning against the jeep was Ryder, who was being watched by Reckless from behind the fence. Mr. Horse's eyes turned from Ryder to me and then back to Ryder again.

I felt a grin spread across my face...I stopped halfway down the steps. Ryder moved away from the jeep and walked toward me. I liked the look on his face. I liked it a lot. He stopped at the bottom of the steps.

I could barely stop smiling long enough to speak... "Long time no see."

"Too long," he said. I liked the way he said it...for about one second. The truck flying up the drive toward us definitely ruined the moment. The driver was the wrangler...the woman who had draped herself all over Ryder the last time I'd seen him. She jerked her truck to a stop and bounded out of it. She was cute; the kind of cute that men find very attractive. She was cute enough to make me jealous. She kept on coming, right up the steps until she could reach out and shake my hand. She gave me a look, and I was pretty sure her eyes were telling me that I was trespassing. Apparently Ryder was her property.

"Hi! I'm Bet. I'm sorry to barge in on you like this, but, Ryder, there's a situation with the delivery this afternoon. Could you ride back with me so that we can get it straightened out?"

There was a situation all right...especially when Ryder turned his attention to her. That's when she did it again—slipped her arm through his. What was it with this girl...did she have some kind of radar where Ryder was concerned?

He didn't look happy, but I didn't care.

"London, I'm sorry, but this is important...I really have to take care of this."

"By all means, take care of your 'situation.'"

I brushed past both of them and gave Reckless his carrot.

"If she comes anywhere near you, give her a little nip in the butt for me won't you?"

Reckless was awfully busy with the carrot, but I was pretty sure he heard me. I never gave Ryder another look.

I shouldn't drive when I'm mad...unlike most people; I drive excruciatingly slowly when I'm ticked. I also shouldn't drive past the grocery store when I'm mad. Stinking brownie bites...stinking "Bet"...stinking idiot me for eating the brownie bites.

I didn't want to get into a conversation with anybody, let alone Sophie. I didn't need any more blows to my ego, so I approached the glass front of the office slowly...trying to see if Sophie was at her desk, without being seen myself. Tall potted plants dotted the lobby in front of the office doors, and I hid behind the tallest, bushiest one I could find. The coast was clear, and I moved as quietly and quickly as I could through the office door. Two seconds after I made it through the door, I saw Sophie coming. Well, actually I saw her *hair* coming.

Sophie must have been bending down behind the filing cabinets in the glass room behind her desk. One minute the coast was clear, the next minute there she was... or rather there was her hair. She hadn't dyed her hair a spy color yet...it was still the same mousy brown...whipped up into the skyscraper of a hairdo she always wore. Watching that hair moving along, sort of floating, was almost hypnotic. I made myself look away, and I admit it...I took the chicken's way out...I threw the envelope addressed to Mike, with the CD in it, on her desk and ran back out the door.

It was only noon, but I'd had it for the day. I was tired and cranky, and when I got home, I gave up; it was official...the universe was out to get me. The proof of that was sitting on my front porch.

"Hey, sweetie!" Trey was up off the steps and waiting for me to get out of the jeep.

"Hey, meatball."

One offensive name deserves another. Trey gave me a confused look and then moved in close behind me as I made for the front door.

"Going to invite me in? I sure could use a cold drink."

I'm not sure when he decided that I'd invited him in, but he was halfway through the door already. Exasperated, I left him cooling his heels, while I tucked my purse away in the bedroom.

"So where you been?"

"Working."

"You're not much of a talker, are you? Look, London, I wanted to talk to you about something...give me a chance, okay?"

I walked to the front door, talking as I went. "Why don't we go outside and sit on the porch? The house is hot, and there's a nice breeze outside."

I don't know why, but I just wanted him out of the house.

"That works for me...okay if I use the men's room first?"

I pointed down the hall and went outside and sat down on the porch swing. I was getting a headache, and as soon as I could get rid of Trey, I was going to take a nap. A few minutes later the screen door swung open, and Trey sat down beside me.

"So London, here's the deal...you and I got off on the wrong foot the first couple of times we ran into each other. I'd like to get to know you better, and I'm willing to do the whole 'let's go on a date thing,' if that's the kind of song and dance you want. I already know what I want, and I'm willing to put in the time to get it."

Well, that was just the most flattering thing I'd ever heard. *Not.* I stood up.

"Get off my porch, Trey." His stupid smile got tighter, and he stood up. He towered over me, and I backed up.

"Come on…don't be so cold…give me a little 'sugar.'"

He reached for me, and that's when I kicked him where it counts. He doubled over, cradling his two best friends.

I left him on the porch and slammed my way into the house. It took at least ten minutes before I heard him start up his truck and drive away. I made sure the door was locked and bolted, took two aspirin, and headed for the bedroom. I needed to vent, and next to Reckless, Handsome had become my go-to guy for spilling my guts. Something was different. Handsome wasn't keeping an eye on the door the way I'd left him the night before. He was back to facing the bed. Something else was different; everything in my purse had been shaken out onto the bed, and the room was trashed.

I'd suspected that Trey had wanted to, shall we say, get in my "drawers," and in one respect he had. Every drawer in my dresser had been pulled out and dumped onto the floor. Panties and socks and bras were thrown helter-skelter all over the room. I needed to breathe; my adrenaline was pumping, and without thinking, I raced out of the house, just in time to see Trey's truck disappear in a cloud of dust.

My heart was pounding with anger as I swung around and returned to the house. Once inside, I slammed the door shut and shoved a chair under the doorknob as an extra precaution. I did a search on the computer for a locksmith, made a call, and knew how I was going to spend the rest of the day...waiting for new locks to be installed on the door and windows. I was a big girl; I could handle this. I could, no problem but man, oh man, I would have given my kingdom for a brownie or a gumball. Now I was the one who wanted a little sugar.

I told myself that changing the locks hadn't been a bit of an overreaction, but after the locksmith finally left, I sat down and reviewed the last couple of weeks. Three people were dead and one person injured, each and every time I had been present. Now I had some muscle-bound goof ransacking my house.

Too much had happened; none of it made sense, and I could feel the cogs in my brain jamming up. I checked the new lock, took a shower, and crawled under the covers of my bed. I didn't want to think anymore...didn't want to worry anymore...I was done with this day.

Chapter 54

The next morning I woke up with a few decisions made. I wasn't going to go anywhere; I wasn't going to do anything, and I wasn't letting anybody into my house.

I did take a call from Mike. He wasn't upset that I hadn't gotten the shot; "Better luck next time" seemed to be his attitude. He still wanted me to get something tabloid-worthy at the gala, and if it involved Jett, so much the better. There was no way I could miss getting something at the gala, according to him. He said that scandalous things always happened at this kind of society thing. It would be a piece of cake. Speaking of cake…it was time for lunch.

I searched high and low but…no cake. Popcorn would have to do. I made way more than I should have and ate every bite of it.

Feeling like I'd swallowed a bowling ball, I decided I needed exercise, so I unlocked and unbolted my door and eased my way out onto the porch. The coast was clear... there was no one lurking in the yard or next to the jeep.

There was something a little interesting going on, though. Reckless was hard at work, trying to get the new latch on his gate open. The minute he saw me walking toward him, he walked a few paces away from the gate and gave me a big innocent stare.

"You can't fool me, mister...I saw you messing with that latch."

I don't think he liked my accusatory tone of voice...he laid his ears back.

"Don't worry, I won't tell anybody. Stand back a bit so that I can open the gate and come in there with you."

His ears popped back up, and he moved over to give the gate room to swing open. Once again I realized I was dealing with one smart horse.

I spent the next hour or so following Reckless as he wandered the field. I didn't ask him for his advice about what was going on, or not going on, with Ryder. I did bring him up to speed on the murders and my visit to the mansion. He seemed to pay a lot of attention to the part about me finding Rey knocked out cold in the wine cellar. I don't know if he found the part about me tossing my cookies interesting or gross, but he pushed his nose against my arm and tossed his head up and down.

"To be honest, I was a little scared down there in the wine cellar. I think I'm going to hire you to be my bodyguard, Reckless…you're big, you're brave, and you could squash someone like a bug if they messed with me."

Reckless walked a little closer and actually rested his head on my shoulder.

"I like you too." I wrapped an arm around his neck and gave him a hug. Just like that, my day improved 100 percent, and I felt more like myself than I had for the last twenty-four hours.

I took my time walking back home, and this time Reckless followed *me* through the field. He stopped just short of the gate and watched me pass through and then secure the latch. I guess he was just escorting me home, because as soon as the latch was in place, he turned and ambled back across the field. His was a big, important, difficult job. It wasn't easy patrolling the ranch *and* keeping track of his red-haired human.

I had left my cell phone home while I was taking my walk, and when I got back, there was a message from CC, reminding me that the next day was the big day…my gown fitting. Now I knew what my plans were for the evening… a nice long soak in the tub and a long overdue date with a razor. The hair on my legs was getting long enough to braid.

It's amazing what shaving your legs can do for a person. To make the end of my day even better, my jeans were slipping on without "extra me" spilling over the top of them…life was good.

Chapter 55

I was a bundle of nerves, awkwardly standing in CC's design area, waiting to see my gown.

"Are you ready?" CC called from the back room. "You're going to be wearing the gown of the season at the gala."

"Ready," I called back.

"Here it is!" CC swept out carrying a shimmering, brilliant gown.

CC took my arm and led me to a dressing area. The moment of truth was upon me...would the dress fit? CC slipped it over my head, and it cascaded to the floor. I turned to look in the floor-length mirror.

The bodice was a halter that wrapped itself around my neck. My shoulders and back, down to my waist, were bare. The skirt of the gown was made of some kind of magic fabric. Every move I made, it responded to. It was like wearing music.

I thought that CC would pick some wild crazy color for the gown, but I was wrong. It was shimmering, luminous silver. It had a heavy dusting of tiny, tiny diamond-like rhinestones scattered all over it. It was as if someone had taken a soft breath and blown fairy dust into the air, letting it gently settle randomly on the gown.

CC had stepped back to get a good look at me. I looked at my image reflected in the mirror and didn't recognize myself. Was that me in the mirror, transformed by CC into Cinderella's time travelling sister?

"This is just what I wanted for you, London…you look like a goddess…and your hair looks like fire! I can't wait until the gala. I'm going to have new clients lined up out the door and down the street. They're all going to want a gown that will make them look just like you…except that they can't. I'm not making another gown like this for anyone else."

"CC, I don't know what to say…" I couldn't find the words to express how I felt.

"Don't say anything. You know I'll get emotional if we talk about real feelings. Now here, I want to give you something."

She reached into her pocket and handed me a very small sterling silver camera. Of course, it wasn't a working camera…but it *was* a work of art. It fit right into the palm of my hand. I turned it over and over. It was heavy and perfect down to the last detail. It had a little diamond on the top, where the shutter release button would be.

"I had 'The love that never leaves' engraved on the bottom. I know that your photography is one of the big loves of your life, and since you collect things that are lucky charms for you, I thought this would bring you luck the night of the gala…I hope it helps you find the billionaire."

I slapped my hand to my forehead. "I forgot to tell you about my trip to the mansion."

"What am I going to do with you, London…how could you forget to tell me? Come on, we're going to get drinks, and you're going to tell me everything!"

CC helped me carefully change out of the gown, and as I put my jeans and T-shirt on, I turned back into regular old London Hart.

We were settled at our table at the Columbia, and CC was on her second drink. I was on my second bowl of guacamole.

"Slow down on the guac, London!" CC had watched me inhale the first bowl and apparently felt that she was my own personal "body" guard.

"Hey…I've done a lot of hard work lately! I've only had a few brownie bites, and I'm only eating four hundred calories a day in chocolate. I've earned this guacamole. The dress fit, didn't it?"

"Yes, the dress fit, but don't forget you still have to get into it for the gala. That's not going to be possible if you keep putting away chips and guacamole as if you're training for the pie-eating contest at the county fair!"

"You stick to your vice, and I'll stick to mine…it's not going to hurt me to take one day off from counting calories."

CC gave me a dirty look and changed the subject.

"So what the hell happened at the mansion? Why didn't you call me and give me all the details?"

"There was just too much going on."

I took a deep breath and recounted the day of the shoot and about finding Rey unconscious. I told her about finding Trey on my porch.

"Katookie! You've had a crazy couple of days!"

"I'm not as worldly as you, CC. What does 'katookie' mean?"

"It's a more polite way of saying a certain four-letter word. You know when you clean up a horse's stall, and you shovel the 'presents' the horse leaves for you into a wheelbarrow? Well…those little 'presents' are 'katookie.'"

I thought it over for a minute and had to agree. "You're right, CC. It's been pretty 'katookie.'"

CC began interrogating me. "First question…who do you think whacked Rey on the head? Second question… what do you think Trey was doing in your bedroom? Third question…why is all this happening to *you*?"

"I don't know who knocked out Reynaldo, but at least he wasn't killed like the other clients were…I wonder if that's because Rey doesn't own the mansion. As far as Trey goes, I'm starting to think he's a freak. Maybe he's just one of those pervos, and he was looking for some of my underwear. Of course, I don't keep underwear in my purse, so that theory doesn't fly, does it?"

CC sat with a frown on her face. "I don't know; I carry extra underwear in my purse all the time."

I restrained myself from getting further details.

"Damn it, London…too much weird stuff is happening. Who can we go to for help? The police are just going to be more suspicious if we tell them someone else was attacked when you were around. To start with, we need to find someone we can trust, someone who knows a little bit about the people who were killed. Like who their friends were, who their enemies were."

"The only person I can think of who fits that description is Mike. He knows a lot of people in town; maybe he can think of a reason someone would want to kill them." I was going out on a limb, but you had to start somewhere.

CC immediately got irritated. "*I am* not going to go talk to him! If you want to talk to him, talk to him, but leave me out of it. He threatened me!"

"He *threatened* you? This wouldn't have anything to do with your overconsumption of white chocolate martini's a while back and your unfortunate experience with Mike, would it?

"You may as well tell me what happened after I left. I'm going to talk to Mike…either about business or to ask for his help, but you'd better tell me…I want to be prepared for whatever *he* tells *me*."

CC's drinks were kicking in...two drinks, and things start happening with that girl.

"*You were there*; you know what happened inside the bar. It wasn't my fault that he got cheese all over his pants! I got my finger stuck in his belt when I was trying to climb up off the floor, and that brute dragged me through the cheese. What kind of man doesn't help a woman up off the floor?"

"I know that part, CC. What happened in the parking lot?"

She was working herself up to an indignant rant, and I was trying to figure out how to stop her. She stood up and turned to the woman seated next to her.

"Hey, honey! Don't 'cha think a man should help a lady get her butt off the floor when she's lyin' in cheese??" She slapped the woman on the shoulder and then swiped her drink.

"What'cha drinkin', honey?" She chugged the drink and slammed the glass down onto the table.

She whispered at me in a voice that would have carried all the way up to Tampa. "Hey, London...she's drinkin' *lemonade*! It's *awesome*! I gotta start drinkin' lemonade! *Ass' the nice bartender what they make lemonade out of!*"

I somehow got CC out to the jeep and loaded her in... she raved most of the way back to the boutique. The way she was going, I wasn't sure she was in any condition to work.

"Do you have any more clients today, CC?" I was praying that she didn't.

"Just that pain in the ass *Prissy*!"

"I thought you two were such good buddies...did that all go up in smoke when your romance with her brother, Eduardo, fell apart?"

"No! It fell apart later! Like the same day Mike and I got in that fight in the rain in the parking lot!"

"Speak up a little louder, CC; I can't hear you, because I just went *deaf* from your shouting."

"WELL...EXCUUSE MEE!" She slapped her mouth shut for about thirty seconds, and then she decided she had more to tell me.

"I liked Prissy until she drove up in that storm and picked Mike up. She said something about being sorry that he had to wait in the bar because she was running late. Then she looked at me and said, 'Shee, shee, darling... you've got a little cheese on your boobs.' She *embarrassed* me! Right out in front of God and *everybody*! Mike is such a jerk...he just kept right on walking toward her car.

"So what are they...*dating*? Can you imagine *them* as a couple? He's a giant, and she walks a pig on a leash. SHE WALKS HER PET PIG ON A LEASH! I'M GONNA GET A PIG AND WALK IT ON A LEASH WHILE I DRINK LEMONADE...WATCH OUT, SEXY MAN, HERE I COME!!"

I'm not sure who "sexy man" was, but I knew one thing...naptime, here comes CC.

"You still haven't told me anything that would have upset Mike enough to threaten you."

"I bit him in the ass, OK?"

"You *what*? *Why*?"

"*I bit him in the ass...I don't have to have a reason! I just did it, and then he got all mean and threatened to call animal control on me!*"

Well, that certainly explained a lot. It didn't take me long to get her up the stairs. I walked her back to the comfy couch she took her power naps on and covered her up with a soft throw that she immediately pulled up to her nose.

"Close your eyes for a few minutes, CC." I gave her a kiss on the forehead. "And thank you...my gown is perfect. You're a true artist, and I love my camera lucky charm."

I walked quietly toward the door, but I heard her muttering from underneath the throw.

"I'm gonna design a gown with a *pig* on it, and then I'm going to put it in the front window with a sign that says, 'Honk if you love *Prissy*.' Maybe I'll put *real* pigs in the window and put little signs around their necks that say, 'My name is Prissy'...*all* the little pigs will be named Prissy... *Prissy Ass*."

Before I left, I found Flor, told him that CC had gone "nighty-night," and told him to trust me and cancel Prissy's appointment for the afternoon.

Chapter 56

did that thing again and drove home, and when I got there, I didn't remember a minute of the drive. I think I spent the whole time focused on the conversation I'd just had with CC. My life used to be so simple; now I was having conversations about murders and living a life that was straight out of a crime novel. Come to think of it, I wasn't the only person with weirdness going on in my life. I realized that I hadn't talked to Brenda for quite a while. The minute I got into the house, I decided to give her a call to see if she'd made any progress with her own mystery.

Stretching out on my bed while I waited for her to answer her phone, I felt the adrenaline rush from dealing with CC start to recede. After eight rings, Brenda answered. She was out of breath, and I could hear several male voices in the background.

"Hi, London! What's up?"

"I called to see if you ever figured out what the accountant next door was up to and if the cop caught you doing any more stalking."

"You won't believe how it's all turned out…Rex and Virgil aren't mob guys; neither is my neighbor, Barry!"

"You know them by name? What in the world has been happening over there?"

"Rex and Virgil, the suit guys, are pro wrestlers! Barry is a video-game designer, and he's creating a wrestling video game. He hired the boys to be consultants. They make sure that everything about the game is authentic looking and sounding. It's really interesting; in fact, I'm with them right now."

"What are you doing?"

"I'm helping with ideas about how the female characters would react to certain threats, and I'm helping Barry come up with costume ideas."

"It sounds like you're having fun, but are you disappointed that they're not mob guys?"

"This is way cooler, and Rex and Virgil are just big old teddy bears."

I had to laugh. "Those were the biggest teddy bears I've ever seen! How did you find out what they were up to?"

"I just happened to be bird watching near Barry's living-room window, and before you ask again, noooo, that cop didn't catch me at it. So anyway, I saw Rex and Virgil choking each other and throwing each other all over the room. I ran back into my place and called the cops…it was crazy!

"Every once in a while one of them would get thrown against my living-room wall, and the third time it happened, two pictures and the urn with Uncle Dean in it fell off the fireplace mantel.

"I was so mad, London! It was scattered all over my sofa, and I didn't know what to do. Luckily that's when the cops pulled up. I ran right out to their squad car and told them somebody needed to clean up Uncle Dean. They made me sit in the back seat behind that metal fence they have between the front and back seats, as if I was a common criminal! It took me ten minutes to convince them that I wasn't having a psychotic episode. After that, the cops went and knocked on Barry's door, and that's when I found out that the boys were just acting out some wrestling moves."

"So what happened with Uncle Dean?" I asked. "Is he all mashed up in your sofa cushions?"

"He's in a much better place now. The guys came over and apologized; then they explained about the video-game stuff. Virgil borrowed my vacuum and swept up Uncle Dean…we shook most of him out of the vacuum bag and put him back in the urn. The boys and I got along so well and had such a good time that they invited me to work on the game with them…and the rest is history!"

"Your life is never boring, is it, Brenda?"

"It's a lot of fun most of the time, London. Now I want you to meet them real soon; you'll love them."

"I'm sure I will…I'll let you get back to what you were doing, but keep me posted on how things are going."

"You got it, sweetie!"

I ended the call and shook my head. Brenda had a knack for falling into the most interesting situations. Video-game design and teddy bear wrestlers…what would she get herself into next?

CHAPTER 57

The night of the gala arrived, and CC and I had our game plan in place. She was going to pick me up, and at the end of the evening, I'd spend the night in her guest condo. Yes, you read that right…I said guest condo. She liked having guests stay with her, but she liked her privacy. If you spent time with her, you lived large.

I was dealing with a case of butterflies again, but it actually felt more like dragonflies were smacking around inside of me this time…I was having *big-time* anxiety.

I slipped into my magical gown; my hair wasn't an issue…I'd had it styled earlier in the day and was still getting used to the French twist. I kind of liked the way the stylist had left long tendrils falling randomly around my face.

I quickly packed my camera into my beautiful bag, along with an extra memory card and a battery. Just as I heard the purr of CC's Mercedes in front of the house, I remembered the lucky charm that CC had given me. I made a quick trip back into the bedroom and, giving handsome a pat on the head, swept up the tiny camera and put it into my bag.

CC had gone va-va-voom with her gown. It hugged her tight in all the right places, and I was surprised that she could manage to drive the car without splitting a few seams.

"This is going to be a lovely night, London...I know I told you that I wasn't very interested in seeing or meeting Prince Brannigan, but I am interested in seeing his mansion. Are you excited about tonight?"

"I don't know if excited is the word, anxious might be more like it. I really, really need to get a shot of Brannigan."

I took a second to focus on the task at hand. I would get a chance to hunt the Prince again tonight. I decided to watch all the dark corners and private places. Who knows, he might sneak out to a back hall with some young debutante and get amorous. Ooooh...and what if Chesty found them! Now *that* would be good tabloid trash. What was happening to me, wishing heartbreak on someone?

We pulled up in front of the mansion and turned the keys of the Mercedes over to one of the valets.

CC oohed and aahed over the beauty of the landscaping and the huge fountain in the center of the drive. The estate was even more impressive and stunning at night. The gardens on either side of the front doors were twinkling with little white lights that wound through the bushes, trees, and flowers. There was actually a small line of people waiting to enter the mansion, because everyone was admiring the garden before they moved through the doors.

As we finally reached the front door, the valet who had parked CC's car bumped up against me. He grabbed my arm to keep me from falling and gave me a quick apology. Slipping CC's car keys onto a special key rack designed for big events like this, he was off the porch and holding the car door open for another arriving guest.

Once we got inside, we had to gently push our way through the crowded entryway and into the great hall...I stopped short in amazement. The room had been transformed...it was filled with large round tables with deep-purple tablecloths covering them. Chairs covered in gold-draped satin were placed around each table, and gold-rimmed crystal wine and champagne glasses stood next to exquisite dark-purple china plates. Towering vases seemed to explode with deep-crimson roses, deep-purple roses, and gold roses, while long strands of some kind of deep-green ivy thing wound through the arrangements and then swept down to the tops of the tables. Additional small vases of red and gold roses were scattered randomly on the tabletops.

The chandeliers were dimmed, and the rooms had taken on a romantic, mysterious atmosphere. Red and purple lights washed the walls up to the dark ceiling. The great hall had become, quite simply, a fantasy.

At the far end of the hall, opposite where the floral oil painting was hung, a stage had been built. It was a small stage, but it was still a stage. Standing close to it were giant champagne glasses, one on each side of the stage. The things looked big enough to take a bath in, and they were filled with what appeared to be pink champagne. Someone had gotten carried away with pouring the "bubbly," because the enormous glasses were almost overflowing. To either side of the giant glasses were tiered tables stacked high with normal-sized champagne glasses, also filled to the brim.

CC and I had become separated almost immediately, but we were together long enough to find our assigned table for dinner. CC tossed her clutch down on the table, plumped up her cleavage, and got a determined look on her face.

"I'm off to find a drink with a man attached to it."

"CC, leave the waiters alone until after we eat...I want them to have the strength to serve our dinner...after that, go ahead...knock yourself out."

"I'm not making any promises...Mama's gonna find herself something yummy."

"CC," I hissed at her disappearing back. "CC!"

"*What?*" she hissed back.

"Thank you again for my gown."

She gave me a dazzling smile and disappeared into the crowd. I took a long look at all the guests and reached into my purse for the camera. I decided to start out photographing the gowns and the women adorned in them, first... there were so many to choose from, but I knew immediately which "vision of loveliness" I wanted to start with.

Chesty Hills had just made a sweeping entrance down the grand staircase, and all eyes were on her. I guess I shouldn't say she swept down the staircase...she minced her way down the staircase. She had forced CC to design the dress to cling so tightly to her legs that she was doing her "Marilyn Monroe" slither/walk thing again.

CC had done her best. The dress was pink...a lovely shade of pink, but it was cut very low...so low that a *lot* of Chesty was spilling out of it. CC hadn't wanted to cut it quite as low as Chesty requested, but Chesty finally wore her down and got her way. The dress shouted, "Look at me! I have absolutely *no* class, and I sure as hell don't want you to miss getting a look at the boobies I bought myself for Christmas."

The hat that "Miss Booblette" had requested had been vetoed by CC. She convinced Chesty to wear a tiara instead of a hat. That suggestion had ended up backfiring on her. Chesty snuck around behind CC's back and had a tiara made that had huge, tacky, brilliant orange crystals scattered in among hot-pink crystals. Chesty loved it, according to CC, and had said that she would feel like a queen among her subjects at the gala. CC's opinion was that she would look like a beauty-pageant contestant gone mad.

Finished with Chesty, I'd taken a lot of shots of the guests within the first twenty minutes, and I couldn't help but notice Prissy. She was standing at the far end of the room under the massive oil painting, deep in conversation with her idiot brother, Eduardo. Something must have happened to upset her, because her face was bright red, her eyes were full of fury, and she was pointing dramatically at someone in the crowd.

I wasn't close enough to hear what she was saying, but Doofus the third apparently had nothing to say. He didn't seem to be as upset as his apoplectic sister...he just looked bored and was licking the last of his drink out of the bottom of his glass. I decided to say hello and find out what had Prissy so hot.

On my short walk over to them, I couldn't stop looking at Prissy's gown. If you looked at it closely, the pattern was created with the embroidered images of pigs! Pigs in every size...all designed to create a lovely pattern, but pigs just the same. CC had gotten her revenge. Nobody embarrasses C. C. Covington by telling her that she's got cheese on her ass and gets away with it.

Chapter 58

I slipped up beside Prissy and whispered at her. "What's going on? You look like you're about to explode."

Prissy snarled at me. "I beg your pardon?"

"We met at CC's…you were just leaving from a fitting, and I was just arriving for mine." Okay, I stretched the truth a bit. I have no excuse…I'm just evil.

"Really, I have no recollection of ever meeting you."

"I'm London, London Hart. CC and I have been friends for years, so that's how I know her. I also work for Mike Brant."

"Ohhhh, you're the one who took the pictures of the mansion for his magazine. Mike told me all about what you're doing here. You've been in his office…you'd probably understand why I'm so furious right now. You've got personal experience."

"Personal experience with what?"

"You know, that airhead Sophie who works for him. If you've dealt with her at all, you know that she's ditzy enough to make a person pull their panties up over their head and scream with frustration. Tonight she's gone too far. She brought her twin sister here tonight, and she's been pushing her at Mike ever since she got here! That little twit with the Eiffel-tower hair had better not mess up what I've got going with Mike, or I'll make sure she regrets it!"

Prissy's eyes were blazing again, and I tried to change the subject.

"I'm glad that the gala was able to still take place despite the tragic happenings of the last few weeks."

"Tragedies…whatever are you talking about?" Prissy said impatiently.

"The deaths of two of the board members, Toni Palumbo and Monique Summers."

Prissy curled her lip. "Tragedies might be a bit of an exaggeration, don't you think? Toni acted as if she ran the whole show, and Monique was always hitting on other people's husbands at the committee holiday parties!"

"I had no idea! They must have made a lot of people pretty angry."

"Oh, they didn't care in the least about other people! I take that back…I think Monique started to care when Chesty made some pretty ugly threats."

My antenna went straight up. "Chesty made threats? Who did she threaten?"

"Why, Monique, of course…she was sniffing around some new man in Chesty's life, and she made it clear that if Monique didn't back off, there would be hell to pay. I wouldn't want to cross her…there are rumors that she has a criminal past!"

"How did you find out about all this?" I asked.

She gave me a haughty look. "What else is a maid for?" Prissy then glanced up. "Oh dear God, here she comes." She charged off, dragging Eduardo behind her.

Almost immediately I found out who "she" was. Bearing down on me was Sophie dragging a woman behind her.

"LONDON!"

"SOPHIE!" Yes, I screamed back at her…I know, pretty unladylike.

"You look like a midnight sky!"

Wow! I had just gotten an actual compliment from Sophie. And then she opened her mouth and ruined it.

"You look like the night sky when it's all silvery and sparkly, and then it gets so full of stars that it looks as if it could explode, and suddenly it isn't pretty anymore, and it gets all scary looking, and then it seems like all hell is going to break loose, you know…like that."

What was it with this woman? She was just completely tactless.

She pulled the unfortunate woman with her forward and introduced her.

"This is my sister, Evangeline. We're twins!"

"*Twins?* Sophie, you never told me you had a twin!"

"Well, you never asked! We're fraternal twins...two eggs in one mommy."

"Does fraternal mean that you share the same personality traits, stuff like that?" I couldn't imagine two people operating on Sophie's mental wavelength.

"That's only if you're identical twins. It's too bad we're not identical; poor Evangeline got cheated...she wasn't born with the charisma and style that I was born with."

I looked at the pained expression on her sister's face and could only imagine the insults she had endured over the years. A wave of sympathy for her washed over me.

"It's nice to meet you," I said. "You both look lovely tonight."

Evangeline's gown was soft blue and had a beautiful bodice and flowing skirt. It made her look very elegant. Sophie's dress was a deep, dark burgundy. It had long sleeves, a very high neckline, and a skirt that poofed out in kind of a bell shape. She had covered up almost every inch of her skin. Talk about a night-and-day difference from the dress she wore the last time we were here. Obviously she was no longer in spy mode.

"Have you seen Mike?" Sophie had to squeak a little louder than usual to be heard. The event was getting noisier as each new guest arrived.

"Not so far. Do you want me to tell him you're looking for him if I see him?"

"Yes! Tell him my sister and I are here and that I want him to meet her, OK? She won't be staying here long. She's leaving for England soon. Eve travels all over the world... she has the most exciting life!"

Evangeline finally did a little talking through her pinched little lips.

"My life isn't all that exciting. I work for a cruise line, and I do training at our overseas 'port of call' offices."

Sophie had been hopping up and down every so often, trying to see over the heads of the people who surrounded us.

"Ooooh, ooooh, I think I see Mike over there by the champagne...come on, Eve...let's get over there before that nasty Prissy gets to him first!"

As she walked away hand in hand with her sister, I heard her squeaking to Evangeline.

"Did you see Prissy's dress? It's got *pigs* all over it! I'm going to ask her why she picked pigs to put on her dress... she must relate to pigs on some level."

No doubt about it, CC was going to be in *big* trouble for designing the secret pig gown.

Once the whacka-doodle, plus twin, had gone on her merry way, I decided that I would grab a few shots of the shoes that were being bid on in the silent auction. I discreetly followed a few guests around the huge continuous circle of tables that displayed the gorgeous footwear. I snapped photos of them bidding on shoes, pointing at their favorites. The amazing collection of heels really *was* beautiful, and I took way too many shots of shoes.

I was drooling over a pair of stilettos with heels about six inches high, even though there was no way I could manage to walk in them. There was no way the ninety-five-year-old woman bidding on them was going to be able to prance around in them either, but she was determined to be the top bidder for those heels. If anybody made a move to write their name on the bidding sheet, she raised her cane and glared at the enemy. If they got so bold as to try bidding again, she rammed them with her scooter. Every last one of them backed away.

I'd reached the halfway point of the circle and came to a dead stop; there seemed to be some kind of traffic jam. I'd run into this a couple of times as I followed people... they'd be moving along, and then they'd all stop and stand so long I'd have to wiggle my way through them to move on to the next group of bidders.

"I want those, Maxie! You *have* to buy me those shoes... I'm going to be so mad at you if you don't buy them for me!"

The cute little blonde, with her arms crossed, pouting, was definitely giving "Maxie" a hard time. His face was getting red, and he did *not* look happy. I bumped into a woman standing just next to him and turned to apologize.

"What's she so upset about?" I figured I might as well ask her...she seemed to be highly amused by the whole spectacle.

"Little 'Miss Entitled' won't take no for an answer; she wants the heels, and poor Max has never been able to say no to her."

"Which heels?"

She took her pinky finger and pointed toward the center of the circle of shoes.

"Those heels."

Smack in the middle of the circle of tables displaying the collection of shoes was a tall column with a glossy black, mirrored base. Sitting on top of the base was a thick glass case with special lights that lit up an absolute work of art...the ten-million-dollar stilettos.

"Are they for sale? I thought they weren't part of the auction."

"They're not, but if I know that little schemer like I think I do, she'll get Max to buy her another pair that are just as expensive."

"She must be quite the manipulator...she looks like the type that gets her way by using sex. How do you know her?"

"She's my sister."

Well, crap. After I apologized and managed to duck when she tried to slap me, I found a different spot to drool over the ridiculously expensive stilettos. A special plaque was placed on either side of the pedestal, describing the jewels that elevated the shoes from ordinary to ten million dollars' worth of *extraordinary*. White diamonds, chocolate diamonds, pink diamonds, yellow diamonds...they covered every inch of the stilettos. I was transfixed, frozen in place, staring at them along with ten or twenty other mesmerized women...until they announced dinner, and then I was off like a shot...I was starving.

Chapter 59

Just as the servers were bringing our first course, CC threw herself into the seat she had saved next to me. I could see that she'd found the drink she'd been looking for...I didn't see a man attached to it.

"No luck on finding a warm body that's both smooch-able *and* yummy?"

"You know, London...I do have *some* class. I don't ca-noodle with just anybody!"

"Canoodle?"

"Don't play stupid with me, girly...you know what I mean...canoodle, fool around with, lock lips with."

"So, in other words, there's been no canoodling...there's not one man in this room who is worthy of a canoodle."

"Well, there might be one, but we haven't actually pro-gressed to a lip-locking relationship just yet."

Well, now there was an intriguing statement. Since when has CC had to establish a relationship *before* she got smoochy with a guy? I was completely absorbed with that mystery until the food arrived, and then I forgot everything but the steak in front of me.

There was a salad, but it had olives in it, and I'd had a bad experience with an olive before. It had pretty much ruined a first date…don't ask. There were two baked potatoes the size of my thumb with some kind of finger-licking good butter on them. And there was the steak…a juicy, big steak. I was just about to cut into the heavenly chunk of protein, when a server came back, grabbed my plate, and plopped a salmon dinner down in front of me.

"So sorry, miss, we gave you the wrong meal by mistake."

"What do you mean, by mistake?" I pouted back at her.

"It says on your place card, salmon. Someone ordered a salmon dinner for you."

I mulled this over as I forked a piece of salmon into my mouth. It had to have been Sophie. She'd made all the arrangements, so she must have ordered my meal. I was feeling a little sulky about the whole situation until they brought dessert. Chocolate mousse! CC had been watching me have my little sulk all through dinner, and she must have felt sorry for me. Silently she slid her mousse over to me. Two desserts! All was right with the world.

Licking the last little bit of chocolate mousse off my spoon, I gave a little sigh of happiness. CC was pushing away from the table. She was off to mingle with the few people *not* putting in their last bids on the various shoes. Having reapplied her lipstick for at least the fifteenth time, she stashed it back in her evening bag. Tossing the bag down on the table, she blew me a kiss and glided off.

I decided that now was the perfect time to get some large group photos and maybe a few shots of the people enjoying the relative quiet of the alcoves. I grabbed my camera and then tried to figure out where to stash my purse. It was in no way as tiny as CC's bag, and I didn't want to clutter up the table with it, so I tucked it down onto my chair and headed out to wrap up my photographer duties.

I had captured some candid shots and was looking for a few more photogenic bidders, when I saw Brenda with her new friends, the wrestlers. They were massive and dwarfed everyone around them.

I wound my way through the clusters of partying guests and tapped her on the shoulder.

"London! I'm so glad you're here. I want you to meet Rex and Virgil."

They spoke at the same time. "Pleased to meet you."

They took turns shaking my hand and doing that fancy bow you only see men do in the movies.

"It's a pleasure to meet both of you." I quickly looked back to Brenda. "I'd love to stay and chat, but I'm supposed to be working…if I don't do a good job, I'm going to look pretty stupid when the boss has 'Don't Hire Her' tattooed on my forehead." *Damn,* why did I have to go and say *that*?

"Not that there's anything *wrong* with tattoos…some of my best friends have them!"

I really needed to shut up. Brenda just gave me a confused smile as I backed away from them and beat a hasty retreat. I hoped I hadn't offended her new friends…they both had a large Superman S tattooed on their heads.

I decided to take a break and wait for the speeches before I took any more pictures. I zipped back to my table and placed the camera safely in my bag. I couldn't resist the flower-scented air just outside of the French doors any longer. I made my way back across the room and tucked myself up against the side of an open door, gazing out at the beauty before me.

The moonlight softly illuminated the gardens, and the breeze tickled the leaves of the trees and flowers. Heavenly.

The silent auction had closed. The bidding sheets had been collected. People were beginning to find their way to the garden, and the spell was broken. I was disappointed… I had liked having the night garden to myself for a little while. I turned and crossed to the far side of the room, hoping that maybe one of the little alcoves would be empty, and I could find a quiet place to sit.

The first alcove I came to had a small group of people chatting just inside the opening. I started to move on to the next alcove, but something caught my eye.

A man was standing quietly off to one side of the chatting group, his back toward me. Is there anything more handsome than a man in a black tux? This man was born to wear a tux. His hair was pulled back tight into a pony-tail, and it gave him an air of cool sophistication. He was focused on...what? He seemed detached...yet calculating. I jumped a little when he turned his head in my direction, and familiar golden eyes locked on me. Ryder.

He was no longer detached...he was, however, calcu-lating. He walked toward me as if there was no one else in the room. He didn't smile...he just came to me, took my hand, and led me back to the garden. He went straight to a secluded spot, far away from the doors, and wrapped me in his arms.

Why hadn't any other kisses in my life felt like his? Other kisses had been fun, sexy, exciting. These kisses were "soul to soul" kisses.

Too soon, he gently put his fingers under my chin and tipped my head back. His eyes searched mine, possessed mine. He wound a long red curl around his finger, and then setting the curl free, he watched it settle itself against my cheek.

"Stardust."

I wasn't sure that I had heard him right.

"What?"

"Stardust...you look like the stardust that you see in the night sky sometimes. Silver and white...*always* breath-takingly beautiful."

His eyes were a deeper, darker golden color in the moonlight, and I couldn't say a word. I just stood as still as I could, drinking in the emotion in his face and those eyes.

I don't think there could have been a more private corner of the garden, but unfortunately someone else found
their way to ours. Prissy's brother, Eduardo, came weaving
along the pathway.

"*Heyyyyy*," he said, careening into Ryder and spilling his
drink, landing on his butt in a bush…"You oughta get inside
and get some bubbly! Chesty and what's his name, the fancy-
pants billionaire, are gonna make a toast or somethin', and
then everybody gets a big ole glass of champagne."

Eduardo raised his now empty glass in a toast…"I already snuck in an' got mine." He held the glass up to his
eye and kept it there.

"*Heyyyyy! This is empty*! I got an *empty* one! I'm goin'
back and gettin' one with champagne in it this time."

With that said, he passed out, fell backward, and completely disappeared behind the bushes. We left him there.

"I guess I should go back in…I still haven't gotten any
pictures of the billionaire for the magazine," I whispered
to Ryder. (I didn't want to wake up Eduardo when he was
having such a nice nap.) "I haven't seen Chesty with a man
on her arm so far, so it looks like this is finally my chance
to get some shots of him."

Ryder looked amused. "So he's hooking up with
Chesty…I have to give him credit; she's more than enough
woman for one man to handle."

I was immediately jealous. "How do you know?
Personal experience?"

He looked down at me with a little grin. "You're something else, Miss Hart...Come on, let's get inside so that you can get back to business."

We had almost reached my table, when a man approached us.

"Ryder! I've been looking for you everywhere. I need your expertise; I'm all set to commit on the purchase of that stallion I told you about, but I want to get your thoughts. Could I have just a minute of your time?"

"London, would you mind if I give Charles a minute? And by the way, this is Charles Manning."

"It's a pleasure to meet you, Mr. Manning. You two take all the time you need; I've got a little work to do."

Ryder gave me a quick kiss on the cheek. "Now don't go disappearing on me; I'll be right back."

He gave me a wink and made his way through the crowd. I couldn't help but notice the looks on the faces of a few of the women he passed. He was easily the most handsome man in the room.

Several women exchanged meaningful glances. Several husbands gave those same women, meaningful glances... they looked like warnings, to me.

CHAPTER 60

The speech giving hadn't started yet, so I decided to take a little stroll around the room. I pulled my camera out of my purse and hadn't gone more than ten feet, when I saw Chesty standing in a corner close to the stage talking with a man. I couldn't see who he was because the two of them were half hidden by a huge floral display. Maybe my lucky charm was about to do its job, and she was with the Prince. I ducked behind a convenient drape by one of the French doors and eavesdropped on their conversation. I didn't want to barge in and take the shot unless I could be sure of the man's identity.

Chesty barely sounded like herself. With a voice as cold as ice, she tore into the man. "I gave you *two* jobs to do, and you screwed them up! Both times you left before you finished the job...and you call yourself a professional."

I got a shock when I heard the fierce male voice that shot back at her. It belonged to none other than Trey.

"I didn't see you putting yourself out there to get things done! I've had it with you. There's one more thing I need to deal with, and then I'm finished…I'm never working with you again!"

Chesty's voice got more threatening. "Be careful what you wish for."

The sound of someone tapping on the stage microphone interrupted the quarrel.

"Chesty Hills…Chesty Hills…are you out there somewhere? We're ready to start our program for this evening."

Chesty threw back her shoulders, and I could see her morphing into the woman I had met at CC's salon.

"I'm here! Coming!" She minced her way out around the side of the stage, and Trey melted away into the crowd.

I was still standing behind the drapery, wondering what the hell they had been talking about, shocked at the anger they had aimed at each other.

Within a minute Chesty was on stage and had gotten the crowd to quiet down enough so that she could introduce the mayor. Tapping the microphone with one fingernail, she whispered, "Testing…testing…can you all see and hear me?"

"YESSSS!" Well, at least the men in the room were giving her their full attention. I hadn't realized it until the spotlight hit Chesty that her dress was so sheer that it was pretty much see-through. Yep, there was no doubt. They could see pretty much *all* of her.

"Thank you all for coming and for your support of this worthy cause. Tonight we have two gentlemen for you to meet. First off, I'd like to introduce our illustrious mayor. He's got a little talk he'd like to give, and then right after that, I'm going to introduce you to a *really* important person."

The mayor stepped forward with a slightly insulted look on his face and began to give a long-winded "I'm the best thing that ever happened to our community" speech. After at least fifteen long, mind-numbing minutes, the speech finally, mercifully, ended. I left the shelter of the draperies and moved closer to the stage…Brannigan was up next, and I didn't have my long lens. I needed to be close to the stage in order to get a good shot of him.

Chesty was back in control of the microphone.

"OK! Now on behalf of the gala committee and all our guests tonight, it's time to offer a *huge* thank you to Mr. Jett Brannigan." She flashed her pearly whites over at a man with extremely blond hair, dressed in a tux with tails. He was also wearing an arrogant attitude. So this was the mystery Prince, handsome in a plastic kind of way. He reminded me of a Ken doll. I snapped a few shots and then a few more when Chesty bent *way* over to blow him a kiss. The men looking up at the stage howled their approval, while the women shot her death stares.

"Now you just march yourself right up here, Jett honey."

Brannigan walked up the steps to the stage…his blond hair almost blinding once the spotlight caught it. I'd fired off a few shots as Jett was introduced and a few more as he ascended the stairs and made his way toward Chesty. I felt myself relax; I had images of that blond head and the body that went with it to take to Mike.

"Here now, come on over here with me." Chesty slithered over and, clasping his hand in hers, pulled him over to stand next to one of the giant champagne glasses.

"Now has everyone taken a glass of champagne from our gorgeous display? Raise your glasses high with me; come on…Dear Mister Brannigan, thank you for all you do for our community. We couldn't be more grateful that you are so hugely endowed, and we are all better for it."

I guess she meant to thank him for the endowments he'd given to the community's various charities, but I could be wrong. Maybe she was sending him a personal message. Chesty drained her glass and planted a huge sloppy kiss on Brannigan. She finally pulled herself off of him and signaled a tiny china doll of a woman to come onstage.

"This is Bebe, everybody; she's wearing a gown made by none other than the famous C. C. Covington, and she's now going to draw the name of the winner of a custom-designed gown made by CC."

Bebe stepped forward and swirled her hand through a large glass bowl that had been brought out onto the stage. Her tiny little bird hand pulled out a pink slip, and she announced the winner in a trembling voice.

"The winner is…Amelia Presley!"

A thrilled scream came from somewhere in the audience, and a woman rushed to the stage. Jett Brannigan waited at the top of the steps and led the thrilled woman back to Chesty and the microphone.

"Congratulations, Amelia! Let's all raise our glasses in honor of Amelia and the fabulous C. C. Covington!"

Chesty drained her glass at breakneck speed, just as she had with her first drink. She got a goofy grin on her face and slipped off one of her six-inch heels.

"This champagne tastes *yummy*!"

Holding the microphone in one hand and glued onto Jett with the other, she lifted her bare foot. Ever so daintily she took that foot and placed just her toes in the giant champagne glass, giving the drink a little stir.

"Ooooooooh...this champagne *feels* yummy!"

It was as if she had hypnotized the crowd. They watched her giggle and then shake the "bubbly" off her toes over the glass. They watched her as she lost her balance and tumbled into the glass. They watched while Jett and a man from the audience each took an arm and tried to pull Chesty out of the glass. They watched both men fall into the glass *with* Chesty.

Tuxedoed man after tuxedoed man ran up on stage and slipped and slid in the bubbly liquid that had been splashed all over the stage. Amelia had the good sense to run back down the steps, taking little Bebe with her.

I watched, fascinated, until I realized that I should be taking shots of Chesty and her champagne-glass companions flapping and flopping in the giant glass. I'd struck tabloid gold. Socialites were slipping and sliding all over the floor, hanging onto each other, trying not to fall. Women struggled to pull their husbands and significant others out of the glass…priceless.

It was getting a little too wet for the safety of the camera, so I made my way closer to our table. Out of the corner of my eye, I saw movement at the top of the floral centerpiece on the table. It was Ralph. The little black snake had found a good place to watch the gala and was now sneaking down the flower arrangement, possibly trying to get a better view of the mayhem on stage.

"If I were you, Ralph, I'd stay right where you are. This is *not* a safe place to be at the moment."

Ralph gave me a dark stare and stopped. The words had barely left my mouth, when a large hand grabbed my upper arm. I turned to look into the eyes of a very menacing Trey.

"You know…you're right; this isn't a very safe place. You've got something I want, London, and I mean to get it…so the two of us are going to take a nice little ride together."

I jerked my arm free of his grasp.

"Excuse me! Just what do you think you're doing?"

I backed quickly away from him, and turning, I started speed walking toward the alcoves. I'd almost reached the first alcove, when I sensed something tall, dark, and menacing coming at me from my right. Behind me, Trey had reached out to grab my arm again. Tall, dark, and menacing turned out to be Ryder, and reaching Trey, he grabbed him by his lapel and stopped him dead in his tracks.

"I'd rethink the idea of laying a hand on the lady again, Trey."

Trey practically snarled at Ryder.

"Really?"

And with that brilliant comeback, he reached out for me again. That's all it took...Ryder threw the first punch, and down they went in furious male combat. I backed away and found myself pushing through into one of the alcoves that had been closed off with a velvet curtain. The room was piled high with boxes and boxes of alcohol and bartending supplies. I bumped into a tall stack of empty boxes, and they fell to the floor, revealing CC and Mike...canoodling. I looked at them, they looked at me, and I backed out the way I had come in.

Trey and Ryder had taken their fight to the other side of the room, deep into doing the whole "I'm going to beat you to a pulp" thing. I shot back down the room to my table to get my purse. I'd had enough...Things were totally out of control, and it was time to call it a night. I reached my bag and wrenched it open to stuff my camera into it. My things were gone...my extra batteries, lipstick, house keys, cell phone...even my beautiful little lucky charm from CC. My things were gone, but the bag wasn't empty. It was stuffed full...stuffed full of glittering, precious diamonds... all attached to one of the stilettos from the glass case.

Five million dollars' worth of diamonds...*in...my...bag.*

Chapter 61

Ralph had managed to get himself down onto the tabletop and was watching me turn into a zombie. The only thing that made me capable of thought was his movement toward the bag. I actually had only one thought running around and around in Zombieland. "What should I do? What should I do?"

Things were settling down a little bit up by the stage, and any second someone could notice that the stiletto was missing. My survival instincts finally kicked in...I grabbed my bag and raced back to where I'd left CC and Mike. I shoved my way past the curtain, and there they were...*more* canoodling.

I shoved my way between them and got straight to the point.

"*CC! Now! We have to go now!*" I grabbed her by the skirt on her gown and started pulling her out of the alcove.

"*What are you doing? Let go of me!*" she demanded.

Then she got a look at my face. I must have looked like a mad woman. I was still standing clutching her gown, and I'm pretty sure I was beginning to turn into a zombie again.

"London? What's going on?" Mike was speaking very calmly, trying to be the voice of reason…but I was beyond all reason. I was going to be arrested as a jewel thief. The police already thought I might be a murderer, now this… they were going to send me up the river. I was going to "the Big House"…who would smuggle cigarettes to me in prison? I don't smoke, but it's the principal of the thing.

CC pulled me over to a corner, and we stood with our backs to Mike.

"London, London, look at me."

I gave her my zombie face.

"Now tell me what's wrong."

I didn't tell her anything. I opened my bag ever so slightly and held it close to my body so that Mike couldn't see what I was doing. CC lowered only her eyes to look into the bag. Her face went white, and she went into action.

"Mike, we have to go. London's had some very bad news. I need to get her back to my place."

She was nudging me toward the curtain, and she ran back to give him a little "canip"…(that's a little kiss. Yes, I just made that up. A "canip"…you know…for when you don't have time for a full canoodle.) She had me by the hand, and we were *moving*; she called back over her shoulder to a totally bewildered Mike.

"I'll call you when we get home."

When we were a good ten feet away from him, CC shook me by the arm.

"Where the *hell* did you get *that*?"

"I picked up my bag, and it was just *in* there!! I don't know how it got in there!"

CC ran her hands through her hair. "We need to get out of here…how are you going to explain this? We need to go somewhere and decide how to return that damn thing without you getting arrested! Let's just walk out of here, nice and casual, and then we'll get my car. The most important thing to do now is to get far, far away from here."

She had taken charge, and we were headed for the front door…trying to look casual, trying not to look like international jewel thieves. We were almost there, when CC pulled up with a jerk.

I started to panic. "*What? What? Why did you stop?*"

"*I've got to go back! I've got to go get my purse!*"

"*You've got other purses…come on!*"

"*I don't have other purses that have the valet ticket and a thousand dollars cash in them!*"

"*Why in the world would you have a thousand dollars in cash in your purse?*"

"I thought we might want to stop and get a drink on the way back to my house!"

Well, that just made perfect sense. I *always* carry a thousand bucks around with me in case I need to stop for a drink. But a thousand dollars is a thousand dollars; we had to go back.

CC did an about-face and raced back toward our table. She had made it about halfway back, when she suddenly stumbled. She had come "this close" to doing a face-plant on the floor and was inadvertently saved by Sophie, who was just passing her. Unfortunately she had grabbed onto the first thing at hand to keep from falling, and it just happened to be Sophie's towering hair.

Sophie shrieked at the top of her lungs. "YOU'RE RU-INING MY SALON-STYLED, MOVIE-STAR-INSPIRED HAIRDO! LET GO!"

CC shrieked back at her. "I CAN'T LET GO! MY RING'S STUCK IN YOUR HAIR!"

At that point CC looked over her shoulder to see what she'd tripped on, and there stood Tralenka. Remember Tralenka? The underage nutso who had spray-painted CC out of jealousy? Well, she was back and, as we were about to find out, still a tad wacko.

"Did you trip me?" CC moved toward Tralenka, dragging the still-attached Sophie with her.

"Who? Me? I don't know what you're talking about, clumsy butt." Tralenka had a grin plastered ear to ear and couldn't have looked happier. She took another verbal jab at CC.

"You need to watch where you're going...women who steal men make a lot of enemies, and you could end up getting hurt."

"Are you threatening me, baby girl?"

Things were going downhill fast, and CC was forgetting what was important.

"CC!"

She snapped back at me.

"*What??*"

I waved my bag at her.

"Don't you ever mess with me again," CC hissed at Tralenka. She reached out and, with one hand, flipped Tralenka's gown up over her head.

Leaving the little shrew standing with the lower half of her birthday suit exposed, CC was off and heading for our table.

I stood staring at Tralenka, wondering when it became fashionable to not wear underwear.

CC was still dragging Sophie, who was clawing at her hair, trying to work it free of the ring. Tralenka had regrouped and looked as if she was positioning herself to make another assault of some kind. She had sidled up next to the manic Sophie. They reached our table.

Suddenly there was a shout from near the stage..."ONE OF THE STILETTOS IS MISSING!"

The entire group of champagne-soaked guests turned as one to look at the now partially empty display. For a second or two you could have heard a pin drop. Then all hell broke loose, and people were shoving and shouting. Some of them were shouting because they were getting shoved out of the way as people ran to look at the scene of the crime. I suppose the rest of them were screaming because they were just screamers.

This was it. In just a very few minutes, they'd lock the doors to make sure no one escaped with the shoe, and we'd be trapped...and I would go to prison...the pokey...the slammer.

Just as the screaming had subsided to a dull roar, and "people in charge" started shouting orders for everyone to stay where they were, I was saved by CC. She had reached the table and was still squabbling with Sophie and ignoring taunts from Tralenka, who was now half draped over Sophie in an attempt to get closer to CC.

"YOU CAN'T FOOL ME!" Tralenka shouted. "YOU'RE A MAN STEALER!" Sophie had finally worked her hair free from CC's ring and was now trying to get herself free of Tralenka's grip. She had latched onto Sophie as if she was a shield and held her between herself and CC.

"YOU'RE A FINK! YOU'RE A POOP! YOU'RE A—"

"SNAAAKE!!!!!!!" CC had met Ralph.

After I'd found the stiletto in my bag and fled the area looking for CC, Ralph had apparently decided that

CC's purse would make a good hiding place from all the craziness.

When CC snatched her bag off the table, she took Ralph with it. He couldn't manage to stay in the purse as she jerked it through the air, so he learned how to fly. He flew the few feet between CC and Sophie and Tralenka.

If I thought the screaming had been loud before, it was nothing compared to the shrieking that was coming from first Tralenka and then Sophie as Ralph landed on them. Take the hysterical reaction of the crowd as they realized that there was a snake in the room and add in the fact that it was actually *on* two people, and you have the sound that I imagine the hounds of hell would make. Without my realizing it, CC had reached me and grabbed my hand.

"Let's go, London, run!"

She was yanking at my hand, trying to get me to move. I looked toward the stage and saw a sea of people, all heading for the front door. It was as if we were on a sinking ship and everyone was headed for the lifeboats. I looked at CC wild eyed, and then we hitched up our gowns and took off running.

Watching the valet hanging up CC's car keys when we arrived ended up paying off. I knew right where CC's keys were, and we plucked them off as soon as we burst through the front doors. Valet ticket be damned; this was survival...no way were we going to stand around waiting for a valet to fetch the car for us. We raced around the side of the mansion, down into the parking garage thingy, found the Merce, and threw ourselves into it.

CC put her foot to the accelerator, and we were up, out, and racing down the driveway, going like a bat out of hell. I don't think we drew a normal breath until we were driving over the bridge back to Sarasota, gulping in cool, calming gulf air.

Chapter 62

CC unlocked the door to her condo and flipped on a few lights. I walked over to the huge floor-to-ceiling window that looked out over Sarasota Bay and the Ringling Bridge. The bridge looked beautiful at night...green lights shining from the bottom of it...white lights illuminating the top of it. I was having a hard time imagining what was happening on the other side of that bridge on St. Armands.

"My hands are still shaking—look." CC held up trembling fingers.

"I can't feel my legs, if that makes you feel any better." I'd been pinching them and nope, nothing. "I think I've had a stroke."

"You haven't had a stroke, London. We need brandy, something...whatever it is they give people when they've had a shock."

"I don't want anything except for that stiletto to not be in my bag."

CC tried to give me a bag of snacky stuff, but I couldn't get my fingers to work. I was thinking they weren't working because of the stroke…then reason started to kick in, and I realized that I'd had a death grip on the "stiletto bag" ever since we left the gala…no wonder they'd stiffened up.

"CC, help me…I can't put my bag down."

"What is *wrong* with your fingers?" CC was trying to pry my pinky finger out straight, but it just wouldn't relax. "Come on, London, relax!"

"I *can't* just relax…my fingers are paralyzed!"

"You're just freaked out. Go sit on the couch…think happy thoughts…you'll relax."

I barked at her. "THINK HAPPY THOUGHTS? LIKE, I'M GO-ING TO PRISON FOR THE REST OF MY LIFE? THOSE KIND OF HAPPY THOUGHTS?"

It took half an hour, but eventually I calmed down, and my fingers relaxed. CC had thrown a blanket over me, and that seemed to help.

After getting me all settled, she had changed clothes and gone back down to the condo's garage to get the bag that I had brought with my clothes, etc. It wasn't long before she was back and making sure that I was still in the land of the living.

"I put all your things next door in the bedroom. Is your brain working yet?"

"It's working…but I'm not so sure that's a good thing. CC, what the hell happened? One minute everything's perfectly normal, I'm taking pictures, eating good food, I find my good friend making out with my boss, and then I find a gazillion-dollar shoe in my bag. That is sooooo not normal. And by the way…what happened to you and Mike hating the sight of each other?"

"I don't know! These things just happen. I had a couple of drinks, and Mike walked by and called me an 'ass biter.' Cupid works in mysterious ways."

I wasn't really listening to CC explain; I had opened the top of my bag *very* slowly and again found myself staring at a glittering mass of diamonds.

I was very close to treating CC to a weeping and wailing, "I'm going to prison" repeat performance but decided I'd do it later.

"CC," I whispered.

"I know, it's beautiful, isn't it?" She reached out a finger and ran it across the side of the shoe that wasn't still hidden in the bag.

"It's unbelievable. You know I didn't steal it, don't you, CC?"

"I know you didn't steal it, London…but how did it end up in your bag? This is *way* too scary. We need to figure this out and figure it out fast so I've come up with a plan. First thing we need to do is get some chocolate in here for you, you know, for medicinal purposes. I'm going to call out for some chocolate for you and some chocolate for me, but my kind is going to have a martini wrapped around it."

She had just gotten up to call the doorman to let him know that there would be a delivery arriving, when the intercom buzzed.

"Why would the doorman be buzzing me at one in the morning?"

I suddenly got panicky. *"He knows! He knows I have the shoe, and he's going to arrest me!"*

"London! He's a doorman, not a cop! Now zip it so that he doesn't get suspicious when I talk to him."

She punched the button on her intercom. "Yes, Anderson?"

"I'm sorry to bother you, Ms. Covington, but there's a Mr. Brandt and his friends here to see you."

CC turned to look at me. Her eyebrows were raised in surprise so high that they were lost somewhere up in her hairline.

She whispered to me, "What do you think? Should we let them up?"

"You can't say no; it would look suspicious."

She jabbed the button again and, in her most gracious voice, instructed Anderson to let them in.

The minute her finger was off the intercom button, she followed me into panic…*"What are we going to do? What are we going to do? Maybe they know you have the shoe!"*

She was flitting from me to the door, back and forth, back and forth.

"WE'RE GOING TO ACT NORMAL!!" I yelled at her.

I took a deep, slow breath. "We've got to stop this, CC. We can't keep taking turns freaking out. I'm losing track of whose turn it is to go crazy."

"OK, OK, OK, I'm relaxed, I'm calm, and I'm cool." She took her own deep breath. "Are you ready? Should I open the door now or wait till they get up here?" CC whispered.

"Wait," I hissed back at her. "I've gotta hide this!"

I pulled the stiletto out of my bag and looked around her pristine living room; there was absolutely no place to hide the thing. The doorbell rang, so I did the only thing I could think of...I threw it under the sofa cushion and sat on it. I stifled a gasp...the spiky heel was digging into my bottom. I grabbed the throw and quickly folding it, put it on top of the cushion, and sat down again. I wriggled around trying to find a position that wouldn't maim me for life and signaled for her to open the door.

Chapter 63

"Mike! What are you doing here and with an entourage no less?"

Sophie; her sister, Evangeline; and Eduardo pushed past Mike and kind of popped into the room all at the same time. Sophie and Evangeline stood over by the window, hugging the wall. Eduardo oozed his way around the room until he sank down next to me on the couch.

"I'm sorry to stop by so late, CC, but I wanted to see with my own eyes that you had made it home safely."

"Why wouldn't I have made it home safely?"

"It was so chaotic and crazy when you and London left me. I was just worried about you."

CC gave her body a little shake. "Getting home was no problem at all, darling; I'm a lot better than I was when I met up with the snake earlier."

"You met *the* snake? I kept hearing that there were *fifty* snakes in the room."

Sophie finally said her first words. She'd been standing as close to her sister as she could, and she looked a little green.

"CC threw that snake on *me*!"

Her face was starting to look really weird. It was getting dark red from what I was guessing was building anger, and that, combined with the green that had already been there, did not bode well. It also wasn't a good look with the color of her gown. Why was she wearing a different gown? That question was never going to get answered because the most important thing at that moment was to calm her down.

"Sophie, CC didn't throw that snake on you guys on purpose; she didn't even know it was there until she saw it in her purse!"

I felt kind of bad for Sophie. She'd been an innocent passer-by in the whole thing. If CC hadn't gotten her ring stuck in Sophie's hair, she'd probably be home right now curled up in some superspy jammies, happy as a clam.

Sophie was now turning an interesting shade of white.

"Evangeline, do you think you could help me over to the couch? I'm scared of heights, and being this close to the window is making me feel sick."

Evangeline helped her creep over to the couch, and she sank down next to me with a sigh. I think she also burped a little. I waved the air in front of my face, just in case.

It had been pretty quiet on the Eduardo side of the couch, so I glanced over, and he looked as if he was going to slide down onto the floor and take a nap...One thing we didn't need was him falling asleep and staying the night.

I jabbed him in the side with my elbow. "If you're here, Eduardo, where's Prissy?"

He gave a little burp and came back from wherever he had been drifting off to.

"My jewel of a sister left me to fend for myself when the great hysteria erupted at the gala. I assume she left with our driver, and there I languished, alone, resting in an alcove. If it hadn't been for Evangeline helping me to my feet and kindly assisting me to the driveway, I'd be lying there still."

"It's quite true, Miss Hart. Poor Mister Eduardo. I thought at first that he was a dead body, and I ran to check his pulse. I was so surprised when he pinched my bottom as I bent over him." She began to blush just the tiniest bit. "He wasn't a dead body, after all. He chased me all the way to the driveway, before I let him catch me."

I liked his version of events a whole lot better than hers. Gag. A change in subject seemed called for.

"So you all came in the same car?"

Mike gave me an excited play-by-play of what had happened after we left.

"You should have seen it! After they discovered the stiletto was stolen, people were running everywhere. They were running out through the French doors, back and forth across the stage...up and down the staircase...it was just pure bedlam! The valets were trying to help people get their cars, but a lot of people just jumped into cars with people who already had theirs. Sophie and I were stuck in a long line of traffic, trying to get off the property, and that's when Evangeline and Eduardo came running across the lawn and hopped into the car with us.

"My car actually got damaged during the whole mad scene! The woman who was using the scooter at the gala came buzzing up beside me and put a big long scratch down the side of my car with her cane! Crazy woman…by the time we got off St. Armands and up onto the bridge, she was already shooting across it and swearing at every car that passed her.

"When I get home, that woman and I are going to have a *long* talk…if she doesn't start controlling herself at these things, Mother is just going to have to move out. It's like living with an abusive two-year-old."

His *mother* was the ninja woman stopping people from bidding on the shoes she wanted? The ninja woman *lived* with him? CC and I were going to have to have a talk. She might want to rethink her new relationship with Mike.

Sophie's color had slowly been returning to normal while she listened to Mike. Eduardo, on the other hand, was not looking so good. He was looking green with a little yellow mixed in. I myself was getting increasingly uncomfortable. The business end of the stiletto was still making a pincushion out of me, and I wasn't going to be able to bear it much longer. As it turned out, I wasn't going to have to.

My purse had ended up on the floor next to my feet when I'd plopped myself down on the stiletto to hide it. Sophie was so short that her feet didn't reach the ground, and she was using it as a makeshift footstool. I'd paid way too much money for the beautiful bag to have it covered in smudgy footprints. I figured I could get it out from under her mouse-sized feet diplomatically, with no fuss, no muss.

"Here, Sophie, let me get that out of your way. Why don't I just tuck one of these pillows under your feet."

I put a nice big puffy pillow down for her and stashed my bag on the floor between Eduardo and myself. *Big* mistake. He had roused himself out of his stupor enough to repeat his tale of woe one more time…even though no one had asked to hear it again. Once again we heard how his sister had so ungraciously left him behind in an alcove. He reminded me of a seasoned war veteran regaling his audience with his daring deeds. He seemed to acquire a surge of energy and put everything he had into the line, "*When the great hysteria erupted!!*"

With that dramatic declaration, he reached down, picked up my beautiful bag, and put *everything* he had into it. *He* "erupted," and the contents of his unhappy stomach were now in my bag. And I'd been worried about Sophie's smudgy footprints getting on the bag…oh hell.

CHAPTER 64

woke up the next morning to find myself clutching the stiletto. I looked at the gleaming shoe in my hand and sat straight up. The Eduardo eruption episode with my purse flashed through my brain, and for a few seconds I got to relive that fun. Eduardo had no sooner done his evil deed in my purse than Mike had him up and out the door. The girls followed Mike, and CC locked the door behind them. After that I didn't remember a lot. Well, I did remember some things. I remembered throwing my befouled bag in the trash. I remembered CC giving me a hug and sending me off to the luxurious condo that would be all mine for the night. I vaguely remembered walking through the beautiful living room in a trance and then into the bedroom. I remembered crawling into bed, still in my beautiful gown.

Now it was morning, and I was awake. I crawled out of bed and put the stiletto under the mattress. Creeping down the hallway, I went next door and let myself into CC's condo. Remembering my manners, I knocked on her bedroom door while I nudged it open a little way.

"Are you awake in here?" I nudged the door open a little farther and peeked my head around the door.

"Sorry! Sorry! Sorry! Sorry! Sorry!" I was backing out of the room as fast as I could go.

Sometime after dropping his band of misfits off at their respective homes, Mike had doubled back and had a sleepover with CC.

I retreated back to my condo and grabbed a quick shower and tried to decide how long I should wait before I went back over and knocked on CC's door again. Since I wasn't going to be able to go over the events of the night before with CC, I was impatient to get home and hide away so that I could try to figure out what the heck was going on with my life. In particular, why people were getting murdered and why a shoe worth a fortune was now in my possession.

Just as I was about to head down the hallway and knock on CC's door again, she knocked on mine.

I gave her a wide-eyed look and my most innocent voice.

"Why, good morning! I didn't know you were up. I hope you weren't afraid last night, all alone in your big bed by yourself...I know you were worried that the shoe thief might come back in the middle of the night and jump up and down on us! I know no one came in and jumped up and down on me. Did anybody come in and jump up and down on—"

"Shut up, London."

Ooooh…she was being so *rude* to me!

She couldn't help herself…she gave me a little grin and fluffed her hair.

"Now don't go getting all obnoxious on me. Mike *was* worried and came back to make sure we'd be OK."

"Well, thank God he did! That measly little doorman weighing three hundred pounds and built like a linebacker, carrying an alarm button that sends an emergency alert straight to the police department is not nearly enough protection."

"Shut up, London! Now be serious for a minute…what are you going to do about the shoe?"

"We can't talk about this with Mike next door, CC. Right now I just want to get home and lock the door so that I can think without a parade of people coming in and out."

"Damn, I really want to talk about this now, and I really want to see the shoe again. OK, here's what we'll do… you take my car and head home. I'll spend the morning with Mike, and then I'll have him drive me out to your place later, and I'll pick up my car. Don't plan on going anywhere when I get there; we're going to figure this all out if we have to eat three pizzas to do it!"

I wasn't sure what three pizzas had to do with anything, but then again, she and Mike had been "sleeping" for a few hours, and maybe she was hungry from all the sleeping.

"Give me your keys, and I'll get out of here before Mike comes knocking on the door. He's not the type to come prancing out here in his underwear, is he?"

Putting her hand over my mouth and the keys in my hand, she said good-bye.

"Out, out, out…no more talk about my manly man."

"Oooooh, he's a 'manly' man! That's such personal information to be sharing. Is there anything else you want to tell me? I wondered about the size of those shoes…is it true—"?

"*Out!*"

I darted out of her reach, went back and picked up my overnight bag in the guest condo, grabbed the stiletto out from under the mattress, stuck it in the bag, and trotted back to her door. Sticking my head back in to let CC know that I was truly leaving, I blew her a kiss and headed home.

CHAPTER 65

I'd been home for an hour, before I came up with a plan for hiding the stiletto in a safe place. I didn't want it in the house in case the police came looking for it, and I *really* didn't want it in the house if the person who stole it came looking for it. I wasn't so worried about the police, but the thought that someone might know that it was *my* purse they'd put the shoe in really scared me.

In the interest of full disclosure, I need to tell you that I did have a partner in crime...Reckless. I decided to hide the fancy footwear in the tree that stood in the field next to the house. Getting into the field wasn't a problem, but getting up into the tree was. I stood and stared at it for about five minutes, wishing I was about three feet taller...then I could have reached the first branch and climbed on up into the tree. Just when I was about to give up, Reckless came ambling up to me and, I kid you not, looked up into the tree...as if trying to figure out what I found so interesting up there. Now was the time to put our friendship to the test.

"So here's the deal, Reckless…I need a way to get up into the tree. Do you trust me enough to let me get up on your back?"

He didn't say no, so I tucked my shirt into my pants and dropped the stiletto down into the back of my shirt. It wasn't comfortable, but at least I had my hands free for pulling myself up onto Reckless.

"Now I'm going to try to get up on you, so come over here by the fence. This is what I'd like to try to do…I'm going to climb up on the fence, and then I'll climb onto your back. Your job, if you should choose to accept it, is to not throw me off."

He didn't say no to this proposal, so I walked him over to the fence and started climbing.

"Here I come, I'm going to get on your back…good horsey…good horsey."

I was amazed…I was actually sitting on Reckless.

"Good boy, now we just need to get over by the tree."

I didn't have any reins, so I pressed my left knee into his side and kind of pulled on his mane, trying to steer him toward the right. He gave a big horse "sigh" and then walked the few feet to the tree.

"Are you ready for the next part, buddy? I'm going to grab the branch over my head, and then I'm going to stand up on your back…it'll be great, you'll love it, you'll be like a circus horse."

I was really hoping he'd feel like a circus horse and not the cannon that they shoot people out of at the circus. If he got tired of taking orders from me, he could buck me off in a heartbeat. I decided to start bribing him.

"I'm going to buy you some great horse treats if you'll just put up with me a little longer. Maybe for Christmas we could find you a nice horse blanket and a fancy name tag for your stall door."

I'd been working on pulling myself up to a standing position using the tree branch the whole time I was talking, and legs shaking, I was now standing upright on Reckless's bare back. Keeping up my stream of chatter, I pulled myself up onto the branch. Woo-hoo! I climbed up a few more branches and found a good place to stash the shoe. I had it wedged into a spot where a lot of branches all came together, making kind of a nest, when I heard a vehicle off in the distance.

I parted the leaves on the tree and peeked out. I wasn't the only one interested in who was coming for a visit. Reckless abandoned his post and, walking a little farther down the fence, looked back up at me.

"Don't look at me! Don't look at me! Whoever it is, I don't want them to know that I'm up here!"

Reckless turned away and looked back toward whoever was coming. I left him in charge of being the lookout, while I tried to stay as still as possible. I heard a truck door slam and held my breath.

"Hey, there...where's your lady friend?" My visitor was none other than Ryder.

I heard him walk up onto the porch and knock on the door…I was tempted to call down, "Yoo-hoo, I'm up in the tree, and I've got a really huge problem," besides being the kind of person who hides in trees. Would he believe me if I told him all about finding the stiletto in my purse and that I had no idea how it got there? Probably not, since I was in the process of hiding the shoe in a tree. I kept my mouth shut and let him knock on the door for a while longer.

Finally tired of knocking and getting no response, I heard his boots on the steps. He started talking to Reckless, and peering down I could see him giving the horse's ears a good scratching.

"Not such a bad life being retired, is it? I'd much rather be spending my day like you are, instead of being in the trouble I'm in now."

Ryder was in trouble? I heard him walk away, and then the truck door slammed shut. I waited until he was gone and began trying to figure out how I was going to get out of the tree. I tried coaxing Reckless back over to the tree again, but would he come over and help a poor girl? No, sir, he would not. I had to make my exit from the tree entirely on my own, so I lowered myself as far as I could and then dropped to the ground.

With the stiletto safely hidden, I turned my thoughts to something Ryder had said to Reckless. Why had Ryder said he was in trouble, and did it have anything to do with the shiny "sparkler" that I had just hidden in the tree?

I was sitting on the porch swing and decided that I couldn't process all the craziness going on...CC would come over later and help me with that. What I could do meanwhile—what I *needed* to do—was take a nap. I wandered into the house, and on the way to the bedroom, I remembered that I had some chocolate syrup in the fridge. I grabbed the chocolate and a few chunks of cheese to drizzle it on (don't knock it until you've tried it) and settled down for a catnap.

It seemed as if my head had just hit the pillow, when I heard someone knocking on my front door. I moved Handsome over and glanced at the clock; I'd been asleep for two hours.

"London! Open the door!" CC was pounding on the door and sounded borderline panicky.

"I'm coming, I'm coming!" I unlocked the door and wrenched it open.

"I've been pounding on your door for five minutes! I was scared to death!"

"Why were you scared to death?"

"Have you forgotten that there's a shoe thief out there missing a shoe? I think it's safe to assume that they're probably kind of anxious to get it back. When you didn't answer, I was afraid that they'd already been here! Don't scare me like that *again*!"

She pushed past me and threw her purse on the sofa.

"What have you got to drink? I'm a wreck; I was so scared for you...anything...I'll take anything...I need to calm my nerves."

"The only thing I've got besides water is an energy drink…in the state you're in, I don't think that would be a good idea."

"Give it to me! They don't bother me at all; I've had five in one afternoon, and they had no effect on me whatsoever."

"CC, I *really* don't think that's a good idea."

"*Give it to me!*"

I gave it to her.

Chapter 66

Satisfied that she'd gotten her drink *and* gotten her way, she threw herself down on the sofa. Pulling a notebook out of her purse and flipping to a brand-new, pristine page, she then fished around in her purse and found a pen. She turned into one serious individual the minute she jammed on the glasses that had been perching on the top of her head.

"Okay…let's get started."

"Started with what?"

"The solving of the crime, the investigating, the figuring it all out. First, where's the stiletto?"

"I'm not telling you."

"What do you mean you're not telling me?"

"I'm not telling you because you'll be safer if I don't tell you."

"Stop being so dramatic, now let the investigation commence. We are now officially detectives, and we're going to figure out at exactly what point in time your life went off the rails."

"I don't think my life has gone off the—"

"Shut up. Your life's gone off the rails. You used to have a normal life, and then the minute you started working for the magazine, it started careening out of control… Oooh! That's it! The starting point was when you started working for the magazine!"

She took her pen and wrote a giant ONE on the left side of the page. I watched as she printed out in capital letters: MAGAZINE STARTS THE SPIRAL OF DEATH.

"What the hell? I'm not in 'the Spiral of Death!'"

"I'm making a totally valid, accurate statement. *You* didn't die, but I can name a few people who have! Does the name Toni the Tuna mean anything to you? I'm pretty sure she experienced the spiral of death. How about Monique? Spiral again."

"Well, if you want to get all picky about it…fine! They got sucked into the spiral of death."

Detective CC was really getting into the deduction game.

"So…if I was a detective, I would think it was really suspicious that every time you go to someone's house to shoot pictures, somebody dies."

"*Hey!* You've been there right along with me…if *I* look suspicious, *you* look suspicious, too!"

"Why would I look suspicious?" CC looked as if the idea had never occurred to her before.

I decided it was time for Twinkbutt to wake up and smell the coffee.

"*You* look suspicious because you wore opera gloves the entire time we were at Monique's place, and you flat out told the police you were wearing gloves. They're going to think you wore the gloves to make sure you didn't leave any fingerprints!"

"They wouldn't think that! Why would a guilty person *tell* them up front that they were wearing gloves?"

"A guilty person might tell the police that in order to make the police think they're just an innocent dope, when all the while they're *actually* a scheming murderer trying to fool 'the man.' But on every show I've ever seen, the cops have been pretty good at spotting liars."

"*Hey! I resent that!*" CC's face was turning red...I took that to be a sign of anger. "*I'm not a liar!*"

"Time out, *time out*! Sorry...that didn't come out the way I wanted it to. I didn't mean that you're a liar and a murderer. I know you're innocent, you know I'm innocent...we just need to figure out who's guilty. Somewhere out there a killer and a shoe thief are running around loose. Not to mention the attacker who's out there."

"An attacker?" CC turned a laser-like stare on me. "What attacker?"

"Well, I never told you this, but the night before we did the photo shoot at Monique's, somebody attacked me."

"*What? Did they hurt you? Why didn't you tell me?*"

"I didn't want to talk about it; I think I just was too scared…I don't know."

"Well, did you at least call the police?" CC's face was getting redder by the minute.

"No. I should have, but I didn't. Nothing's happened since then, so let's just forget about it."

"Nothing's happened since then…*nothing's happened SINCE then? Just Monique getting killed, Rey getting knocked out, and a gazillion-dollar shoe being planted in your purse! You're totally right…nothing's happened since then!*"

I didn't say anything. What could I say? She was absolutely right, and I felt absolutely stupid.

"I'm adding this to our list of incidents…and we're not done discussing this…we need to tell the police this…and by the way…you're an idiot." CC gave a sniff and started clicking her pen furiously.

"Okay, let's start over…we need a clue…any little thing to get us started."

Crisis averted…she was still speaking to me.

CC went to the fridge to get another "Volcano." Make fun of the name all you want, but if you need energy, that's your drink.

I needed a couple of things, and none of them was an energy drink. I needed to figure out how the shoe ended up in my bag…the murders the police could deal with. I needed to figure out how to get the shoe back to whoever owned it or else turn it into the police without anyone knowing that I was the one who returned it. Briefly a thought crossed my mind…Would I have been better off to have just held up the shoe at the gala and yelled, "Oh hey! Here's the shoe! In my purse! Can I keep it?" I was never going to know how that would have turned out. The fact was I had the shoe…it was in a tree…I had to get rid of it.

"London…" CC was clicking her pen again. "We need to go over what happened at the gala, see if we noticed anything or anybody that looked suspicious. Do you think you've got any pictures on the camera that would help?"

"I always check the images I've taken as I go along… there's nothing on there. I *did* hear quite a few people say weird things, and as far as I'm concerned, they were *doing* weird things."

CC sat up straighter and drained the rest of her drink.

"Who said weird things?"

"Trey and Chesty."

CC me her full attention. "No way…what did they say?"

"They were having an argument, and she was really letting him have it. She said something about giving him two jobs to do and that he messed things up. He called her out for not helping him and said that 'once he finished the job,' he never wanted to work with her again."

CC stared off into space. "She gave him two jobs to do…and he's not finished yet…Oh dear God…could they be the murderers? Two *jobs*! Two murder scenes! Maybe Trey's a contract killer, and Chesty hired him, and London…*he still has one killing to go!*"

"I just remembered something else, CC. I was talking to Prissy earlier at the gala, and she told me that there have been rumors that Chesty has a criminal past. You told me yourself that she has an edge to her...that she might be the type to get violent."

CC took the pen and with shaking fingers wrote down, "Chesty and Trey." She cleared her throat and muttered "dear God" to herself.

"We don't have any proof that they've committed the crimes, so that's a problem that we're going to have to deal with, London. We can decide later which of us is going to start stalking them or if we're both going to do it. So you said that somebody had been doing weird things. Who was that?"

"Back up the train just one minute, CC. Neither one of us is going to start stalking people who we think might be murderers!"

"We're detectives, London; that's what we do!"

"*We're not detectives, CC!*"

She sniffed and ignored me. "The person doing weird things?"

"Trey. He's not just been saying things that are weird... he's acting weird, threatening. He and Ryder got into a fight at the gala after Trey got nasty with me."

"Trey got nasty with you, and they fought?"

"Big time. He grabbed me by the arm and said I had something he wanted. He was going to make me leave with him. I thought he was drunk or something, and I pulled my arm away from him, but he wasn't taking no for an answer, and all of a sudden Ryder was there. Talk about a testosterone festival…they went after each other like cavemen. I took off, and that's how I ended up interrupting your 'moment' with Mike. Now here's another weird part…that's not the first time he's acted strangely."

"He did something *before*? I want to hear what happened, but we're definitely talking about the testosterone festival later…that sounds intriguing."

"Trey came over to the house one afternoon. At first he was just really flirty, and when that didn't work, he got annoying."

"*What?*"

"Yeah, he showed up here and just followed me into the house. I was in no mood for his 'macho man' garbage, so I suggested we go out onto the porch. I really didn't want to get stuck in the house with him. He said he needed to use the men's room, so I went outside, and while he was supposedly in the bathroom, he was actually searching my bedroom…for what, I don't know. Anyway, when he came outside, he made it clear that he wanted us to be together, and as he so eloquently put it…he was willing to play 'the dating game' in order to get what he wanted. I told him to leave, he got pushy, and I kicked him in his 'nuggets.'"

"*Whoa!* I like your style, Ms. Hart…I like your style."

"If I'd known that he had just trashed my bedroom, I would have kicked him a whole lot harder. What could I possibly have that he'd want? I barely know the guy."

CC took her pen and wrote a large TWO on the side of the page. Then beside it she wrote…WHAT DOES TREY WANT LONDON FOR BESIDES SEX?

"Cross out that sex part! Just seeing it on the page freaks me out!"

"*No!* Sex stays in…sex is *always* involved in a crime… *always.*"

"You do realize that what you just said makes no sense at all, right? I mean, if somebody shoplifts a pack of gum, is sex involved in that?"

CC popped the top on another "Volcano" and chugged some down.

"Sure, sex is involved. People steal gum so that their breath will smell good…why do they want their breath to smell good? They want their breath to smell good so that people will find them attractive. If a person steals *two* packs of gum…*bingo!* They want to have sex."

If I didn't get her interested in another motive, her logic was going to make my head explode. Her detective skills were veering more off course with every energy drink she consumed.

I threw out my own theory. "Aside from the sex component as a motive, I know I've heard that money could be one…don't you think that's the motive with the stiletto at least? I mean somebody had to be looking to make money off it. They were probably going to somehow get the jewels off and then sell them."

"Unless the thief was planning to sell the shoe to a crazy shoe collector, I don't know what else they could do with the shoe besides sell off the diamonds." CC shot out the sentence at breakneck speed, and her thought process seemed to go right off the rails.

"Although, jealousy is always a really big motive...and don't forget revenge...revenge is *really* big in the motive department! How about *betrayal*? I think betrayal could be a motive!"

I sat there watching her, getting more and more confused. She'd jumped up from the couch and was pacing furiously back and forth. Suddenly she whirled around...she had been flipping her pen back and forth between her fingers so fast that when she changed direction, it went whipping out of her hand and knocked a picture off the wall.

Without missing a beat, she screamed at me...

"WHO DID YOU BETRAY?"

She kind of took me by surprise with that one, and I screamed right back at her. "I DIDN'T BETRAY ANYBODY...! AND WHAT DOES BETRAYAL HAVE TO DO WITH STEALING A SHOE?"

"EXACTLY! Exactly? Sorry, I'm getting the shoe thing mixed up with the murder thing. I don't know what's going on in my head...I'm just so wired all of a sudden."

"I think *you* are experiencing a little revenge...the revenge of the Volcanoes. You really shouldn't drink any more of that stuff."

She plopped herself back down onto the sofa and fanned herself. "I'm hot...I'm, like, totally overheated. Can you turn the air conditioner up a little?"

I got up and walked over to the thermostat thingy on the wall and poked at the dial. It was right next to the front door, and I nearly jumped out of my skin when someone knocked loudly on the door.

CC jumped up from the couch. "Be careful, London... it could be the shoe-fetish person! Aaagh! *Why is it so hot in here? I'm so hot!*"

She was also *so* nuts. Just as I opened the door to find Ryder standing there, CC pulled off her blouse. Well, crap. I was really hoping that the sight of her wouldn't make *him* hot.

Chapter 67

It turned out I didn't have to worry about that...the moment Ryder registered what he was looking at, he did an about-face and walked right back out the door. Once he'd reached the safety of the porch, he covered his eyes and turned his head toward me.

"London, could I talk to you for a minute?"

I slipped out onto the porch and pulled the door shut behind me.

"Nice show you've got going on in there."

"Come back at ten...that's when she juggles poodles."

He reached out and wrapped his hand around mine. Pulling me closer, he didn't say another word. He just gave me the searching look that was now becoming familiar and gave me a long, lingering kiss. When I came up for air, I had to take a step or two backward.

We just stood and looked at each other. The look and the kiss were different from the others...the look we shared said, "I know you; I've been waiting for you."

This sounds so corny, but in those moments that our eyes did all the talking, something was settled. It sounds ridiculous, but right then and there, I knew. The look in his eyes had told me he would always be there. The searching look was gone, and if I had anything to do with it, it would never come back. I thought I needed a second kiss, when the door behind us burst open...CC's eyes were bugging out of her head...not her best look.

"GET IN HERE, AND FIX THE AIR CONDITIONER!!!" At least she had her blouse back on.

I have to hand it to Ryder...he walked back into the house and right up to CC.

"We haven't met...I'm Ryder; it's nice to meet you." He reached out to shake her hand, and she latched on to him with a grip so tight I saw him wince. Somehow she managed to flap the bottom of her blouse up and down with the other hand.

"Did it just get a whole lot hotter in here?" She was totally checking Ryder out from head to toe. She could have stopped with the blouse flapping any time as far as I was concerned. Every time she lifted her blouse, we got a peek at her taut, toned abs.

Ryder pried his hand out of hers and with a polite "excuse me," eased himself around her and into the house. We both watched him stride into the kitchen and head for the refrigerator. Grabbing the orange juice, he found a glass in the cupboard and helped himself. He turned around to find both of us watching him.

"Sorry. I've been on the move all day, and I haven't had time to eat or drink anything."

"Will a frozen pizza help? I'm pretty much out of everything else."

I set the oven to bake and started pulling things out of the fridge to use as toppings…I always like to add a few extras…extra cheese, extra pepperoni. The last topping that I decided to add was my new favorite…cherry tomatoes.

CC had gone off to find a cool cloth to put on her forehead, so it was just Ryder and I—alone—in the kitchen. I decided to see how good his memory was, so I washed the little tomatoes off and laid them on the counter. I took my time finding a knife to slice them with. I didn't make eye contact with him or say a word, but I felt him move in next to me. He passed the memory test.

He stood for a moment, studying them, and then he picked up the tiniest tomato. Turning to me, he reached out a finger and tugged the top of my blouse toward him just a bit. Just like that, he dropped the ripe little morsel into the opening. I could feel it slide down and come to rest nestled in my cleavage. *Wowza!* Now *I* was feeling hot.

Timing is everything…CC pranced back into the kitchen, and she looked a little cooler. I, on the other hand, had a little problem…I had a tomato in my blouse and burning cheeks.

"Did I miss anything while I was gone?"

Keeping my face turned away from her, I made an excuse to get out of the room.

"Nope, not a thing…I'll be right back; I need to get something out of my purse."

I kept my back to her and made sure not to make eye contact with Ryder. No way could I look into those eyes right now.

I zipped into my bedroom and retrieved the tomato from inside my blouse and placed it next to Handsome on my night table. I was going to keep it forever. It was my favorite lucky charm of all time. At least I thought I was going to keep it forever, until CC appeared next to me, picked up the tomato, and popped it into her mouth. She moved it to the inside of her cheek and talked around it.

"So what's going on between you and 'His Hotness?'"

She hadn't taken a bite out of the tomato yet, so there was still a chance.

"CC! Spit that out!"

"Spit what out?"

"The tomato! That was a special tomato!"

She took my hand and spit the tomato into it.

"A little less spit would have been nice!"

My hand was totally nasty, and I ran into the bathroom to wash it off. My special tomato disappeared down the drain.

I stood at the sink for a moment…mourning the loss of my tomato.

When I came back into the bedroom, CC was still there, manically fluffing up Handsome's mane.

"You didn't answer my question. What's going on with you and tall, dark, and delicious?"

"Let's talk about this later, when he's not standing five feet away, okay?"

"Fine...have you noticed how good he smells?"

"Keep your nose to yourself. From now on, I'm the only one with 'sniffing' privileges."

I took Handsome away from her and dragged her back into the living room.

Ryder gave us both a look. "After you two are done deciding who gets to smell me, we need to talk."

Oh, what the hell...I did what I considered to be a sexy little walk over to him and sniffed his neck. "Please...talk away."

He didn't smile, and that made me nervous. I sat down on the sofa next to CC and held my breath.

"Were you two together last night?"

"We drove back to CC's, and I spent the night there."

"Were you together the entire evening?"

"Well, sort of...she stayed in her condo, and I stayed in her guest condo."

I guess I gave the wrong answer, because Ryder rubbed his hand across his eyes and looked even more serious than before.

"Damn."

I didn't like the sound of that word at all, and the look on his face wasn't inspiring confidence.

"What's going on, Ryder?" I didn't get an answer, just another question.

"What's the last thing that you saw when you left the gala last night?"

"I don't know about CC, but I saw Ralph draped over Sophie and Tralenka, and then the whole room just went nuts."

"That's what I saw, too," CC volunteered. "It was like a massive stampede; people were totally freaking out. I mean *totally* freaking out!"

"Who's Ralph, and why was he draped over two people?"

"Ralph is a black snake that I've seen at the mansion the two times that I've been there."

"What happened to Ralph after he landed on—who was it—Sophie and somebody?"

Luckily for me, CC had an answer ready for him. I was beginning to get nervous, and the less I said, the better.

"We didn't stop to look; we just kind of got swept up in the tide of people running."

CC gave me a look…just a little warning look to make sure I wouldn't blurt out that, in reality, we were making our escape with a multimillion-dollar piece of footwear in our possession.

"Look, Ryder, I don't know about, London, but you're making me nervous. Why all the questions about where we were and what we saw? And why do you want to know what happened to the snake? Is the snake part of the gang of thieves? Is the snake a *pet* that belongs to one of the thieves? I wish we'd taken that snake with us so that we could question it."

I gave CC a closer look; she sounded as if she really did want to know if the snake might have belonged to the thieves.

Ryder brushed off the snake questions.

"Last night, someone managed to steal one of the stilettos…right in front of about five hundred potential witnesses. So far the police can't find anyone who saw anything.

"I was still there when the police came, and I ended up getting questioned. Everyone who was still on the property did. You'll probably get a visit from the police pretty soon; they're going to want to know where you were at the time of the theft." He gave a sigh and ran his hands through his hair. "What a mess."

I was turning all this over in my mind and wondering just how long it would take for the police to show up. I also hoped that it wouldn't be a windy day when they did come to question me…it wouldn't be cool to have the stiletto fall out of the tree while they were knocking on my door. Maybe I could go down to the police station and "volunteer" to tell them what little I knew. Well, everything except the stuff about the shoe. *My* mama didn't raise no fool.

CC had been twitching around in her chair while we learned about the police and the questioning. As soon as

Ryder paused for breath, CC was peppering him with questions again.

"Where were *you* when the shoe was stolen, and why are you acting like *we're* the thieves? And another thing... did you really go after that guy Trey and punch his lights out? Who won the fight? Did you have to rip your shirts off in the heat of battle, because your abs and pecs were all *sweaty* and *glistening* in the glow of the chandeliers? You can answer that later, but right now I *demand* that you apologize to us. Who are *you* to impugn our dignity? Insinuating that we would *steal* from a charity event? Do you really think that we would do something so *heinous*, something so *vile*, something so *low*? I am *offended*, sir! I am *offended* on *so* many levels! I am *offended* on behalf of my sweet little friend London here *and the entire human race*! I am *offended* on behalf of *Ralph* the snake! Such an *innocent*, such a *lamb...I am...*not feeling so hot."

She had her hand on her chest, and the color of her face didn't look so good. Getting up off the couch, she staggered back to my bedroom.

Ryder had listened to her tirade without any change of expression at all, until she put her hand to her chest. He was suddenly on high alert. He watched her make her exit, and then he followed her quietly into the bedroom...I was right behind him.

Chapter 68

CC had curled up on my bed and taken her shirt off again. Ryder didn't even seem to notice. He approached the bed.

"I'm going to see how many miles an hour your pulse is going, just lie here quietly." He gently took her wrist and felt for her pulse.

"Have you taken anything, CC?"

She snapped at him. *"Are you asking me if I did drugs?"*

He ignored her and turned to me. "Has she taken something, London?"

"Way too many energy drinks."

"Well, that would explain the runaway heart rate."

"What should we do? Should we take her to the hospital?"

CC barked at us, *"Hey! Hello! Anybody want my opinion?* I'm *not* going to the hospital. They'll take blood and urine samples, and I don't give away my bodily fluids to just *anybody,* thank you very much!"

Ryder spoke quietly, "Tell you what, CC. I'll make a quick call to a friend of mine…he's a cardiac specialist up in Sarasota. He can tell me if you need to get checked out at the hospital…if he says you need to go, you go, deal?"

She made him wait for an answer for one full minute, and then she caved. "Deal."

Satisfied, he went back into the living room to make the call, and I sat down on the bed next to her. Her beautiful face was flushed, and her eyes seemed to be vibrating. I held her hand, all ready to comfort her and calm her. My nurturing instincts didn't last long.

"*Holy cow! How could anyone resist those eyes?* If he turned on the heat behind them, a girl could just go up in smoke. There's something about his voice too…when he lowers it and talks softly like that…oooh baby! And his bedside manner! Have you made an appointment with him for a complete physical? I'm telling you, London, he could play doctor with me *any* day!"

I dropped her hand as if it were a hot potato. "You should never, *ever*, drink that energy stuff again."

Ryder's timing was perfect. His return forced me to stop before I said something that I might regret. The news was good…the cardiologist said her pulse was definitely elevated, but she could avoid a trip to the hospital if she stayed in bed and stress free for a bit.

As soon as Ryder gave her the news, CC took charge of her "recuperation" and gave us our orders.

"Both of you, *out*! I have to have quiet, and you two are just *total* drama queens. You're sucking the life forces out of me with your drama. You heard my cardiologist's orders...I'm not to be disturbed...I'm in a fragile state... *Leave me in peace!*"

She didn't have to ask me twice...I was *more* than happy to give her some space. I was out of there faster than you could say, "My friend is a total loon."

We were sucking the life out of *her*? I felt like someone had removed everything resembling a muscle in my body and my brain...dealing with her manic behavior had exhausted me.

The pizza had long ago gone cold, but it was still calling my name...I pulled two plates out of the cupboard and transferred two slices onto each one. Ryder had poured us each a drink and led the way back into the living room. This was a "park your feet on the coffee table and your plate on your lap" kind of night.

I don't think we said a word until we were both done. One...we were both so hungry that talking would have definitely gotten in the way of devouring our food. Two...I don't think either one of us was brave enough to risk disturbing the bitchy bear in the next room.

Finished with his pizza, Ryder began to communicate without speaking. He put a finger to his tongue, licked it, and, reaching out, dabbed up dried pizza crumbs that were scattered across my chest. Well, two could play that game. I grabbed his finger and licked the crumbs off; I don't know why.

You should have seen the look in his eyes when I did that…I get shivery all over just thinking about it. I put a finger to my lips and whispered at him.

"Behave yourself! I need to talk to you, and I can't if you get me all distracted!"

He whispered back at me, "Woof."

"Don't try to sidetrack me with that kind of sexy talk, mister…this is serious."

I concentrated on giving him my most stern look and took our empty plates out to the kitchen.

I'd just rinsed them off, when I felt two hands slip around my waist.

"Woof."

The warm breath that sent the word into my ear had me leaping across the kitchen to a safe zone, to be precise, a zone safe for him. He had been a millisecond away from me starting to act like a monkey with a cupcake. He, of course, would be the unfortunate cupcake.

I had decided to confess almost all of what had been going on with the shoe, but he was definitely making it difficult to focus. I took a deep breath.

Maybe it was the carbs from the pizza making me feel all calm and trusting…I don't know. Something had changed my mind about confiding in Ryder…it was either the pizza or the kiss out on the porch. I couldn't explain it; regardless of the reason, I just trusted him. I took a deep breath and tippy-toed into a more realistic version of the truth about "stiletto night."

"Ryder, you know how CC and I told you that we just got swept up in the mob of people trying to get out of the mansion? Well…we did…but we thought we had more reason to run than everybody else."

"You thought *you* had more reason to run than everybody else. What reason?"

"A *really* good reason…at least we thought it was a good reason…I mean, everybody has their own idea of what makes a good reason. Oh crap…there's just no good way to say this. The shoe was in my purse. I found the stiletto in my purse, and I don't know how it got there! Almost everything that had been in the bag was gone, and instead, the freaking shoe was in there!

"I kind of went into shock, I guess, when I found the shoe, and I didn't know what to do. I mean, would anybody have believed me if I just walked up and said, 'Oh hey, this megabucks shoe just magically appeared in my bag.' I just felt like everyone would think I'd taken the stiletto and that I'd gotten cold feet and decided to give it back. I figured if they called the police, I'd get arrested. All the police need is for me to be involved in one more suspicious situation and they're going to be convinced that I'm a total criminal. I started to panic, so I found CC, and she decided we should sneak out and go to her house and decide what to do. I know this doesn't sound good, *but I didn't steal the shoe!*"

I was pretty proud of myself. I'd laid the facts before Ryder, most of them anyway, and he hadn't even blinked.

And then he blinked.

And then he stood up.

And then he started looking through my kitchen cabinets.

"What are you looking for?"

"Scotch."

So maybe things weren't going as well as I thought. After I'd dug out my emergency Scotch and poured him a drink, he got back down to business.

"So you had the shoe, and you went to CC's place. And then what happened?"

I just couldn't bring myself to tell him that the shoe was up in the tree outside. I'd thought earlier that I could totally trust him, but I couldn't help myself...I chickened out.

"We went to her place, and when we got there, the stiletto wasn't in my bag anymore."

"Where was it?"

"Well, somewhere between the mansion and CC's in Sarasota. I mean it *could* still be at the mansion, but I doubt it. When CC and I took off running, a valet guy bumped into me...maybe the shoe fell out then. Now that I think about it, when we ran around the house, back to the parking garage, we took a shortcut through some shrubs, and my purse got caught up in some sticky things. I had to yank on it really hard to get it loose, so it could have fallen out then. I don't know how it happened, but the stiletto is gone."

I know…I lied…I lied to him big-time. Having concocted my little web of lies, I sat waiting for Ryder's reaction. It was all I could do to keep myself from putting my hands over my eyes and then peeking out through my fingers at him. Just like a little kid afraid to see what was going to happen next. Luckily for me, his cell phone rang.

"Do you mind if I take this?"

I shook my head no and took a second to go listen for sounds from my bedroom…CC wasn't making a peep. Hopefully, the volcanoes had worn off a bit and her manic behavior was a thing of the past. I really hoped she'd stay asleep until Ryder left. I needed to tell her about lying to Ryder; we needed to have our stories straight.

I turned around to find Ryder standing almost right behind me. Something was wrong…very wrong. His eyes had gone deep and dark and dead serious.

"What is it? Ryder, what's happened?"

"Jett Brannigan's been murdered, and the police are looking for you. They're up at the ranch office, and they'll be here in about a minute."

CHAPTER 69

I **was on** the porch swing watching the squad car pull up in front of the house, while Ryder waited at the bottom of the steps. I had decided that there was a better chance of not disturbing CC if I talked to the police outside. I hoped we'd have a nice little chat, and then they'd be on their way. Two officers climbed out of the car and walked toward the steps.

"Hey, Ryder…we missed you at the Brass Rail Thursday night."

Now this was an interesting turn of events. The Brass Rail was a bar that not too many "civilians" frequented. It was pretty much a cop hangout…and it sounded as if Ryder was an honorary member…like I said, interesting.

"Sorry I missed it, Coop. I heard Martz got handcuffed naked to a telephone pole on Albee Road. You trying to hurt Pelican Sunset's business by spoiling the customers' appetites?"

"Don't look at me; I'm pleading the fifth…I had nothing to do with it…I was never there!"

Having declared his innocence, the cop named Coop looked over at me and put on his cop face. (Say that ten times real fast.)

"Are you London Hart?"

I got a little dizzy, but I managed an answer. "Yes, I'm London."

"Ms. Hart, we're here to take you down to the station for questioning in regard to the death of Mr. Jett Brannigan."

To tell the truth, I really wasn't too worried about going downtown. The sooner we left, the better as far as I was concerned. The wind was picking up, and the leaves of the "stiletto tree" were starting to rustle in the breeze. Rustling in the breeze was okay…the tree swaying back and forth in the wind and dropping the stiletto to the ground right in front of everyone was not okay.

"Can I just take a second to leave a note for my friend? I don't want her to wake up and worry about me being gone."

I guess I didn't look like too much of a flight risk, because Coop gave me a nod, and I headed into the house. "Back later" written on an envelope was the most CC was going to get. I grabbed my bag and locked the door behind me on the way out.

Before I could make a move to get into the patrol car, Ryder reached out and took me by the elbow. Making it look totally casual and natural, he steered me toward his truck.

"Since you're all just going to have a little talk, we'll meet you boys at the station."

His cop buddies looked a little disappointed. Maybe they'd been hoping for some friendly conversation on the drive back into town…you know, like a full confession.

I climbed into Ryder's truck and cleared a spot in the straw that was scattered all over the seat. I felt kind of like a chicken settling down into my nest. Ryder pulled in behind his Brass Rail buddies, and we sped away from the ranch. We were headed for Sarasota on I-75, ripping north.

"What's with these guys? They're driving kind of fast."

Ryder had a grim look on his face yet again.

"The murder of Jett Brannigan is a high-profile case. There's going to be national and international repercussions, so the sooner they can announce that they've got a suspect on the five o'clock news, the better it will be for them."

We were almost back to Sarasota, and traffic was forcing our little motorcade to slow down.

Ryder reached over and squeezed my hand. "Do you have a lawyer?"

"Do you think I'm going to need one? I wasn't anywhere near Brannigan last night."

"I believe you, but from what you told me, you were in CC's guest condo without an alibi for a few hours."

"Damn, damn, damn. You're right."

Ryder gave my hand another squeeze. "Remember this while they're talking to you. If you're not being charged with a crime, you can leave at any time."

I thought about that the rest of the way there.

Ryder found a space in the "guest" parking lot, and I slid out of the truck and walked to the building. He hurried ahead of me to hold the door, but I waved him in first...no sense in hurrying to my doom.

I'd barely gotten through the door, when people started laughing and whistling. I was in denial for about half a minute, but there was no ignoring the finger pointing... they were definitely laughing at *me*! I could feel my blood start to boil as the laughter got louder, and I almost jumped out of my skin when I felt someone run his hands all over my bottom. What the hell?

Ryder was behind me and was so close that he was almost in front of me. Obviously he was "the groper."

"Excuse me, but this is a helluva time to play 'grab ass,'" I said as I slapped his hands away.

That's when he held up his hands...they were full of straw.

Damn! I turned in a circle, trying to see my backside. How could I have not noticed? I had straw all over my rear and inside the legs of my jeans. I looked as if a scarecrow had thrown up on me. Why does this stuff always happen to me? I want to glide through a room, grace and beauty personified. Instead I usually look as if I've been pulled through a hedge backward. My lying, two-faced bathroom mirror makes me think I look good before I leave the house. I get outside and drive two miles, and that brutal bitch, my rearview mirror, tells me the truth.

My new cop pals got down to business right away. They got me all comfy in a metal chair with a rigid back. Being questioned was fun...not. I learned some stuff...they learned almost no stuff.

I learned Jett was found in his bed wearing nothing but a neat little hole in his head. I learned my beautiful little camera lucky charm from CC was sitting on the nightstand next to his bed.

They had already learned that "The love that never leaves" was engraved on my little lucky charm.

I learned that right next to my now "unlucky charm" camera was a framed photograph of me.

They learned that I wasn't going to do a whole lot of talking.

They did a fair amount of talking.

"Were you sleeping with Jett Brannigan? When did you become lovers? Did you have a lover's quarrel? Was he awake when you put the hole in his head? What'd you do with the gun? Did he find out that you stole the stiletto and so you had to kill him to shut him up? Did you kill him because he had a tattoo on his butt that said 'I love Mona?'"

Trying to keep my voice from shaking, I gave them answers.

"No, we weren't lovers; I didn't know the man. There was no quarrel. I didn't put a hole in his head. I never had a gun. I didn't 'steal' the stiletto. Who the hell tattoos 'I love Mona' on their *butt?*"

I had a question for them.

"Am I under arrest?"

Coop looked sad. "No."

"Then I'm out of here."

Chapter 70

had finally started to relax as we drove back onto the ranch, but as it turned out, that wasn't going to last long. We opened the front door and found CC standing over Trey. It didn't take a rocket scientist to figure out that she had beaned him with a brass horse that she stood holding in her hand. I'd been using it for a doorstop and was really surprised that all along it had actually been a weapon.

"He was breaking in!" CC whispered. "He was breaking in, and I did what I had to do. No jury in the world will convict me."

"CC, in case you haven't noticed, he's not dead. There's not going to be any jury."

Trey was slumped against the wall holding his head, and in a split second Ryder had him. Taking him by the front of his shirt, he dragged him up the wall to a standing position and held him there.

"I'm sure that you have an excellent reason for break-ing into London's home."

Trey just shook his head no.

"Now listen up. I didn't get to the gym today, and you've got punching bag written all over you. Tell me why you broke in here."

If Ryder had looked at me like that, I would have told him my entire life history. There's also a distinct possibility that I might have been so scared that I would have tinkled a little.

Apparently the blow on the head had damaged Trey's sense of self-preservation, because he lifted his middle fin-ger and aimed it at Ryder.

That did it for me. I figured the time for talking was over, and I kicked Trey where it counted, just like I had the last time he was in my house. He slipped from Ryder's grasp to the floor and rolled up into a little ball of "ouchy."

"What are you doing here, Trey?" I demanded.

"Protecting myself," he squeaked out.

"What do you mean, protecting yourself?"

He took a shallow breath and squeaked some more. "I wanted to get hold of the images you took at Monique's house."

"And why would you want to do that?"

"I wanted to find them and get rid of them before the police came looking for them."

"And they would come looking for them because…?"

"They think there might be a picture of the killer in them."

I won't say that a light bulb went off in my head, but somehow a candle got lit, and I knew why Trey wanted the images.

"You were there when I was there, weren't you, Trey?"

Trey had recovered some and was stretched out on the floor. Ryder stood over him, fists clenched at his side.

"No way! No way was I there!"

"I feel like kicking something again, Ryder, should I?"

"OK! I was there! *I was there!* Monique and I had been having an affair, and she didn't want that rat bastard of an ex-husband to find out. She expected to get a lot of sympathy when the article came out. She wanted to be seen as the poor pitiful wife, betrayed by her husband and best friend. Being seen as an equally guilty adulterer was *not* part of the plan."

I shot CC a look. "Looks like that virginal gown Monique wanted for her wedding was an even bigger joke than I originally thought." I tried to make my voice drip with sarcasm as I turned back to Trey. "Please go on with your story; *so* sorry to have interrupted."

"I overslept that morning, and Monique was freaking out because you were driving up to the house. I kept trying to sneak out, but you were always in my way. When you went upstairs, I slipped out a side door, got my car, and left."

"We didn't see any car. Did we see a car, CC?" All I got from her was a silent shake of the head.

"I parked a couple of driveways down. Monique has a friend who lets people park their guests at her place when they have parties and stuff and need more parking."

"So you're saying this woman is your alibi…she can back up your story…she knows the exact time that you left her driveway."

"No, damn it!" Trey sounded panicky. "The friend is gone all the time; as far as I know, she didn't see me."

"So what did you do after you got your car? Where did you go?"

"I drove back to the ranch. All the way there I was ticked that you might have taken a shot with me in it. I knew that Monique would be furious if you had gotten a shot, and we'd kept our relationship a total secret up until she was killed. She was afraid if her ex found out that it was me she was involved with, he'd start putting two and two together and know she'd been cheating too; then he'd go after *her* and try to get revenge."

"If he found out that she was marrying you, why would he leap to the conclusion that you two had been having an affair while he was still married to her?" I asked.

"Because something happened while they were married…something that he might remember, and from there he could connect the dots."

"The suspense is killing me," I prompted. "What was the thing that happened?"

"He and I played high-stakes poker together from time to time over the years. A group of us went to Vegas for a tournament; some guys took their girls, and some took their wives. The ex caught me coming out of his room one night in just my boxers. I thought he was in a game that should have gone all night. Me and Monique figured it would be safe to be together, that we wouldn't get caught…we figured wrong."

Ryder asked the obvious question. "What happened when he caught you coming out of the room?"

Trey shrugged. "I pretended I was sleepwalking, and he bought it, took me back to my room, and tucked me into bed. What a chump."

"So what do we do now, Trey? Turn you over to the police for breaking into my house or for murdering Monique?"

Trey put his hands over his eyes, and big fat tears plopped out from underneath his fingers.

"I didn't kill her. I *loved* her," he said, sobbing.

"Oh, stop with the tears," I snapped. "I'm not going to waste one minute of my time on sympathy for you. You just broke into my house! You acted like a goat in heat on multiple occasions, you threatened me at the gala, *and you went through my underwear drawer!*"

"Hey," he smirked. "The flirting…it's just what I do, you know? The thing at the gala was just a misunderstanding…now the underwear, that was a bonus."

"Hold me back, Ryder," I snarled. "There's about to be another homicide."

"Well, what was I supposed to do?" Trey protested. "Monique was killed! Murdered! If I turned up in one of your pictures, the police would come after me for sure. It didn't matter anymore that her husband might find out that we were having an affair, but I sure as hell didn't want to get put away for murder just because you accidentally took my picture! I decided to come out here and get all flirty with you, distract you. I was hoping I'd get a chance to do a quick search in the house while you took a shower after we, you know, fooled around. But before any of that could happen, you were trying to make me go back outside. I had to make an excuse to get into the house, so I pulled the old 'I need to use the men's room' routine and did a fast search."

Ryder was moving closer to Trey, but he didn't seem to notice.

I was focused on only part of what he'd just said.

"What in the world made you think we'd be fooling around?"

"Are you kidding me? Desperate women like you *never* turn me down."

Ryder's eyes lost a lot of the gold and bronze in them, and they went deep black. He moved another step closer to the idiot. Trey simply put his hands over his privates. I shook off the moment and decided to put an end to the fun and games.

"Here's the deal, Trey. I've gone over the images, and you're not in any of them. Why don't you take yourself home, ice things down, and think about this…if you ever show up around here again, I'll have a gun, and I'll aim for below the belt."

At first it was painful to watch him inch his way out of the house. He did little screams going down each step to the driveway, and then a vision of my underwear drawer popped into my head. I stopped feeling sorry for him.

CC had been like a fly on the wall the entire time. She'd been standing near the bedroom door, clutching the brass horse, never saying a word the whole time Trey had been "chatting" with us.

Once he'd left, she piped up. "Do you think he was telling the truth? Do you think he came here to kill you, London? Are you supposed to be the last murder victim?"

I suppose watching the color drain out of my face made CC realize she could have been a little more tactful when she asked me that question. Ryder just put his arm around me and said nothing.

She started babbling as she put the brass horse back down on the floor where it belonged and headed for the front door. "Between the energy drinks and whacking Trey on the head, I'm starving. Did we ever eat that pizza? I can't remember eating that pizza. I'm calling Mike, and we're going to go get white chocolate martinis and grouper nuggets." She continued babbling her way out the door.

"I hope they've got those little muffins; I just love those little muffins. Maybe I'll order that salad with the panko-crusted chicken and the goat cheese. We'll get a double order of muffins. I could eat about five muffins all on my own. I'll have the martini and the muffins and maybe some onion rings…." Her voice drifted off into the distance.

I still had one guest left, and I wasn't sure what to do with him. Fortunately he knew what to do with me.

"CC needs to learn to think before she speaks," he said as he gave me a long, long hug and kissed the top of my head.

"You've had way too much excitement the last twenty-four hours, London. I'm going to head home, and you're going to see me out, lock the door, and go to bed."

I walked him to the door, and as he left, he said the sweetest thing.

"Sleep tight, sugar bug."

Don't tell anyone, but I kind of liked being called "sugar bug."

CHAPTER 71

I thought I'd sleep forever, but once again...no such luck. I dreamt that I was locked up in jail and that Trey was prancing around with a sling, protecting his "privates." Next to him, Jett Brannigan was trying to talk to CC, and Ryder was saying, "I need to find London...she knows how I died." Slowly he turned toward me as I stood in a jail cell and, with his eyes burning into mine, he said, "Forever and ever, you'll dream of me." I woke up covered in sweat.

A half hour later, I was digging through my purse, looking for my car keys. Ryder had texted me at six thirty to see if I was awake. He wanted to meet at the jetty so that we could talk and have at least *some* privacy. He got there before I did, and together we found a bench well away from the fisherman who had gotten an early start and were throwing their lines in. I sat and waited for him to start the conversation.

"Yesterday, you told me what happened when you found the shoe and left with CC. Do you mind going over some of the stuff that happened before the gala?"

"I don't mind. Do you want me to begin with my childhood? I had a really cool, pink, kid-sized swimming pool and a hula-hoop that I just couldn't live without. I'd really rather not go into the trauma of getting stuck in the mailbox at the post office."

"I have no doubt that your childhood was fascinating, but I was thinking more along the lines of starting with the first murders."

"I told you about all that, didn't I?"

"Humor me, refresh my memory."

"CC and I went to Toni and Dick's house. They started arguing, she started throwing stuff, he threw a bloody fish, CC got knocked out and then I did. I came to, and they were dead."

"Did you ever see *anyone* else there?"

"Just the maid and then the police when they got there."

"What happened on the next job?"

"CC and I went to Monique's on Manasota Key, and bingo, she ends up dead. We didn't see anything, hear anything, nothing. It's kind of weird to know that Trey was there when we were. It turns out, by the way, that he was telling the truth…he didn't kill Monique.

"CC sent me a text after you did this morning. She's a friend of the woman who lets people use her drive for extra parking. She *does* let Trey park his car there. She's not a fan of Monique's ex-husband, and she said she was more than happy to help keep Monique's affair with Trey a secret. It turns out that the woman's gardener saw Trey leave in his car. The guy always takes a siesta at the same time every day, and Trey drove away twenty minutes before Monique was killed."

Ryder let out a frustrated sigh. "So we've got murders number one and number two and then murder number three. We'll get to Jett Brannigan's murder in a minute. Are there any more murders that I *don't* know about?"

"Well, there aren't any more murders, but somebody did get attacked."

"When and where did this happen, and who did it happen to?"

"It happened while I was at the mansion."

"Do you mean when you were doing that photo shoot for publicity pictures?"

"Right...Sophie and I went, and she ran interference for me while I took pictures."

"What do you mean 'she ran interference?'"

"She flirted a bunch with the butler and got him all distracted. I just wandered around by myself to get the shots, hoping that I'd run into the billionaire."

"And did you?"

"No. I did meet Ralph the snake for the first time, and Reynaldo the property-management guy for the estate."

"How did you meet the property manager?"

"He was the one who got attacked. I found him knocked out cold in the wine cellar, at which time I threw up on his shoes."

Ryder put his head in his hands.

"Don't worry; he was fine. I got Reynaldo upstairs, and we got him all fixed up, and I saw Ralph the snake on the way out. After that I went home; I was pretty bummed out…I was going to have to tell Mike that I didn't get a shot of the billionaire."

I stopped talking. I wasn't going to tell him about my getting attacked on the beach path. I knew he'd be angry that I hadn't told him before, and I just couldn't deal with that. Now it was Ryder's turn to talk if he wanted. I looked out at the gorgeous blue water and watched the waves build as they rushed to crash against the rocks. I jumped when Ryder finally spoke.

"Either someone's worked very hard to incriminate you in these murders, or this is the most bizarre series of coincidences that I've ever heard of. We've got our work cut out for us, London. We need to find out who's behind all this and whether they've targeted you intentionally. We also need to eliminate you as a suspect and do some digging into Trey's background."

"But there's already a witness who can prove that Trey wasn't at Monique's when she was killed."

"Witnesses can be bought."

"Shoot…you're right…how are you going to check out Trey? Are you going to hire a detective?"

"Can you keep a secret, London?"

"Yes...cross my heart, my lips are sealed. I'll put it in 'the vault'; mum's the word."

That made him laugh. I loved that laugh...it made his eyes sparkle.

"Here's the secret...they have these amazing things called computers...I actually *own* one."

"Real nice, smart guy."

"Seriously, though, I'm going to see who and what our buddy Trey really is. There's something wrong about him. He makes the hair on the back of my neck stand up."

My brain asked him a silent question: "Would it be okay if I ran a hand over that hair on *your* neck?"

Ooooooohhh...That wasn't my brain asking the question...I was afraid I had just said it out loud. Ryder's posture and focus hadn't changed a bit as he watched the waves. I let myself breathe again. If I'd said that out loud, I would have felt like a total fool. Then again, who knows what might have happened. The jetty can be a pretty romantic place. He might have kissed me right out of my sandals, ripped his fingers through my wind-tossed hair, and proclaimed to the world that I WAS HIS WOMAN!! Ryder stood up, and I yanked my brain back to reality.

"I've got to get back up to Sarasota this afternoon... more ranch business. I'm also going to make a few phone calls about Trey. I may find some stuff on him on the computer, but I bet somebody at the ranch knows what's up with him."

"If you're going to do that, I guess I'll run down to Matlacha and stop by some of the local bars and restaurants. I want to see if I can find any dirt on Richard and Toni the Tuna. If I don't find somebody else for the police to suspect soon, I'm afraid I might be accessorizing my outfits with handcuffs."

We stood up and walked to our cars. Ryder moved in close, and my senses went on high alert.

Touch me, hold me, *kiss* me. There was an epic battle going on between my brain and my hormones. Guess which side was winning.

Ryder moved in even closer and whispered in my ear, "Want to run your hand down the hair on the back of my neck before I go?"

Well, crap. I *did* say that out loud.

Chapter 72

It would take me awhile to get to Matlacha, and before I left, I needed to pick up a few odds and ends for my purse. Whoever emptied my purse left me without a small mirror. I liked to have one with me just in case I was stranded somewhere and needed a rescue plan. What? I watch those survival shows…they use the mirror to reflect the sun so the rescuers see it flash.

I drove downtown and pulled up in front of Brenda's. I knew right where to find the little mirror that I wanted, but I couldn't just ignore the jewelry…now, could I? I spent ten minutes checking out the new items they had gotten in. Just as I reached the back of the shop, Brenda popped out of her office.

"London! Aha! You are officially in the doghouse. CC told me you found an amazing man. She said he's got this fabulous hair and a body to die for. Now do it in the right order…tell me about his body first and then his voice…she said his voice makes your clothes fall off. His hair, we'll get to later."

I could feel my ears get hot. They were so hot it was painful.

"BRENDA!"

"Don't yell at *me*! I'm just repeating what CC said!"

Since I was busy plotting ways to kill CC and hadn't answered her, Brenda forged ahead.

"So is she right? I mean about the clothes falling off? Do I know this man? Can I meet this man? Can I be in love with this man?"

"BRENDA!"

"*Again* with the yelling! Come on, honey, let's get you checked out, and then you'll tell me all about him."

She rang up my purchase and followed me out onto the sidewalk.

"So come on, out with it…I want all the details. If you'd like to start with any sexual details, that's fine by me."

I'd barely opened my mouth, when she put her hand up to stop whatever I was going to say.

"I know…you're not going to tell me anything…some friend you are."

She gave me a big hug and turned to go back inside.

As I turned to leave, there was a man around fifty years old standing near the curb on the sidewalk, and he was watching us. The minute he made eye contact with me, he went into action.

"Hey…Hey, girls! I've got something to show you!"

Brenda froze like a deer caught in the headlights. He was turned toward us and had started messing around in the vicinity of his belt. I slammed my hand over my eyes and turned my back to him. Brenda didn't bother to cover her eyes *or* turn away from him.

I tried to be polite. "No, thanks, we're not interested."

"No, no! It's nothing like that…I'm just tucking in my shirt. I'm Wally, this is my friend Jack, and we're just waiting here for our wives. You're gonna love this. Now watch!"

I turned around just in time to see him put his hands down onto the sidewalk and flip himself up into a beautiful headstand. His hat fell off his head, and his shirt fell over his face.

You see all kinds of stuff in Venice, but usually the people *doing* the weird stuff were standing upright…especially *adult* people.

I looked at Brenda, and when we stopped laughing, I asked her the obvious question.

"What's wrong with this picture?" I started to laugh again. "At a certain age it's time to…"

"Time to what?" Brenda prompted.

"What's wrong with this picture…?" I whispered to myself.

Why hadn't I made the connection before? Trey's attempts to get to the images I'd taken, the words I'd just spoken…there was something about the phone call I'd received from Reynaldo. My brain was playing with a clue, and it wouldn't let me have it, but I knew how to get it.

I had grabbed Brenda by the arm without realizing it, until she started trying to pry my fingers off her.

"London, London, let go...you're pinching my arm!"

"Sorry, Brenda," I stammered.

I turned and ran toward the jeep, leaving Brenda standing on the sidewalk, rubbing her arm. I jammed the key into the ignition, and in a matter of minutes, I swerved into the magazine's parking lot and raced for the front door.

Barging into Mike's office, I found it empty, so I threw myself into his chair and settled for the next best thing. I yelled for Sophie.

"You bellowed?" Sophie hippity-hopped into the room, lugging her purse.

"Where did Mike put the CD? The CD that has the images from our photo shoot at the mansion?"

She plopped her bag down on the desk with a thud. Squeezing in next to me, she gave my chair a shove with her little hip. I don't know if Mike greased the wheels on the thing or what, but I went slamming up against the side of his credenza.

Sophie pulled open a drawer in the small filing cabinet under Mike's desk, and opening a folder, she pulled out the CD and shoved it into the computer.

"So what are we looking for?"

"I'm looking for an image from the shoot, and I think it might be a clue, the first clue I've come up with so far."

"A clue to what?"

"A clue to who the psycho murderer is, a clue to who knocked out Rey."

Her bag was blocking my view of the computer screen, so I dragged it off to the side of the desk.

"Sophie, your bag weighs a ton! What have you got in there, a bowling ball?"

"A woman is *supposed* to have a heavy bag…haven't you ever seen those TV shows where the woman has to empty her bag to find something? There's always a ton of stuff in her bag. She'll have gum and tissues and, of course, her car keys and lipstick and a compact and maybe a bottle of perfume and—"

"Sophie! Shush!"

She sniffed an offended sniff and took her purse and herself to the chair on the other side of the desk. She sat down and proceeded to bounce up and down on the edge of the seat like an excited little kid.

"If you find anything, will you show me? I won't tell anybody…I promise! I know if I tell anybody I could jeopardize the case. I learned that on that TV show…SUV."

"The show isn't called *SUV*, Sophie; an *SUV* is a type of car thingy."

I was only partially paying attention to her. I had been scrolling through the images and found the one that I wanted. I stared at the image and felt my stomach drop.

My face must have dropped just like my stomach, because Sophie got up and came back around the desk to look over my shoulder.

"So what are we looking at, London? Wine racks down in the wine cellar? Come on...show me."

I put the tip of my fingernail on an image. I had zoomed in on a mousey poof of "something" rising five inches above the top of a wine rack. There it was...the top of Sophie's insane hairdo. Just as I had while watching Wally do his headstand, I said the words, "*What's wrong with this picture.*" Yes...I said that out loud.

Sitting there I remembered noticing something wrong with the image when I first reviewed it. I'd just zoomed in on the picture to examine it more closely, when Rey had called to thank me again for helping him after he'd been attacked. I'd never gone back and finished proofing the image. If I had, I wouldn't be sitting where I was...right next to a crazy woman and her gun. She thumped me up beside the head ever so slightly with what turned out to be a very pretty pearl-handled revolver.

"If you had let me finish my sentence a minute ago, I would have told you that a lot of times on those TV shows, the woman has a gun in her purse."

Chapter 73

Sophie sighed and then turned her attention elsewhere. She used the hand that wasn't holding the gun to smoosh down her hair. She used sharp vicious jabs, but the hair just sprang right back up to its original height.

"This freaking hair. I *cannot* believe that this freaking hair nearly ruined everything. Now that I don't have to play the part of a ditzy screwball anymore, I'm cutting this mop off!"

Unfortunately, all too soon her attention came swinging back to me.

"All right, London, let's have the CD."

I ejected the shiny piece of evidence from the computer and handed it to her. Laying it on the floor and using a heavy brass paperweight that was sitting on Mike's desk, she smashed the CD into teeny tiny pieces.

"Thanks for showing me what you were looking at. Like I said, I'm not going to tell anybody about what you found. I definitely don't want to jeopardize the case. I'd rather *destroy* the case. Now let's take a ride to your house, and when we get there, we'll get the stiletto. Won't that be fun?"

I wasn't worried about whether or not it would be fun. I was worried about whether or not she was going to delete *me* once she was sure all the images were destroyed and she had the shoe in her hot little hands. I got up, picked up my bag, and walked through the office and down to the jeep, with Sophie breathing down my neck.

Traffic was fairly heavy, so we inched our way through town. Sophie hadn't had a word to say once we left the office. I flinched when she finally screeched out a sentence.

"Oh look! There's your fancy schmancy friend… DeeDee…or is it Dodo?"

I glanced over to see CC and Brenda deep in conversation on the sidewalk. I focused my brain and prayed that I would telepathically reach them and that somehow they would sense that I needed help.

Sophie had cracked herself up with her little name joke, and she laughed until she choked. I gripped the steering wheel harder and kept my mouth shut. I drove at least a half mile, wishing that I were one of those brainiac detectives in a movie or TV show. You know the kind. They act all quiet and harmless, but their mind is going a million miles an hour formulating an escape from the evildoers.

My mind was on a slow boat to China without a paddle…totally stalled out. I was down to scanning the sky for a superhero to come help me, when my cell phone rang unexpectedly. I nearly drove off Highway 41 and straight through the hot-dog diner.

"Answer it, London; put it on speaker, and don't screw up…my trigger finger is getting itchy."

"Oh my Lord, Sophie…nobody says their trigger finger is getting itchy anymore."

"Plenty of people watch old gangster movies and say it. Now don't make me scratch my itch. *Answer the phone!*"

I sighed and picked up.

"London? It's CC. I need to see you right away. I was talking to Brenda, and she told me about the guy who stood on his head for you. She said his shirt came un-tucked and fell over his face. Where are you? I want to talk to you about something you said. If you're home, I could swing by your place in just a few minutes. From the way Brenda said you were acting, it sounds like maybe you figured something out about either the killer or the thief."

"Sorry, CC, I can't talk now…I'm in a meeting with Flor, and I won't be done until late."

"You're in a meeting with Flor…hang on a second, London." I could hear muffled conversation, and then CC was back. "I've got to go, London…did you know Brenda has a sugar addiction? The people from the fudge shop are out on the sidewalk, yelling at me to come get her. She's behind the counter, and someone said she's licking the big giant slab of fudge that was just put on the cutting table. I'll call you later…I still want to know if you figured anything out. Damn! I've got to go; they've got Brenda by the legs, and they're trying to pull her off the table."

I hadn't even gotten a chance to lay the phone down, when Sophie went into a mini rant.

"BLAH, BLAH, BLAH, BLAH, BLAH, BLAH, BLAH! That woman drives me friggin' crazy."

"How do you know CC?"

"She designed my gown for the gala. The gown they made turned out fine, but what a bunch of snobs. She's got a bunch of idiots working there. If she farts crosswise, there's some weird guy in tight pants telling her it smells like roses. And that fake French bitch. She just about came unglued when I told her I wanted pockets in my gown."

I had a momentary sense of panic. I hoped that she didn't know that the guy in tight pants was Flor...she'd think I was trying to get CC to call the boutique to see if I really was in a meeting with her assistant. Actually that *had* been my lame-ass attempt to raise a red flag with CC. I also was having a sudden flashback to hearing the demanding, deep-voiced client arguing with Bobbi at CC's. Who would have guessed that Sophie's voice could go that low? Well, that was one more mystery solved. I decided to see if I could solve a few more.

"Why was it so important for your gown to have pockets?"

A smile spread across Sophie's face.

"My gown needed to have pockets, *large* pockets, because you can't fit a stiletto into a normal-sized pocket."

Mystery number two…solved.

Sophie continued. "This whole experience has been so much fun. This last part has been a little frustrating, because it didn't go according to plan, but everything else… perfection. I wish I'd taken up the robbery stuff a long time ago. My life is so much better, now that reality TV has gotten popular."

"What has reality TV got to do with it?"

"There's this amazing show where all these rich people get drunk, and then they go out and steal fancy cars from other rich people. Usually they know the people they steal from, so it's pretty easy. I got to thinking…I'm *way* smarter than those people. I knew I could come up with a plan to steal even better stuff than cars. If I could pull off a big enough robbery, I could live just like those idiots."

"Sophie, you know those shows aren't real, don't you? I read that they have it arranged ahead of time for them to 'steal' the cars from their friends. When the episode is over, they give the cars back."

"*The show is real!* They wouldn't call it 'reality' TV if it wasn't!"

It was like talking to my grandmother…in the pre-reality TV era, she always thought that what happened on soap operas was real. She thought the actors were living their real lives in front of the whole world. The good news is, my grandmother never decided to lead a life of crime. The bad news is, she always thought she had an evil twin living somewhere in Chicago. She used to have a little glass of brandy before bed so that she wouldn't have nightmares about "Sister Evil." Now that I was all grown up, I suspected Granny just liked to have a snort.

I couldn't help myself. I really wanted to know everything that Sophie had done. Did she just steal the shoe, or had she made the leap to becoming a murderer?

"So when did you decide to make such a big career change, Sophie?"

"I guess about a year or two ago...I'm not sure. I'd been visiting Evangeline, and I told her what I was thinking. Having a twin sister is awesome...they think like you do, and with her help it was as if I had a 'super brain.' I came back from vacation with a plan. I'd heard about this big shoe auction thing, and we decided that was going to be our target. If I could steal *one* shoe, we'd be set for life.

"After that, I'd only do robberies if I wanted to have some fun. So anyway, step one was to find a way onto the committee for the gala. That way I would know just how the shoe would be transported...where it would be displayed, how it would be displayed...you get the idea."

I was getting the idea.

"So what did you have to do? Just ask to be on the committee?"

"Ohhhh, no, no, no, no, no. I felt like I was back in grade school. Getting into the committee was like being in a popularity contest. Every time an opening came up, they'd put somebody they were friends with into the position."

"Well, then how did you finally end up getting on?"

"I killed enough people."

"You *killed* people?"

"I don't know why I didn't think of it earlier. I just started knocking off people who were on the committee. Toni the Tuna, Monique…Toni's husband was just an added bonus. I never liked that guy. I'd suggest using their houses in the magazine; 'Mike the dope' would fall for it hook, line, and sinker, and then I'd just set everything up for you to do the shoot. I'd follow you there, and when I got my chance, I took them out. Speaking of following you to Toni and Richard's…I had fun following you through the woods that night."

"You were the one in the woods that night? Why did you attack me? I never did anything to you!" I tried to stay calm, but I was furious.

"I thought it would be fun to mess with you. You're so ridiculously clueless. I never could resist an easy target." Her face beamed with satisfaction.

So there it was, as simple as that. Sophie had just wanted to mess with me that night. I would have liked to have messed with *her*, but now wasn't the time.

"So anyway," Sophie continued, "with you on the scene every time, I provided the police with an obvious suspect and that kept them busy.

"After I finished off Monique, things finally fell into place. The committee had a hard time finding someone to take her place…murder has a way of making people nervous. That's when I finally got my chance, and they put me on the committee."

I gave an involuntary little shudder. Each time CC and I had been on a shoot, Sophie had been lurking somewhere close by…waiting to kill.

Chapter 74

"**You believe in** luck, don't you, London? Well, lady luck smiled on me big time when I met Jett Brannigan."

"You knew Jett Brannigan?"

"Knew him? We were lovers, partners in crime."

"How...what?? I thought he was involved with Chesty!"

Sophie barked out a laugh. "She thought he was, too, but he was just using her. No...Mr. Brannigan was all mine."

"How did you meet him? No offense, but I can't see you rubbing elbows with billionaires on a regular basis."

"We met at the Sarasota Airport. My sister's employer has a private jet. That's how they get her from job to job. She worked it out so that I could hitch a ride on it to see her. One day when I was trying to drag my stupid ass bag across the tarmac, Jett came up and helped me with it. He'd just gotten off his plane. I couldn't believe my luck when I found out that he owned the mansion where the stiletto would be auctioned off. I flirted with him, and before you know it, he was 'in love.'

"At a committee meeting I learned where the stiletto would be positioned in the great hall. All I had to do then was get access to the room that would be directly below the display case for the shoe. That's where my relationship with Jett started to really pay off.

"I got him to give me a tour of the place, and I told him I wanted to see everything. We covered every inch of the place, every inch except the room next to the wine cellar, the room I needed access to."

"Why didn't you see that room?"

"It was locked. Jett said he didn't have a key for it; he never had. When he bought the place, it was locked. He had plenty of space and no curiosity, so he never bothered to get a locksmith in."

"I guess that since you did manage to steal the stiletto, you found a way to get into the room."

"Brilliant deduction, Detective London. I did indeed find a way in."

"Did you use a hairpin, or did you kind of swipe a credit card down the side of the door over the lock?"

Sophie reached over and flicked me in the forehead with her finger.

"No, stupid, I got hold of a key."

It took everything I had not to flick Sophie in the forehead, with my fist, but there was still the matter of the gun in her hand.

"So how did you get a key?"

"Jett was gone a lot for business, so I talked him into letting me spend my weekends there. I told him it would make me feel as if he was close to me if I could sleep in his bed while he was gone. That's all I had to say...he ate that kind of sappy romantic stuff up with a spoon. So while I spent weekends there, I watched the routines of the staff in case that knowledge came in handy sometime. One day I hit the jackpot. I saw Rey making his rounds and followed him, right to the locked room. He pulled a chain with a key on it from under his sweater and unlocked the door."

"Did you follow him in?"

"No, you moron...I didn't know what was in there. Besides that, the minute I walked in, he'd see me. You'd never make it in this business, London. You don't think things through. Of course, that was the night that I screwed up, so I shouldn't be so hard on you."

"How did you screw up?"

"I was pretty psyched that I finally knew where the key was. I was just so wound up. Jett got back from his business trip that night, we had too much to drink, and I told him that Rey had the key to the room. After that, I had to explain why I'd been stalking Rey, and I ended up telling him the whole story. He wanted in on the deal, and actually, he turned out to be really helpful. He came up with the idea of using Chesty as a distraction."

"Jett Brannigan was in on it with you?"

"Sure, we were just like the three musketeers… Brannigan, Evangeline, and me."

I was trying to process the fact that, "Mr. Magnanimous," the selfless giver of oodles of money to charity, was a thief. Sophie was going to have to help me make sense of it.

"Why would Jett Brannigan get involved with stealing, when he's already a billionaire?"

"For the thrill. Jett was bored; he'd done it all and seen it all, everything except something criminal."

I was all set to make another brilliant deduction, when Sophie waved the gun at me.

"Pull into the ice-cream place…just up here on the right. I want an ice-cream sundae."

How could Sophie want ice cream at a time like this? She was kidnapping somebody, and you'd think that would kind of kill your appetite. I know I couldn't bear the thought of food.

"Go through the drive-through…you want anything? It's my treat."

Seriously? Oh, what the hell…it might be the last time I got to have sugar.

"I'll have one of those parfait thingies with the peanuts on it."

"Well, don't tell me, tell the voice coming out of the box."

"We'd like a parfait thingy, the one that has peanuts all over it, but hold the peanuts and add extra hot fudge."

I'd barely gotten the words out of my mouth, when Sophie leaned across my chest and shouted into the ordering box.

"I WANT A DOUBLE-SCOOP VANILLA CONE, DIPPED IN CHOCOLATE. WAIT FIVE MINUTES BEFORE YOU MAKE UP OUR ORDER, WE'RE COMING IN TO GET IT!"

My heart was in my throat. The whole time she was leaning into me, the gun was pressed against my stomach. I needed to calm down. If I didn't, it would be a miracle if I could eat more than half of my treat.

I pulled into a parking space, thinking that maybe it was a good sign that Sophie bought me an ice cream. Maybe she *was* just going to have me get her the stiletto, and then she'd tie me up, and off she'd go, treasure in hand. I figured keeping the conversation going was a good idea…be her buddy, I told myself. Bad guys don't kill their buddies.

Sophie got talkative again. "So here's how I got the key. I knew Rey's routine, so the day that you and I went out to shoot the mansion, I was ready. Jett and I waited until we knew Rey would be down in the wine cellar, which was a good place to get to him, because nobody's ever down there. Jett snuck up behind him and whacked him on the head…he went down like a ton of bricks. All I had to do then was pull the key and the chain out of his shirt and make an impression of the key. Once I had that, I tucked the key back under his shirt, just the way it had been. I was positive that it would never occur to him that the key was what we'd been after, and I was right. Jett did what he was supposed to do, he got back upstairs to get rid of the sterling silver candlestick that he hit Rey with. Then he opened one of the doors that lead into the garden, and one of the garage doors. Everyone would think that the assailant or assailants, had left the house, wasn't that a brilliant idea?"

I didn't care what Jett had done after he got upstairs, something else was bothering me.

"Wait a minute…I came down the steps while you were still in that room; Jett would have had to pass me on the stairs."

"Ever hear of an elevator, honey? There's one tucked away down at the far end of the hallway. It was designed to blend into the wall, almost like a secret passageway."

I was blown away by that tidbit of information, but I went right back to questioning Sophie…the whole damn thing actually *was* fascinating.

"You made an impression of the key with what?"

"I learned this on TV too…I had a little metal gift-card container that I filled with wax. All I had to do was press the key down into the wax, and I had a perfect copy of the key. There's a guy at the hardware store, who has a little crush on me, so I talked him into making two keys for me."

"How many guys do you *have* running around after you with their tongues hanging out?"

"That's a really personal question, London. How would you like it if I asked you what brand of tampon you use?"

Well, that just made no sense at all. She kills people, knocks people out, steals things, and then gets offended by me asking her a simple little question. Nut job.

Sophie opened her car door and gestured at me to do the same. "Come on, I have to use the little girls' room."

I climbed out of the jeep and walked inside with Sophie just two steps behind me. We walked straight back to the ladies' room, and I realized we were going to have a problem.

Chapter 75

"**So how is** this going to work, Sophie...there's not room in there for both of us."

The stall had sidewalls that stopped two feet before they got to the floor, and there was only room for one person in the cramped space.

"You're going to get down on the floor and slide yourself under the sidewall."

"*What?*"

"Get down there, and crawl under the wall. Slide your head into the stall next to mine, and keep what's not in the stall with me, in the stall next to me on the other side."

"And just where will you be?"

"I'm going to go into the stall and use your back as a footstool. If you try anything funny, I'll shoot you."

I couldn't argue with her reasoning, so I got down on my stomach and wiggled under the stall partition. I was now stretched out flat in front of the toilet. Well, great... talk about humiliating.

"Now lay still. Your back isn't level, and I don't want to twist my ankle standing on it."

She got seated, and the door to the bathroom opened. I heard someone walk past the stall Sophie was in, and then the door where my head was, opened.

"Is this stall occupied?"

I shot back an answer. "Doesn't it *look* occupied?"

She slammed the door and walked back past Sophie's stall and opened the door to the stall with just my legs in it.

"Move your legs" was all she said as she kicked me and sat down on the toilet. Oh good...another nut job.

All I wanted was to burn my clothes and cut off my hair after I finally got to get up and off the bathroom floor. Sophie marched me back out into the dining area, ignoring the glare from the girl holding our order and shoved me out the door to the parking lot. I decided it would be wise not to complain about the fact that I didn't get my treat. I led the way back out to the jeep and climbed in. I started digging through the console, and Sophie grabbed my hand.

"What do you think you're doing?"

"*I* think I'm looking for my hand sanitizer. I have this weird ritual...I'm kind of OCD about it. Every time I lay on a public bathroom floor, I wash every exposed surface of my body afterward."

She shoved my hand to the side and dug out the sanitizer.

"There's no need to get all crappy about it. Here, wash your face."

I used up most of the bottle and got back down to business.

"Sophie, you were supposed to be distracting Mr. Adam while I was going through taking pictures. How did you manage to get away from him long enough to sneak downstairs and do all that stuff?"

"Simple, Mr. Adam was in on it."

"Are you telling me that you ended up with *four* people working on this robbery?"

"Let me help to clear this up for you, London. There was never more than the three of us. The Mr. Adam that you met…that was Jett in disguise. Didn't he look ridiculous in his long braids? He hated that wig, but we had to cover up his blond hair somehow. We couldn't have anybody knowing that we knew each other. The fewer connections between us, the better."

"So you two were putting on an act until I left to take the pictures; you were just having a good old time, weren't you?"

"Jett was so charged up that day. He couldn't wait to knock out Rey, because he was so mad at him."

"Why was he mad at him?"

"Because he'd had a key to that room the whole time and never told Jett. Rey worked for the previous owner of the estate, and by rights, that key belonged to Jett. You should have seen how mad Jett got when I told him that I saw Rey use a key to go into that room; I thought he was going to blow a gasket.

Anyway, I'd given Jett a key so that he could get into the room on Rey's day off. He figured out which ceiling tile would be directly under the stiletto pedestal; luckily it would be sitting on a wood floor. He removed the ceiling tile and cut an opening in the floor above him big enough for a shoe to drop through it, he did so good you couldn't even tell it was there.

"All he had to do was press the piece he'd cut out, gently back into the opening and it looked like normal. I knew where the display for the stilettos was being stored, since I was on the committee, and one night I let Jett into the storage place. He made a trap door in the bottom of the pedestal and rigged the stand that would hold the shoe. If you pushed on the stand from the bottom, it would fall through the open trap door, bringing the stiletto with it."

"Before I forget, Sophie, Rey's room; what needed to be kept so secret that the room was locked all the time?"

"It was so lame. Rey had a little 'lounge' set up. He had a pool table in there and a big old flat-screen TV. I don't know if you noticed, but there aren't TVs anywhere else in the house. I guess it was just his little hideaway."

She stretched and then waved the gun at me.

"Come on, detective...time to get back on the road."

I pulled back into traffic and asked Sophie something that had been bugging me.

"You said Jett came up with the idea of Chesty being a distraction...what was that all about?"

"We were going to need a distraction the night of the gala. So we had to find a really good one, and Jett suggested using Chesty. She'd been throwing herself at him for months, and so we decided that he would wine her and dine her and profess his love for her. He told her that he didn't want anyone else to introduce him at the gala…only his true love would do. What a dope, she fell for it hook, line and sinker."

"So how was she supposed to be a distraction?"

"If I was going to be able to steal the stiletto with all those people there, we needed something that would keep them looking in the direction of the stage. We couldn't have people randomly milling around, so we got Chesty up there with her great big 'distractions,' and I don't think any man in that room heard a word the mayor said. All the women were keeping their eyes on their men."

Sophie had gotten a dreamy look in her eyes.

"Everything was going so well. Evangeline had her cellphone ready, and I had mine. The minute the mayor walked on stage, Eve ducked into the powder room and put on a wig that looked just like my hair…if anybody noticed her, they'd just assume it was me, and I'd have an alibi. Jett had an alibi because he was waiting at the side of the stage to be introduced. Eve was going to tell the police that she was taking care of Eduardo in an alcove, if they asked. He was so drunk he'd believe anything she told him. Poor Eve, she'd had that damn wig tucked up between her legs until it was time to use it. She told me she has hives all over her thighs now."

I was driving as slowly as I could, and so far Sophie hadn't seemed to notice.

"I took off for the lower level and used the key to get into the room. Those big pockets worked just like they were supposed to. I wore gloves to make sure I didn't leave fingerprints. I carried them in the pockets of my dress, along with a collapsible baton, and my cell phone. Once the shoe was in my possession, there would be room for that too. Things worked like clockwork. Jett, being the smarty that he is, brought a stepstool down to the room right before the party started. You might not have noticed, but I'm not all that tall, and I was going to need to be able to reach pretty far up.

"Once I got in the room, I climbed up on the stepstool and used the baton to push up on the ceiling tile, and when I quit pushing, the panel dropped down. Next I pushed on the piece of the floor that Jett had cut, and *boom*, out it came. I could see the trap door Jett had cut into the pedestal, so all I had to do then was take the baton and push up on the trap door in the bottom of the pedestal. It fell open, I pushed up on the shoe stand and the stiletto dropped down and landed at my feet. What a rush! I felt *incredible, just incredible!*"

I felt as if I'd been in the room *with* Sophie, just from listening to her talk.

"What happened next, Sophie?"

"I speed-dialed Evangeline's number when I got close to the top of the stairs. That was her signal to go back into the powder room and take the wig off and wait by the front door for me. I had the stiletto in my pocket, and I hadn't gotten fifteen feet away from the staircase, when the head of the committee, Zandra, grabbed me and dragged me over into an alcove. The mayor was still droning on in the background, and she didn't want to attract attention. She said that Bebe was supposed to model one of CC's gowns right after Chesty introduced Jett, but someone had just bumped Bebe and spilled red wine down the front of the dress. She knew I was wearing one of CC's designs; I was the only person as small as the 'model,' and she insisted that I give my gown to her to wear up on stage."

"What did you do?"

"I pried my arm out of the death grip she had on me first. It was going to look suspicious if I refused, so I told her to give me a minute and that I'd slip into the powder room and trade dresses. As soon as Zandra left, Eve showed up. She'd been watching us from across the room, and I told her that we had a problem. If I didn't have my dress, I didn't have my big pockets, and there was no way to get the stiletto out without being seen. That's when lady luck struck again. I looked down, and there was your big bag tucked down in your chair, the perfect solution…at least for the moment.

I had Eve walk over and get it and bring it back to me. I took all of your junk out of your bag, and Eve stuffed it in hers. Then I put the stiletto in your bag, and Eve left to put it back in your chair.

I had to put the collapsible baton and the gloves under a seat cushion. As soon as I switched gowns, I was back near your table, waiting for Chesty to introduce Jett. The minute she did and everybody was straining to get a look at Mr. Billionaire, I was going to walk by, pick up the bag, and Eve and I would be out of there."

"Why didn't you get the bag? What stopped you?"

"I was all set to make my move, when Chesty ended up in the champagne. Everyone was watching her, and then people started getting involved in that freak show, and I knew it was my moment. Just as I started toward the bag, *you* showed up at the table and grabbed it! What a *freaking* disaster!"

She didn't need to tell me what happened next; I *lived* what had happened next. Finding the shoe, trying to get out of the mansion with CC, Ralph flying through the air. All along Sophie was trying to get close enough to us to get the shoe, and she ends up wearing Ralph. Her version of the events explained a few things.

"Did you get Mike to stop by CC's condo so that you could try to get the stiletto?"

"Once again your powers of deduction amaze me. After you left, people were running all over, and by then they were screaming that there were fifty snakes loose in the room. Someone else was yelling that there were five guys headed for the mansion to rob everybody. Mike ran up to me, looking for CC, and all I had to do was lie and say that I had seen some shady-looking guy follow her out the front door. He took off running, and I ran right with him, straight to his car." She shifted in her seat and gave me a dirty look.

"So tell me, London, since the shoe wasn't in your bag when we got to the condo, where was it?"

I suddenly remembered Sophie moving over to the couch and putting her feet on my bag...she'd been checking to see if the shoe was in it.

Chapter 76

I knew Sophie wasn't going to be happy when I told her where the shoe had been the whole time.

"I was sitting on it."

"Bitch."

Well, that went better than I thought it would. We'd been getting closer and closer to the ranch, and my stomach was starting to hurt. Stress always goes to my stomach. I was trying to ignore the building "distress," when Sophie suddenly made a spinning gesture with a finger that wasn't locked onto the gun.

"Turn around."

"*What?*"

"Turn around, and pull into the grocery store. I need something in there."

She was in the middle of a kidnapping…she'd already stopped for ice cream; what else could she need? Maybe she wanted to get a roll of duct tape to put over my mouth when she tied me up. She probably needed some rope too, because I knew she didn't bring any with her, and I sure didn't have any. I got parked, and we paraded into the store. My stomach distress got a lot worse thinking about the rope and the duct tape. I was going to need to find a bathroom.

Sophie gave me a little poke in the ribs.

"Go over to the bakery department."

"The *bakery* department?"

"I want some of those brownie bites…they're divine."

"Buy me one, Sophie; they're my favorite. Actually, could you buy me five?"

Who knew how long I was going to have to go without food after she tied me up and put duct tape over my mouth. A girl could starve to death.

She sneered at me. "So that's where your huge butt came from. I only eat one of those at a time. I need to watch my figure. I want to look good in a bathing suit when I'm rich and lying on the beach in Cabo San Lucas."

Well, great. She had just told me where she was going after she got paid for the stiletto. Maybe she *wasn't* going to just tie me up and leave me. Maybe since I'd be dead, it didn't matter what I knew. That was it for my stomach.

"Sophie…I need to use the bathroom."

"You can wait…we'll be at your place soon, and you can go there."

"I'm telling you, Sophie, *I can't wait.*"

"I SAID YOU'RE GOING TO WAIT!"

The woman putting the brownies in the bag for Sophie didn't even raise an eyebrow. *They see bratty kids all day, acting just like us.*

"NOT WAITING!"

I took off running for the back of the store. Sophie was running behind me with little baby steps, holding tight to her bag of brownie bites. That would have been a great time to escape; I could easily have outrun her, but all I cared about was making it to the bathroom in time. I slammed myself into a stall, slid the lock shut, and sat down. Two seconds later Sophie barged into the bathroom and came sliding underneath the stall partition. By then she had her gun out and was pointing it right at me.

"You can stay if you want to, Sophie, but I wouldn't recommend it."

"Oh, I'm staying *right* here."

"Don't say I didn't warn you!"

I won't go into all the dirty details, but after the first explosive expression of my stomach's dismay, Sophie disappeared from my stall. But did she leave the bathroom? Nooooooo. She sat on the seat in the stall next to me and proceeded to have a conversation with me.

"I don't know what it is about bodily functions...other peoples, I mean. They just don't seem to bother me. Take, for instance, when Eduardo threw up in your bag. That didn't really bother me."

Of course, it didn't; he didn't throw up in *her* bag. I heard her sigh, and then I heard the sound of the bakery bag being opened. *She was going to eat, at a time like* THIS?

"Oooh, London, these are *so* good."

The woman was pure evil…who would *do* that to someone in my condition?

"I hope you didn't really want one; I'm not going to be able to save you any."

"I didn't want *one*…I wanted five…and you'd better pay for those!"

"Don't get your knickers in a twist…I'll pay for them!"

I heard her sucking the chocolate off her fingers and the bag being crumpled.

"It would have been so nice to stay home after Mike dropped us off at our place, but I had to go back to the mansion to see Jett. He called me after all the cops left and everyone was gone. I guess Chesty almost messed up our plan. She was all over Jett earlier that night. He had always been with her in hotels, and she was trying to convince him to let her become 'mistress of the manor' and stay the night. I guess she changed her mind after she fell into the champagne glass and turned into a makeup-smeared, soaking, dripping mess."

Sophie laughed. "Chesty is such a train wreck…she thinks she's going to be some big-time criminal. I've been keeping an eye on her and her big dope of a brother."

"She's got a brother?"

"Oh yeah…Trey…I believe you've met."

"Trey's her brother?"

"Oddly, yes. There's no love lost between those two, from what I've heard."

"I thought Trey was trying to kill me…I heard him talking to Chesty, and she said she gave him two jobs to do and that he messed them up. He said something about a last job, and then he tried to kidnap me at the gala, and *then* he broke into my house. I thought *I* was the last job."

"Those two couldn't pull off a murder if their lives depended on it. Chesty's just a small-time kleptomaniac, trying to make a career move into robbery. During the time that I was trying to get on the committee, I had lunch with Toni Palumbo. We talked about the meetings, and she started sharing gossip. It seems that after every meeting, someone would report that an item had been stolen out of her purse. Alexandra DuPone threw a fit because a diamond-covered cigarette case that her husband had given her was taken.

"Toni knew what the case looked like, and at a cocktail party, she saw Chesty with it. She decided that two could play Miss Chesty's game, and she stole the case out of Chesty's bag when she wasn't looking. Just before Toni left the party, she caught Chesty's eye and waved the cigarette case at her.

"I imagine that one of the jobs that Chesty sent Trey out on was to get the case back. Right after I took care of business at the Palumbo's, I tucked back into the foliage around the pool to wait and see if you and CC really were unconscious and, as a result, hadn't seen me…if you were just pretending to be knocked out…well, we wouldn't be having this conversation right now.

"It was only about two seconds later that Trey came sneaking through the house and out onto the lanai with the cigarette case in his hand. He took one look at the 'pool party,' dropped the cigarette case, and ran. He definitely let Chesty down on that one. I have to say, I was disappointed in Toni for keeping the case and not returning it to Alexandra. It had sentimental value, after all!"

I did a mental eye roll...the murderer and thief who was kidnapping me had issues with the bad moral choice of one of her victims. What a hypocrite.

I pulled myself together and left my stall. Sophie slammed out of hers.

"Do you want to know the rest of the story? I'm having fun telling you all this...it's been killing me to keep all these secrets."

"By all means, Sophie, continue."

"Let's see...oh yeah, so we left CC's place, Mike dropped me off at my house, and I headed back to the mansion. I was supposed to pick Jett up, and then he planned for us to leave the country in his private jet. We were going to fly to a private island and deliver the shoe to a collector who was going to pay handsomely for it. When I say 'we,' I mean Eve and myself. Jett didn't know it, but he wasn't going along for the ride."

I washed my hands, and we headed out the door. Sophie herded me past the checkout stands and out the front door. I *knew* it! She'd been lying about paying for those brownies!

I swallowed my irritation and picked up my questioning. "So you never intended to take Jett with you when you left?"

Sophie smiled. "The plan had always been that the only people leaving with that shoe would be Eve and myself. Anyway, when I got to the mansion, Jett had champagne poured, all ready for a toast to our success. Of course, he wanted me to show him the shoe right away, so I had to distract him and then take care of him."

I already knew how she had taken care of him, but I wanted details—just in case I came out of this whole thing alive.

"What did you do?"

"I used sex. I used my kitty-cat voice."

"What's a 'kitty-cat voice?'"

"Oh, you know…the books always say, 'She purred the words into his ear'…that kind of thing. Whispery, sexy, whatever. Anyway, I talked all sexy and said, 'I learned something tonight. Success gets me all hot and bothered. The shoe can wait, but I can't.' I could have said 'I feel sexy when I take the trash out', and I would have gotten the same reaction from him. He was all over me."

"Ewwwwww…you shot him while you were having sex?"

"Please, London, what am I, a savage? I led him upstairs to the bedroom and told him to get into bed while I got more comfortable. I still had a lightweight coat on and my purse, so I went into the master bedroom closet. I told him I was going to hang up my things." She smiled a creepy smile and looked at her gun.

"That's when I got you out of my purse and got you all ready to shoot Jett, didn't I, Pearl?"

She looked away from the gun and looked up at me.

"I named her Pearl, because she's a pearl-handled revolver."

Oh Lord, she had named her gun…and she *talked* to it.

"You should have seen his face when I walked out pointing Pearl at him. I said 'I don't love you anymore' and pulled the trigger. After that I took a picture of the two of us together."

Chapter 77

had reached the ranch, and we sat parked in front of my house. Sophie was in no hurry to get out of the jeep, and neither was I. She seemed to be enjoying the process of revealing the details of her grand scheme. She could take as long as she wanted, as far as I was concerned.

"You know, London, one of the things that I love about this gun is what a nice little hole it makes. I couldn't use the gun on Monique, and I regret that. She didn't look pretty after I got done using that metal stick thingy I found in your car. People still look nice after you shoot them with a little bullet…well, most of them anyway. Some people are just ugly, with or without a hole in their head. You don't have to worry, London…you're going to look pretty when you're dead. I'll make sure that I add a little makeup around your eyes before I take your picture."

"Thank you, Sophie, that's such a relief…here I was, thinking, if I'd known you were going to kill me today, I'd have worn more makeup. I don't suppose you could change my underwear while you're at it, could you? I broke the most important rule my mother ever taught me today. She always said, 'Wear clean underwear; you never know when you're going to meet your maker.'"

Somehow I'd managed to irritate her…not a good idea.

"Excuse me, London, did I say you could talk? My gun…my rules…the person holding the gun gets to talk."

"I don't suppose I could hold the gun for a minute?"

My answer was a poke in the ear with the gun. She held the gun there for a minute, and then she pulled the gun away and tapped her teeth with it.

"Now where was I?"

I took a chance and talked anyway.

"You were putting makeup on me and taking my picture."

"Oh yeah…I love taking pictures…I always kind of wanted to be a photographer, like you are. I never sell any of my photos, though. I just do a lot of scrapbooking with them. I'm going to really enjoy having a picture of you. I'm kind of proud of how I framed you for the murders. In fact, I framed you one more time, right at the end. I put a picture of you in a frame on the nightstand next to the side of the bed Jett slept on.

"I also put the cute little camera that we took out of your bag, next to 'your' side of the bed. Just like that… anyone would get the idea that you and Jett were lovers."

"Well, your plan worked, Sophie; the police think we were having an affair."

"I know! I was here at the ranch when the police came and took you away. Actually I was here *way* before they showed up. When I first got here, your dopey friend, CC, was in the house, and I hoped that she'd leave, but that didn't happen. Then that beautiful man showed up, and *he* stayed forever too. I finally gave up when the police showed up, and you got an escort into Sarasota. You made my life so much easier today when you just waltzed into the office."

"So what do we do now, Sophie?"

"I get the shoe, you get dead, and Evangeline and I get rich."

I didn't like that answer *at all*.

"Damn, there's that horse looking over the fence at us. I don't like horses…they're mean, and they smell, and they throw you off if you try to ride them."

I was still keeping a firm grip on the steering wheel, and Sophie reached over and rapped me on the fingers with the gun.

"Time to get the shoe, London. Get out."

I climbed out, and she kept the gun on me the whole time. She came around the jeep, and her eyes got ugly.

"Where's the stiletto?"

"I can give you the file with the picture of you in the wine cellar, but I don't have the stiletto."

"Don't play this game, London. I've been out here watching the house, and I've seen you walking around the fields with that horse as if he's your best friend. If I don't get a straight answer right now, I'm going to shoot that freaking horse. *Now where's the shoe??"*

I felt my heart start to hurt.

"It's in the tree next to Reckless."

"Well, now, aren't you the clever one? Well, go on, get your ass over there, and get it."

I walked to the gate and let myself through. Reckless watched me and then watched Sophie.

"Make that damn horse stop looking at me!"

I coaxed Reckless over to the fence.

"Come here, boy…I'm going to need you to help me again."

I climbed the fence and got onto his back. He knew the drill this time, and he walked right over to the tree and stood waiting under the big branch that I'd used before. I thought my legs had been shaking hard the first time I tried this stunt. I could barely stay upright this time; they were shaking so hard. I managed to pull myself up and into the tree. A couple of branches later and I had the stiletto.

It was a little dirty but still amazing. The light was bouncing off the diamonds, and it looked as if the shoe was on fire. I nearly fell out of the tree when Sophie's voice barked at me.

"Bring the shoe to me, and don't get stupid! I've got this gun trained on that horse, and he's too big to miss. And just for your information, I *never* miss."

I slipped out of the tree and rode Reckless over to the fence. Sophie backed away from it, never taking her eyes off me. I slid off Reckless' back and stood next to him for a moment. He obviously felt the tension in the air. He was pawing at the dirt and tossing his head, leaning into me.

I couldn't help it…I could feel tears burning in my eyes.

"It's all right, boy." I wrapped my arms around his neck and pressed my face into the warmth of him, drawing strength from him.

"Oh, boo-hoo-hoo. Could you be any more dramatic? Get your ass out here!"

I pressed my forehead into Reckless one last time and then walked out through the gate, latching it shut behind me.

"All right, little Miss Sentimental, give me the stiletto."

I handed the shoe to her, and she moved in behind me. Pushing the business end of the gun against my back, she gave me a little shove.

"Now we're going to take a nice little walk to the beach where it's private and the surf is real loud. Someone standing fifty feet from us won't be able to hear a thing."

We walked to the far side of the house and followed the path to the beach.

"You know how they say taking a walk is good for you, London? Well, I totally agree. This walk is the beginning of a whole new life for me! This fabulous piece of footwear is going to make me a *very* rich woman. Of course, this walk isn't going to be good for you at all…how ironic, a whole new life for me and *no* life for you."

My life wasn't flashing before my eyes. I wanted it to…
if it would just do it, then I would feel as if I was getting the
chance to say good-bye to everyone and everything that I
loved. I stood and faced the gulf, and Sophie stood behind
me.

"Any last words, London?"

I didn't have an answer…I closed my eyes, and my
heart saw Ryder's eyes. I focused on the sound of the waves
and listened to them pound the beach. I felt myself relax
as they pounded louder and louder. The horrific scream
wrenched me back to the here and now. I should say, the
scream and the sound of a shot. I wasn't dead…who'd been
shot? I turned in the direction of the scream and realized
that the pounding that I'd focused on had been the pounding of Reckless' hooves. The enraged horse had blood all
over his chest, and he went for Sophie.

I scurried backward, away from her and what was
about to happen. I tripped over my own feet, and as I fell, I
saw Reckless rear up and start to bring his hooves down on
Sophie. I'm pretty sure that's about the time that I fainted.

Chapter 78

was so warm...you know, the kind of warm that you feel on a summer day when the sun is shining and the temperature is perfect. For a second I was totally relaxed, and then the commotion around me came into focus. Ryder was sitting in the sand, cradling me in his arms, and all around us there were police officers and medical technicians. The technicians really didn't have much to do.

Aside from passing out, I was fine, and the medical examiner's people were dealing with Sophie. As I watched, they zipped the bag shut that contained her body and prepared to carry her off the beach and back to a waiting ambulance. The police were bagging up the stiletto...it had been lying in the sand, just a foot away from me. I struggled to stand up with Ryder's help.

"Ryder, where's Reckless? He was bleeding! He was bleeding... Sophie shot him! She shot him, Ryder!!"

Ryder pulled me close and didn't say anything for a few seconds, and I started having trouble breathing.

"It's going to be all right, London…the wranglers are following him, and they'll get him home. He charged off down the beach, but I'm sure he's going to circle around and come back. He saved you, you know."

"He did? I wasn't quite sure what he was going to do… all I saw was him going for Sophie after she shot him!"

"She never hit him, London…she missed. He broke the gate down getting to you. That's why there was blood on his chest."

I buried my face in my hands, and tears rolled down my cheeks.

"I thought she killed him; I was sure she'd killed him."

"I'm pretty sure he was afraid that she was going to kill *you*."

"Ryder…did he…what did he do to her?"

"He took her out. He pretty much finished her with one blow. I got down to the beach, just as it happened. As soon as she went down, he walked over and stood by you until I reached you both. I'd already called the police, and the sirens must have spooked him, because that's when he took off down the beach."

"I need to get back up to the house, to the barns…I need to know if they've found him."

We made it about halfway up the path, when CC came racing toward us…wailing all the way.

"LONDONNNN!!!!" She ripped me free of Ryder's supportive arm and hugged me until it hurt.

"It's okay, CC. I'm okay. Could you just loosen your grip a little?"

She started shouting at that point.

"WHERE IS SHE? WHERE'S THAT EVIL WITCH, SOPHIE? I'LL KILL HER! HOLD ME BACK, RYDER, I MEAN IT…I'M GOING TO KILL HER!"

I touched her face. "Calm down, CC; you don't have to worry about Sophie…Reckless killed her."

She looked at me with crazy eyes. "*What?*"

"Reckless killed Sophie."

It took us a minute to bring her out of her fainting spell, and then we helped her get back to the house. I gave her the key and told her to go in and wait for us…we were going to go look for Reckless.

She shouted at us as we drove toward the barn. "THAT HORSE DESERVES A MEDAL! *A MEDAL, I TELL YOU!!*"

We were almost to the barn, and I needed to know something before we got there.

"Ryder, how did you know that I was in trouble?"

"CC called me in a panic. She said she and Brenda saw you driving through town with Sophie, and when she called you and asked you where you were, what you said didn't make any sense. Brenda had just told her that you were acting funny and took off in a rush just a short time earlier. So when they saw you driving down the street with Sophie, and you lied and said you were with Flor, CC knew something was wrong. No way were you in Sarasota with Flor; she had just seen you. I told CC not to worry, and I headed for your place. When I pulled up to the house, Reckless was flying down the path to the beach. I ran after him...and found all of you."

Pulling up in front of the barn, we were shocked to see the crowd that had gathered. There were cars and trucks all over the place...media people. When we got stopped, the reporters crowded around the truck. Ryder wore a deep frown and pulled his cowboy hat down lower over his forehead. He shoved his door open, and I did the same. We pushed our way to the barn door where one of the wranglers stood blocking it.

He stepped aside for us. "Just trying to keep the vultures out."

"Thank you, Randy...Did they find him?"

"He's in there. The vet is looking him over right now."

Randy let us in, and closing the door behind us, he went back to keeping the reporters at bay.

The barn was unusually quiet as we made our way to Reckless' stall. Normally the horses nicker, snort, and move around in their stalls. Every horse we passed was standing as close to their door as they could, head turned in Reckless' direction, listening.

I ran the last few feet. The vet was just pulling the stall door shut, but when he saw me, he silently opened it. I stopped before I walked into the stall and made myself calm down. The minute I walked in, Reckless tossed his head up and down and walked toward me. I stood totally still as he came to me and rested his muzzle on my shoulder. I bawled like a baby.

CHAPTER 79

It had been just a few days since Sophie had nearly ended my life and Reckless had saved it. My hero had made a full recovery and was busy mowing the pasture with his teeth while I leaned on the fence watching him. The gate had been repaired where Reckless had broken through it, and the original latch had been put back on. It was nice to know that if he ever needed to be a superhero again, he wouldn't have to break the gate down. He could just open it and walk through.

I heard the crunch of tires on gravel and watched Ryder drive up to the house. I enjoyed watching him walk over to us. He just had this way of walking...very sexy... very male...very him.

"You two aren't cooking up any trouble, are you?"

"What? You don't trust us? We lead such boring lives, you should know that."

"Right…you…leading a boring life…if only it were true."

"So what's up?"

"I found out a couple of interesting things from my buddies at the precinct."

"Interesting how?"

"Well…Trey's second 'job' for his sister was to steal some money from Monique that she kept in a safe. Trey was all ready to take it while you did the photo shoot, he knew Monique would be distracted. He could never get to the safe, though, because every time he tried, either you or CC would get close, and he finally gave up and left. Turns out that after Monique was killed, he realized that he really did love her. I think the thing he needed to finish was to get a copy of your images, not to prevent the ex-husband from finding out about their affair but because he wanted to see if there were any last shots of Monique on them. He'd never had a picture of her; he wanted one to remember her with."

"The heart of a criminal changed by true love…sort of," I said. "I think Trey is always going to cut corners as long as he's around his sister. What other interesting things did you find out?

"I found out something about Jett Brannigan. A family member, an uncle, came to claim his body. The guy came all the way from Scotland, and when he got to the morgue, he wasn't happy."

"I don't suppose he *was* happy…a member of his family was dead, after all. Not exactly a happy time for anybody."

"That's the thing…the dead guy wasn't family."

"What do you mean he wasn't family?"

"It turns out that the man who Sophie shot…wasn't the real Jett Brannigan."

"Are you serious?"

"They took Jett's uncle down to the precinct, and they checked out all his credentials. He's the real deal…the man in the morgue isn't."

"Who the hell is the guy in the morgue?"

"The dead man's name is Alfred Pratt. Jett and Alfred were roommates when they were attending Oxford. Because of Jett's wealth, he got a lot of media attention, and he was frustrated with his inability to lead, what he called, a normal life. Five years after they graduated, Jett contacted Alfred and asked him if he'd consider a job offer. The job was pretending to be Jett…living in his home, keeping a low profile. All he had to do was to act a part…and he'd be paid handsomely to do it. Jett's uncle said he was uneasy with the arrangement from the beginning and warned Jett that the whole thing could blow up in his face. He told him that he'd better take a lot of precautions to protect his assets, and himself, in case Alfred got too comfortable being Jett."

I gave Ryder a little info that I'd forgotten to share with him. "From what Sophie told me, it sounds like the real Brannigan didn't have to worry. Alfred was ready to go start living his own rich, fabulous life once he and Sophie had sold the stiletto. Have the police talked to the real Jett to get his side of the story?"

"Apparently they haven't. He's not a suspect, so they really don't have a legitimate reason to bring him in. The uncle never thought to try and reach Brannigan by phone when he got the call from the police that his nephew had been murdered. Coop said they let the guy call Brannigan's number once they discovered that there was an identity issue with the corpse. The uncle called, and Brannigan answered. He was not happy to hear about the unraveling of his elaborate plans for privacy, but he assured his uncle that he was alive and well.

Since the murder, he's gone even further underground because of all the media interest, but at least his uncle knows he's alive. The guy must be seriously freaked out by all this…it sounds like he's pretty much of a hermit and can't take a lot of turmoil in his life."

"I'm glad for the uncle, but I wish there was a way to wrap up the loose ends in my life. Sophie confessed to me, but I don't think the police believe me.

"They know she was trying to kill me, but what about the others? There's no proof that I didn't kill Richard, Toni, Monique, and Jett…Alfred…Jett, whoever."

"You don't have to worry about that anymore. Sophie's cell phone was next to her body on the beach, and there were "trophy" images on it from each murder scene. Not just of her victims but also of her *posing* with the deceased. She made 'bunny ears' behind the head of each one of them."

"I don't know if she was going to do the bunny ears thing behind my head, but she *was* planning to do my makeup afterward. Creepy little nut job. Did they pick up Evangeline and bring her back?"

"Yep…they said you'd hardly recognize her. She'd dyed her hair pink and was dressed like some middle-aged hipster. It's lucky that someone was able to recognize her and called the cops. I guess some reality TV show wants her to sign a contract with them, if she gets released, which isn't going to happen for at least five years.

"It's pretty ironic that Evangeline could end up being on a crime reality TV show. That kind of thing is what inspired Sophie in the first place. And look where it got her."

Ryder steered the discussion in a slightly different direction. "Speaking of themes for shows…did you ever watch that one where someone would pick a date without ever seeing the person…they were hidden from them by a sort of wall?"

"You're talking about 'date me up' or something like that."

"I've got an idea, and it has pretty much nothing in common with that show, except one thing."

"Why, Mister Ryder, just what *do* you have in mind."

"I think we should go out on a date…a real date. I don't call the times we've been together, dates. I'm old school… I'd kind of like to start over. Not *all* the way over, we're at the perfect stage of our relationship in at least *one* area."

"When did you want to go out on this date?"

"I'm an impatient man...how about tonight?"

"What a coincidence...I'm an impatient woman. Be here at seven."

CHAPTER 80

I was dressed in a classic little black dress. Ryder's only hint about our evening was that I would probably want to wear heels. Miracle of miracles, I actually had a pair of heels that I loved. They were black with a tiny sprinkle of crystals on them…tasteful but with just enough bling to make me feel sexy. My crazy red hair was actually behaving, and I'd gotten it into a nice French twist.

I was as ready as I'd ever be…after I'd checked my bra for cereal crumbs. What? I like to snack on cereal, and I don't add milk to it…I just eat it with my fingers. Sometimes I find crumbs down in my bra later…don't you dare sit there and act as if you've never had that happen to you.

The doorbell rang, and I hurried to let Ryder in. When he walked into the house, I could feel myself blush. He was wearing a tux again…and he was devastatingly handsome in that tux…again. He stood and looked at me, and I blushed some more.

He had a way with words. "You look…"

"I look what?"

"I don't…"

"You don't what?"

He had me in his arms, and I was breathless.

"I'm in trouble," he whispered into my ear.

I pulled away from him.

"You're in trouble?" I'd heard him say that the day I was up in the tree, hiding the stiletto.

"What kind of trouble?"

"I think I might be a little bit in love with you."

I moved back into his embrace.

"You *are* in trouble."

He bent his head down and nuzzled my neck. "How about you, are you in trouble?"

"Let me put it this way…I think I need to call 911…I'm having a love emergency. I'm afraid this might be more than I can handle on my own."

I'm not telling you guys anything else. Well, okay, just a little more. There was kissing…and more kissing…and some heavy breathing. And…and that's all I'm going to tell you. If we wanted to actually *go* on our real date, I needed to slow things down.

"We'd better stop, like, right now, cowboy."

He straightened his tie and squared his shoulders.

"Just don't look at me with those green eyes; they tell me things."

"What things?"

"Heart things, sexy things, and they also tell me when you're keeping a secret."

"Oh really…and what secret have I kept from you?"

"I knew you had the stiletto from the day that CC got high on Volcanoes."

"*What?* How did you know?"

"Like I said, your eyes tell me everything. That and the fact that I saw you up in the tree hiding the shoe."

"All this time you've known that I was keeping that a secret from you?"

"Yes, all this time, so from this point forward, no more trying to keep secrets from me. It won't work. All I have to do is look into those big green eyes, and I know everything."

"Well, excuse me, Mister Mind Reader…it's not like I can't tell what's going on by looking into those eyes of *yours*."

It was weird…at the very moment I said the words, I could see something being hidden away in those eyes.

"*You're not telling me something right now!* You just said no more keeping secrets, and you're keeping a secret! Are we doing this honesty thing for real, or am *I* the only one who's supposed to do it?"

He took my hand, and I saw the guarded look disappear from his eyes.

"I'm sorry…you're right. The 'no secrets' policy applies to both of us. I want to give you something, London."

He turned and picked up a velvet bag that I hadn't noticed when he came in…that just tells you how seductive he looked in that tux. He silently handed me the bag, and I slowly opened the top of it. Reaching into it I pulled out a replica of the stiletto…it was about half the size of the original gem-encrusted beauty, but it glittered just as brightly and brilliantly.

"This is for me? It's…how did you ever find this? I've never seen anything like it!"

"I bought it from the gentleman who created the original…he always makes a copy of each shoe he designs."

"Ryder…getting back to that 'secrets and truth' stuff. These diamonds look real."

"They're real…you're the most 'real' person I've ever known…I couldn't give you something that wasn't."

I stared down at the beautiful little shoe.

"How in the world…this must have cost a fortune!"

He leaned back against the front door and lowered his head. His hair had never looked so black as it did at that moment. I raised my hand to brush it back from his forehead, and just before I touched his hair, he raised his head. His eyes were liquid light…the gold, brown, and bronze in them washed over me. I couldn't read them at all. He put his hand on the doorknob and paused in the act of opening the door for me.

"You asked me if the gems were real…but you didn't ask me what my secret was."

I could see the beginnings of a smile playing at the corners of his lips.

"All right, tall, dark, and handsome…what's your secret?"

He opened the door to reveal a long, sleek, black limo waiting for us in the deepening dark of the night.

"My real name isn't Ryder…It's Jett Brannigan."

THE END.

Made in the USA
Monee, IL
22 March 2021

62658981R00288